A Distant Call

The Fateful Choices of Hattie Sheldon

LANE DOLLY

The image of a young girl used on this book cover comes from an anonymous 19th century tintype. It represents the sincerity and intensity of the real-life Hattie Sheldon, whose early life story is the focus of this work.

International Standard Book Number: 978-14943-6066-5
Printed in the United States of America

Editorial development and creative design support by Ascent:
www.itsyourlifebethere.com

To my sweet mother,
whose influence, character, and good memory
encourage my writing. She sets a noteworthy example of loyalty,
faith, love, and perseverance that has kept me going.

To my late father,
for his passionate personality,
accomplishment-oriented lessons, unyielding belief in our
forefathers' wisdom, and untiring interest in history.
He handed down many of the traits and pithy fortitude
that Hattie Sheldon brought from Utica, New York
to Indian Territory, the forerunner of
our home state of Oklahoma.

Introduction

Hattie Sheldon sprang from history into my life through her own written words and documented stories about her fearlessness and intelligence. With a famous legacy linking her to the Deerfield Raid of 1704 during the French and Indian War, Hattie had leadership and heroism in her blood. The Sheldon family later distinguished itself during the Revolutionary period, as well. Hattie's father, an ardent Presbyterian and abolitionist, established a successful saddle, trunk and harness business that lasted more than a century in Utica, New York.

Women had just begun to follow their dreams when Hattie was a girl. She wanted to do more than keep the home fires burning, but an undertaking as ambitious as hers was still rare before the Civil War. Gaining admission to prestigious schools, she completed a rigorous, academic program that armed her with knowledge and skills. However, women in her era could pursue little beyond teaching or missionary work. Faith happened to be Hattie's driving force, so she accepted the challenge. There was no stopping her. Proof of Hattie's pioneering leadership was just waiting to be discovered.

The research that motivated this book also offers readers a magnifying glimpse into the customs, expectations and influences that motivated Hattie to step outside of tradition. From abolitionism to Indian removals, Hattie's story travels through the tempest of politics and public discourse as slavery ravaged America. She made life changing decisions amid societal upheavals and groundbreaking change in the nation prior to the Civil War. Learning about her and her era brought inspiration, resolve and thankfulness into my life. I hope others will love her as much as I do.

—*Lane Calhoon Dolly, McLean, Virginia*

CONTENTS

CAST OF CHARACTERS

The Sheldons—a family in Utica, New York

Harriet Ann "Hattie" Sheldon—the protagonist. Age seven in 1840.

Ebenezer Sheldon—Hattie's father. A Massachusetts native. Owner of a saddle, trunk, and harness business, first in Burlington, New York, then Utica, New York.

Helen Sheldon—Hattie's mother. A New York state native.

Amanda—Hattie's older and only surviving sister. She is married to LeGrand Moore. Their little daughter is named Mary.

George—Hattie's oldest brother.

Albert—Hattie's middle brother.

Artemas—Hattie's little brother.

Mary and Cornelia—Hattie's late, older sisters who died during a two-month period of sickness when Hattie was just a young girl.

Margaret—Hattie's girlhood friend. A composite fictional character.

Reverend Philemon Fowler—Hattie's Presbyterian pastor.

Moses Bagg, MD—the Sheldon family physician.

The Worcesters—a missionary family in Park Hill, Cherokee Nation, Indian Territory (pre-state of Oklahoma).

Reverend Samuel Austin Worcester—a pastor and linguist whose service to the Cherokees is legendary due to the famous Supreme Court case, Worcester v. Georgia. His first wife, Ann Orr Worcester, died in childbirth when their sixth child was born. He remarried Erminia Nash.

Erminia Nash Worcester—second wife to the missionary preacher and teacher. A New York state native and former mission school teacher at a neighboring mission in Indian Territory.

Ann Eliza Worcester Robertson—Worcester's oldest daughter.

Sarah Worcester Hitchcock—Worcester's second daughter.

Hannah Worcester Hicks—Worcester's third daughter.

Leonard—Worcester's oldest son.

John Orr—Worcester's youngest son.

Mary Eleanor—Worcester's youngest child, born just before her mother died.

Aunt Mary Brown—Ebenezer Sheldon's sister from Amherst, Massachusetts. Her second husband is Jason Brown.

Professor Alexander Colquhoun—a retired ex-professor at Amherst College. A fictional character.

Professor Cornelius Thorne—a troubled professor at Amherst Academy. A fictional character.

TIMELINE

1808 U.S. outlaws legal importation of slaves. Smuggling of slaves continues, however.

1820 **Missouri Compromise**: Congress seeks to keep slave and non-slave states equal. No slavery is allowed in subsequent territories north of latitude 36°30′.

1830 Congress passes the **Indian Removal Act** allowing the government to force tribes off their ancestral lands. Reservation land, called Indian Territory, was set aside for them hundreds of miles to the west.

1833 *Hattie Sheldon is born into an abolitionist family in the state of New York.*

1835 A leading Cherokee citizen claims to represent the whole Cherokee Nation when he and several others negotiate a secret treaty to give up their ancestral lands. **The Treaty of New Echota,** ratified by the U. S. Senate, accepted an offer of $5 million in exchange for moving to Indian Territory. When the majority of the tribe found out, they vowed to stay on their land and fight to keep it.

1838 The U.S. Government, breaking all former treaties and promises, orders the Army to remove the Cherokees and other tribes from their homelands in the southeastern states. This forcible removal was called **The Trail of Tears**.

1839 Retaliation murders in Indian Territory take the lives of the small Cherokee minority that negotiated the Treaty of New Echota. A deep divide within the Cherokee Nation grows deeper.

1848 **The Seneca Falls Convention**, the first women's rights convention organized by women, is held in Seneca Falls, NY. The featured speaker, a Quaker orator from Philadelphia named Lucretia Mott, told women it was time they fought against the unacceptability of speaking in public. Other issues the women argued against were the tyranny of patriarchy, lack of property rights, dearth of educational opportunities, and low wages.

1850 Congress passes the **Compromise of 1850** to balance northern and southern interests in the slavery debate. The Fugitive Slave Act allows slave catchers into free territory, which antagonizes and emboldens abolitionists. *Seventeen year old Hattie Sheldon attends Amherst Academy in Amherst, MA.*

1852 **Uncle Tom's Cabin**, an anti-slavery novel by Harriet Beecher Stowe, becomes a bestseller in the anti-slavery North but is banned in the pro –slavery South. It sells 300,000 copies within one year. Slavery remains legal in Indian Territory. Hattie Sheldon continues her schooling in a class of 92 young women at Utica Female Academy.

1856 *Twenty-two year old Hattie Sheldon graduates from Utica Female Academy*

1

Underground Railroad Rescue

In complete silence, the exhausted runaway slaves darted toward the waiting escape wagon, obscured by darkness and passing October cloud shadows. Their number and ages were undistinguishable as a chilly wind hurried them. Weathered branches of a craggy tree scratched forebodingly against the barn that had hidden them. Riveted by curiosity from her assigned spot in the carriage only yards away, seven year old Hattie Sheldon gripped the dash tensely and willed herself to memorize what she could see of the silent transfer.

One Negro man's tattered shirt gapped open in the back, fairly hanging off his emaciated frame. Uneven rows of long, mounded scars marked his exposed skin. Limping beside a second fugitive, a skinny woman struggled to keep hold of his hand. Hattie cringed, because instead of shoes, the woman's feet were wrapped with bloodstained rags. For that matter, none of the slaves wore shoes. Making their way across the farmyard, they ran barefoot over sharp stones, thorny stubble, and hard clods of dirt.

The escapees Hattie's family was rescuing from one secret station to the next seemed almost close enough to touch. But she knew not to move, and had to keep silent for their sake. Her initial excitement about tonight had evaporated since she laid eyes on the runaways. Her young heart comprehended more than most seven-year-old girls. From their looks, the escapees must have suffered in untold ways she hadn't anticipated. No longer just characters in one of her father's gripping stories, they became real people all but overcome by injuries, fear and exhaustion.

Beside his escape wagon, Hattie's father, Ebenezer Sheldon, held up a lantern whose glow revealed the low trap door to the hidden compartment that would conceal the runaways. Running half the length of the wagon bed, the door to the shallow little crevice was bolstered by hidden hinges. Opening it, he motioned silently for the escapees to bend and slide in, one by one. They soon had precious little room to even move. When he stepped between the lantern and the scene, Hattie lost sight of the escapees. How many were there? Shortly, he moved, but they were out of sight. Then he extinguished the lantern.

Only flickering moonlight illuminated the scene now. Hattie had a clear enough view, however, to gauge the reaction of two of her three older sisters as they exchanged looks of amazement. Riding above the secret compartment in the wagon bed, ten year old Mary, and eight year old Cornelia's assignment was to make the operation look like an innocent family outing. From their expressions, Hattie saw that they, too, realized how deadly serious this mission was.

She couldn't imagine how the runaways could endure such a

narrow crevice for the long ride to the next station. Were they able to breathe any fresh air? It must feel so cramped. Would they get to sleep in a bed later tonight?

But there were no answers to these and many other troubling questions. Tension rose, sensed even by the horses that strained against their harnesses. Hattie knew she must remain silent and wait, her spot fairly protected at her mother's feet. Soon, their carriage would follow the wagon and the journey would begin.

Ebenezer Sheldon had been active in the Underground Railroad for several years by this fall night of 1840. The organization's efforts had paid off, but grown more risky. He prided himself on being a careful man, however, and reminded the family that nothing had ever gone wrong.

"This is the Lord's work. Sacrifices by the free are often the only hope for the oppressed," he had explained at supper, while extolling the virtues of freedom. "We are privileged to serve and blessed that New York is a free place, a refuge for escaping slaves." During Hattie's young life, he must have said a hundred times that the movement was growing rapidly in central New York State. She hung on every word as he graphically described the conditions escaping slaves endured. To get away from their tyrannical Southern masters, they first had to risk death itself by escaping their masters and tracking bloodhounds. If they survived that, they tramped hundreds of miles, swam frigid rivers and maneuvered through dangerous, unfamiliar territory. Fear compounded their fatigue, demanding the secrecy that cut their risk of capture.

Ebenezer's vivid descriptions led Hattie to picture herself right beside the escapees. What must it feel like to hide during the day in sweltering, makeshift shelters or cobweb-draped barns? How awful that their only option was traveling at night, which slowed their pace and doubled their time in ominous, dark places. As they trudged blindly through thick woods, they faced hazards. Some fell in unseen holes as if the night swallowed them. Ensnaring thickets ripped at their clothes and bodies, especially when they tripped over old logs and fell into thorny bushes. To make matters worse, their skin became a mass of swollen, itchy insect or spider bites. If they reached New York, her father had said, it was the job of the Underground Railroad to make them whole again. To a person, the gaunt escapees suffered from hunger, weakness, and ill health resulting from lack of sleep or shelter.

When her parents arrived home one evening last week after visiting a sick friend, Hattie heard them pull up. Swaying on the rope swing under the big tree beside the house, she jumped down excitedly and crossed the dewy grass to the carriage. Ready with a little sing-song greeting as she approached from behind, she nevertheless came to an abrupt halt upon hearing agitated whispers. Her parents seemed to be having a disagreement. She kept silent and listened.

"I'm not questioning the moral value of what you taught the children," her mother, Helen, reproved, not knowing Hattie could hear. "Of course all men are created equal. Believing it differs greatly from enforcing it, however. The children need to *believe* it. But they're too young to do this kind of work."

"They're old enough and it's time," her father countered

persuasively. "They'll also provide much-needed distraction, especially if anyone pursues us. Remember, there's safety in numbers. Trust me."

Hattie's mother sounded extremely agitated. "That's not enough. I am terrified by your idealism. You must promise you'll protect *our children first* if anything goes wrong," she disputed, exhaling at length.

Hattie comprehended a concerning degree of tension. Through her lens of curiosity, however, she gathered that something exciting was going to happen. Turning to tiptoe out of sight, she began to imagine herself involved with the Underground Railroad.

The farmyard fell into utter darkness after Hattie's father extinguished his lantern. Until the moon reemerged from cloud cover, nothing but sound would guide the rescue. Squatting by the carriage seat, she squeezed her arms tightly around her legs. As each tense minute passed, the lack of light brought foreboding feelings. She couldn't hear her mother's breathing, but thank goodness she could feel the hem of her dress. Hattie was glad she wasn't alone.

The wait began to grow tiresome after a while. Restless, Hattie stretched her legs sideways. This new position revealed that she could crawl beneath the carriage seat for more obscurity and the illusion of safety. That's where the black cloth was stashed, just in case her mother needed to hide or cover up something unexpectedly.

Without telling anyone, Hattie had brought along a little rag doll, the one she loved best and slept with. Why ask permission when she knew the answer would be no? Her doll wasn't in the way and made for good company. Since it was bedtime, Hattie kissed the doll lovingly, tucking the black cloth up close to create a sleeping place. Nobody needed to know how much comfort her doll offered or what a good listener she was. Hattie might be the youngest girl in the family, but she wanted to look as mature as her sisters who had outgrown their dolls.

Earthy aromas of soil, livestock, and hay filled the air, now heavy with evening dampness. Hattie tried to be patient, but the eerie quiet of the secretive operation soon wore thin. Concurrently, the worry of being caught grew and began to weigh more heavily. If only Hattie and her mother could talk about what had happened so far. Everything Hattie had seen was now seared into her conscience. After merely hearing about the Underground Railroad for so long, it had sprung to life tonight. Without her family's help, these people might die.

Hattie jumped when a barn door creaked on its hinges in the breeze. The familiar sound of horse's grunts echoed from her father's team, which always responded to his calm demeanor and time-worn training. He knew horses like the back of his hand. Hattie recalled sitting beside him time after time as he fitted horses with new harnesses.

Then, thankfully, the darkness gave way. A full moon broke through heavy cloud cover to reveal her father's wagon again. It looked ready to go. He glanced from side to side, as if doing a final inspection, then hoisted himself onto the seat. Finally, they were making their departure.

Suddenly, from nowhere, urgent rustling and knocking noises signaled something unexpected. Ebenezer pulled the horses to a halt and sprang back down. Scrambling around to the hidden compartment's trap door, he pried it open again.

To her surprise, Hattie heard a small child crying. Instantly, her mother swiveled toward the sound. Who was crying? Her sisters were too old to cry like that. She looked up and searched her mother's face, only to find a petrified expression.

Within seconds, her father began to march toward Hattie and her mother in the carriage, his boots pounding hard against the soil. As he came into focus, her mother drew in a quick, sharp breath. Hattie couldn't tell what was wrong. She struggled to remain silent as he approached the carriage.

Dim, filtered light revealed that her father was carrying something alive and moving. Hattie heard a little moan and tensed unexpectedly. Her mother's questioning eyes revealed shock just as her father placed a tiny Negro girl right beside her. The child, delicate with huge round eyes, was even smaller than Hattie. Her tattered clothing looked like old cleaning rags. Hattie froze in place.

In the softest voice her father had ever used, he gave clear, brief instructions.

"This is Sena," he introduced, almost pleading with Hattie through raised eyebrows. "Do not leave her side, Hattie. You must protect Sena. Her mother could not keep her still in the secret compartment. So she must go with you. Don't play or make any sounds. Stay still and hide under the black cloth."

Awed, Hattie searched the faces of one parent, then the other. Her mother's mouth fell open in distress, but she nodded silently. Her father returned to his wagon. Reaching down, her mother placed a warm hand gently on the back of Hattie's neck for a minute. It seemed to say, *I have confidence in you.* Then she patted little Sena and ran her hand softly across the child's bony shoulders.

Hattie felt important to be given such a mission at only seven years of age. Immediately following instructions, she crouched close and took Sena's hand, which was icy. She had never made friends in the dark before.

"My name is Hattie. Let's keep quiet together."

This new and unexpected situation quickened Hattie's senses. Her former excitement was replaced by uneasiness. Why had nobody mentioned Sena? If anyone stopped them on the road, could she keep Sena safe? How long would tonight's escape take? Could Sena keep quiet? But then she remembered her father's multiple assurances in the previous days that things would be all right if she did exactly as he instructed.

Before the family departed woodsy, rural Burlington, New York, to undertake tonight's rescue, her father had prayed to Almighty God at supper for protection and success. Never before had circumstances compelled the entire family to help with an Underground Railroad rescue. He had detailed the strategy, which left the children hanging on every word. When he emphasized safety, Hattie's mother had looked away, unable to hide her furrowed brow. Lost in thought, she stared blankly around the neat but worn home they had all but outgrown.

The plan was clear in Hattie's mind, as were the special words her father used to describe the mission. The escaping slaves, called *baggage*, were to be delivered to the next Underground Railroad connecting place or *station* near Utica, a farm in this instance. Sometimes, a group of escaped slaves was called *a load of potatoes*. Rescuers like the Sheldon family were part of the *forwarding,* a term for the movement of slaves through the countryside.

Without secrecy, all the escapees were in great jeopardy. Once they reached the *station*, which Hattie must never speak about, they were closer to that coveted, free place up north. There, the escapees could be certain that nobody would ever beat them again, work them into the ground, or treat them like animals, let alone sell them away from one another.

During the rescue, Hattie's sisters, Mary and Cornelia, would ride in the wagon bed. Their job was the work of distraction. If anyone approached the wagon, they were to talk, laugh, and act like all was well. Seventeen year old George and twelve year old Albert, her oldest brothers, were given assignments, too. The transfer to the next Underground Railroad secret station was merely to look like a family outing that had lasted until late.

"Behind my wagon, mother and Hattie will follow in the carriage," her father had instructed. "George, you and Albert ride your horses alongside. Be ready to create diversions."

After the briefing, every member of the family understood the plan. Hattie's thirteen year old sister, Amanda was to remain at home with her four year old brother, Artemas. They accepted the importance of each person's role.

The whole family was to work as a team, especially when it came to the alternatives if anything went awry. And plenty of things could go wrong. Bounty hunters might track and confront them. They must use caution to avoid accidents. Even the weather might change suddenly. A gushing rain could create mud and bog down the wagon or carriage.

"Do we need to go over the plan again?" Hattie's father questioned in conclusion. "If you have even one question, ask it now."

❋ ❋ ❋

Sena had fallen fast asleep by the time Hattie's father finally snapped the reins and steered his wagon away from the farmyard.

Taking a deep breath, Hattie smelled the familiar aromas of dust, leather, and horsehair. They hadn't been caught. The first part of the rescue was successful!

With a light snap of the reins, her mother's carriage began to follow the wagon. A great relief washed over her as the bumpy pace began in earnest. Hattie lay back down under the black cloth, hot as it was, and nestled close to Sena. Maybe she could take a little nap, too.

Before long, however, her arms and legs began to itch. Why this year's heat and insect invasion had stretched unbearably into late October was anybody's guess. It was the stuff of talk downtown and in newspaper headlines, her father had said. As she scratched, she couldn't stop thinking about the swollen, stinging mosquito or ant bites all over the escapees' skin. But, on second thought, insect bites weren't as bad as dog bites. Without question, her very worst fear was mean, slave-tracking bloodhounds.

Too energized to shut her eyes, Hattie's thoughts returned to little Sena. She must keep Sena quiet. Had her sisters heard Sena cry and alerted father? Maybe he worried that Sena's cries would get them caught. Yet, she must count on George and Albert to remain on guard. There were ample numbers of eyes and ears, and their plan was sound. Hattie pictured her brothers riding silently through the night, alert to all possibilities. Her father had called them young sentries doing God's work in the Underground Railroad.

The journey grew long as they traversed mile after mile of dirt roads. Surely they had traveled for hours rather than just minutes, Hattie concluded. The wheels made popping sounds as they bounced over soft rocks that gave way or broke in two. Sometimes she smelled weeds, sometimes brackish water. Finally, she relaxed and dozed in the darkness.

Before long, however, she awakened confused, and began to pat around under the black cloth for her doll. Her finger caught one strand of its yarn hair by chance. But, to her surprise, her doll rested in the arms of little sleeping Sena. Slowly pulling the doll free, Hattie stroked its hair reassuringly as she worried about the escapees under the wagon.

A distinct pine aroma moved through the breeze. They must be far into the country by now. The trees made swishing sounds.

"Mama, how much farther?" she whispered, gently tapping on her mother's shoe.

"It won't be much longer. You've been so good. Be patient a few more minutes."

Hattie shifted uneasily. If only she could stretch. Then, to her relief, the pace of the carriage began to slow down. She didn't smell as much dust as before. Encouraged, she sat up as the carriage continued a few yards, then came to rest.

When she looked out, the full moon highlighted a shabby little farmhouse next to a weathered barn. In two of the house's windows, the warm glow of candles kept vigil. Her mother looked down and frowned at Hattie, who was all eyes.

The silence was broken when a man opened a squeaky door and stepped out of the house. He was holding a long musket. The man looked toward her father's wagon, waved the gun silently, and motioned toward the barn. Just then, Hattie's mother reached down and pulled the black cloth back into place, obscuring Hattie's view. She wanted to cry in frustration, but put her head back down instead. Listening intently, she heard whispering, many more footsteps, a cough, and the rustling of hay.

The next second, the unmistakable yelping bay of a bloodhound energized the hushed atmosphere. Hattie stiffened to listen with all her might, gripping the doll for comfort. A mean dog was nearby! But how far off?

As the barking continued, a chain clanked. What if someone had released the dog so it could attack them? The idea of its dripping jaws made the hair on the back of Hattie's neck stand up. For the first time, she felt real fear. Burrowing back under the black cloth, she grabbed Sena's hand and held on tight.

Suddenly, a deafening shot tore through the air. Hattie heard its echo and smelled gunpowder. There was no question but that the escape operation had just grown more dangerous. Who had fired? Someone tracking them with a dog? The man at the farmhouse? Her father? Was anyone down?

Frenetic barks filled the darkness, along with the rustling of dried corn shocks. Hattie worried that her father might have been shot. Then, from fairly nearby, a gravelly voice began to shout obscenities she had never heard before. The voice sounded angry and depraved. Her skin went clammy, and Sena began to shake all over.

Instantly, Hattie had doubts about minding her father's instructions. Were they really protected under the black cloth? If she peeked, would she risk exposing them? If she didn't, how could she be of any help? She had to make a choice.

Mustering all her nerve, Hattie parted the black cloth to find out what was happening. Suddenly, a young Negro woman appeared from the shadows and ran toward the carriage. She was the one with rags for shoes. Hattie's mother jumped from the carriage to meet her.

"Here's all the thanks I can give, ma'am," the scared woman whispered to her mother, pressing something into her mother's shaky hand. "The cross brought us this far. I pray it keeps your family safe, too. God bless."

Hattie's mother gasped, looking from the woman to the unexpected gift now in her palm. Then the Negro woman turned and hobbled off. Hattie watched her mother follow and help the woman across the stony farmyard into darkness.

Instantaneously, the wild barking began again in earnest. Stricken, Hattie shuddered to hear the ragged snorts. All she could picture was the huge bloodhound biting her. From the sounds, she knew the dog was growing ever nearer. As she turned in fear, galloping horses approached the carriage.

It was Albert and George! Her brothers had come to the rescue! Tearing the black cloth away, Hattie waved for the boys to pull her and Sena to safety. Yet darkness threatened to overtake the scene again. It was worsened by a choking cloud of dust raised by the commotion. Coughing, she caught sight just as Albert's horse reared. He leaned in and yanked the reins, then circled to get his horse under control.

Simultaneously, George disappeared behind the house and then returned with a torch of fire. Its glowing, gold flames provided new visibility so his brother could approach the carriage again. Before she knew it, Albert was back. His horse seemed calmer. But, in the angry flare of the torch, Hattie saw that Albert's face revealed confusion.

"Where's that little girl?" he whispered anxiously to his brother, craning his neck nervously.

"Under the seat with Hattie," George cried. "Hurry. They're almost here!"

"Draw your gun," Albert ordered. "I don't have enough hands to shoot that dog!"

Barely controlling his horse, the torchlight allowed Albert to spot the little girls. He lunged wildly to grab Sena, but only knocked the seat off its bracket. To make matters worse, his horse sidestepped in obvious agitation over the bloodhound's approach.

Scared and exposed, Sena yelped. In an instant, Hattie clamped a hand over the child's mouth to stop the scream that nearly escaped. Then Albert reached for the child again.

"Sena," he coaxed, motioning with his free hand, "climb onto the horse in front of me! Hurry!"

Hattie wanted to help, but just couldn't stop herself from looking for the dog. Its thrashing and the sound of breaking cornstalks left her in a state of near panic. By now, it had to be only steps away. The idea of being devoured made her shudder.

Then, she was jolted back to attention. Sena had grabbed for her instead of Albert! The little child must be just as terrified as Hattie. Why did she shy away from her rescuer? Hattie tried to think fast and nudged her forward, but Sena recoiled and sank down into a heap on the black cloth.

Unnerved, Hattie couldn't stop herself from looking again. Instead of seeing the dog, however, she caught sight of her beloved doll tossed aside. In that instant, she realized that the child had probably never owned a doll. Sena had fallen asleep with it earlier, so it was obvious what she wanted. In that split second, Hattie decided she could easily give up her doll if it saved them from the bloodhound.

"You can have this if you get on the horse with Albert," she urged through chattering teeth. Then she handed the doll to Albert.

Sena fixed her gaze on it and reached up. Just as she enclosed her tiny hand around the doll's waist, Albert leaned perilously low, pulling her safely onto the saddle. Turning rapidly, he dug sharp spurs into the horse's ribs. Seconds later, they had all but disappeared behind the barn.

Hattie's heart nearly beat out of her chest. They had gotten away! It had happened so fast. Breathless, she turned to get approval from George. But, torch still in hand, he turned his horse and began to follow Albert. That left Hattie all alone in the carriage. Her mouth went dry. Having no protection now, she was too terrified to call after him.

Suddenly, a flash of brown came into her peripheral vision. The huge dog tore out of the cornfield and pounded forward, kicking up dust. She heard its guttural growls and flinched before realizing it was not headed toward her. It was racing headlong for George on horseback. She wanted to scream, but couldn't utter so much as a cry of warning.

The animal all but flew the last few feet toward George's leg, catching his boot in its vicious jaws. George let out a howl of anguish and fear. To make matters worse, his horse lurched in panic and thrashed. George held on for dear life. So did the dog, its teeth firmly clenched around George's boot. Then the horse began to back up, dragging the dog.

Despite the intense physical struggle, George managed to remain in the saddle. But he dropped the torch, which promptly caught scores of dry grass sprigs on fire. The flames merged. Blown by a breeze, they threatened to lick dangerously close to the wagon and carriage. Hattie looked around wildly for help. She dare not jump out of the carriage or the dog might attack her next.

Seconds later, her father rushed out of the barn. That moment, a picture of David rushing to fight Goliath formed in her mind. As the moon reemerged, her father showed no fear of the commotion or the fire in the farmyard. Her heart jumped with hope. He looked so sturdy and brave, so undaunted in silhouette against the flames. Approaching George, who still battled the obsessed dog, he raised his right arm to reveal a huge bullwhip.

With precision, Ebenezer Sheldon aimed the braided leather body of the whip for the dog's midsection, and then flicked it back powerfully. A deafening crack like a gunshot knocked the dog from George's leg to the ground. It yelped in pain, falling sideways and looking stunned as George galloped off.

Hattie had only seen a bullwhip once before. It was in a bin of leftover leather in the workroom of her father's shop. After she had mentioned it, he removed the whip and changed the subject. When she asked George later, he expressed surprise and said their father would never sell whips. Then he dramatized the power of its snake-like, coiled construction.

"In seconds, it can rip the flesh of man or beast to shreds," he had whispered to his wide-eyed little sister. Back then, she felt he was just exaggerating. Now, she wasn't so sure.

Tail between its legs, the dog slunk away, leaving drops of blood in its wake. Poor George rode toward the barn, a hand nursing his injured leg.

With the dog out of commission, Hattie's father made fast work of the fire. He dunked a nearby bucket into a water trough and doused the flames. In seconds, nothing was left but a little smoke. Hattie blinked, in awe at her father's heroism.

The intense situation resolved, he turned and ran after George. Hattie's mother reappeared and in what seemed like one swift motion, replaced the seat, scooped up Hattie, and spread the black cloth onto their laps.

"Everything is all right," she sputtered breathlessly to Hattie, hugging her close.

Hattie was so relieved she broke into tears, which stung her face as they streamed down. Her father had come to the rescue! He had saved the family from the bloodhound! And her mother was back. But was George all right? What if he was badly hurt?

Drawing a ragged breath, her mother looked nervously toward the shadows of the adjacent wagon. Then she called across the way toward the wagon.

"Girls," her raspy whisper ordered as she smoothed her hair and disheveled dress, "someone is coming. Sing some rhymes!"

It was comforting to hear the girls sing, even though they began weakly. Her mother's expression, however, revealed precious little encouragement. But she dried Hattie's tears and reached into her dress pocket. Hattie was amazed when she retrieved the little handmade cross, the one the slave lady had risked her life to offer as a token of appreciation.

"I want you to have this, honey," her mother soothed through damp eyes. "Albert said you gave Sena your doll. I think it saved her life."

Suddenly footsteps crackled from the cornfield. Hattie and her mother turned just as a grizzly, sweat-drenched man emerged. He was swinging a chain in one hand and carrying a gun in the other.

"You stay still or I'll fire," he shouted at her mother.

Hattie's attention was riveted. Because of the large chain she figured he must be the dog's master. The man approached the carriage while calling for the dog. To Hattie's dismay, it reappeared and crept to his side, emitting an injured whine. The scowling man surveyed the dog's bleeding injury then clamped a collar and the chain around its scruffy neck.

Immediately, the dog strained and thrashed in a half circle. The collar must irritate its wound. Writhing, it nearly knocked the man's gun out of his hand. Droplets of blood flew in all directions. The man swore at the dog while struggling to get it under control. With each surge, the dog practically overpowered him. Finally, he managed to hit it with the butt of his musket. The dog let out a pained cry and cowered as the man secured the chain to his belt.

Throughout the scary ordeal, Hattie's mother neither reacted nor spoke. She held her head high and wrapped Hattie in her shawl. Looking truly evil, the man swaggered nearer and circled the carriage slowly. When he leaned close and looked inside, the dog raised up, too, its huge front paws bringing blood, slobber, and dirt with them. Hattie drew back in fear. But her mother kicked at the dog's head and waved it off.

"Your mongrel dog bit my son," she seethed.

"You had no cause to whip him," the man retorted as he glanced down at the dog's wounds, his musket at the ready.

"I'd have shot him if I had a gun," her mother retorted righteously. "Leave us alone."

"Where's your load of potatoes?" he challenged menacingly.

"Our friends have taken sick and can't host us as originally planned," Hattie's mother explained in a remarkably calm voice.

"Oh yeah? Who's the man of this family?" he confronted angrily.

"My husband is helping out, and then we're heading home."

"That's a pack of lies," the man spit, rushing across the farmyard to peer in the escape wagon. "You don't fool me."

As Hattie's sisters continued to sing nervous but effective bars of a favorite old hymn, the man scowled, looking a bit confused. Just then, Hattie's father emerged from the barn, looking every bit in control of the situation. The dog whined nervously, but Hattie saw no sign of the whip. Her father strode confidently as he carried an old harness toward his wagon.

"What's all the racket?" he inquired, as if the dog and his master had intruded on nothing of particular interest.

"I know who you are," the man grumbled forebodingly as he moved toward Hattie's father. To Hattie's surprise, however, the bloodhound had other plans. It began to pull at the chain that was still attached to the man's trousers. The dog's strength quickly overpowered him, virtually dragging him toward the barn. The man cursed and uttered threats as he struggled to stay afoot and keep hold of his musket.

"I'm the law," he lied in a screaming voice. "You wait for me!"

Laughing, Hattie's father retorted. "No, you're not."

Checking on her sisters, Ebenezer Sheldon threw the harness in the very back of his wagon. Swiftly, he jumped to the reins and motioned for the carriage to follow. With that, they were off.

"That disgusting bounty hunter will search the barn in vain," Hattie's mother muttered as the carriage picked up speed. "He has no right to track those defenseless people all the way to the state of New York."

Hattie had never seen her mother like this. All eyes, she breathed a sigh of relief as Albert appeared and galloped ahead just as George emerged farther along. In a few seconds, they were fifty yards beyond the farmyard and well on their way.

When Hattie peeked back one last time, the bounty hunter was emerging from the barn, having unhinged himself from the bloodhound. No longer was there a musket in his hand. He tried to run after their wagon, but gave up in utter failure.

"Hey," he screamed frantically, "someday, the likes of you won't get away with hiding another man's property. We know who you are, Ebenezer. One day, you'll go to jail for helping escaped slaves!"

But Hattie's family had gotten away. As they disappeared into the clear night skies, only an empty farmyard remained after the rescue. Finally safe, Hattie's head began to spin from all that had happened. She sank back down under the seat onto the black cloth.

She wished the whole family could crowd around the table and talk about every last detail of what had just transpired. How had the others managed through the tension and uncertainty? What had they seen? Where had the farmer taken the runaways? What had her father done with the whip? When were they going on another rescue?

As the minutes passed and the rescue's successful conclusion sank in, Hattie began to feel euphoric. This had been the most thrilling event of her entire life. None of her friends had ever done anything like this. She was so glad her father had allowed her to take part. Most of all, she wanted to know if he was proud of her. If only she could sit next to him right now. He would answer all her questions with his usual reassurance and animation.

Maybe mother would have something to say. Before asking, however, Hattie thought back to the night her family had gone over the plan. She recalled her mother looking away and acting distracted. She seemed much less excited than her father. But now, after tonight's success, surely the rescue had convinced her otherwise. She must be gratified by the outcome.

Rising onto all fours, Hattie leaned sideways to look up at her mother's face. But, her mother was trembling all over, tears streaming down her face. Her hands shook so badly it seemed she could barely keep hold of the reins. Hattie shrank back, instantly abandoning her idea to discuss the excitement. Why was mother crying? Feeling puzzled, Hattie slumped down further under the seat. There were so many things about her mother's reaction that she didn't understand.

This journey home in the dark gave her time to ponder many things, since she couldn't ask questions. As she thought back over detail after detail, the little cross rested firmly in her hand. The slave woman had made it from two tiny, jagged sticks bound by braided grass and a skinny piece of oiled leather. Running her fingers over it,

Hattie decided the differences in texture seemed to represent all that had happened. Some parts of the night were dusty, a few were smooth, and others were bumpy. She must keep it forever as a reminder of this life-changing night.

God must have arranged and blessed every part of the runaway slave rescue. God had allowed her to help Sena. Everything had turned out fine. So why was her mother so upset? What would cause her to feel anything but joy over helping the slaves get free?

The next day, Hattie wondered who had carried her to bed in the middle of the night. The room she shared with her sisters was already drenched in full daylight. The girls must be at breakfast already.

As she rubbed sleep from her eyes, a memory of the bloodhound from the night before crossed her memory. Wait—how was George's leg? She was dying to know how badly he was injured. Had someone gone for the doctor? Bounding out of bed, she rushed to find out. With any luck, her father would also add new insights about the rescue.

But the comfortably shabby little parlor was empty. There were no welcoming traces of bacon or coffee. Breakfast was long over and her older siblings had left for school already. Even worse, her father's stained hat and lightweight coat were missing from the coat tree by the door. What time was it anyway?

Voices and water sounds revealed that her mother was doing laundry. She must be talking with the neighbor lady, Mrs. Chambers, who was a gardening enthusiast. Hattie knew she couldn't interrupt to talk about the night before. It was a family rule never to discuss abolition activities with a non-family member.

Moping, she poured herself a glass of fresh milk. Today was not off to a great start. On top of that, the temperature suddenly felt very chilly.

She peeked in Artemas' room where he had made a mess constructing something with bits of leather and twine. Days like this always became so boring, what with her older siblings gone to school and only Artemas to play with. His idea of fun had nothing in common with her interests. She could not bear to stack wooden blocks into buildings and then knock them down time after time. It didn't seem fair that neither she nor Artemas could attend school yet.

Frustrated and isolated, Hattie surveyed the sky and the swaying tree branches from her window. The day was grey, blustery, and a little foggy. If she asked to play outside, her mother would surely turn her down. She had warned just last week that cold weather was coming, so it was time to guard against a stopped-up nose. Hattie certainly did not savor staying inside or playing quietly all day. The hours were going to drag so slowly.

After getting dressed, she grabbed a golden biscuit. Out back, she spotted a mound of clean laundry below the line strung between two maple trees. To Hattie's relief, there among the gold and orange leaves stood her mother, hanging clothes to dry. She looked like her old self and was alone.

Watching closely from the kitchen window, Hattie could see no remaining traces of last night's tearful shaking. As a wisp of hair caught her mother's eyelash, she casually whisked it back into her loose bun. This might be a good opportunity to ask some pressing questions about the runaway slave rescue.

"Mother, I overslept," she apologized. "What happened at breakfast? Did everyone talk about last night?"

Her mother was halfway finished hanging the clothes to dry. Smiling, she reached down and pecked Hattie on the cheek.

"Good morning, sweetheart," she replied warmly but with a rather distracted expression. "Where's Artemas?"

No sooner had she spoken, however, than Mrs. Chambers returned, chatting about next spring's peonies. Hattie cast a longing gaze toward her mother. She wanted so badly to talk over all the exciting details. Her stare was really a silent plea, but her mother only patted her and sent her off to play. Soon there would be no time to chat, because her mother had to make a trip to the butcher shop and then prepare for supper. Her mother had too much work, which meant Hattie would get precious little attention.

Why did it always turn out that the rest of the family was off pursuing interesting activities and duties while she was stuck at home? Her mind was brimming over about last night. How maddening that nobody could listen and respond.

On occasion, her mother had Mrs. Chambers keep Hattie and Artemas when she had more chores and errands than usual. This turned out to be one of those days. Mrs. Chambers, who had no children, seemed to relish the chance to have them around. Hattie wasn't thrilled, as she would rather have gone downtown, where there was more activity.

Nevertheless, as instructed, she and Artemas marched across the back yard and were met with a savory stew for dinner, which they couldn't complain about. After that, the afternoon flew as they drew pictures and sang songs with Mrs. Chambers. Hattie was learning her letters and could make out a few words in Mrs. Chambers' books. She had to admit that Mrs. Chambers was patient and always so kind.

When she next looked up from her projects, it seemed the afternoon was all but gone. Hattie grew impatient and almost jumpy with anticipation. After her family sat down to supper, surely they would relive the details of last night's rescue, just as they had reviewed the carefully laid plans for it ahead of time. Her siblings must be just as impatient as she was to hear what their father had to say. Most of all, Hattie was anxious to know if he was pleased over her handling of little Sena. She practically itched with curiosity.

Soon, the familiar sound of their mother's little bell grabbed Hattie's and Artemas' attention. With so many children playing all over the neighborhood, her mother had devised this system to call them to supper. All she had to do was step out the back door and ring her bell. Always hungry, the Sheldon children came running.

So Hattie and Artemas thanked Mrs. Chambers, ran home, and slid into their places at the table. Everyone else was already seated.

Bowing his head, their father began to say grace. Hands folded reverently, Hattie struggled to keep her thoughts on being thankful. Concerns and inquiries pressed into her prayer. Had her father received word about the runaway slaves or their whereabouts? How was George's leg after the grizzly dog bite? She couldn't wait to start asking these and many more questions.

As soon as the prayer ended, however, her father introduced an unexpected topic. He had something else on his mind beside the thrilling rescue. This was not the usual, raucous atmosphere of everyone talking at once. First, he offered an unusually long monologue about the blessings of family. He seemed serious and remained in firm control of the conversation, so no time presented itself for the children to bring up other interests.

Another noticeable element was her mother's particularly silent and sober attitude. Only occasionally did she even nod as she sat stoically with nervous, pursed lips. Helen Sheldon offered not a single word as her husband conducted the conversation. To Hattie's growing chagrin, neither parent mentioned the Underground Railroad rescue, but it had to be on their minds.

"Tonight I would like to hear from each of you children," her father announced after everyone had filled their plates with roast duck accompanied by potatoes and stewed pumpkin. "In recent days, I admit I've become too absorbed outside our family. While we're together and I'm able to give you all my attention, it's a good time to hear about your schoolwork, your teachers, and the status of your education."

How boring. Hattie moped as her siblings began to whisper and formulate their comments as they ate their supper. Without delay, her father began to call upon them one by one. Sitting still while listening to five dull reports seemed like torture to Hattie. She ignored her food and stared out the window at the swing on the big tree. Why did they have to do this tonight? What was so important that they couldn't talk about the rescue mission? All she wanted was to hear about this one, terribly pressing issue.

Next to her, little Artemas sat propped up on some big books so he could see over the sizable table. He must be as bored as she was. She turned semi-attentively when he reached over and tugged at her ruffled sleeve.

A very precocious little fellow, Artemas smiled widely with big, innocent eyes and gestured that he had a surprise for her. Opening her hand, she held it out to the little rascal in complete trust. But all Artemas deposited there was a watery glob of something slimy. Hattie screamed and dropped it.

"That's not fair," she wailed, jumping up from the dinner table and drawing everyone's attention. "I wanted to talk about last night, but all I get is a dead tadpole."

Looking strangely relieved over the commotion, her mother came to her side and brought back order.

"Please excuse us," she apologized, taking Hattie and Artemas' hands to escort them upstairs.

❖ ❖ ❖

Hattie pouted while waiting for her mother. It seemed to take forever to tuck Artemas in. The lamp's wick glowed brightly, reflecting from the window as she stretched out on her patchwork quilt. She traced the initial "H" in the condensation on the window nearest her bed. Her thoughts returned to the excitement of getting away from the man with the big gun and the mean dog. In detail, she relived the whole event, its sounds and smells and shadows.

As the minutes grew longer, Hattie also began to entertain exciting, new expectations for the next rescue mission her family would undertake. Why, at any time, they must be likely to receive word about another group of runaway slaves, or even a family needing their help to move closer toward freedom in Canada.

In her mind's eye, Hattie had already transformed the real frights from the rescue into something quite different. The fear from the night before, and even the memory of it, was disappearing quickly. She couldn't even recall being that scared. Now, in the glow of the rescue's success, the night had been full of pure excitement.

How had she been so lucky, as the youngest girl in her family, to go on such a grand adventure? She knew one thing for sure; she would never, ever forget it. And as proof that it happened, she held tight to the little cross the slave woman had fashioned. As she contemplated the future and her dream of more rescues, Hattie knew she must take the woman's gift and its message seriously.

Saying her prayers, she tucked the cross under her pillow gently and curled up. She could picture the woman placing the cross in her mother's hand and saying thank you. Just last Sunday, the preacher had said the same thing the Negro woman had said: the cross brought us this far and saved us. So Hattie made a vow then and there that, as long as she lived, as long as she could help anyone, she would let the cross do the work in all future rescues or adventures.

This decided, she stretched and yawned, forgetting completely about the upset at the supper table. Her eyes felt sleepy, and she lost track of time as she relaxed against the warmth of her quilt. The next thing she knew, it was completely dark outside. But the sound of voices had jolted her awake. Sitting up, she wiped sleep from her eyes and realized that the voices weren't happy. They were agitated and they were out in the hallway.

Cracking the door, she peered through the slit into the upstairs hallway. It was too dark to make out the difference between the papered walls and the dark woodwork. The voices weren't coming from downstairs, because her older siblings were laughing and talking there while playing a game at the table. The voices speaking in raised tones must be upstairs.

She peered to the end of the hall. Only the thinnest crack of light appeared from under her parent's bedroom door. Hattie decided to walk down the hallway to see if they were in there. Maybe she had just dreamed about a heated conversation. Her parents were probably asleep, but why not walk on tiptoe to keep from waking them? She knew exactly where the squeaks were located in the flooring and was careful to avoid those spots just in case.

Reaching the wall outside their bedroom, she suddenly heard a stern, whispered exchange. They were arguing!

"Nothing happened, Helen," her father urged. "Not a hair on their heads was touched."

"But we came excruciatingly close," her mother replied tensely, emphasizing each syllable.

"That doesn't count. It's over, so there's no reason to belabor the issue."

"Oh, there is every reason! Things could have gone wrong in seconds," her mother countered firmly. "I can't get that out of my mind. It haunts me. I can't sleep."

"Then I'll do it alone from here on out."

"That won't work either," her mother replied. "You got them energized. They expect to help in the future. You'll look disingenuous if you go around their backs."

"You're giving me few options, Helen," her father muttered. "Why are you tightening the noose? What has happened to you?"

"I'm perfectly fine and don't use the word noose," her mother returned. "You know I believe that the work is worthy. I also know we've been watched. In the future, someone else can do this work."

"How can your conscience accommodate that?" Hattie's father countered. "It sends a truly selfish message to those who remain committed and active. Our concerns are no better than theirs, yet they support the network. "

"I don't owe them or anyone else an explanation," her mother retorted in a trembling voice. "My job is to protect the innocents in our care. No matter how worthy this cause of yours is, I could never get over it if something should happen. Don't you have any fear?"

"It goes against everything we're taught, dear," her father replied slowly. "I choose to have faith instead."

"Faith is fine, but I want safety. No matter how you disguise it, we were almost apprehended," her mother whispered excitedly. "They came within an inch of violence. Never again, do you hear me? Never! I want them safe!"

Afraid of being caught, Hattie quickly returned to the girls' bedroom. What had made her parents so upset? They were using so many big words. Try as she might, she couldn't completely understand what they were talking about. What did accommodate and innocents and apprehended mean? Why was her mother so concerned about violence?

Crawling back into bed, Hattie hoped she would learn more tomorrow. Compared to the excitement of the rescue mission, however, this minor upset between her parents was nothing. Of far greater importance was the fact that Hattie now had a sense of purpose. Her number one priority was the next rescue mission and getting prepared for the challenge. She wanted to be much more involved with planning all subsequent rescues.

On the other hand, her mother's words about safety began to make sense. Safety must be very important, because it had prompted a level of words and emotions from her mother that Hattie had never before experienced.

One day, these two forces would struggle within Hattie herself. The memory of this night, of her father's heroism and sense of purpose, would hang in the balance beside the slaves' terror.

2

No Resolution, No Discussion

Years passed before Hattie got any satisfying answers. In the meantime, her father moved the family and his business some forty miles north to Utica, New York, a growing city with wide, handsome avenues on the shore of the Mohawk River. Before long, her siblings seemed so grown up. George became their father's young partner, while Albert threatened to quit school and join the militia. Alongside her sisters Amanda, Mary and Cornelia, Hattie spent endless hours laughing and swapping stories. Often, they took turns spoiling their youngest brother, Artemas.

The Mohawk River's link to the miraculously engineered Erie Canal brought waves of travelers through Utica, making it a leading transportation center. Close to the river's hustle and bustle, their needs led the Sheldon saddle, trunk, and harness business to thrive. Hattie's father often joked that explorers' money expanded his pockets.

Traders, explorers, and even troublemakers needed the leather goods Ebenezer Sheldon crafted. For the first time in the young nation's history, he said, people had ventured beyond their dreams. Finally it was possible to travel from the Atlantic to the Pacific. They were headed west on newly proven routes from places like Boston, Montreal, and even Great Britain. Many believed fortune awaited them on the frontier. Those seeking more modest goals passed through Utica on their way to territories created from the Louisiana Purchase's vast acres, where they intended to put down roots.

❁ ❁ ❁

Just a few blocks from the handsomely painted front entrance of Ebenezer Sheldon & Son, the shore of the Mohawk offered many beautiful places to walk or relax near magnificent tall trees and grand rocks. Townspeople gathered there to picnic on nice days. A handful of folks always congregated to watch the colorful procession of ships and smaller boats. Most were curious to learn what was happening at the docks, as well.

After church on Sundays during warm weather, the Sheldons sometimes joined their closest friends, the Twimbleys, for an afternoon of relaxation and conversation down by the river. They were like-minded, faithful friends who shared a commitment to abolitionism. Ebenezer Sheldon and Daniel Twimbley attended the Utica Anti-Slavery society meetings together. Hattie knew that her father took quiet pride in supporting the Society's political and humanitarian crusades. He said it was the right thing to do.

"This movement is unmatched previously in the history of America, or the world for that matter," he bragged to his children.

As she matured and became more observant, Hattie realized

something else. Her father and Mr. Twimbley kept watch. They were vigilant about every move and every word for fear of being noticed by spies who could unravel the Underground Railroad's secret network. Discovery remained a constant threat, so the careful relaying of information was vital. Spies could lurk around any corner. Even one careless word could get people killed, so tense was the disagreement between pro and anti-slavery folks. Unrest and even riots had become more common in Utica as some supporters of abolition were caught, identified publicly, and pushed before angry street crowds demanding an account of their actions.

The Twimbley's youngest child, Margaret, was Hattie's best friend and confidant. Having reached the ripe old age of nine, the girls now saw themselves as mature, but they still compared notes to gain a better understanding of the adult world they didn't quite grasp. As much as they wanted to stay abreast of the talk between their mothers, occasions presented themselves so rarely to snoop into their fathers' business. They took advantage of an innocent opportunity one day while picnicking together by the river.

After feasting on chicken, the two men had separated themselves from the ladies to discuss private matters. They didn't seem to take notice that Hattie and Margaret were seated nearby, pretending to play a quiet little game. Hattie's interest grew when she heard the words "splintering of the movement."

"Did you read the editorial?" Ebenezer commented, his pipe smoke curling upward. "I found the language less than helpful."

Daniel nodded. "And I quote: 'To their great disdain, the minds of many on the one side began to be swayed against the extreme and even seditious acts by a few on the other side.' You heard that two were wounded, didn't you?"

"You mean just last night?" Ebenezer questioned, a look of controlled concern on his brow.

"The bloodhounds lost them after they slipped into the river," Daniel explained. "A number of shots were fired, and two separate trails of blood led to the river's edge."

Hattie's stomach took a jump of alarm. She wished she had been a rescuer last night. What would she have done when the escaping slaves were wounded and jumped into the river? What would her father have done? She wondered how many were shot. It must have been horribly painful to feel river water in a gunshot wound! Hattie couldn't imagine enduring the pain, yet pushing forward to freedom. What a valiant thing!

Any talk of freedom always reminded her of her father's undying faith in the union. He often told stories of the revolution when America had to fight for her freedom. Sometimes, Hattie had a hard time lining up her understanding of how that was threatened by slavery. But always, she returned to the fact that her father stressed his firm biblical principles over and over. Those beliefs reminded her how freedom and slavery were opposites.

"I see a dangerous trend developing overall," Ebenezer summarized, tugging nervously at his chin whiskers. "The papers report more unrest every day. I fear for our movement. For the brave . . ."

"Or are we the foolhardy?" Margaret's father questioned, a grave expression shadowing his comment.

❖ ❖ ❖

"Come along, Hattie," her father called from the workroom of his shop. "We're going to the docks on a delivery."

Hattie was thrilled. She loved how deliveries turned into adventures. Her father's customers at the docks and beyond represented the most intriguing swath of humanity she had ever encountered. Every sort of person could be seen at the docks—tall, short, fat, skinny. They sported all manner of whiskers. There were cranky people and jolly, laughing people. She liked to compare their faces, the sounds of their languages, and their unusual attire, among other traits. The dark faces of the Indians were as intriguing as the nearly albino faces of Scandinavians. To Hattie, the people of the world were a source of endless color, culture, and variety.

To Ebenezer, however, the most notable thing these people had in common was progress. Because they were on the move, he said he could make a good living. Once the ships, canoes, rafts, and commercial boats docked, the people and their belongings or the businessmen and their wares were met by buggies, carts, wagons, and everything in between. A good number of them needed something Hattie's father manufactured and sold at his shop.

Ebenezer Sheldon's acumen at sales, along with his exuberant personality, attracted buyers for his custom saddles, trunks, and harnesses. In addition to the big items, he saw possibilities where other merchants might just see scraps. After he had hammered in the last tack to complete a saddle or trunk, he scooped up the leather leftovers. Ebenezer turned these into affordable small goods like wallets, satchels, or pouches that were desirable to passengers. Some of the intrepid travelers, at least in Hattie's view, looked so dirty or threadbare they must have no money. But after her father pointed out their obvious needs, they produced cash from soggy or well-worn pockets.

Arriving at the river for the delivery, Hattie wiggled with excitement while watching the bustling activity the dock brought to town. If her family hadn't moved from little Burlington to Utica, she would never have seen any of this. Each time she watched a boatload of relieved but tired emigrants disembark, she knew they carried many hopes and dreams. A few unknowing, disenfranchised souls, especially those on crowded ships, also carried a deadly stowaway called disease.

In January of 1846, following the arrival of several troubled vessels, an outbreak of rashy illness began to plague Uticans and their children. The disease struck just when endless snows had tamped down the community's spirits. Rumors sounded foreboding, so Ebenezer directed his children to stay warm, dry, and close to home.

"After school, you steer clear of that dock," he warned.

But nobody knew for sure how to avoid the threatening illness called measles. It continued to come closer. After treating the victims, doctors agreed that, for unknown reasons, children in large families were more susceptible than those with few siblings. This single fact turned the happy Sheldon children into invisible threats toward one another.

Stricken first was Mary Sheldon, a fifteen-year-old brunette secretly smitten with a handsome neighbor boy. Mary first complained of a sore throat and then developed a burning fever. For a couple of days, before she broke out in the red rash, no one thought her illness was serious.

Hattie viewed Mary as her role model. A lively personality, Mary was like a second mother. She braided Hattie's hair every morning and let her go along sometimes when she went to visit friends.

Within days, three more of Hattie's siblings also became ill. Amanda, eighteen, fell ill with a dry cough. Cornelia, thirteen, first noticed a runny nose. Artemas, nine, found himself unable to remain in any room with bright light. He said his eyes hurt.

But Mary's malaise was the most serious. Before long, she complained of many more symptoms, including a profusion of strange spots in her mouth on the inside of each cheek. Feeling weak and uncomfortable, she stayed in bed.

Hattie watched the situation with tremendous confusion, wondering if she was next. But nothing happened. She remained perfectly well and wondered why she had been spared.

Soon, it became clear that Mary was deteriorating further. Time didn't seem to bring healing. Each hour dragged on and on, the January bleakness encouraging more worry. Hattie wondered if it wasn't a silent warning sign when some ladies came over to help. Until then, she hadn't realized that her mother had cared for her siblings round the clock.

Hattie listened to every word the ladies muttered. Something about the way they whispered in the corner alarmed her. It sounded too secretive. When people whispered like that, it meant they had something to hide. What were the ladies hiding? Their expressions were solemn, their tone serious. Were all her siblings growing sicker? Frightened after her mother finally went to bed, Hattie ran to her father for comfort.

"When will they be well?" she implored through misty eyes. "I'm scared."

"Why, there's nothing to fret over," her father assured her. "The ladies are here to change linens. After fever sweats, clean, dry sheets will help the children rest better. When someone's sick, it's also important to bathe their foreheads. Mother needed rest, so the ladies are helping. Don't worry. Artemas is already perking up."

Hattie dried her eyes as she went to bed, but still sensed

seriousness. The next morning, the girls looked and sounded more frightening. Hattie wanted her mother, but minded when the ladies separated her from her ailing siblings. Something must be terribly wrong. They explained that they had doctor's orders, which she'd never heard of.

"You can sleep down here by mother and me," her father soothed. "I'll make you a special place. Once everyone's better, you can go back to sharing a room upstairs."

For the longest time that first night, Hattie couldn't get comfortable on her little pallet. To make matters worse, she found herself unable to fall asleep because of her father's snoring. She didn't like being kept from her sisters. A strange sort of homesickness troubled her into the night. In her whole life, she had never slept anywhere but next to her sisters.

Hours later, uncertain if she had slept or not, Hattie discovered that her mother wasn't there.

"Father, wake up," she whispered, shaking his arm gently. "Where's mother?"

Ebenezer rubbed his eyes, then hugged her and sat her on the edge of his bed. "Mother is just being a mother," he explained. "She's taking care of the girls."

"Well, if she can go in with them, why can't I?" Hattie fretted.

"I'm sorry, but you must stay here. It's not wise for you to go into the sick room with the others," he explained softly as he tucked her into her pallet again.

The next morning, Hattie jumped up to find out the latest. At breakfast, she learned that she would continue to be separated from the other children. This was unwelcome news. On the other hand, she was encouraged to hear that Amanda, Cornelia, and little Artemas were better!

The ladies began to take food upstairs again. Someone had made an aromatic chicken soup, saying it would make everyone well. However, when she walked by the kitchen later, Hattie overheard that Mary had been moved to a separate room at the end of the upstairs hall. A worried-looking woman in a wilted blue dress said nobody was supposed to take any food to that room. Hattie's mind raced. Mary wasn't eating? She had been sick for days. Surely she was weak from hunger.

The next time Hattie's mother came downstairs, her morose expression sent an alarming signal. The level of tension in the house rose precipitously. Hattie fell silent and waited, but not patiently. The ladies, heads down, had ceased to whisper among themselves. Previously full of life, the house grew deathly quiet except for a few creaks on the stairs when someone went up or down.

Mary's further decline brought confusion and heartache, then horror when her symptoms became grave. Hattie's father paced and puffed his pipe constantly. Mr. Twimbley brought over a loaf of bread as a kindly gesture. Instead of inviting him in, Hattie's father stepped out on the frigid porch for a few minutes. She heard his voice break as he talked with his friend.

"Mary's got shortness of breath. She suffering more nosebleeds and jerking movements," he whispered, wiping his eyes with his handkerchief.

"Heaven bless her," Mr. Twimbley replied, shivering. "Can I help?"

"I doubt anyone can. This is in God's hands," her father returned soberly.

As light snow began to fall that night, Mary died.

❧ ❧ ❧

In the days that followed, Hattie felt much older than her twelve years. Not only were the skies in Utica grey and the winds sharp, but her emotions felt the same. She had known that death was final, but hadn't ever realized what final felt like. It was far sadder than her wildest dreams envisioned. Her face felt tight, as if the tears had made permanent tracks down her cheeks and shriveled her skin.

If only she could have told Mary goodbye, could have let her sister know how much she adored and admired her. But maybe Mary would have been alarmed to hear such talk, especially if she didn't know she was going to die, Hattie realized. *It might have upset her if I said things like that. What should I say to the others?*

When they weren't at work, George and Albert spent nearly every hour at the house. But Hattie felt the family seemed disconnected and far away even as they sat together in the same room. Most of the time, they just stared silently.

Home didn't feel much like home anymore. The glow of the lamps was not warm, the cushions not soft, the rooms not friendly. Even conversation seemed superfluous. There really was nothing to say, although her parents tried when people came to pay their respects.

Finally, Hattie grew so disconnected that she sneaked upstairs to talk to Amanda, who was weak but much better. Pale Amanda couldn't stop crying. This broke Hattie's heart to an even deeper degree. Amanda said over and over how she wished she had died instead of Mary.

"Mary was a better person than I am," she told a somber, speechless Hattie.

Then there was poor, listless Artemas. He, too, couldn't seem to dry his tears. But Hattie knew Artemas couldn't stop crying because he was confused as well as ill, poor little fellow. Like her, he had adored Mary and couldn't understand why she had died and he had lived. Still sickly in the next bed, but with less acute symptoms, Cornelia continued to sleep most of the time, her dark curls flattened by the pillow.

In Hattie's estimation, the tables seemed to turn about who was taking care of whom in this unbearable, grief-stricken state. Upon losing Mary, her parents were barely able to notice, much less comfort their other children. Her mother just stared unfocused out the window through swollen eyes. Her father shut himself in the bedroom for a while.

After a few hours, Hattie was grateful that the church ladies brought food, because her mother certainly wasn't cooking. After he emerged from the bedroom, her father just sat glassy eyed and looked blankly at the newspaper he was holding, but not reading. She had never seen her parents like this. It felt like the world had ground to a sudden halt.

Hattie was too young to have experienced the ritual of death. It came as a shock when her mother appeared in a rather formal black dress she had never seen before. Black was said to be customary for mourning, but Hattie didn't want to dress like that. In fact, she had always wanted a white dress, especially for her upcoming baptism. After she happened to mention this timidly, a new white dress suddenly appeared. She had no idea where it had come from and didn't intend to ask. But it felt tainted, especially after her mother insisted that it be adorned with an armlet of black ribbon.

For such a terrible occasion as a funeral, Hattie didn't want to wear that special dress. She also did not want to see her beloved sister in a coffin, but there the coffin sat in the front drawing room embellished with black crepe draping. Periodically, she broke away from the people who came to visit and peeked around the corner at the coffin. Each time, she hoped the nightmare would prove to be a bad dream.

Looking around at the funeral, Hattie studied sad, familiar faces as they marched soberly up the aisle and into the pews. Most avoided eye contact. Even if she had wanted to talk with them, it was obvious they didn't know what to say. Seeing them this way helped her accept that Mary really was gone.

The church bells, which always rang with the loveliest tones, echoed somber and dark. She decided these were the saddest sounds she had ever heard. Repetition made the gloominess worse, as did the minor key of the melodies. The bells seemed to cry out, "Mary's gone, Mary's gone."

Aching emotion followed the gloomy procession out of the church. Step by step, the horses drew the coffin higher up the frozen ground to the old cemetery on the hill. The snow had stopped, but the frigid wind remained, cutting bitterly at Hattie and the other mourners. Soon, they stood in a half circle around the grave.

Reverend Philemon Fowler, the Sheldon's pastor, took his place before the family to offer words of comfort. Hattie closed her eyes against the wind and the hurt, hoping she would remember as little of it as possible. Instead, she thought of going to church with Mary not so long ago. Mary's bright smile that day had given away how much she harbored a secret affection for the boy who would never get to become her beau.

❁ ❁ ❁

By the time Hattie got home from the cemetery, her feet were all but frozen and throbbed painfully. The family dissipated to individual corners of several rooms. Hattie took wooden, clumsy steps up the stairs to the girls' bedroom, longing to be where she could warm up and release her sobs.

Falling asleep upon a tear-stained pillow, she missed supper. Nobody came after her. The next morning, she didn't wake up until ten o'clock, something unheard of in the household.

❁ ❁ ❁

The Sheldon children had always taken their cues from their father, the acknowledged leader of the family. But after Mary died, something shifted in an unspoken way. Their mother, who didn't seem like herself, now began to exert new influence, to accommodate less conversation when it came to decision-making. It wasn't obvious at first, at least while the family wandered in its initial fog of disbelief and pain.

As the days passed, silence and sadness gave way to talk of everyday things. The children came to understand when it was best to show support with a hug rather than words. They were more helpful and cooperative about chores. Still, their mother seemed to inhabit her own world, and they wondered sometimes if she even knew what day it was.

❖ ❖ ❖

"I heard my father talking about the Underground Railroad again," Margaret shared the next week when Hattie went back to school.

"So did I. But it was so confusing," Hattie returned in a dejected tone. "Promise you won't tell?"

"Cross my heart and …" Margaret promised, and then interrupted herself. "I almost said 'hope to die.' Sorry."

"That's all right," Hattie forgave, looking wistful. "We say the wrong thing around mother all the time."

"But what did you hear?" Margaret pursued.

Hattie weighed her words. "Something put our rescue work to a stop. I think Father wants to start again. But Mother's beside herself over losing Mary and told father she can't bear any more loss."

❖ ❖ ❖

Once the family was reacclimatized to community and church, Hattie found out they were not alone in their bitter tears. The illness that killed Mary had also taken the lives of many others in Utica. Thank goodness that Amanda, Artemas, and Cornelia survived! How blessed Hattie felt about that fact, especially when Artemas, then Amanda, got back on their feet.

Amanda was always best at reading their mother's mood. As her energy returned, she began to help with household duties once again. But their mother, who was looking drained and listless, wouldn't allow her or Hattie to take care of Cornelia, who remained sickly and weak.

Helen Sheldon kept a vigil over Cornelia, to the point where

Hattie watched her father frown at her mother a little too often. Sometimes, her mother seemed disinterested in any of her other children's needs or activities. But other times, when they thought she seemed happier, she might rise up unexpectedly and scold them for the slightest thing. They didn't know where they stood with her and grew uneasy, but forgiveness covered over those rough spots for a while.

❖ ❖ ❖

Through the support of their church family and one another, healing came, although slowly. After a few weeks, Hattie found diversion from her sadness at the shop. The routine of sweeping and organizing her father's worktable brought a renewed sense of usefulness and value. She felt like her old self and paid attention in a heightened way.

Working at the shop exposed her to action and activity, to movement and dreams. All the explorers' colorful stories rang with new insights and prompted fresh ideas. Each day, Hattie soaked up a more graphic picture of life beyond Utica. Tales from remote places revealed the world to be profoundly exciting, full of abundance, and lush with variety. The people in the shop proved to be more diverse than anyone she had met before. What did the rest of humanity look and feel like?

Hattie didn't come to a sudden realization that she wanted adventure. Rather, she slowly comprehended that it was the right future for her. She desired a fresh brand of wisdom that people in Utica didn't seem to have. Those who impressed her had traveled and learned lessons that weren't taught locally.

In the light of comparison, it was sad how poor Mary had been robbed of her chance for a future and opportunity to enjoy adventure. Mary would never spread her wings. Would Hattie? When? What if she got sick, too? There were so many *what if* questions.

Slowly, Cornelia seemed to improve. One day when her mother fell asleep, Hattie fed Cornelia some soup and took her for a little walk around the bedroom. After that, she was allowed to help more often. It felt like happier days, and their closeness grew. A mere shadow of her former self, however, Cornelia's once bright eyes lay dark and hollow in their sockets. But her spirit was strong.

Cornelia wanted to get well and spoke of her future. Hattie regaled her with tall tales from the shop. Once again, the sound of laughter lightened spirits in the house. With a sigh of relief, the Sheldon family took heart. A time followed in which no one took the others for granted. Happy times together were almost sacred.

As March arrived with warmer winds, the weeks of grief gave way. A growing sense of normality returned to the family and, with it, routine.

"Hattie, come right home after school, because I'll need your help," her mother directed one day as Hattie gobbled a savory breakfast of fried eggs and toast.

"But I promised Margaret she could go with me to the shop," Hattie complained.

"You know its laundry day," her mother reminded. "It's got to be done."

"Then why can't Cornelia help?" Hattie argued.

"Why, Hattie, you know she can't!"

"Then Artemas can do it for a change," Hattie retorted.

"That's enough now. Boys don't do laundry. I need help I can count on. Do as I say."

Before the Sheldons even realized they had overcome the worst of their grief, the happiness within reach was broken again suddenly. No sooner had they returned home from their mid-March church supper than Cornelia complained of abdominal discomfort. She confided to Hattie that their mother worried about her too much. So she had hidden her growing nausea for the last twenty-four hours. After she had been out and grown tired, it became worse quickly.

Five long days of decline ensued at a time when Cornelia's defenses were still low. Certain that improvement was just around the corner, the family kept up hope despite her deterioration through diarrheal cramps to fever and dehydration. Everyone stayed quiet and prayed constantly.

Hattie's mother seemed to suffer Cornelia's relapse in a way that eluded comfort. When the ladies came on duty again to relieve her, she refused food, wept openly, and wandered the house looking listless. Later, she resumed her exhausting bedside vigil, only to fall asleep when she thought a period of quiet meant Cornelia was improving.

Cornelia died during that silent interlude. It was the blackest, most bitter night of the late winter. Before dawn, Hattie's sleep was shattered by her mother's screams upon discovering Cornelia's demise.

The Sheldon family was devastated. Losing two precious girls in two months was unthinkable. Icy winds and sleet made the second funeral more miserable than the first.

3

Safe

The summer of 1846 came and went without any merrymaking. Deep, overwhelming grief hung like heavy smoke over Hattie's family. The unnoticed summer was followed by a rather dull school year. The Sheldons plodded along and struggled to overcome their sadness. Hattie continued to feel more comfortable at her father's shop than at home.

By the fall of 1847, right after she turned fourteen, Hattie found every possible opportunity to rub elbows with grizzled travelers and colorful fortune seekers at the shop. Their rough edges never intimidated her as they shopped among the wares. Her father's business having grown, two newly hired craftsmen now produced popular styles of traveling trunks and leather satchels. Customers snatched them up as soon as they reached the sales floor. Transactions were always more brisk in cooler weather, so her father had worked many late nights that humid summer to be ready for his growing customer base in the fall.

Some buyers, wide-eyed over the size of the Mohawk River valley, had jumped off the railroad for just a few hours, swapping stories of the 1840s with Ebenezer and bragging about the hard use their new leather goods would endure. Hattie envied their anticipated quests in the great, uncharted west. What they didn't know was that she had more than a few far-flung ideas on her own horizon.

"We're almost adults now," Hattie reminded Margaret as they whispered about the changes in their bodies that had happened so fast. "I've been thinking about the future. The other day, a man in the shop said his wife was only sixteen when they married. Can you imagine?"

"We couldn't attend the Utica Female Academy if we got married that young," Margaret agreed.

"I know. My hopes are still set on getting into that school. But afterwards, we could go out West. I'm dying to see new territories and ride river rapids and feel fur pelts! That sounds far more exciting than settling down."

"To be honest," Margaret confessed, "since my sister got married and had babies, it's pretty obvious she's not happy. Raising children can be monotonous."

"But she was so madly in love."

"Well, it didn't take long for that to fade away."

"I never thought of it like that before."

"Neither did I until she begged me not to tell," Margaret revealed. "Mother would kill her. She'd be in hot water with your mother ... and everyone else's mother who thinks we just need to get married and have babies."

Hattie blinked soberly as she envisioned crying babies, laundry, cooking, and staying at home. "I think I'd rather go to school longer."

Through discussions like this, Hattie had begun to question why old customs limited young women. Although her ideas about life's prospects were only partially formed, she could name more girls in recent years that had broken with tradition. Most continued their education, while some traveled and others taught school outside their home sphere.

With their examples in mind, Hattie anticipated many explorations, certain that her future held possibilities for stretching the boundaries she encountered so often. Would she ever again rescue escaping slaves with the Underground Railroad? What about becoming a teacher in a school? Maybe a missionary society might accept and station her among foreign people with great needs.

Flying out the door to school, Hattie brushed past some little yellow blossoms near the gate as she escaped the confines of home. She disliked the growing regularity with which her mother called her back to help around the house. Ordinary chores and cooking were so solitary. She had come to realize she just wasn't oriented toward staying at home. There were so many things to do and a growing list of needs at the shop. She couldn't wait for the months ahead when she would spend every summer day there.

"Hattie, come back," her mother called anxiously from the back porch.

Hattie stopped and turned around, an annoyed expression on her face. "Why? I'm in a hurry."

"Your father's working late tonight," her mother explained. "I need you to come home after school and take his supper to the shop."

"Oh, not again! It's out of the way to come back here before going to the shop. Why can't you take his food?"

"I've got a committee meeting at the church, dear. Now, promise me."

Nodding with frustration, Hattie agreed. But she wasn't happy to be assigned this chore.

"After he's been fed, you come straight home," her mother continued. "I've made a list of things you need to do."

Hattie's countenance dropped, and she sighed disappointedly. Then she turned on her heel and disappeared. Coming home to get her father's food was an extra trip she didn't want to make. But since it was for him, she would follow through.

❋ ❋ ❋

The roast beef and potatoes she was carrying smelled marvelous as she ambled down the street. It was worth the long walk if the food pleased her father. The day was perfection with high, thin clouds wafting by. Hattie looked across the street at the regal Second Presbyterian Church, its magnificent, grey steeple reaching skyward. An alert observer, she watched a squirrel scamper along a thin tree branch. In his wake, a few leaves fluttered down to the sidewalk. Despite the annoying logistics of her errand, a feeling of energy and worth made her march with intention. The day, the work ahead, and the city felt invigorating.

If she climbed on one of the many doorsteps she passed and stretched as tall as possible, the Mohawk River came into view, its greenish teal water carrying ever more new customers to the shop, the railroad, or the Erie Canal. Utica possessed a sense of movement, as if nothing stood still.

Hattie had begun to brush elbows daily with merchants. The traffic around their shops thrilled her, as did the speaking acquaintances.

She envisioned getting up the nerve to ask the shopkeepers about where their customers came from and what news they brought. More women and young ladies had begun to shop unaccompanied downtown, which was an encouragement for an independent-minded girl.

Approaching Bagg's Hotel, Hattie paused to review the scene before her. A white-aproned man was busily washing its front windows. Her father often spoke of the writers, artists, and diplomats who had slept there. She hoped he would take her inside for a look one day.

Rounding the corner onto the busy thoroughfare called Genesee Street, a woman with a heavy basket full of potatoes crossed the street. Horses with switching tails stood dejectedly behind their blinders, waiting to take a load from a shop here to a home somewhere else. A man threw a bucket of cloudy water into the street.

Near him, Hattie noticed a strange-looking cart unlike any she had seen before. The cart's wood looked old and its design had a low, crude construction. Most carts were open, but this one was enclosed with a door at the back whose opening was covered with heavy, bent wire. As Hattie pondered what kind of animal it must transport, a thin black hand reached through the wire. She gasped, stopping cold. A human being was inside that awful cart.

A split second later, shouts signaled some kind of trouble. In her peripheral vision, something large came hurtling through the air toward her head. Hattie ducked, her reflexes instantaneous and lifesaving. She responded so rapidly that not even a yelp had time to escape her lips. Smashing against the cobblestone street the next instant, a chair splintered into scores of jagged pieces. Next to it, Hattie lay dazed and shaken, but unhurt.

Angry voices filled the air, followed by the unmistakable sound of breaking glass. Looking around warily, in ten seconds time,

Hattie had focused on the doorway from which other troubling noises poured out. She heard the screech of moving furniture, angry shouts, and the scuffle of irregular footsteps. Without question, more violence was coming. Dusty and tingling from the scare, she stayed down and crawled a few feet before rolling flat against the building for safety. She forgot all about her clothes in the process of trying to keep her father's food from spilling.

The fight had started inside Warnick and Brown Tobacco Company, whose door barely hung on its broken hinges now. Suddenly, more threats and guttural cries erupted onto the street as three men exploded out the door, landing in a gnarled heap. This wasn't just any fight, Hattie realized, as she continued to inch away as fast as possible.

At eye level, she looked straight into the faces of two filthy, disheveled bounty hunters who were battling a Negro man fighting back unsuccessfully. One of the wild white men jumped on top of the Negro and grabbed the poor man's hair, smashing his head to the ground. The other attacker pounced to hold the bleeding man down. Both began to punch him with brutal, hard blows about the chest and abdomen, obviously fueled by fierce strength and anger.

Dazed, the outnumbered man's eyes rolled back, and he lost consciousness. This allowed an easier effort for the bounty hunters as they rolled him onto his stomach, then pulled and tied his arms back so strenuously that they must have come out of their sockets. Hattie's stomach retched at the brutality of the attack.

"Your taste of freedom just came to an end, boy," shouted one of the hunters who looked like a mad, mongrel dog. "You don't belong up North," he fairly spat.

"We're here to take you back home, back down South," the other laughed haughtily, a disgusting curl coming to his crooked lip.

After they opened the door to the horrid cart, Hattie saw the terrified faces of other captured Negroes, some half lifeless. Inches from the fray, her heartbeat thudded heavily into her throat. If only she could help them. But she knew she faced getting caught up in the violence. Looking for a way out, she saw her one option and knew she must take the risk to run.

In a sudden daring move, Hattie abandoned the food and jumped up to dart around the men. Bursting to full speed past the cart, she couldn't avoid a particularly filthy part of the street, replete with mud liquefied by a recent thunderstorm. Under foot of horses, carriages, and wagons, the rain had mixed dirty hay and horse waste to form the muck that everyone in town sought to avoid. In no time, Hattie was heavily soiled yet out of sight, no longer a part of the hateful attack to steal the Negro man's hard-fought freedom.

Never frightened for her personal safety, Hattie lost no time heading for her father's shop. It was not hard to grasp the meaning of the roundup she had just witnessed. She knew exactly what she must do. With each step, she grew angrier about what was happening.

All families involved in abolitionism knew they must help the North's free Negroes who feared being kidnapped back into slavery by unscrupulous hunters. Episodes like this roundup were becoming more commonplace in Utica and beyond. Gaining strength, Hattie realized she hadn't raced this fast in a long time.

Reaching the shop out of breath, she paused to peer through the front window and check for the presence of customers. Seeing that the shop was empty, Hattie burst through the lettered door and began to shout to her father.

"Quick, there's a slave roundup!" she cried as loud as her winded lungs would allow. "Some awful bounty hunters are capturing Negroes down the street. They're headed this way."

In a split second, Ebenezer Sheldon jumped from his workbench and ran to lock the front door. Rushing into the back room, he grabbed his hat and coat.

"Silas, we must run," he called to the free Negro man who worked in the back at his saddle shop. "Get in my carriage and hunker down. We still have time." Turning back, Ebenezer shouted instructions to Hattie as he grabbed the reins and turned the carriage toward the street.

"Hattie, keep watch at the front and don't unlock the door unless you know the customer. Just say that I've gone on a delivery."

Dismayed, Hattie was shocked that her father departed so quickly. There hadn't been a split second to think, much less express her expectations. She had wanted to be part of the getaway—to play a useful, life-changing role as she had as a little girl. While she was running toward the shop, she anticipated facing the kidnappers or helping summon other local merchants to take a stand. But her part in this effort was now completely over, long before she wanted it to end.

Hands on her hips, Hattie paced the floor for want of any other way to deal with the overwhelming frustration. It flooded her entire being as she remained there alone with the trunks, saddles, and harnesses. How had she ended up left behind? *Why didn't I speak up*, she griped angrily to the air.

The last place she wanted to be was out of the action. Maybe she should not have run from the fight around the corner. Could she have faced the kidnappers herself while her father helped Silas get away? Probably not, she allowed. Her mind felt cluttered as she thought through different options. It was the first time she had ever hated being in the shop. For that matter, it was the first time she had been left in charge of the shop. If only she could ride in the carriage with her father and Silas. She wanted to feel the wind on her face while saving another innocent soul from the desperation of slavery.

❖ ❖ ❖

Hattie sank down on her father's seat at the workbench. Why was she so often disappointed just because she was a girl? She had always pictured adventure for herself. But, lately, other people emphasized comportment, stifled settings, rigid rules, and quiet conversation for her.

Such limitations had coincided with other changes she and Margaret weren't prepared for. In a surprisingly short time, they had grown to the point where people treated them differently. Their clothes no longer fit the same. Their frames had taken on a different shape. People began to comment and call them "young ladies." Neither of them quite understood, as they were the same they had always been in spirit, intention, and personality.

Hattie felt there was a link between those changes and this situation that denied her the excitement of going with her father. Brooding over her changing fate, she absent-mindedly picked up a hammer and began to pound tacks into a scrap of heavy leather. It just wasn't fair. If she were a boy, she was sure she wouldn't be sitting here all alone and away from the excitement.

Suddenly, rapid knocking at the front door shook her back to attention. Were the kidnappers here already? They had arrived so fast. On high alert, she searched her surroundings for a weapon to protect the shop, to show that she would use force. Dropping the hammer, she grabbed a piece of lumber from a trunk project and held it up in the most threatening way possible. This would show the kidnappers she meant business. If only there were a gun in the shop.

Taking a deep breath, Hattie left the back room on tiptoe, sliding into the shadow along the side wall where she couldn't be seen from the front. If a confrontation was coming, she was ready.

From her vantage point, she spied the silhouette of a person at the door. It fell as a murky shadow through the frosted glass onto the floor. Hattie stopped short. Something wasn't right. She surveyed the outline. This was not a large person like the bounty hunters.

The knocking grew more urgent, which brought doubts. Why would bounty hunters knock anyway? They had crashed through the door at Warnick and Brown's.

Then a familiar woman's voice called her father's name. Hattie recoiled, feeling something like dread. To her great regret, the impatient person at the door was her mother! Her heart sank over what was going to happen. It was almost worse than if a bounty hunter had arrived. She would have much explaining to do.

Moving quickly toward the door, she unlocked and pulled it open. As expected, her mother drew back defensively and then stared at the piece of wood Hattie was still holding.

"What are you doing with that board? Why was the door locked?" her mother challenged.

Shrugging, Hattie took a deep breath and withdrew her weapon, hugging the piece of lumber under her arm as she walked away from the door silently.

"You didn't follow my directions to come home," her mother scolded.

Hattie turned back to see her mother rip at her bonnet ties and cast off her shawl. Then her mother stopped short. "What in the world has happened here?"

"It's a long story," Hattie sighed, her shoulders wilting.

"You look frightful," her mother said as she noticed Hattie's soiled condition. "What is all over your clothes and face?"

Hattie waved a hand in the air silently, hoping to avoid the confrontation she knew was coming.

"Answer me! I've come here sick with worry because you didn't come home! Now you're filthy and sullen. What is wrong?"

"Something terribly more important than looking dirty," Hattie retorted righteously. "A slave roundup is underway downtown. I almost got hit, but managed to run so I could warn Father. He immediately took Silas to safety. THAT is the meaning of this!"

Helen Sheldon's eyes reflected nothing short of horror. "Your father left?"

Then she stopped, cocked her head, and looked around, a suspicious expression on her face.

"YOU'RE HERE ALL ALONE?" her mother cried.

Hattie exhaled, almost growling. She felt trapped, but began to relate the details, one by one. Her mother reacted with disbelief, then rising emotion.

"There are *violent kidnappers* down the block, and he left you all alone?" she repeated, growing pale. "I cannot bear this. We are leaving for the safety of home right now!"

"No! I'm in charge of the shop," Hattie argued, tears streaming down her face. "I don't want to let him down."

"Oh, I can assure you it is QUITE the opposite," her mother returned in a hostile voice, as furious as Hattie had ever seen her. "What if those awful men found you here alone? What if they kidnapped you because you could identify them to the authorities? What if there were more of them and they converged here? What if they had gotten a tip that your father was an abolitionist? There are plenty of pro-slavery troublemakers who use violence against the innocent. They would just love to send the Underground Railroad a painful message. If they did something awful to the little Sheldon girl, it would threaten the whole network. But you couldn't realize that because you're a child. Children belong at home, not protecting businesses."

"Well, they haven't shown up yet," Hattie countered, wide-eyed at her mother's explosion. "I'm sure father will be back soon and then we can leave."

"No. We are leaving this very minute. Forget the shop. You belong at *home.* And not one word about this when we get there." she commanded, pulling Hattie toward an uncomfortable, uncertain future.

The discussion that night would remain in Hattie's memory as one of the most intense of her lifetime. As she traced the pattern of the wallpaper absentmindedly with her finger, she was sure tonight marked a turning point, if not in her actual life, then in her thinking and expectations. She wanted to do something great. Something memorable that was out of the ordinary. She didn't know what, but she realized that her inner drive to do it was growing every day. It had grown by leaps and bounds until her mother pulled her out of the shop and corralled her at home, isolated from people and activity.

Hattie began to see a solid black line dividing her future. Whatever it was, she wanted to choose and follow a vision still in its germination stage. She wished to formulate a clear picture of what would make her dream come true and then act upon it. On the other side of the black line, however, was her mother's idea about what Hattie's future held. She didn't think their ideas were going to intersect.

Today had provided a situation of ample severity to show Hattie the kinds of twists and turns life presented. After she avoided the chair that came hurtling for her head, she knew what to do. As she ran to the shop, the risk had motivated her. New ideas came to mind as she met the challenge. If she could do this, perhaps she could do other more exciting things. But there would probably never be a time when her mother could understand this. Admitting this deep chasm between them brought confusion and a little grief, an emotion already too common in their household.

In anticipation of her father's arrival, Hattie felt a little helpless. All she could think about was how to explain her terrifying experience to her father. She knew he would burst through the front door feeling invigorated. He would instantly share the exciting story of how Silas had been saved from the reaches of the destructive kidnappers. Instead, he would meet with something much less triumphant, much more troubling, and many times more personal.

Hattie had watched her mother prepare for his arrival. She had fed the children simply and sent them to their rooms. The others knew nothing of what had transpired. Crouching on the stairs to listen, Hattie knew something was going to happen the moment her father arrived.

"How could you?" her mother confronted under her breath. "Hattie was left alone at the mercy of whatever wild, uncivilized characters came to the shop."

"Helen, it was about protecting Silas, not Hattie. We may even have saved his life," her father argued.

Hattie knew he didn't yet realize the extent of her mother's agitation.

"Hattie was never at risk," he continued. "I gave her instructions so she would be safe."

"Safe?" her mother fumed, throwing her hands in the air. "NO ONE is safe with these slavers in town. NO place is safe!"

"All they want is Negroes, Helen," he returned resentfully, his voice rising.

"I have worried about your unsavory customers and their influence. But they are nothing in comparison to these bloodthirsty, insane bounty hunters. They are lawless, mad, heathen invaders. Our city and our lives are threatened with violence. They would have overcome Hattie in an instant to search for old Silas! Don't you understand that? Hattie could have been KILLED!"

"That's far-fetched and you know it," her father argued. "It's over. Let's not ruminate on what might have happened."

"What about next time? I am aware that your activities have continued, you know. What about the time after that? No, I cannot live this way. Too much has already been lost. I will not allow anything that threatens another one of our children, do you hear me? I'm not allowing Hattie to be at the shop EVER AGAIN."

At this, Hattie nearly screamed out loud. It took all her might not to speak in her own defense. She had only rarely disobeyed her parents' orders in the past, and she had never debated them on a point this crucial.

On second thought, she couldn't stay silent over something as unjust as this. The shop was her refuge, the place where her future vision was taking root. Maybe it was time to stand up for herself. In her estimation, her mother was unreasonable and using overblown emotion. Her mother wanted to win the argument, which meant limiting Hattie. Emotion welled up inside her and took over. She couldn't bear the idea of remaining at home, like a prisoner.

Rushing down the stairs, she audaciously interrupted the argument. "The shop is my favorite place in the whole world," she cried. "The bounty hunters had an awful cart and locked the Negroes inside like animals. If you keep me away from the shop, it will feel just like that."

Her mother exploded, throwing her hands in the air. Hattie was stunned, but held her ground. Was the outburst a response to her explanation? Or was it because Hattie had interrupted? Whatever the case, her mother sounded like a wounded animal finding that its babies in the nest were all dead. It was almost a primal cry. Within seconds, it brought Amanda running toward the confrontation. When she saw the tearful, unsettling scene with her parents and Hattie, she went silent.

Standing next to Hattie, her father grew upset when Artemas rushed into his arms, alarmed to tears. Hugging him, Ebenezer seemed to study his horrified children, then turned and walked toward their mother. Taking her in his arms, he enveloped her in the strangest way. Hattie couldn't tell if he was comforting her or holding her back. But her mother grew quiet as she relaxed in his hug, breaking into sobs. Hattie and Artemas embraced and walked toward Amanda. The three children stood frozen in place, too awed and confused to move.

❖ ❖ ❖

To Hattie's great distress, her mother did not forget the vow, nor did she change her mind. From the day of the slave roundup forward, she insisted that Hattie return home after school daily instead of going downtown to the shop. It was almost too much to endure. Hattie suffered the change painfully, daydreaming about the old days of meeting raucous storytellers and other travelers. Some days she just sat on the front porch and stared at the street. The silence at home grated on her nerves, often leaving her irritated.

Her dissatisfaction grew. Sometimes she schemed about escaping. Maybe she could slip out and enjoy a little secret time with her father. But how would she get back into the house unnoticed? With great heaviness, Hattie wept that she might never again join him on errands and deliveries or hear all the unusual people's stories.

4

Lucretia Mott's Example

Some time back, Hattie had been so puzzled by grief. Unlike her mother, her father appeared more adept at recovering from grief. He somehow was able to divert his attention to more constructive and encouraging affairs. The same thing happened when he was frustrated. Almost as an act of will, he could control it.

Hattie wished she could, too. But so far, her nerves grated at every thought of the confines of her mother's boundaries. Perhaps she should try to emulate her father, who made a point of commenting on positive things. As family optimist, he took his role seriously. Within a few minutes of arriving home to a quiet, subdued household, he could divert all attention and raise the family's spirits singlehandedly.

After work some days, he stopped into Bagg's Hotel, which still claimed to be the largest hotel in New York State. Hattie knew it was a place to hear lively stories. Her father shared them, along with other fascinating information to brighten the evening. The hotel, he reminded the children, had existed before the city of Utica had a name. And Utica, which once was old Fort Schuyler, had been around since before the Revolution. Her father loved history, which informed his decision-making and animated his verbose storytelling.

"The American dream is coming of age, and the frontier is wide open," he exclaimed with broad gestures.

It was rumored that explorers were searching for gold as far on the distant frontier as a man could travel, in California. Many were racing there with big dreams. But her father warned that explorations for profit were often ill fated. Instead, he suggested other, more noble reasons.

"Americans have a manifest destiny to expand into the vast West," he narrated. "We who have been blessed have an obligation to democracy and to our God. We must take freedom and Christianity to the far reaches of our land."

Back in 1845, an article touting that very ideal had been published in the *United States Magazine and Democratic Review*. It seemed to so capture his imagination that the term "manifest destiny" was a permanent fixture in his vernacular. He spoke of it so often that Hattie mouthed the magazine's name silently when he began to speak it each time.

Hungry for the outside world, Hattie nevertheless hung on to every word of the stories he told at dinner. Her father had a clever way of describing the details of explorers' action-packed adventures, whether on horseback, across deserts by wagon and stage, over rivers by barge, or around mountains by rail. She could put herself right into the stories, picturing how she would cope and what she would say in difficult situations.

Yet, the stories of the American dream that her father narrated featured only men. Hattie noted the discrepancy, yet gave little credence to it. Her imagination was so full of musings and ideas that his characterization couldn't become a hindrance to her dreams. Many women were proving that they could blaze new trails.

Sometimes, her father's true tales gave way to overt exaggeration at mealtime. Maybe he did it on purpose. Whatever the case, he was effective at diverting the family's attention, especially during the early days of their grief. He created mischief, intrigue, and even rescues that never existed. But it worked. Hattie was in the palm of his hand as she forgot her sadness and learned more than a little history. All the children seemed happier and healthier after being engrossed in his stories.

Suppertime was actually Hattie's favorite time of day. Alongside the stories, other topics crept into the conversation temporarily, but never dominated. Her father told tales with moral and even religious lessons, even if he had to withhold dessert to get the children's attention.

"Enjoy the food of information. I intend to nourish my family back to an even keel," he confirmed openly.

Hattie admired his resiliency. So did her mother, she comprehended with curiosity. It was obvious that her mother hung on his every word just like Hattie did. Even so, her mother had continued to be an unknown entity ever since the girls died. Although Hattie felt stymied and sometimes disagreed with her mother's decisions, she still felt thankful to have a loving mother. Many of the children at the orphanage where she had begun to volunteer had no parents whatsoever.

❖ ❖ ❖

Most afternoons, Hattie daydreamed about the old days at

the shop. How she missed hearing her father say, "You're my little shadow!" He had said it hundreds of times over the years, kissing her on the cheek as she puttered with a little project at his bench.

The raw materials of his creations were endlessly fascinating. She liked to experiment with tacks using his hammer. There were possibilities for things she might make with brass fittings and wood shavings, different grades of leather, or saddle oil and wax. Nothing reminded her of the shop and her father's love more than the magnificent aroma of leather.

When she had been quite small, he gifted her with little bits of leftover leather from a trunk project. Hattie fashioned the scraps into doll accessories, which pleased him. He encouraged her creations, even when, more recently, she made unexpected things. Quite often, she had gotten new project ideas from people who had merely walked through the shop. There was the one-legged man who used leather to strap a peg-leg on his stump. Another man who had lost an eye needed a comfortable leather eye patch. She wondered what her father would do if a toothless person asked for his help.

Memories of such characters made her pause. She might not be at the shop, but she intended to pursue things beyond Utica and break out of tradition. How far she had digressed from her former level of freedom, she fretted. What could she dream up to release herself from the feeling of being in prison, of being separated from her father and the shop, of being held back from the world? But all she could hear was her father's voice from the past.

"*Harriet Ann Sheldon! What have you made there?*" he would ask his youngest daughter.

❖ ❖ ❖

Time intervened. School and other pursuits eventually filled her time. Then came a deciding day. A clear, new resolve urged her to make a point. Hattie had no idea where the idea came from. How she got the nerve to push back, she wasn't sure. But that day, she used her little project to send a powerful message.

"What have you made there?" her father inquired.

"A pair of leather covers for the handles of Artemas' new bicycle," Hattie snipped with a peeved expression. She wasn't allowed to ride any bicycle.

"Hmm. Why?" he questioned rather innocently. "I thought you were reading back here."

"No. I was making these to bribe Artemas," she explained, chin up rather defensively. "It's the only chance I might get to ride his bicycle."

"Oh—now, now, let's not go that far," he balked, a forced smile on his face. "Your mother will have my head if that happens. Leave Artemas to his bicycle and you focus on ladylike pursuits."

But Hattie plowed forward anyway, her willful nature leading.

"Why does everyone insist that bicycles are only for boys? You and mother keep saying girls shouldn't do this or that. But I know it's just because mother can't forget the girls' deaths. Well, I'm tired of being held back. I'm alive and healthy. There's no good reason why I shouldn't be the first girl in town to ride a bicycle!"

"Disrespect is uncalled for, Hattie. You must realize you're as pretty as a picture and almost grown. Young ladies do not ride bicycles. Why do you push so hard?" he returned, slightly annoyed.

"Because I want to be different than other girls," she returned, suddenly serious. "They're silly. They have no ideas and they're annoying. They don't care about learning or traveling like I do."

"Oh, I'm not so sure about that," he argued halfheartedly.

"More young women than ever are trying new things and getting a good education," she justified. "Didn't you hear about those big conventions for women only? Margaret and I loved hearing all the details. We plan to fight against old-fashioned limits and help women get the vote."

Ebenezer stared at his daughter in bewilderment. "Well, sweetheart, I hardly know what to say. But I'll try harder to understand. Yes, I have heard of those women pushing against tradition. And I guess your mother's work with the orphanage is fairly progressive, like those women you admire."

"But mother only helps at the orphanage to get away from her grief," she returned.

"Are you seeing yourself in that kind of setting someday?" he inquired quietly.

"Yes, and far beyond that. I would *die* if I grew up only to sit around embroidering at home with gossipy women. That isn't my idea of a useful life," she confirmed. "I've just got to try new things. You've forbidden me to ride a bicycle. Mother forbids me to work at the shop. So, what's left that I can do?"

"I have a good answer for you," he replied, perking up. "You can sharpen your mind. I recommend that you focus your attention on reading. And in the meantime, I'll give some other thought to the fact that you need a change."

Hattie thought long and hard about her father's suggestion. It wasn't actually a new idea. She had long since been a reader. But now it occurred to her that fresh and innovative outcomes could result from serious reading. After all, study always brought insight and know-how.

In a few more seconds, she was able to bring the idea of determined reading full circle: the only way to win her side of the argument was to be smarter. And to be smarter, she had to be better informed. Maybe this was the way around her growing frustration over too many limits. Suddenly, she felt a renewed sense of hope about the days ahead. It would behoove her to read whatever she could get her hands on.

Then, out of the blue, an option dropped right into her lap from Margaret.

"Remember the other day, when your Mother said how much she admired Lucretia Mott, the celebrated activist and speaker?" Margaret whispered just minutes before class began.

"Oh yes. She follows Miss Mott's example closely," Hattie confirmed.

"Well, I just learned something interesting about last summer's Seneca Falls Convention that caused such a stir. Evidently, all the husbands in Utica were mad when their wives left town to hear her speak! Mother's friend said Miss Mott told the attendees they must push forward in life. She even insisted women can become writers. She said to start by reading everything in the library."

The last sentence was music to Hattie's ears. This was the same thing her father had recommended. Only he hadn't mentioned the library. "I didn't think girls were allowed there," she questioned.

"I didn't either. Maybe we could ask," Margaret suggested. "Nobody has ever said we can't go inside. Let's stop on our way home from school and see what happens."

Hattie's spark was lit. "If they approve, I could claim to follow Miss Mott's advice! How can my mother possibly complain about that?"

But inside her heart, she questioned why her mother held her back, even as Miss Mott promoted more opportunities and roles for young women.

"I can't wait," Margaret gushed. "The library must have hundreds of books. I'm sick to death of *Pilgrim's Progress* and *Oliver Twist.*"

"So am I. Think of all the newspapers they must have!"

❖ ❖ ❖

Hattie proceeded tentatively on that first, secret trip to the City Library on Franklin Square. While most of the library visitors were men, a small number of women were also there. With little effort, approval was granted for her and Margaret to have open library access with all the adults. Hattie wanted to leap for joy. Her life had changed for the better. An incredible number of fascinating books was readily available.

At first, Hattie just wandered up and down the long aisles of books, perusing as many titles as she could absorb. The library had a particular silence to it and smelled like a combination of leather and dust.

Next, she removed a few volumes from various shelves and flipped through the pages, mesmerized before she knew it. The content was so rich that she couldn't choose what to read. She memorized several titles before she and Margaret emerged wide-eyed.

"There are over 1,700 volumes in there. What do you think you'll read first?" Hattie whispered after they were seated on the bench out front. "I keep reminding myself I can choose anything. There are no limits!"

"Did you see *The World and Its Inhabitants*?" Margaret asked.

"No, but it sounds more interesting than *Pleasant and Profitable.*

As I flipped through that one, a sentence caught my eye. It said reading inappropriate types of books—or the avoidance of reading altogether—could keep a person out of heaven."

"I wonder what Lucretia Mott would say to that idea," Margaret retorted sarcastically.

The two looked seriously into each other's faces for a moment and then burst out laughing. Gathering their belongings, they continued to compare notes while they sauntered home.

"I looked at *A General Atlas of the World*," Hattie shared after a minute. "Then, out the corner of my eye, I saw *A Handbook for Travelers in Spain* by Richard Ford. It details places on the map, like Andalucia, Ronda, and Catalonia. Don't they sound utterly fascinating?"

"Yes, and romantic. But the one I want to read first is *A Summer in Scotland* by Jacob Abbott," Margaret concluded.

Armed with newfound resources, Hattie arrived home with the realization that she had already overcome a large portion of her restlessness. Never again would she waste a single minute thinking about her limitations. From that day forward, she and Margaret would pore over all kinds of publications.

Gaining access to the library had been so easy. Hattie and Margaret began to go there almost daily. Shadowy corners and elegant wood shelving more than begged them to discover the secrets and stories inside each volume. They loved wandering among the leather-bound books, stacks of periodicals, and layers of newspapers.

At first, Hattie brought books home on loan. Then, she began to read at the library and remain a few minutes longer each day.

Something about it seemed so right that she couldn't even formulate why it would displease her mother. As the new daily habit grew, it began to outweigh the risks of upsetting her mother. It might be happening right under her mother's nose, but, to be truthful, she felt justified about the library.

Meanwhile, Hattie's mother gave herself substantial liberty. Hattie heard her say that Mrs. Cornelia Cooper Graham, the chief promoter of the orphanage, had mentioned a need for more help there. Mrs. Graham was known all over town for her charitable work and infectious personality. The next thing Hattie knew, her mother was going to the orphanage almost every day.

So, Hattie kept going to the library. When she casually mentioned it one day, her mother registered no objections. Suddenly, she felt free in a brand new way, gaining strength through a profound appreciation for freedom. The knowledge she was gaining was as valuable as golden treasure. In a way, the library was almost like a new kind of home. A door had opened onto a world previously unknown. Hattie had to pull herself away each day when it was time to leave.

At a supper some weeks later with Reverend and Mrs. Fowler, as well as the Twimbleys, Hattie chatted with her sister, Amanda, and Margaret. Something caught her ear, however, in the midst of the adult conversation. Turning, she confidently offered an informed opinion that employed a new vocabulary. She also referenced editorials in two state newspapers. Obviously stunned, every person at the table turned to stare at her. She noted their reaction in wonder. They seemed so flabbergasted that they forgot to eat the food on their forks.

Once revealed, Hattie's newfound pastime of reading at the

library was accepted. The family accommodated it as the factor that had transformed her entirely. In a few short months, according to her father, she had taken on quite a scholarly demeanor. Hattie was thriving and she knew it.

However, she also comprehended that her new status left her parents in a delicate position. There was no denying the fact that she now desired and was capable of more serious education. Her academic performance had always been strong. Now, she won accolades at school and grew more confident of her academic capabilities. Should a debate occur about her future, she believed she could convince them to continue her schooling. At a better school. And soon.

But Hattie worried how her mother would cope when their big conversation about education took place.

"What if mother tries to keep me home and tied to old fashioned expectations?" she whispered to Amanda.

"I think father would stand up for you," replied Amanda, who had decided to marry and pursue a traditional life.

"But I'm not sure if he'll win," Hattie worried. "If his standpoint clashes with mother's, what will happen? I am counting on him. He believes in education and has encouraged all my reading."

As this issue swirled in her head, Hattie resolved to continue pressing. By using her tenacity, she would cite her literary accomplishments and provide many examples of her facility with words.

"This is the best idea you've ever had," she remarked to Margaret one afternoon. "Coming to the library has improved my life beyond all expectation. Neither of my parents question the hours I study here."

"Sometimes you sound smarter than the teacher," Margaret returned with a laugh. "I can tell that the librarian is amazed about how many books you've read."

"I forgot to tell you something," Hattie continued, a wide smile on her face. "Last week when you couldn't come with me, I lost track of time and stayed late. The librarian brought me an apple! She said she was worried that I was hungry from so much reading!"

Glowing from within, Hattie had never felt better. All in all, she decided that *Webster's Unabridged Dictionary* was her favorite book, even though it didn't have many pictures. But it answered her endless questions and led to revealing discoveries, including how women around the world lived their lives.

In America, women had arrived in the field of education, and they weren't leaving. She also extrapolated that the women profiled in newspaper articles fueled their accomplishments with a new type of inner motivation. It made her smile, as inner motivation was her middle name. And she was motivated to learn more and more every day.

Time passed quickly once Hattie found her stride and nurtured her educational hunger. It brought change just as it fostered maturity. The library took priority in her efforts. Of course, she did well in school, but she realized more and more that the curriculum was limited. The school could no longer meet her needs. Nevertheless, she still outpaced her classmates, except for Margaret. Thank goodness for Margaret.

Then, a day came in 1850 when the unexpected brought a deep hurt. Hattie knew something was terribly wrong when Margaret came to school in tears. Through deep sobs, Margaret broke the news that her father was moving the family from Utica to Hartford, Connecticut. Both girls came unhinged over their impending separation.

After her sisters' deaths, Hattie ached to think she would also lose her best friend. Not even the delights of the library could fill the empty hole in her heart or calm her loneliness after Margaret left. All Hattie could do was carry on—and wait for a letter.

❖ ❖ ❖

Without Margaret, the hours dragged. Adjusting to her absence wore heavily. Hattie loved the library, but longed for a new hobby. Surely she could be useful somewhere.

She had always loved children, which was probably inherited from her mother. This prompted the thought that, like her mother, she also had a soft spot for orphans. Why couldn't she help at the orphanage, too? Lending a hand there would keep her within her mother's purview.

"Mother, I just had a wonderful idea," she offered one day thereafter. "You always say the orphanage is short of helpers. I need more to do. It's a place to be useful. We could even go together. That way, you would be secure that you know where I am."

"For goodness sakes, Hattie," her mother reacted impatiently. "The orphanage is no place for you. I'm doing you a favor by keeping you focused on our home and family. Those poor children have neither."

❀ ❀ ❀

March 7, 1850
Hartford, Connecticut

Dear Hattie,

This letter is long overdue, but nevertheless sincere. Hartford feels so far away from you in Utica. Leaving was painfully hard and I miss you terribly. Yet, I am trying to look for the good. I like our new house and have a nice room. Hartford is a promising place, but it is still not home like Utica.

I am making friends at my new school, Hartford Female Academy. You would love my school, Hattie. It offers so many more subjects than either of us ever imagined before. That is thanks to our headmistress who founded the school, Miss Catherine Beecher. Her father is Lyman Beecher, the famous Presbyterian preacher who was mentioned so often at church.

Miss Beecher has written great things you would appreciate, including a treatise on how women's roles are underestimated by society. She is known here for breaking new ground. She believes that children should be educated by women, not men. All my new classmates intend to follow in her footsteps. Just like you and I talked, Miss Beecher thinks women today have a higher calling. Oh, Hattie, I wish you were here. This is a school you would truly value. You've just got to find a school like this and convince your parents to send you. Please write me soon and I will continue to stay close by post.

Your loyal and loving friend,
Margaret

A school like this. Those were Margaret's words. And as they sank into Hattie's mind and heart, she took strength from the fact that Margaret was on her side. It was true. Hattie did need a school as focused upon her future as she was, a school that could open doors rather than push her into a future distinguished by nothing beyond tradition.

❖ ❖ ❖

"How was your day, my dear?" Ebenezer asked at dinner, passing the saddle of mutton.

"I got a letter from Margaret today," Hattie replied animatedly. "She's living my dream."

"What accounts for it being so wonderful?" he inquired.

"I'll read you the letter if you want," Hattie offered.

"She's a lovely girl. Let's hear what she wrote," her mother interjected warmly.

Without stopping, Hattie read every word of Margaret's letter to her family. With each phrase, her imagination pictured more clearly the school and Miss Beecher herself. When she had finished, Hattie looked up, smiling broadly in anticipation of their reaction. Her father was grinning and nodding, obviously glad for Margaret's good fortune. But her mother had turned her head to the side and was looking down at the floor, biting her lip. For a long moment, Hattie looked at her in anticipation of her support.

Suddenly, her mother awoke from her reverie, cleared her throat, and looked at Hattie somewhat indirectly.

"Well, Margaret is young and excitable," she said blandly. "There's no school like that here in Utica, Hattie. Once again, let me remind you that you need to focus on the here and now, rather than all that big talk."

Hattie's smile faded instantly and the wind in her sails died a sudden death. What possible reason would her mother have for throwing cold water on this happy news? As she began to puzzle over her mother's reaction, Hattie looked sideways at her father. He would understand. He would be able to read how Margaret's news sparked a light in her.

But he, too, looked down. Then he began to fumble with his napkin and blotted the corner of his mouth politely before extending an open hand toward Hattie.

"Well, I'm awfully glad that Margaret has been in touch, dear," he replied in the kindest of voices. "She was your faithful companion all these years. And, you know, when she mentioned Lyman Beecher, I had a recollection of having shaken hands with him a couple of times. He is a force of nature, and all the more a force for temperance."

Then he uttered a quick excuse and stood, changing the subject as he reached to tweak Artemas on the ear. In the blink of an eye, supper had ended, and they left the table. Hattie stayed in her chair wondering what had just happened. She felt as heavy as lead. After another uncomfortable silence, her mother stood silently and walked into the kitchen with her plate. Hattie was left alone at the table, her half-full plate of food as cold as her heart.

The whole encounter left her incredulous. Whatever had just happened was crucial to her future plans and wellbeing. That much she knew. But what else did it reveal? Leaving the table purposely without clearing her plate, Hattie crept up to her room, feeling dejected. She didn't understand how things had suddenly turned in an unconstructive direction. Her mind clouded as her emotions dampened. Soon, tears ran down her cheeks. Unable to concentrate, she cut the lamp's flame and lay in the dark, struggling to process what it all meant.

A foggy period of time passed. She became aware that she had fallen asleep, but wasn't asleep any longer. Thinking hard there in the dark, she concluded that her inner person was not asleep, but still smarting over the episode. Hattie needed to resolve it or she knew it would rob her. For a long time, she filtered various aspects of what had and had not happened. Her thoughts came to rest on her father moving the topic off the letter and onto Hattie's loyal and long friendship with Margaret.

What was the reason for his overly formal, polite words? Why had he been so indirect, which wasn't like him at all? Hattie felt a strong sense of intuition that something more complex existed but wasn't expressed. Holding that idea inside her heart, she began to comb through the entire scene that had played out at supper. Recreating each word, glimpse, and expression, she finally concluded that she was correct in believing something was working against her right in her own home.

After she had finished reading Margaret's letter, her mother's response had numbed her. It was so unsupportive that she had turned toward her father after about ten seconds to see his reaction. She remembered him nervously folding his dinner napkin. His face became flushed, and then went redder still as he spoke, a sure sign that he was provoked. No amount of fumbling with the dinner napkin could hide that.

Therein she found a clue. Her father's reaction suddenly meant everything to her. All indications pointed to the fact that it was not a response to her or to the letter, but rather to her mother's sour attitude. His words and actions were a direct outgrowth of being perturbed by her mother's reaction.

Hattie searched her own actions and words, but could find that she had done no wrong. Nor did she have ulterior motives by reading the letter aloud. Her mother would likely not agree with that conclusion, she realized. But on that point she gained a new insight. And with the insight, she began to understand.

Hattie could see that her mother's reaction had more to do with her *mother's* agenda than with Hattie's life, ideas, or plans. The obvious was quite hurtful: her mother didn't care about Margaret's opportunities. And it looked like the reason was because Hattie had been influenced.

What all was behind her mother's staunch, restraining attitude, Hattie wondered. Why did she want to keep Hattie away from so many things? Her mother was not a mean person, after all. But she was a changed person. Things had never been that way until the girls died.

On this point, Hattie stopped. There it was again. Those deaths. They had changed everything else, so why not her mother's attitude, too? Memories of all kinds flooded her thoughts. Their family had been happy, carefree, and devoted before. Why hadn't her mother acted that way recently? She had been so warm in the past.

Maybe I'll never understand, Hattie told herself. *Maybe she doesn't know how hard it's been to get along with her.* Even after all that had happened, Hattie knew deep in her heart that her mother loved her very much. But there was no denying that her mother thought differently and treated the children differently.

She had been somewhat aware of it when they were planning Amanda's wedding. Her mother was not excited about that, either, and had expressed regret that Amanda would leave home. Amanda recoiled when their mother had said, "How can I possibly let you go?

Then there will only be Hattie." Those words had made both girls pause.

Now, it seemed the clues were as plain as the nose on Hattie's face. Fate had been rather unkind. Helen Sheldon had lost two daughters to illness and a third to marriage. She couldn't bear losing all her daughters, and Hattie was the last one left at home. This acknowledgement loosened the grip on Hattie's heart. Her mother didn't want to restrain her on purpose, she reasoned, but rather to preserve her only little girl. Almost desperate, she wanted to keep Hattie from leaving, to keep the family as much like it had been in former years.

As the hurtful puzzle came together, Hattie began to release her feelings of frustration. Maybe she could see her way through the situation. It would require untangling her mother's flawed view, however.

Hattie decided that her rebellion against the tightening grip was not wrong, just misplaced. Morally, she knew the right choice was to remain patient and forgiving. But if she did, her mother would get the wrong message. In fact, her mother could conclude the exact opposite of Hattie's intentions. It appeared that only a steady pressure from Hattie could convince her mother to give up the unrealistic hopes and dreams. Keeping Hattie cooped up in Utica forever as the perpetual youngest daughter was not going to work.

Hattie decided she must act sensitively, but on the line of registering an offense. Only something challenging would get her mother's attention. This conclusion energized her. She finally felt armed with enough understanding and preparation to deal with it. When a wrong had been committed, she had heard somewhere, you sometimes had to fight to make it right or nothing would change. Hattie knew what her choice was.

5

Forced Relocations

While Hattie devoured more and more of the library's contents late that spring, her challenges gave way to a ray of hope. Stories of great conquests and survival at sea helped her see that people overcame big obstacles every day. As her perspective deepened, new stirrings of her vision for the future took root. When it came right down to looking at facts, she was sixteen years old and looking forward to so much. She just didn't know when or where her future would unfold.

One day she noticed that her parents seemed to have lost interest in quite a bit of reading material they used to value highly. For as long as Hattie could recall, her parents sprinkled dinnertime with quotes from respected Presbyterian publications and other newsletters that arrived in the mail, including *The Missionary Chronicle*, *The Mother's Magazine*, and *The Missionary Herald*. Now, however, a large number of unread issues had begun to stack up in the dining room corner. Her mother used to read every word, often clipping bits from one or discussing recommendation from another. Issue after issue, her mother followed the detailed instructions about raising children and made that clear to them.

This was sometimes annoying. Not so long ago, as Hattie read a new book in the sunniest corner of her room, her mother had interrupted, directing her to put down her reading and help with household chores. Hattie had kept her mouth closed, but she fumed inside because that kind of work used up so much time. She found no redeeming value whatsoever in dusting, scrubbing, and folding laundry. To her chagrin, it had taken several hours away from her progress in a particularly interesting book. When she finally broke her silence and complained, her mother had a ready answer, as always.

"*The Mother's Magazine* knows what is best for young ladies, Hattie. This kind of work helps you form good habits. Did you know that habits create character? Your chores must have a cost, dear, or you'll never value the tenets of the faith."

Hattie knew better than to press the subject, even though her mother's rationale didn't make much sense; trying to link chores with religion felt like a stretch to her. But there was no point in questioning it. Besides, most of her friends' mothers also read *The Mother's Magazine* and used the same tactics with their daughters. The last time the girls had glanced through the magazine together, they didn't like an article entitled "Hints to Young Ladies—No. 2." Its premise was that women were inferior to men.

Looking again at the corner, the unread newsletters and magazines prompted Hattie to frown and ask unsettling questions. *Why isn't anyone reading them any longer?* she asked herself. *For that matter, instead of mother, why am I the one cooking supper for our whole family?*

"There just aren't enough hours left in the day," her mother had commented breathlessly that morning when assigning supper to

Hattie. Then she had rushed out the door, full of chatter about all that awaited her at the orphanage.

Confusion clouded Hattie's view of her mother's interest in the orphanage. When a compromise had to be made, it seemed her mother usually gave time to the orphanage rather than the family. She just wasn't around home enough in Hattie's estimation. In fact, she didn't seem to like being home much. Why should Hattie have to cover her mother's responsibilities? She wanted to live her own life instead of fulfilling the kitchen apprentice role for her mother.

Completing supper preparations amid these troubling concerns, Hattie tidied the kitchen. Soon, the oven began to waft savory aromas of onions and roasting potatoes into the house. She ambled over to the corner and sank down into her father's cushiony chair. It was by far the most comfortable chair in the house. A tufted style, her father had taken a whole year to make it from leather remnants. She loved its soft, enveloping comfort. The rest of her siblings always wanted to sit it in, too.

A late ray of sunshine cast itself through the lace curtains onto the corner where she relaxed. Hattie picked up several newsletters from the big stack and began to flip through the pages. One had an item about the Underground Railroad that looked interesting. She folded down the corner of the page as a reminder to read it later. Several issues later, many good articles awaited careful attention. But because of her responsibility for making supper, she mustn't take time to read in depth.

As she hurriedly turned the last issue's pages, a riveting pen and ink illustration grabbed Hattie's attention. It pictured hollow-eyed, half-clothed Indians who appeared to be shivering in the snow around a dying campfire. One man grimaced with upraised shoulders and looked ill. He was barefoot. Not far from his side, a weeping mother leaned against a stark tree stump cradling a lifeless looking child. The horrific scene stabbed Hattie's heart. A ghastly portrayal, she shuddered as she pictured her own mother's lost children. The idea of it sobered her there in the cozy corner of her secure life.

A second later, the article's headline jolted her back to reality. In ominous, bold letters it read "Forced Relocation of Indians and its Repercussions." What was a forced relocation, she wondered, looking back to the drawing. The Indians it pictured were obviously on the move. Where were they going in the decrepit wagon hitched to starving oxen whose bones practically protruded through their flesh?

Full of questions, Hattie began to read. She told herself she should only skim the article and follow up later. It was well past time to retrieve the dishes and set the table, but she wanted to read just a few more sentences. Then she would stop. But with each unconscionable fact, more disbelief flooded her. Soon, her attention was totally captivated.

A devastating story cried out from between the words. After President Andrew Jackson had signed a measure called the Indian Removal Act, he used the military to force several tribes off their land beginning in 1831. Why had she never heard of this before? In all her reading at the library, she had not come across a story quite like this. Reading on, Hattie could barely accommodate the fact that most of the Indians who were relocated, at least the ones who lived, had *walked* an astonishing 800 miles. Many had no shelter whatsoever and precious little food.

She immediately recalled the runaway slaves who also had no home, shelter, or food until the Underground Railroad helped them attain freedom. But, unlike the slaves, the Indians held a desperate desire to remain in their ancestral Georgia, Alabama, and North

Carolina homelands. Through President Jackson's land grab, however, the government disregarded them. Previous promises and carefully negotiated treaties that had been lawfully agreed were systematically broken.

Losing all their possessions in the resulting mayhem, as many as 60,000 Indian people had been moved against their will. Hattie could not imagine such a number and struggled for a standard of comparison. Until last week, for instance, she had thought the City of Utica was large. But, over dinner, her father had indicated that Utica was undergoing transition.

"Many believe the number of residents in Utica is now only about 10,000," he had explained.

"But that's huge, at least compared to Burlington," Hattie interjected from her own point of reference. "Ten thousand people sounds like so many! Isn't that how many were led out of Egypt in the Bible?"

"Goodness, no," he corrected. "That involved hundreds of thousands! We're not on a biblical scale, dear. Our population used to be 12,000. It matters, because any drop is a threat to our business."

Hattie found herself unable to imagine moving six times the number of people in Utica. She pictured the Indians marching in the cold over muddy, rutted roads. They had had no choice. But she had yet to learn why President Jackson uprooted and moved them. Herded like animals, no wonder many succumbed to illness, exposure, and even starvation. Try as she might, it was impossible to imagine their suffering.

After arriving at the remote region newly designated as Indian Territory, how had they started their lives again, built homes, planted crops? Hattie couldn't help but contemplate the shocking contrast between her safe, comfortable home, complete with lots of wonderful food like the supper she was cooking, versus the Indians' wilderness suffering. They endured hunger while huddling next to a meager campfire with no roof over their heads. In her entire life, she had never slept anywhere but a nice, warm featherbed. Dislodged from all comfort and tradition, the Indians had slept upon nothing but the cold ground. She could almost feel the aches of their bodies.

But what was their plight today? Who was helping them? As Hattie formulated questions, something she had never felt before welled up within her. It was part hurt, part anger, and mostly compassion. Wasn't this article published so others would learn the truth and try to help? Without question, those Indian people still struggled. She felt sure of it, in a most compelling way.

No force of nature could convince her but what fate had led her to read this riveting story about Indian removals. With great seriousness, she took the matter to heart. As a girl wishing to use her life meaningfully, nothing had ever drawn or motivated her more than this.

Suddenly, Hattie smelled smoke and looked up from her reading in alarm. Jumping up, she dropped the newsletter and rushed into the kitchen, hoping supper wasn't completely burned.

Over the next weeks at the library, Hattie grew intellectually. She watched the ways of the world even as she didn't understand everything entirely. But she was coming to understand herself better.

Soon, summer blossomed and beckoned her to remember childhood days playing with Margaret. They had loved the swing beside the house on the big branch. As she anticipated the arrival of her seventeenth birthday in August, those carefree play times seemed a long ways away. Instead of swinging and playing with dolls, she now spent her time studying. Before her, the newspaper at the reading table noted that June was mid-year and 1850 was mid-century. It said the world was modernizing at an escalated pace, which filled Hattie with a sense of urgency.

❧ ❧ ❧

The next Sunday, as the Sheldon's wagon rolled through their tree-lined neighborhood on the way to church, Ebenezer steadied the energetic horses to an even pace. Summer was perhaps the most beautiful time of the year on Genesee Street, the widest thoroughfare Hattie had ever known. A profusion of trees and bushes in many shades of green framed the houses and reached toward the street as if to greet residents.

She should be happy, yet the loveliness of nature left her melancholy. Without school or Margaret, the warmest months would be the quietest this year. Of course, she had other friends, but few shared her interests like Margaret had. The days ahead could grow monotonous, especially since she couldn't go to her father's shop.

Perhaps it's time to set some new goals, she mused. *If I examine every possible option and commit some plans to paper, maybe summer will go faster. I'll feel better if I can make some solid accomplishments. I need something to look forward to.*

Thinking hard, she began immediately to explore every idea her mind could imagine. Maybe she could read some of father's favorite books and initiate a discussion with him. That seemed like an excellent idea to strengthen their relationship, perhaps even making up for the distance she felt because the shop was off limits. Just as she was about to ask for his five favorite books, he suddenly broke the silence.

"Listen up, my dears," he called to the family, sounding unusually chipper. "I have a surprise for you. I'm certain you will like it."

All heads turned immediately. There was an extended pause. It continued longer than Hattie's patience could understand. Was he milking their anticipation? If so, he definitely had their complete attention.

"Haven't we all taken to heart the many stories I've brought home," he prompted with a flourishing gesture. "Think of the gallant explorers and intrepid travelers in search of everything from the fountain of youth to the Northwest Passage to gold in distant territories."

"Oh, yes, Father," Hattie responded immediately, beginning to tingle. She watched him closely and wondered about such flowery talk.

"Of course we have," her mother nodded, glancing at Artemas, whose eyebrows rose out of interest.

Ebenezer reacted with an exaggerated nod and a curious expression of satisfaction. "Marvelous. I'm thrilled to see that we all agree. It encourages me to know that you have been listening."

With that, he grew silent and, holding his chin high, adjusted the reins unnecessarily. Hattie decided his wrinkled brow indicated feigned seriousness, even though he appeared to take stock of the world and make determinations about it.

Hattie, Artemas, and their mother waited patiently, expectant gazes practically boring a hole through him. Surely he intended to continue. Yet after his initial attention-getting question, he was strangely silent. Had another thought preoccupied him? He seemed completely unaware that they were waiting. The delay grew markedly tenser by the second, yet he still held them at bay. Finally, Hattie could stand the suspense no longer.

"Well, what else, Father?" she pressured impatiently. "What about the surprise?"

"Oh, my goodness," he reacted as if he had nearly forgotten. "I was momentarily distracted. Yes, yes. Where was I?"

"Father, stop," Artemas cried, shaking his father's sleeve. "Tell us!"

"Why, of course there is a surprise," Ebenezer teased, looking sideways at Helen, who had closed her eyes and pressed her brow impatiently with a thumb. "Do you want to know now or later?"

"NOW," the three cried in unison, straining their necks and drawing closer.

"All right, then. What I want to share is that, soon, we are going to see some extra special people . . ." Ebenezer mouthed these words slowly, leaving the last word on an up note. He wasn't finished.

Nobody moved. But they did frown impatiently, holding their breath. Artemas leaned forward and stared. Hattie wondered if they were going to host visitors. Then, suddenly, Ebenezer added two more definitive words.

"… in Massachusetts."

Helen Sheldon was the first to let out a delighted cry of joy. Close behind her, Hattie clapped her hands over her head and began to stamp her feet. Hattie was already hugging Ebenezer by the time Artemas unfroze and began to jump up and down.

They were going on a trip to Massachusetts! The very idea of visiting a new branch of the family in Ebenezer's home state of Massachusetts was the furthest thing from Hattie's expectation. It was a long journey, but now that train lines connected the miles, it had become a possibility after all. Hattie felt as elated as she could ever recall. Her dream of going on an adventure was actually going to come true.

Many years had passed since anyone had seen Aunt Mary Brown, Ebenezer's sister who lived in Amherst with her husband, Jason. Hattie had only been a baby the last time she and Aunt Mary were together. The prospect of becoming closer suddenly cast away all her worries about the summer. Because of this one trip, she could endure just about anything, she decided.

"All right, let's not spook the horses," Ebenezer reacted with a chuckle, trying to calm their excited reactions.

"When, father? When are we leaving?" Hattie begged, her heart beating faster than it had in a while. "I'm so excited I can't think. We will be elbow to elbow with other travelers! I can't wait to see Massachusetts. Can we just keep on going to the ocean?"

"How long can we stay?" Artemas followed without waiting for his father's response to Hattie. "Can I take my bicycle on the train?"

"I should think we can leave within the week," Ebenezer responded thoughtfully. "I've been working ahead of myself to meet customer demand. Things are well on target, so we'd best get going before something comes along to postpone us."

6

Deerfield Raid of 1704

Ebenezer kept his word. In exactly five days, during which the last cool breezes gave way to hot summer sun, the Sheldons boarded a large, coal-powered steam train in Utica. Pulling away amid its black cloak of smoke, it left behind the bustle of Genesee Street, the wide Mohawk River, and everything else familiar to Hattie. The flag atop the train station fluttered gracefully like waving goodbye and wishing them luck.

The train picked up speed and headed east. Hattie pressed her nose against the window, counting the houses they passed. How many of those residents had been to Massachusetts? If they had the chance to leave their gardens and their farms and their families, would they want to go as badly as Hattie did?

This trip was so important because it fulfilled her dream. She was going somewhere new and exciting. The docks were now behind her. Likewise, the Adirondack Mountains began to recede in the distance. In her imagination, she was saying goodbye forever, wondering what it would feel like to leave Utica and live somewhere else.

Hattie had anticipated many things as she packed, deciding to keep a detailed diary of the many sights, sounds, and smells. But, most of all, she wanted to talk with attention-grabbing people. This was her first genuine adventure, and she would make the most of it. Surely the diary would help her relive it afterwards. She vowed to record all that her senses could perceive while away from the ordinariness of Utica.

To quantify her enthusiasm, Hattie tried to conceive of a standard for comparison that represented how she valued this chance, this unexpected foray into her dreams. How rare it was for someone her age to explore another region's exciting history, enterprising people, varying culture, unusual food, riveting newspapers, political passions, refreshing topography, and even, perhaps, a variety of splendid trees.

Quite by chance, an uninvited thought struck a few minutes later. It brought her a profound sense of where her life's priorities now stood. She would not miss her favorite pastime *in the world*, which was reading wonderful things in the library. When a person could give up her most treasured pastime, surely it signaled the virtual attainment of adult-level reasoning. Books had been a conduit that readied her to see and touch, feel and hear for herself.

Later that day, when another passenger mentioned that they had crossed over into Massachusetts, another realization came. As of today, when she was all but seventeen, Hattie's first *actual* journey of exploration held a special distinction. It was just the first of many more she intended to take.

ALBANY AND WEST STOCKBRIDGE RAILROAD

Formerly known as the Castleton and West Stockbridge Railroad, the Company was organized April 9, 1830, but nothing was done under the first name. The name of Albany and West Stockbridge Railroad was assumed May 5, 1836. The road was opened from Greenbush to Chatham, December 21, 1841, and to the State Line, September 12, 1842. It was leased to the Western (Mass.) Railroad on Nov. 18, 1841 for the term of its charter, and later was operated as a part of that road, including the ferry at Albany.

The city of Albany at different times issued bonds for $1,000,000 to aid in building the road, the lessees paying the interest and $10,000 annually toward the sinking fund. It connected at Albany with Springfield and Boston.

❊ ❊ ❊

Hattie felt she knew Aunt Mary Brown from her colorful letters. Years back, when Ebenezer went west from Massachusetts to Burlington, New York, Mary had remained behind in their home state. Over the years, she had only been able to visit them one time. Ebenezer told Hattie how Mary had adored her as a tiny baby back then. But, of course, Hattie didn't remember. Now, she couldn't wait to drink in the wonderful addition of an auntie from afar with whom she could become friendly.

"You may not recall, but her treasured daughter died a couple of years ago," Ebenezer whispered quietly to Hattie. "Since you didn't know her, and given our own sadness, I said little at the time. It nearly broke Mary's heart though. That's a tender subject, all right?"

Hattie nodded sympathetically. She knew all too well how a loss like that shattered a family. Conversing about it served no purpose. The hurt remained fresh. Probably, it would always be that way.

❖ ❖ ❖

It took no time at all for Aunt Mary's long-ago affection to become mutual. From the first hug, Hattie felt a kinship toward her smiling, salt-and-pepper–haired auntie. The connection was personal, which might relate to the death of her daughter. Hattie hoped to help fill the void. Maybe they could become close in time.

To make matters warmer, Hattie and Aunt Mary shared a strong family resemblance. Their brow lines, arrow-straight noses, and hair texture were identical. Hattie laughed about her less than ideal hair. Aunt Mary replied jovially that, while her father had had heavy whiskers, he was cursed with a paltry head of hair. A family trait was at work, so they all laughed about it.

From the sound of Aunt Mary's chirping observations, encouraging comments, and thoughtful questions, it seemed she genuinely wanted to know Hattie inside and out. She kept Hattie close to her side those first few days in Massachusetts, which pleased Hattie beyond words. It was the perfect arrangement, as Hattie's parents went to visit her father's old school mates and the few surviving friends of his late parents. Luckily, Hattie did not have to trail along.

Aunt Mary's inviting house was filled with her colorful handiwork. Hattie wanted to learn about all her creative projects and help with chores. In the cozy Massachusetts kitchen, they peeled potatoes, dressed chickens, and made a big, multi-layered Lane Cake from an old recipe. Aunt Mary just giggled over mishaps such as spilling flour on the floor. Hattie felt secure in her auntie's presence.

Aunt Mary was also easy to talk with. The quality of her

questions and insights proved to Hattie that she was a woman of genuine character. Without question, Christian values were the primary determinants of her thoughts and actions. Aunt Mary also liked to read, and spoke about reading in a way Hattie didn't expect.

"My dear, there's no question but what reading saved me. If I hadn't been a reader, I wouldn't have overcome my first, dear husband's death ... and more recently, the loss of my daughter," she confided quietly.

Hattie felt sad for her grief, but also uninformed to learn that Aunt Mary's current husband, Uncle Jason, was a second husband. How had Aunt Mary endured the death of her first husband? As the facts unfolded, she learned that awful event marked the time when Aunt Mary had determined to educate herself and become better informed. She had enjoyed virtually no educational opportunities in her day, as most of the schools then were only open to young men. Undeterred, she read everything in sight and borrowed books. Today, she called herself a "self-educated woman."

This new insight opened the door for Hattie and Aunt Mary to talk about learning and school and the growing number of opportunities for young women.

"What do you envision for your future, Hattie?" Aunt Mary asked lightly the next morning while steeping tea.

"I want to learn enough to live in a faraway place and help people there," Hattie responded instantaneously. Her words and the certainty with which they flew from her mouth surprised even her. She felt comfortable sharing her growing vision of the future. Hearing herself, she comprehended the clear connection between her dreams and intentions. And she couldn't think of anyone she would rather confide in than Aunt Mary.

"That's a wonderful and lofty vision," Aunt Mary responded

with interest. "Help me understand where this came from. Are you saying you don't want to stay in Utica near your family?"

Hattie responded slowly. "The world is so big and so full of need. It's not that I want to be away from anyone, but rather to be closer to a need that I can fill. I don't want to sound critical or ungrateful, but I find Utica full of limits."

Aunt Mary nodded respectfully. "Like what? Give me an example."

"Boys can ride bicycles and be in competitions. They get to talk after dinner with the educated men who have traveled. Girls have to go off in a corner or stay quiet or help in the kitchen. I've heard what travelers experience, and that adventure beckons me."

"Where would you rather go then, if you leave Utica?"

"Hopefully, a place without limits, where I can be useful," Hattie responded, feeling like an adult. "Ordinariness isn't for me. Honestly, most of the girls in my class have no desire to achieve anything. All they talk about is their imagined husbands. There's more to live for than a husband. I also want to live for others."

Aunt Mary blinked at Hattie's words and then looked thoughtfully out the window, apparently processing her niece's intentions. Drying her hands, she slowly set aside her tea towel and turned to take a seat at the kitchen table across from Hattie. For a long moment, she looked deeply into Hattie's face.

"You're young to have such selfless determination. It's honorable," she complimented. "I'm impressed that you want to affect the lives of others. And I see purity in you. That's a powerful combination."

"You really think so?" Hattie queried, feeling flattered. "After reading so much at the library, I began to imagine lots of things."

"When you're there, what subjects draw you the most, dear?" Aunt Mary probed. The question helped Hattie realize just how many volumes she had digested. In a relatively short time, she had attained a bigger picture of the world at large.

"I absolutely love studying about foreign cultures and customs. It would be so exhilarating to travel. My favorite book was an unforgettable story about one man's amazing experiences in Spain."

"You lose track of time when you're reading, don't you?" Aunt Mary smiled knowingly.

"Yes! The day I read that one, I forgot to eat, but didn't feel hungry," Hattie chuckled. "I felt I was actually in Spain."

"I know that feeling," Aunt Mary nodded. "You forget your troubles when ideas come alive."

"It's also like that when I read a world atlas or even *Webster's Dictionary,*" Hattie agreed. "Something changes within me. I feel free and useful."

"You're already useful, Hattie. I surmise that, at the library, you're seeking freedom," Aunt Mary encouraged, giving Hattie's hand a squeeze. "I expected to hear about your school mates, flirtations, or little ups and downs. But you're thinking beyond ordinary girls your age. You have great depth, as well as vision. I'm excited to watch your future unfold."

❧ ❧ ❧

The next day, Artemas was almost late for supper. He had been at a creek with some neighbor boys he'd met out back. As he and Hattie washed up, he teased her.

"I heard something from my new friends that you don't know and could never guess!"

"Did those boys have a raccoon skeleton or something?" Hattie returned, bored at her brother's revelation.

"Go ahead and stick your nose in the air, Hattie Sheldon. But you'll be sorry when I see the graves of our ancestors before you do," Artemas jeered in response.

"That's nothing special, I can assure you," she continued. "You're just exaggerating."

"No I'm not. There's a big secret about them because Uncle Jason confirmed it."

"Artemas, it's no secret that generations of Sheldons are buried in Massachusetts."

"Oh, I know. But some died violent deaths. There were murders," he whispered with extreme emphasis, coming nose to nose with her.

"Is that so?" Hattie reacted, trying to hide her genuine curiosity. "And just who was responsible for the so-called murders?"

Artemas glanced from one side to the other to make sure their parents were not listening. He wasn't usually on guard like this. It suggested he might really possess secret information.

"You know who murdered whom," he baited, obviously energized. "Indians! They murdered one of Father's long-ago great-grandmothers and kidnapped all her children to Canada. Then they burned down the town. Now what do you have to say, Miss Know It All?"

Hattie's jaw went slack as she reacted. But Artemas had turned on his heel and walked away without revealing anymore details.

Having long been away from Massachusetts, Hattie knew her father harbored a deep desire to reconnect with two of his cousins in particular, even as he hoped to see all his Sheldon blood there. His late, favorite Aunt Sybil had two daughters, Sybil Snow and Huldah Cushman. Aunt Sybil had helped pull him through a threatening bout of childhood illness years and years ago. He had never forgotten her or his cousins. Hattie was excited to accompany him on the visits to see Mrs. Snow and Mrs. Cushman.

Meanwhile, she felt driven to follow up on the story Artemas had related. Was it possible that some ancestors had actually been murdered? What about kidnapped by Indians? Surely it wasn't both. Since the shock had registered, more questions came to mind. She had begun to doubt Artemas. It was very possible that the local boys had twisted some facts.

But then Artemas shared one more critical fact with her. The cemetery containing the graves of the dead was not in Amherst, but up the road in another town called Deerfield. There, where the story took place, the Sheldon name was well known.

Hattie liked being competitive with Artemas, especially when she felt she could win. In this instance, she knew something important that she purposely didn't share with him. Cousins Sybil and Huldah lived in Deerfield, and on her visit to them Hattie was determined to become a sleuth and find out the real story. There were challenges, however. Her father had no knowledge whatsoever of her intention to uncover the truth while in Deerfield.

Hattie organized her conclusions. To begin with, Uncle Jason had confirmed the rumors. Second, the most curious clue was silence. There was some truth to the story. Since her father had never, ever mentioned a word of it, his reticence told Hattie that the murders might really have happened. He was not a man who ever spoke negatively about family. It sounded like him to protect something sad. Was it possible he just avoided a particularly dark chapter in the Sheldon family's past?

❧ ❧ ❧

The next morning, Hattie nibbled half-heartedly at her breakfast and thumbed nervously through one of Aunt Mary's books. The conversation around her went from one topic to the next. Sometimes she listened with one ear, but her attention was elsewhere. She was itching to leave for Deerfield on Saturday.

Later, over second cups of coffee, Aunt Mary made an unexpected suggestion.

"Helen, there are some inspirational people here in Amherst I'd like you to meet," she said in a complimentary tone. "We don't have an orphanage, so your knowledge and experience could greatly benefit our interest here."

"What a kind thought, Mary," Hattie's mother responded. "I'd be happy to. It would be gratifying if my humble familiarity could help anyone."

"Lovely. I'll invite a few ladies to join us for tea, then," Aunt Mary continued. "Saturday is the best day. Correct me if I'm mistaken, but I gathered you had little enthusiasm for the trek to Deerfield."

"Very perceptive," Helen laughed. "I don't think Ebenezer will object. He can take Artemas for company. Hattie and I are much better suited to stay here and meet the ladies."

Hattie suddenly jolted to attention and looked up. Had she heard correctly? A tea? Who cared about an old tea? She was all set to go to Deerfield. Fretting, she fell speechless and wasn't sure what to do. Was the much-anticipated trip suddenly out of her grasp? She looked back at Aunt Mary with a desperate expression, which Mary didn't seem to grasp. Even so, under the table, Aunt Mary grabbed her hand and offered an expression that looked intriguingly like she had something up her sleeve.

What if Uncle Jason had told Aunt Mary that Hattie and Artemas wanted to know about the murders? Could that cause trouble? But Hattie had told no one about her sleuthing intentions in Deerfield. Aunt Mary must have innocently concluded that the tea was a perfect idea. Hattie excused herself from the table to think. What misery!

Stepping outside, she reeled at what had just taken place. Her most fervent goal for this trip was adventure. She couldn't have dreamed up anything juicier than murder and kidnapping right in her own family. Such a story was a dream come true for an explorer. Now, out of the blue, the opportunity had been plucked from her.

This boring tea was unwelcome and unexpected. It just didn't add up. Why would Aunt Mary think anybody wanted to hear about the Utica Orphanage? This was the worst possible outcome. Now Artemas would be the one who got to solve the mystery.

❖ ❖ ❖

Out of respect for Aunt Mary, Hattie pasted a smile on her face and acted interested. She did her very best to contain her disappointment as her father, Artemas, and Uncle Jason left for Deerfield. Next, she had to pretend to enjoy the tea while missing the chance of a lifetime.

Aunt Mary needed help baking scones and icing a cake. Hattie jumped in to assist, which helped chase away her frustration. She knew her attitude must be cheerful by the time the guests arrived. The last thing she wanted was to act small-minded and spoiled. For Aunt Mary's sake, she must do the right thing.

Before long, a small crowd had gathered. Hattie shook hands with half a dozen interesting and well-spoken women who were friends of Aunt Mary. She took a cup of tea and a piece of cake. Then Aunt Mary approached her again with a young woman at her side.

"Hattie, I'd like to present Miss Helen Fiske. Helen, this is my niece, Hattie, from Utica, New York," Aunt Mary offered with a friendly gesture.

Hattie nodded warmly and began to make polite conversation with Miss Fiske, who appeared to be a few years her senior. Miss Fiske was visiting Amherst from New York City, where she attended school at the Abbott Institute. Hattie had never heard of the Abbott Institute, so she wondered aloud how Helen Fiske found her place there.

"Tell me about your school," she inquired politely. "Are you originally a native of New York?"

"Actually, I was born here in Amherst and just love to come back," Miss Fiske responded. "After my parents passed, I was sent to an aunt in the city. I had dreamed of attending Amherst Academy here before going to higher school. But I'm happy in New York now."

"Oh, I'm not familiar with Amherst Academy," Hattie returned with growing interest. "Is it near here?"

"It's just down the road. Most consider it a top-notch preparatory school before going to seminary," Miss Fiske explained. "Young women learn from the same texts as young men. Its female graduates secure important opportunities each year, just like they do at my school."

Another guest approached, so Miss Fiske was obligated to respond. It gave Hattie a moment to pause. At Miss Fiske's unexpected mention of opportunities, Hattie's interest suddenly grew. Maybe there was more to hear at this tea after all. Perhaps the day wasn't a total loss.

"How do you do," her mother spoke to someone a few feet away. Turning, Hattie watched Aunt Mary present yet another guest to her mother.

"I'm happy to know you, Mrs. Sheldon," the woman replied. "I'm Beatrice Hutchinson. My family has been in the tannery business here for generations. I heard your daughter asking about Amherst Academy. My daughters are students there."

Hattie watched her mother nod politely and smile, but she did not pursue the topic.

"Our family wants to be part of the movement to build an orphanage," Mrs. Hutchinson continued.

Hattie stopped. Up to this moment, the issue of the orphanage had bored her. But now, she realized there were people in the room who cared about education for women, as well. In the last five minutes, two of the guests had mentioned this place called Amherst Academy. She decided to pay closer attention.

Eyeing the door, Hattie watched more interesting and attractive women arrive. All were greeted by Aunt Mary, who alternately introduced them to Hattie or her mother before they took a cup of tea and found a seat. The final guest to arrive was a tall, smiling lady whose coming seemed of particular interest to Aunt Mary. Right away, they crossed the room toward Hattie.

Aunt Mary took Hattie's arm and introduced the congenial lady as Miss Anna B. White.

"I'm very pleased to make your acquaintance, Miss Sheldon," Miss White offered.

Nodding courteously, Aunt Mary continued. She began to speak about Hattie in unusually complimentary terms. Her words were so encouraging that Hattie almost gaped in surprise. She couldn't believe her ears when Aunt Mary bragged about how advanced she was for her age. She detailed special measures Hattie had taken, over and above school, to attain stature and knowledge.

"That's the kind of story I find most interesting," Miss White responded approvingly. "As Preceptress of Amherst Academy, I keep my ears open for young women like you."

What? Hattie reacted silently as her pulse began to race. *Did she say Amherst Academy?*

Before they could visit more, someone else approached Miss White. The bustle of people and conversation interrupted them. Hattie politely took an empty chair and began to talk with another guest, but her mind was filtering all that had just been said. Why would this interesting Preceptress come to learn about a Utica Orphanage? Aunt Mary had only introduced Miss White to Hattie, not her mother. How curious. It almost seemed that some people were invited to talk with her mother about the orphanage, while others like Miss White were included to tell Hattie about education for young women.

After a short time, the guest seated next to Miss White stood and thanked Aunt Mary, saying she was needed at home. Hattie realized that something was afoot when Aunt Mary caught her attention and gently motioned for her to move to the empty chair and talk to Miss White. Suddenly, she grasped what was happening. How clever Aunt Mary was. She had planned for Hattie to get acquainted with this school leader! It was so extraordinary that Hattie forgot all about the murders in Deerfield.

For the next half hour, Hattie and Miss White carried on a fascinating exchange.

"The Female Department at Amherst Academy has both Classical and English courses," Miss White explained. "Maybe you've heard of some of the texts. The first division of the English

Course uses Day's *An Introduction to Algebra*, Gale's *Chemistry*, Upham's *Elements of Intellectual Philosophy*, Newman's *Rhetoric*, Goodrich's *Outlines of Ecclesiastical History*, Alexander's *Evidences of Christianity*, Wilkin's *Elements of Astronomy*, Levi Hedge's *Elements of Logic*, and Wayland's *The Elements of Moral Science*."

"I've actually studied from three of those already," Hattie replied eagerly. "The Rhetoric book has been of particular help in my schoolwork. Is it really true that men and women study the same texts?"

"Oh yes. And I hope that integration of the curriculum and of the student body will grow, even though Amherst maintains two separate schools. Here in town, we have Amherst College for gentlemen and Amherst Academy for ladies."

Just as Miss White finished, Hattie caught her mother's reflection. She looked into the handsome wall mirror behind Miss White's head, but hoped Miss White didn't notice. Hattie realized that her mother was watching their conversation intently, but didn't know the mirror gave Hattie's a bird's eye view.

There was no mistaking that Helen Sheldon was frowning and shifting in her chair, clearly uncomfortable. Was she unhappy about the tea or about Hattie? Already guessing the answer, Hattie vowed it wouldn't dampen her spirit. She was still there talking with Miss White and was going to make the most of it.

"It pays off to have your kind of lengthy exposure to a library," Miss White added encouragingly. "What are your plans for the future?"

"I hope for an opportunity that combines my love of other cultures, travel, and benevolence to societies in need," Hattie explained in the smoothest of characterizations. "Before that, I intend to apply for admission to the Utica Female Academy."

"In that case, you're in the right place at the right time. Have a look at Amherst Academy while you are here visiting," Miss White invited. "It offers ample qualification for admission to higher institutions like the Utica Female Academy. I'm sad to say that we are already closed following the end of last term, however. But do feel free to explore the grounds and see what you think."

"How kind," Hattie responded. "Thank you. I will. Is it near Amherst College? We passed by there."

"Yes. Did you know the two institutions have a common beginning? Amherst College is an outgrowth of Amherst Academy. In the past, when men's debate societies were still active, the college was well known for debate. They still have marvelous public lectures and exhibitions. You might aim to visit again and attend one. It draws a large crowd."

"Oh! Debate," Hattie exclaimed. "I've wondered where Lucretia Mott and other lecturers at the women's conventions learned to speak publicly. Hopefully, women will one day hold office and teach about representative government."

I hope so, too," Miss White replied. "I'm working hard on that. In the near future, I want Amherst Academy to offer oratory for young women."

Just then, Hattie's mother approached. Her expression was a little pinched. Hattie wondered what she would say to Miss White.

"I'm Helen Sheldon," she said courteously. "How do you do?"

"I'm pleased to make your acquaintance, Mrs. Sheldon," Miss White smiled, looking interested. "It's been a joy to talk with your daughter."

"I apologize for interrupting," Hattie's mother continued, nodding graciously. "Forgive me, but I need to introduce Hattie to a couple of people across the room."

Horrified, Hattie maintained her smile, but kept her eyes on Miss White's face. To her relief, Miss White seemed unaware of what was really taking place. She smiled at Hattie and reached to shake her hand.

"I'm afraid I must be going anyway. I'm happy to meet both of you. Visiting with you has been a pleasure, Miss Sheldon. I hope we meet again."

From the moment the last guest left the tea, Hattie began to time her next move. Maybe her mother had tried to keep her from learning more about Amherst Academy, but that would not be the last word. Jumping in to help, she removed dishes from the dining room to the kitchen. After Aunt Mary washed them, she dried them.

Thankfully, both women went upstairs for a brief rest before starting supper. The moment their bedroom doors were closed, Hattie looked to be sure she wouldn't be detected, then headed straight down the street as fast as she could walk. Fate may have prevented her from chasing down the murders in Deerfield, but she wasn't going to miss seeing this school that Aunt Mary liked. Hattie's primary focus had suddenly shifted to Amherst Academy.

Amazingly and without doubt, Aunt Mary had done her a very big favor. Hattie had underestimated her aunt, never thinking that Aunt Mary would be just as talented politically as Ebenezer. But perhaps capabilities ran in families. It was no small feat to host an event with two different goals in mind, but that's exactly what Aunt Mary had done. Some guests had been invited specifically to meet her mother and learn about Utica's orphanage, while several were there just to meet Hattie and talk about Amherst Academy.

Hurrying along, she counted on the fact that she would not be recognized. This was not her home, after all, so if Amherst was as provincial as Utica about young ladies being accompanied, then anonymity was on her side. If anyone stopped her, she could easily think up scores of excuses for her venture alone from Aunt Mary's house.

A fairly detailed description of the school informed Hattie's search. Thanks to Miss Fiske, she knew to look for a striking white building at least one story higher than the tallest house. In her mind's eye, the stately structure rested atop a hill looking regal and respectable. Its appearance was an outward sign of quality.

As she approached the main street, where an intersection of two busy roads required a decision, Hattie wondered whether to turn left or right. Passing several enormous oak trees and emerging into a clearing, she saw that no choice was necessary. There, just across the street, Amherst Academy stood at attention on an expanse of green lawn behind a handsomely lettered black sign. Beautifully constructed, it was framed by a number of attractive tall trees, green and handsome in their summer leaves. Like a soldier honored for valor, Amherst Academy's façade looked spotless with its large windows as evenly placed as brass buttons.

What would it feel like, Hattie mused, to sit next to those windows during a class, the light shining onto her paper as she took notes? To quote Shakespeare, it would feel like the world was her oyster. In other words, it would be the finest thing she could imagine. Any girl could count herself privileged to attend Amherst Academy. The character and quality of its Christian students was known far and wide.

❁ ❁ ❁

Hattie's father, Artemas, and Uncle Jason did not return from Deerfield until late. Consequently, she had no opportunity to ask how fruitful the trip had been. Sunday morning presented no opportunity, either, as breakfast was a group conversation. After that, the focus was on organizing everyone to attend church amid a downpour of much-needed rain.

After the mid-day meal was over, the men could be found snoring, so Hattie still had no answers about the murder and kidnapping rumors. Truth be told, she was uncertain just how to broach the subject with her father. In the event that Artemas learned little in Deerfield, however, she would have to. He didn't usually have much drive for solving mysteries.

At supper, once the family crowded around Aunt Mary's table, the food looked so good that Hattie temporarily forgot her urgent questions. She also hadn't talked enough with Aunt Mary about the tea or Miss White or her clandestine visit to see Amherst Academy. Finding a time to chat was difficult, as her mother was always there.

Hattie's mind was brimming over about these things that had happened in Massachusetts. She was lost in thought and didn't even know it as several conversations continued around her. But during a lull, Uncle Jason, who was usually quiet, spoke up. It was just as Aunt Mary was serving dessert. His innocent question suddenly suspended Hattie's breathing.

"Ebenezer, something has come to my attention," he began, his voice low and relaxed. "Some local children playing nearby have plied your children with stories. They brought up an old myth that I've heard and even believed for years. Mary and I don't know if it's completely true or not. I wonder if you would comment. We need to know the truth."

"A myth," Ebenezer repeated, looking puzzled. "What myth am I capable of addressing?"

Artemas' eyes looked nervous with anticipation as he glanced guiltily at Uncle Jason and then back at Hattie. For her part, Hattie could not conceal her own darting glance at Artemas, which was equal to an admission of knowledge, if not collusion. Their father did not miss the glances, she realized, as he noted the unspoken signs that his children had a role in the inquiry.

"Hattie, my dear," Ebenezer began warmly, unexpectedly drawing her into the situation. "Before I begin, would you be so good as to share the background about what you were told and where it stands?"

If Hattie could have fallen through the floor, it would have been preferable to everyone staring in anticipation of what she might say. Out of options, she swallowed hard, trying to force a bite of mashed potatoes down her throat, which felt constricted. She grabbed for her water glass and took a big swallow before speaking.

"Some neighborhood boys told a tale to Artemas, and he shared it with me. We thought it was just silly talk at first. But Artemas asked Uncle Jason, who said there probably was some truth to it. The boys said Indians murdered a seventeenth-century great-grand-mother of yours and kidnapped her children to Canada."

At this revelation, Hattie's mother drew in a sharp breath one second and emitted a small moan of dread the next. She looked trans-fixed at the disintegration of propriety in the supper conversation, her napkin partially hiding her nose and framing her horrified eyes.

"I see," Ebenezer continued, looking serious but not annoyed. "And Artemas, is Hattie's account accurate?"

"Yes, Father," Artemas squeaked, sliding down in his chair. "That's all we know."

"Very well, then," Ebenezer began, straightening himself and putting down his fork gently. "I owe our hosts an explanation, if not an apology for the way this rumor has interrupted things. But first, I need to offer a word of apology to Helen, Hattie, and Artemas."

"Why?" Hattie questioned before she could stop herself. "We're the ones who are sorry for stirring up trouble. Why are you apologizing to us?"

"Because, my dear," Ebenezer responded in a more relaxed, matter-of-fact way. "The rumors are true. I take responsibility for a lack of judgment. I kept a sad but notable chapter of our Sheldon family history in the shadows too long. You children were so young. We had sadness and loss over losing the girls, so I never brought it up. But, if you'll indulge me, I'll put the rumor to rest and tell you the facts. After all, the story is part of our collective past as a family."

The tale that Ebenezer revealed encompassed the entire history of Deerfield, Massachusetts, from its first settlement to that evening at the dinner table.

"In the 1660s, one of Mary's and my forefathers, John Sheldon, went north from Northampton, Massachusetts, to settle in Deerfield. There, he played a pivotal role in the work of a plantation. After marrying a young woman named Hannah Stebbins, he was prominent in the community, the military, and the church. A few years into their marriage, he built a famous historic dwelling. Its main feature was a large and heavy door, which he believed would keep his young family safe from intruders."

Hattie gulped and looked around. Every eye was fixed on her father. He continued.

"This was the time when Deerfield and many colonial settlements were British property. The British wanted to expand their territory endlessly. But there was an imperial rivalry between them and the French over land and money. The Indians who had been the original occupants of the land got caught up in many feuds. Both sides were so certain of their mission that they prioritized their goals at the expense of the Indians.

"At a crucial point, the warring Iroquois Indians ceded land to the Queen of England, much to the chagrin of the aggressive French. In response, the French incited other tribes against the English, hoping that no tribe would ever again become English allies or trade partners. Often, especially in this story of John Sheldon's family, the Indians allied with the French. It got quite complicated, because each side attacked the other, carrying equal blame for much death and destruction.

"On the night of February 29, 1704, French soldiers had made a plan of attack that involved the help of many Indians. Together, they had traveled far south from Canada in the dead of winter to the English settlement of Deerfield. Despite the terrible cold and snow, they crept up to the sleeping village and found a way to attack. The people of Deerfield were aware that danger existed; most had decided to live inside a protected, enclosed fort encompassing their individual homes. Sadly, the night watchman fell asleep that fateful night. The attack that followed was violent and deadly.

"John and Hannah Sheldon, who had a sizable family, were filled with fear. The attacking men used great force against their big door that made a gaping hole. A pointed gun fired through that hole killed Hannah instantly where she was seated on a bed. That door has been preserved for posterity, by the way. Miraculously, John Sheldon escaped, as did John Junior. A daughter-in-law sprained her ankle and was captured, along with John Senior's little girl, Mary, and two other sons, Remembrance and Ebenezer.

Tragically, little three-year-old Mercy was killed. Ebenezer, as you might guess, was my great-grandfather.

"The captives from the Sheldon and other families were marched through the snow, even crossing frigid rivers, on the trek to Canada. Some people from other families were murdered along the way, while others died from various injuries or exposure. The children, in particular, caught the interest of the Indians, who began to reacclimatize the children to their own culture. Because they were not allowed to speak English, many of the children soon took up the Indian language, which further separated them from their families of origin.

"In the weeks and months after the captives reached Canada, John Senior was sent there by the governor. He completed several long, dangerous missions to get the people of Deerfield back. His heroic efforts were largely successful. He redeemed all his family members and brought them home. Some families weren't that fortunate. The Indians kept a number of children."

When her father paused, Hattie realized she had forgotten to breathe. The story was not only true, but compelling in a personal way. For the second time in her young life, she was grateful to acknowledge that her life existed because family members had persevered through devastating obstacles. Her parents had protected her from the measles, which killed her two sisters. This earlier ancestor, John Sheldon Sr., had persevered and actually redeemed the man who was her great-great-grandfather! She was alive today for a good reason. Its significance seemed perfectly linked to the importance of getting educated, of finding a worthy mission, and of making a meaningful life as a show of gratitude.

Utter silence encompassed Aunt Mary and Uncle Jason's dining room. Every person at the table seemed to ponder how fate had smiled on those who escaped and lived. Yet Hattie took it one step further. She had a profound feeling that related to something she had read. There was no way to keep from connecting this story with what she had learned about Indian removals from states farther south.

Without question, she concluded, the early days of the nation were treacherous times. She was grateful to live in America, enjoying many more freedoms than generations before had ever dreamed possible. Simultaneously, however, she could not help but contemplate the fate of native peoples. Maybe the Indians from Canada were like the Indians in the article who had been removed to Indian Territory in recent years. Had treaties been broken with the eighteenth century Indians, too? Were they lied to or manipulated?

She could not stop thinking about the fact that Indians had inhabited the land before settlers from England, France, and other countries had come and started wars. What had the Indians felt as their land was taken over by people who wanted to turn it into a new nation? Suddenly, their longstanding way of life came under attack and their lands were slowly or violently or dishonestly taken away. The whole picture left her totally off balance.

7

Amherst Academy

The remaining days of Hattie's much-prized adventure finally slowed down. After unearthing the Sheldon family's ancestral tragedy, she focused once again on Aunt Mary. Their many wonderful conversations found a place in her diary, practically word for word, alongside the Deerfield Raid of 1704 and the discovery of Amherst Academy. She now knew that Amherst was the school for her. But how was she going to get herself there?

The day of departure for Utica came much too soon. Saying goodbye was a bittersweet experience, even though she had vowed within herself to return, somehow, some way. Bringing her suitcase out the front door, Hattie watched Uncle Jason's buggy pulling up. He and Ebenezer jumped out to help. She hadn't noticed them leaving earlier and wondered where they had gone. In another hour, her father said, the family would depart for the train station.

Hattie's mother happened to have begun one of Aunt Mary's books in recent days and couldn't put it down. Even though Aunt Mary begged her to take it, she insisted on reading to the end upstairs in her bedroom. Hattie didn't mind staying longer, and Artemas was outside with his friends. Her father seemed busy with the luggage and train tickets.

To pass the time, Hattie sat in a well-worn rocking chair, protected in its own little corner, and began writing in her diary. It was dim, but she was too engrossed to light a lamp. Perhaps because she wasn't actually rocking, her presence went undetected.

Soon, she heard a whisper and realized that Aunt Mary was trying to get Ebenezer's attention. He responded, and the two of them went out onto the back porch together. Hattie followed silently as far as the door, but dared not go any closer. She had no idea what they were doing. Hearing a conversation in low voices, however, she realized that a nearby window was open slightly. She could overhear their conversation. Crouching against the wall, she listened intently.

"What did you think of Amherst Academy?" Aunt Mary asked Ebenezer, excitement in her voice.

"If the exterior is any indication, it must be an outstanding place," he returned. "When did you formulate this idea? How did it gain steam so quickly?"

"I knew from the moment Hattie arrived and spoke so intelligently," Aunt Mary explained eagerly. "This child has promise, I tell you. She needs and wants better schooling. I can't think of a more wonderful place for her."

"I don't argue with that," Ebenezer continued cautiously. "But the decision is not solely mine. Helen is very attached to Hattie. Losing the older girls left her holding on for dear life. I am confounded over how to convince her to release the constraints. She just cannot accept the fact that Hattie is rejecting an ordinary life in Utica. It's a delicate matter."

As her father's words fell on her ears, Hattie all but squealed in delight. Her father not only understood, but he was on her side! So was Aunt Mary. Surely this meant that her mother wouldn't continue to be the only dissenter. There just had to be a way, against all odds, for her to attend school at Amherst Academy.

"I understand, I truly do," Mary responded sympathetically. "Perhaps I can appeal to her, like I did about the orphanage last Saturday. Were you aware of that? Several ladies came to tea genuinely interested to meet Helen. Our town needs an orphanage. But I also invited the Amherst Academy headmistress to meet and assess Hattie as a potential candidate for admission."

"Why, Mary," Ebenezer exhaled, clearly amazed at his sister. "I had no idea. You and Hattie really are kindred spirits in the way you strategize. Thank you. And undoubtedly, Helen benefitted from the attention, as well. I am sure your efforts blessed them."

"Well, dear one, I love both your wife and your daughter and want the best for them," Mary whispered, sounding emotional.

Hattie's entire being tingled with excitement at what she had just overheard. Lest she give herself away, she began to slowly and quietly back away from the window. By the time Aunt Mary and her father entered the house again, she was in the rocking chair, pretending to write in her diary.

Aunt Mary was a worker of miracles! She was an astute observer, as well. How could any girl be so lucky as to have a loving advocate, and all the more, one who lived so close to a marvelous school? It even sounded like her father supported the idea of her attending Amherst Academy. Hattie felt like dancing for joy. The battle was halfway won. Aunt Mary had a strong chance of convincing her mother. She wondered if they would talk about it yet today? The possibility left Hattie willing to do days or even weeks of household chores, or any other task for her mother, without even being asked.

❀ ❀ ❀

"Hattie, dear, I'm afraid it's time to go," Ebenezer called after a few minutes. "Where is Artemas?"

"I'll find him, Father," she responded. "He's probably just out back saying goodbye to his friends."

Leaving the house, Hattie crossed Aunt Mary's orchard and departed the back garden. She could hear voices and soon found Artemas and his friends not far away. Like her, he would have preferred to stay in Amherst longer. But, saying his goodbyes, Artemas accompanied Hattie back through the orchard and around the side of the house to where Uncle Jason's wagon was waiting to take them to the train station.

To Hattie's great surprise, there stood Miss Anna B. White, preceptress of Amherst Academy, talking to her parents. Her presence stymied Hattie, leaving her both excited and worried at the same time. She wasn't quite sure what to do, but since this might be an opportunity, she would approach Miss White and act interested.

"Well, hello, Miss Sheldon," Miss White said amiably, offering her hand. "I have been thinking about our conversation ever since the tea on Saturday."

"So have I," Hattie responded. "I have actually given it a great deal of thought."

"Miss White has come to say goodbye," Ebenezer interjected, smiling. "She says complimentary things about you, which your mother and I appreciate greatly."

"In particular," Miss White continued, "I couldn't let you leave without interceding on behalf of the school. You see, I have such a sense of your academic promise. It compelled me to come and urge your parents to consider sending you to Amherst Academy."

Hattie had never considered what she would do when something intangible, like a dream, suddenly took the form of a person. In this instance, her heart was inclined to overflow with words of thanks and gratitude, almost like a fervent prayer. She wanted to thank Miss White, Aunt Mary, and her father over and over again for believing in her. But then she looked at her mother. To say that her mother's expression was negative would misrepresent the truth. She was not very interested, Hattie could tell, but managed to appear attentive, yet silent. Her expression was open, Hattie decided, and could be described as neutral.

In that moment, Hattie decided that neutral was something of a victory. It was better than a frown. And, strangely enough, she found herself able to sympathize with her mother's point of view, however flawed it seemed in logic. After overhearing what her father said to Aunt Mary, Hattie tried to put herself in her mother's shoes, even as she felt her own compelling excitement about Miss White's encouragement.

This much she comprehended: her mother could be hurt if Hattie appeared too eager to leave her. Therefore, this moment was pivotal to her future plans. She must respond in a way that was sensitive to everyone's position.

Her mind racing, she thought, *Why not show a type of gratitude and praise like Miss White's, only focused on mother?* She could bolster her mother, show her how meaningful she was. That was it! Instead of acting tepid and uncertain, Hattie needed to encourage her mother. If she displayed loyalty and empathy instead of rebelliousness, maybe her dreams would unfold in a new way. Hattie wanted her mother to grasp that, no matter where she went or what she did in life, she would always be with her mother in her heart.

So, like a mature young woman facing both her future and

her mother's doubts about it, Hattie drew on a new type of inner strength and compassion. Walking past the others, Hattie looked only at her mother. Helen Sheldon registered uncertainty, even as her eyes followed Hattie lovingly.

"Thank you, Miss White," Hattie said with great composure as she placed a warm arm around her mother's shoulders. "Thank you from the bottom of my heart. You're wonderful for taking the time to come by today. It's so kind of you to talk with my parents about Amherst Academy. They are the most important people in the world to me."

The train's steady pace lulled the Sheldons to rest as they steamed westward from the rolling green hills of Massachusetts toward New York. Their wonderful trip had left each family member with more memories than they could ever have imagined. Hattie, in particular, found herself running out of room in her diary. Her heart contained more emotions than she could count. She had an inkling that her mother had made progress in understanding that the future would bring change. Perhaps this quiet moment on the train was a good time to talk about it.

"Mother, what did you think of Miss White?" Hattie asked, hoping to hear that Miss White had impressed her.

"I found her to be an engaging conversationalist," her mother responded. "She is quite an educated woman."

"I want to be just like that," Hattie asserted. "She inspires me. Have you given any more thought to Amherst Academy?"

"No, I haven't, Hattie," her mother added in a slightly sour tone. "I wasn't prepared to be followed to Massachusetts by this issue of your leaving to go away somewhere to school."

"But surely Miss White's interest got your attention," Hattie challenged, a little alarmed. "Aunt Mary and even Father held onto her every word. That school is right for me. I can just feel it."

"This was supposed to be a vacation away from pressures," her mother returned rather indirectly. Her tone showed that she had no intention of discussing Amherst Academy. "Focus on something else, Hattie. Read a book or write a letter."

Hattie stared at her mother, crestfallen. Her cheek twitched, a signal that tears wanted to flow. Why was her mother consciously ignoring all that had happened in the last week? There was no denying that she was trying to avoid the issue. What was the right response?

Since something had to be done about it, it might as well start now, Hattie thought. There was absolutely no possibility she could endure the rest of the summer with these back-and-forth emotional swings that always left her uncertain. This was no time to give up. She was tired of being deterred. She must win her mother over on this issue somehow. The longer these dead-end conversations continued, the more her mother was becoming entrenched in her stance. So, she decided to reason through it aloud, bit by bit.

"I can hear the reluctance in your voice," Hattie began tentatively. "You still don't want to face the issue of my future. But neither one of us can stop God's work or the desire He has put in my heart. My passion for more education is a gift, after all. And I value it to the bottom of my heart ..."

"Now, Hattie, I said this was not the time for such a discussion," her mother reiterated.

But Hattie couldn't afford to be deterred by her mother's

feelings. She knew that persistence was the approach she must take, no matter how unpleasant things grew or how much her mother protested. Some points needed to be brought to light.

"I understand. You don't want to talk about it. And that confuses me," Hattie returned, gaining strength and finding her words. "Most of the time, you position the topic of my education *between* us, like a battle line in war. On one side, I'm armed with every argument I can muster for more education. You stand across the fence ready to do battle. It feels like you want to capture me over to your side, to imprison me as a little girl forever. There's no reason for us to be enemies. Why do you see me and my hopes that way?" Hattie concluded, no longer flushed or nervous.

"No, that is not accurate," her mother returned uneasily. "My priority is not taking you away from anything. It's about keeping you safe."

"You want to keep me close so you can keep me alive," Hattie summarized, speaking low and evenly. "Because the girls died, you plan to watch after me so closely that I won't die, too."

"I said nothing about dying," her mother protested emotionally in a wavering tone. "I meant what I said. It's about safety."

Hastily removing his jacket upon arriving home from work, Ebenezer brushed determinedly through the hallway, even bypassing his favorite chair. Usually, Hattie watched him gather his thoughts and read the news leisurely. But today, he was obviously not in that frame of mind. As he strode to the kitchen, he offered an agitated monologue to whomever happened to be present, such was his state of distraction.

"Out of the blue comes the astonishing news that our new President, Mr. Taylor, is dead already," he announced nervously, waving the newspaper. "He's been in office just over a year. Today's newspaper says he collapsed from a stomach ailment and died on July 9th. I hardly know what to make of the future now."

"Oh my heavens," Helen exclaimed, wiping her hands on her apron. "He must have gone suddenly."

"You didn't vote for him, did you Father?" Hattie inquired, rushing to her father's side. She was already deep in thought over the development. "Or, I meant to say, you didn't think he was the best man for the office. How will Vice President Fillmore do as his replacement?"

"That's at issue, too," Ebenezer acknowledged, distracted. "I hadn't gotten that far. For the moment, I'm simply stunned over the potential disruption. This North versus South logjam in Congress is tedious, and the debates far-reaching. It's the divisive hand of slavery, yet again. But his death is sorrowful news. Forgive me. We must be respectful and hold President Taylor's family and the nation in prayer during such an upset."

"Didn't you meet the vice president once in Buffalo?" Hattie reminded. "Thank goodness he's a New Yorker and not a slaveholder."

"That's a good point. While I respected Taylor's office and military accomplishments, I disagreed with his politics," Ebenezer continued, pulling at his whiskers. "It was impossible for me to accept that yet another of our presidents was a slave owner. Looking forward, even though Fillmore is a northerner and a New Yorker, when I survey his qualities, I don't think he will be a strong enough leader. He might give in to the extreme pressure. What that could mean for us, I shudder to think."

The conversation sent Hattie's mind spinning with questions. Her father had just expressed little confidence in the new thirteenth president of the United States. It was more than unsettling. To Ebenezer, the fact that the new president came from their home state of New York was not enough. Did he mean that, even if Fillmore's political value system was strong, his character was too weak to uphold it? And what had he meant by "extreme pressure?"

The next day, Hattie's feet carried her as swiftly as possible to the library. There, she reached behind the headlines to study the unprecedented debate generating heat for months in Congress. On January 29, 1850, Sen. Henry Clay had presented a compromise because so many issues muddied progress. As a result, a series of bills now sought to keep the northern Free Staters and southern supporters of slavery on equal footing.

California desired statehood and had already held a constitutional convention, which outlawed slavery. Texas was embroiled in a land dispute. A vast number of acres acquired through the Mexican War lay in the balance. The most controversial of the measures, however, dealt with fugitive slaves. The South demanded their return. Hattie knew all too well that many had fled and built free lives in the North or Canada.

Her thoughts returned to the Underground Railroad rescue in her childhood. She still had the little cross. What had happened to the woman who made it, she wondered? If she had reached freedom, which the South had no intention of honoring, slave catchers might have kidnapped her back to a cruel life. The idea agitated Hattie, so she went outside to shake it off before continuing with her study.

After returning, it took a few minutes to get her thinking focused again. What exactly was the leadership requirement that her father felt Mr. Fillmore was lacking? Pulling from a number of sources, Hattie learned that Fillmore had been against the admission of Texas as a slave territory. That sounded like something Ebenezer would support. Fillmore also had endorsed a policy in which Congress would stop the slave trade between states. That resounded in her. These two seemingly strong stances from his earlier career in Congress must have prepared him more than adequately to become president. But had something happened to change his mind since that time?

Soon, she came across some articles that revealed the answer. President Taylor and Vice President Fillmore did not see eye-to-eye on another slavery issue. When it came to allowing slavery into western territories that had come into United States' possession following the Mexican-American War, it was the slaveholding Taylor who wished for the new states to be *free*! How unexpected. Furthermore, the anti-slavery Fillmore, hailing from the free state of New York, was *in favor of slavery* in those new states. *What a reversal*, Hattie puzzled. Fillmore's rationale for his position, according to the newspaper, was "to appease the South."

Suddenly, Hattie sat up at attention. Appease? Appease the South? Those were fighting words to an abolitionist like Ebenezer. Now that she had uncovered a flaw in Fillmore's moral position, Hattie knew she was on the right track. She must continue to study until she uncovered more about the source of her father's doubt. After all, if she could discuss such a matter cogently at the dinner table, surely her parents would see that she deserved higher and better education.

It took several more painstaking hours of hard study to find enough information. The day grew rather long in the stuffy corner she inhabited, but she pushed through the temporary discomfort. On occasion, she stopped reading to compare something she read against her father's declared value system. Without question, Ebenezer would not respect any leader, president or not, who gave up on a morally grounded position for mere political reasons. He demanded that the elected officials for whom he voted must hold their ground for causes they said they championed. Actions had to accompany their words.

In this case, Fillmore was obviously unable to uphold his own anti-slavery beliefs. So, Hattie concluded, when he had served in Congress, long before assuming the Presidency, he had *already* caved in to political pressure on slavery. And, now, even though he had only been president for one day, Hattie could see that her father knew it would happen again.

One day shortly thereafter, Hattie's mother came into the house holding a letter. Her expression was bewildered; its impact on her was different than anything Hattie had seen before. From her spot in Ebenezer's chair where she had been reading the final paragraph of her book, Hattie watched her mother clutch the letter and then stare blankly at an empty wall for a long moment of deep, disturbed thought.

Hattie liked her own privacy these days when a letter arrived in the mail, especially one from Margaret. Sometimes, she didn't want to share the contents and found her mother's inquiries annoying. It dawned on her that the same must be true for her mother, as well; asking about another's private correspondence was bad manners. So, she kept quiet and watched silently. It was time to go to the library anyway, so she gathered her things, called goodbye, and dashed out the door.

❧ ❧ ❧

Settling down after the trip to Massachusetts had been very difficult. Hattie's heart was full of Amherst, but her summer days were dragging. This frightened her slightly and forced renewed efforts to plan her future. At the library, she found herself pondering anew her decision in Massachusetts to honor her mother's perspective. She still struggled with the limitations on her freedom and harbored some residual resentment.

Hattie's new attitude was filled with intention. She reminded herself again that she mustn't go silent. Doing so would be giving up on her dreams. Only if she maintained a vocal presence about her wishes would there be a way to realize her dreams. She would continue a continuous but positive bombardment of her mother with ideas, plans, suggestions, and any other thing that came to mind.

However, too few options were presenting themselves. She couldn't just use the same old rationale and wording over and over. Yet nothing more persuasive came to mind.

At length, she began to grow impatient and frustrated about reiterating her desire for freedom. Why did it have to be like this? Why must she turn herself inside out so often? For several hours, she toiled without results and then began to shift uncomfortably in her chair. Before long, a pesky backache told her she was too tense and worried.

To make matters worse, others at the library table kept whispering, which interrupted her thoughts. She had no interest in conversation. Besides, it was against the rules. But the eager whisperers persisted.

"What have you read lately?" an unknown woman asked her.

Hattie tried to suppress a frown. The last thing on her mind was losing her focus.

"Oh, too many books to count! You'll find many, wonderful books," she replied a bit too curtly. "Why don't you ask the librarian? I've got some work to complete."

The minute the words escaped, she knew she had sounded rude. This might be the woman's first visit to a library. She had deserved better from Hattie. Smiling apologetically at the woman, she excused herself to stretch and think.

Nothing satisfying had resulted today from her efforts at planning. As hard as she had willed new ideas to spring into her brain, every other force in the world seemed to be intruding. She felt ashamed to have brushed the innocent woman off.

Rather than continue to spoil the day, she decided to put the pressure aside and leave the library. What could it hurt to go home early? In fact, a nice walk might be therapeutic. Perhaps ideas would flow once she got some fresh air and focused on the leafy shadows and stately homes in Utica. She would resume her strategy another time.

Walking toward home, Hattie kicked a stone while deep in thought. She waved as a neighbor passed along busy Genesee Street in a shiny, new carriage she had only spotted from afar until today. It always felt good to see people who looked happy. Turning the corner, she glimpsed another carriage as it pulled up in front of Reverend Fowler's home. It took a moment before she realized that it was her mother's carriage.

For a reason she couldn't really explain, Hattie suddenly jumped sideways to hide behind a tree trunk. She felt a little stumped by her own desire for concealment. Out of sight, she watched intently as her mother disembarked and walked toward the house wearing her good blue dress and matching hat. Her pace was brisk. Why was she hurrying so fast with her head down? What did this mean? Something was out of the ordinary.

Late afternoon was a rather odd hour to pay the pastor a call. Usually, preparations for supper would be underway at home about now. If there were an emergency, Ebenezer would most certainly have been there, too. But he wasn't. Hattie puzzled over how much her mother looked out of place.

Had something troubling happened? Hopefully no one had taken ill. Or was the visit related to something emotional? Reverend Fowler often provided counsel to his parishioners, she knew.

But then, recognizing how questionable her own position looked there behind the tree, Hattie stopped. She, too, was of place. Perhaps it would be best to cover her tracks. Reaching into her leather satchel, she pulled out a sheet of paper and the pencil Aunt Mary had given her in Massachusetts. Then, leaning casually against the tree trunk, she pretended to write something down. If anyone approached, she could always make some kind of excuse about capturing the grocery list before she forgot.

Voices caught her ear. Reverend Fowler himself had come to the door of the conservative, ivy-fronted parsonage. Hattie noted that he expressed surprise and delight upon seeing her mother. This suggested he had not expected her. And he must not believe the visit was sad or disturbing, either.

So, Hattie mused, the meeting was unplanned. It was not about anything troubling, because her mother smiled and carried herself in a confident way. She knew very well how her mother acted when she was bereaved. The behavior she now displayed was not similar to that in any way.

After her mother went inside, Hattie watched for what seemed a long while. Luckily, days were quite long in the middle of summer, so darkness would not come for a few hours. Then, a new thought pierced her conscience. She wouldn't want anyone to think she was spying on her own mother. That would not only look disrespectful, but odd.

It was time to leave her spot. There would have to be some other way of solving this mystery. Retracing her steps, she returned to Genesee Street and found her way home via an alternate route.

Upon entering the house, she was greeted by both Artemas and her father. They just stood there side by side looking quite sheepish. Their expression brightened momentarily like she brought a glimmer of hope.

"Do you know where mother is?" Artemas asked first.

"Well, um, I haven't ... spoken with her since this morning," Hattie replied, struggling for words that were actually the truth.

"We can't imagine where she could be," Hattie's father added, frowning and putting his hands on his hips. "There doesn't appear to be any preparation for supper."

"She didn't mention cooking to me," Hattie replied, eyebrows raised in false concern, hopefully to make her look innocent. "If she wants me to make supper, she always tells me in the morning."

Ebenezer and Artemas looked at each other and then back at Hattie. Any worry about a crisis was temporarily forgotten as Hattie stifled the urge to laugh. The men who lived in this house looked utterly and hopelessly lost. Their routine upset, they couldn't seem to make sense of things. Both were obviously ravenous with hunger.

"Why don't I find something for you to eat?" Hattie offered, striding confidently toward the kitchen. "Surely a little bite or two will tide you over."

Luckily, her mother had baked bread that morning. Hattie cut thick, nutty slices and placed them on the table alongside a dish of fresh yellow butter and a generous helping of Aunt Mary's delicious blackberry preserves. She poured tall glasses of fresh milk and called for Artemas and her father to come to the table. Seating themselves, the three of them momentarily experienced an awkward silence.

"Did anyone tell good stories at the shop today?" Hattie inquired, seeking to bring their anxiety down.

Light conversation followed as the men ate their bread and Hattie picked at hers. Even though she knew they were worried, she resolved not to tell what she had seen earlier. Something about her mother's choices signaled a need for privacy.

When they finished, Artemas went outdoors and Ebenezer returned to his reading chair. Hattie could tell that her father was upset, but he maintained a confident façade. He was quite a loyal person. Hattie realized that, as long as he had too little information, he would not speculate in a way that compromised her mother, especially to the children.

Second, even if something was wrong, he wasn't one to overreact or jump the gun. He maintained his comportment like a Christian man, showing that he had faith in positive outcomes. But Hattie wasn't that sure.

After a few minutes, she grabbed the clean laundry and went upstairs to fold it. All the while, her ears remained alert for her mother's return. Usually, her room was a peaceful refuge where she could read, relax, or strategize. But it brought no comfort tonight. Good thoughts didn't come easily.

There had been a break in the family routine. It meant something, but she wasn't sure what. At length, she sighed about the distraction as she folded the laundry. Soon, there was a small stack for each family member, which she began distributing to their individual rooms.

When she reached to place her mother's things on her dressing table, two crumbled lace handkerchiefs lay there. They partly covered a folded sheet of writing paper. Curious, she pushed the hankies aside carefully. The handwriting on the page was Aunt Mary's! When had it arrived? Why hadn't she said anything?

Hattie was dying to read the letter. It drew her with the most compelling pull. She couldn't explain it. But first, she stopped to think. Was this letter what had caught her mother off guard earlier? Hattie gulped, her heart thumping from more than a little intrigue.

She listened for signs that anyone might catch her. When silence met her ears, she carefully raised the page and began to read.

2 July 1850
Amherst, Mass

Dearest Helen,

Ah, the happy days we had together with you during your wonderful visit to Massachusetts. It was the highlight of my year. Do remember us to Albert, as well as George and Amanda and their spouses.

It cheers my heart that your family is happy again after unbearable losses and grief. How I admire your strength of character and faith after losing precious Mary and Cornelia. It is unnatural to survive one's children. Rest your heart now, as they reside in paradise, forever safe from pain and woe.

I'm glad that Amanda's marriage earlier this year was a source of great joy. Hattie described everything with such skilled words. What a special girl Hattie is, Helen, with great understanding for one her age. Much of that depth came from the inexplicability of being among the surviving children in your family. She wishes to live a "useful" life outside the ordinary. "We can't know how many years God grants us," she told me.

Helen, her response to loss brought up a new question after your months and years of suffering. Will you allow me a question about your reaction to loss? Every mother instinctively preserves her family, all the more after children perish.

If I may be bold, I observed you protecting Hattie in a most direct way. And yet, that was not so for Artemas, as endearing a little fellow as I've met. Despite his bruises and bumps, getting lost, and encountering a snake, he was allowed to roam out in the woods with local boys we do not know well. In short, he was free, while Hattie was restricted.

Your Hattie has unusual gifts with great capacity to do well in our fallen world. She possesses lofty dreams and the talent to make them come true, choosing to study independently so that her knowledge outpaces others twice her age. In short, dear, I draw close to you because, in my estimation, Hattie will go far and wide, yet never meet your expectations. Rather, she will exceed our wildest dreams.

Like me, you picture living out your days near family, hoping to be surrounded by grandchildren and focused on the home. But, a word of advice: turn to your other children more than to Hattie. Her keen mind and compassionate heart must take wing, carrying her to an undefined mission. I think she will land well beyond the home fires. Allow her to fly, even in an untried direction.

In a spirit of love, Helen, I have a special request. Would...

Breathless at Aunt Mary's compliment and awed at the letter's brave approach, Hattie turned the page over looking for the rest of the letter. It was not there, nor was it on the dressing table. *Oh no*, she cried desperately to herself. *Where is it? I just HAVE to read the end.*

But she saw no other pages anywhere. Hattie knew better than to search further. She'd best not disturb any more of her mother's private things. She read the first page again. Aunt Mary's words were bold, if not gently confrontational. She had put structure to crucial details on Hattie's behalf! How fortuitous, especially since Hattie had drawn a blank earlier at the library. Aunt Mary's arguments were convincing in a way that Hattie could never have formulated on her own. It seemed clear that she was leading up to something that might be important.

Was this letter what drove her mother to turn to Reverend Fowler? Perhaps the omission of this page happened in a rush. It was easy to picture her inadvertently grabbing the rest of the letter amid tears.

Hattie held her hand over her mouth out of confusion. The circumstances made it hard to think. She had an advocate—one who dared to say things her mother needed to hear. She also had a detractor in her own mother. Now what?

After recovering her wits, she gently laid the letter back down, her heart still beating wildly. How had the page looked when she discovered it? She could not give away the fact that she had broken a rule of propriety and read someone else's private correspondence. But how Aunt Mary's letter made her hopes rise!

Spying the two hankies again, she gingerly placed them back on top of the page. Then, seeking to cover her deed further, she laid her mother's folded laundry directly on top of the letter that had cried out in her behalf. Hattie tiptoed back to the door and looked carefully before leaving her mother's room. Feeling breathless, she returned to her room and shut the door.

At first, she paced back and forth from the foot of her bed to the wall. Lighting her lamp, she bit her lip, then her fingernails, which was most uncharacteristic. If only Margaret could help work through this mystery. On the other hand, she should entrust her excitement and concerns to Amanda. But that would have to wait for morning. The pressing matter now was what might happen when her mother finally returned home.

Hattie reclined on her bed, glancing absentmindedly at several library books she meant to read. Impatiently, she began to flip through the pages of Charles Dickens' *Dombey and Son*. The librarian had recommended it, but this was the first time she had actually opened the cover. Having read the first paragraph three times, she put the book down. Distracting thoughts made concentration impossible.

Aunt Mary's letter prompted so many wonderful memories about Amherst and the trip. Hattie took deep breaths to calm herself while picturing the fun time she had cooking with Aunt Mary. She could recall every detail of the house, the rooms and the fireplace adorned with pottery bowls. She imagined herself walking out the back door and through the orchard.

Smiling, she recreated the moment at the tea when she had realized that Aunt Mary intended for her to learn about Amherst Academy. What an extraordinary favor. How quickly Aunt Mary had become her friend and confidante. Now, the letter seemed to go further. Aunt Mary had become her advocate, even approaching Hattie's mother on her behalf. It was remarkable.

Finally calmed down, Hattie's heart was full of gratefulness. She had replaced the trepidation over the letter with loving feelings for Aunt Mary. Rising momentarily, she padded over and opened her door a crack. She would be wise to keep track of what was going on downstairs. Then, picking up her book again, she became engrossed within a few minutes.

The familiar sound of the front door hinge brought her to

attention. No voices could be heard, however. Hattie extinguished her lamp. Glancing out the window, the dark July sky confirmed that her mother had arrived home later than at any other time in her life.

Met with no greeting, conversation, or fanfare, Helen Sheldon closed the front door and began to climb the stairs. As Hattie strained to hear, the fabric of her mother's dress swished past her door and to the end of the hallway. In less than thirty seconds, she disappeared into her bedroom and closed the door quietly. Hattie remained perfectly still. This was no time to speak or move.

In another few seconds, there came the unmistakable sound of her father's boots on the stairs. His pace was normal, so he must not be upset. After he passed Hattie's door, the smoky scent of tobacco trailed him. When he reached the master bedroom, he opened the door, went in, and closed the door behind him.

Hattie could hear nothing from behind the closed doors. She waited, expecting her parents to reemerge. But they did not. Quietly, she crept down the doorway and took refuge just inside Mary and Cornelia's old room. Even after straining to hear some conversation or movement, not one sound came from her parent's bedroom.

The next morning, rather than going to the library, Hattie threw on a cool, cotton dress dotted with tiny flowers and walked directly to Amanda's house. The two of them hadn't had time to talk much because Amanda was expecting a child and was busy with preparations. Hattie needed her sister's discerning interpretation.

"Last night, mother skipped supper and came home late after a mystery visit to the pastor's home," she began before exploding with all the details.

"Was she crying?" Amanda queried, shocked at Hattie's story. "Maybe she's grieving again."

"No, I don't think so," Hattie replied thoughtfully. "She walked with intention. Her head was down as if she were deep in thought. I didn't think she looked sad at all."

"Perhaps there's some kind of problem at the orphanage," Amanda continued. "Or maybe she wasn't visiting the pastor at all. She could have gone to see Mrs. Fowler, you know."

"That's possible," Hattie allowed. "Dr. Fowler answered the door himself. He was pleased to see her and she reciprocated."

"I'll tell you what," Amanda offered. "This afternoon while you're at the library, I will find Mother and see if I can glean any information about what might be happening."

❖ ❖ ❖

That night and all the next day, Hattie felt completely in the dark. Her mother spent many hours at the orphanage and then carried on at home as if nothing was wrong. She could not detect any disagreements between her parents. Nor had Amanda come to the house. The absolute quiet gave birth to new theories, some of them doubts.

Maybe her mother was hurt by Aunt Mary's letter. Some of the sentences, while kind, were still unflattering. It was also possible that the problem might be extremely private. What if her mother had questions about faith? Maybe she asked some of the same questions Hattie asked herself privately. The most concerning one was why God had let the girls die. Any problem of a religious nature like that wouldn't be shared with anybody but one's spouse or the pastor. Why, for that matter, there even existed a possibility, Hattie allowed, that some kind of impasse might exist in her parents' relationship. That was so far off limits that she didn't want to know anything about it. The very idea of trouble between her parents was threatening. She would much rather be happily ignorant if that was the source of her mother's concern.

Hattie mulled over the state of their family. She hadn't given much thought to how couples solved their problems until Amanda and LeGrand Moore began courting a few short years back. Hattie had been closer to their problems than she wanted to be, but glad to be trusted with her sister's confidences. Some of the conversations Amanda shared had challenged Hattie's youthful understanding of marriage. Learning of the depth that couples had to trust, understand, forgive, and really know their spouse made her take notice in a whole new way.

Hattie had never before analyzed her parents' marriage. In many ways, doing so felt almost sacrilegious. Yet, it was naïve to believe her parents had no problems even though they maintained a united front. They had argued in front of the children occasionally.

Finding a spouse was serious business, Hattie allowed. Very few of the silly girls at school seemed to realize that. All they talked about was courting. In their view, the decades ahead held nothing more than romance. But Hattie didn't feel that way. It was why she wasn't even remotely ready to think about courting.

"Hello, honey," Hattie's mother called from the doorway as she approached. "Did you have a good day at the library?"

Hattie nearly jumped out of her skin. She felt like her mother could surely have read her thoughts.

"Oh, mother ... you startled me," she stammered, looking up

from her reverie. "I guess I wasn't expecting ... anybody ... to be at home."

"I'm glad you're back, dear. Can you help me?" her mother inquired, putting an arm around Hattie's shoulders. "Everyone's coming to supper."

"Really?" Hattie replied, trying to act excited but feeling confused. "What's the occasion?"

"It's not really an occasion. I just wanted all the family here. Let's call it a time of growth," her mother replied, looking slightly wistful. "We'll talk about it at supper."

Hattie couldn't wait for what would be revealed, whatever it was. Maybe her mother felt better or had reached some conclusion. It could be many things. For now, Hattie was just relieved that her mother seemed to be like her old self. It was nice to be happy together for a change, to work side by side with her mother in the kitchen. And her mother was humming. Something felt different, but Hattie couldn't put her finger on it.

A cool Mohawk breeze blew through the house that evening, promising less humidity. Before long, supper became a delightful time of storytelling and laughter. Ebenezer narrated all the events of the Massachusetts trip. It turned out that Hattie's brother-in-law was considering partnership in Ebenezer's saddle, trunk, and harness business. Equally as exciting, Artemas revealed that he wanted to be a part of the family business one day, as well.

Then, Hattie noticed a small signal of unspoken communication, a nod of recognition. It passed between her parents, even as everyone else was still laughing and talking.

"All right, my dears," Ebenezer said, clearing his throat. "May I please interrupt and have your attention?"

All eyes turned toward the head of the table. Ebenezer Sheldon made eye contact and nodded to acknowledge that he had something to share.

"Your mother asked me to find the right time for her to say a word or two," he continued, gesturing toward his wife. "So the floor is yours now, dear Helen."

Hattie's mother rose slowly from her chair at the other end of the table. She smoothed the skirt of her pastel dress in front, as if ready to make a formal presentation. Looking up, she glanced around the table at her family, surveying them, one by one. Blinking nervously and licking her lips, her hands came together, almost as if she were trying to bolster herself.

"It is true that I have felt a need, for some time, to come to terms with something," she began, clearing her throat nervously. "But I didn't understand that so many people were concerned about it. I don't intend to speak in riddles, so allow me to be direct. For a long while, our family has suffered. Losing the girls was the worst torture I could have endured. I'm afraid I have taken the longest to overcome my grief. You have been most patient and understanding as I found a way to inhabit my own life again."

"But just this week, I was made aware of something I had overlooked. I'll call it a blind spot, for want of a better term. The perceptiveness of a person outside our family circle challenged me, so I have done much soul-searching. As a result, I owe an apology to you all, but to one in particular. You see, in healing from our loss, I gave myself a wide berth. The orphanage became a lifesaving effort that helped me focus on others and forget about myself for a while. But I neglected you. Also, I entertained fear, worry, and even a bit of panic at times. I gave myself freedom, but when others yearned to be as free, I reacted negatively.

"So, I wanted all of you to be present for what I have to say. I know it's the right thing to do, even though I'll have to *continue* to confront myself about my fears. Yet for dear Hattie, this must be a night of celebration. I was wrong to control you so tightly, dear, and I am sorry. Your Aunt Mary has petitioned me that you may be allowed to attend Amherst College. I know it's the right decision, even though I secretly pray you will outgrow such big ideas about foreign cultures and faraway travels. Just promise you will come home, attend Utica Female Seminary and rejoin the family so we can-—"

But Helen was cut off from completing her sentence. An excited squeal, then a shout of joy suddenly filled the room. Everyone's attention immediately shifted off Helen and in the direction of Hattie. She could not believe what she had waited so long to hear. Even the lamps flickered in amazement.

Without knowing it, Hattie had raised to her feet. She leaned forward, hands on the table, and stared at her mother with a most astonished expression on her face. Next, she lost track of herself and emitted a sound that must have been heard all the way to Amherst, Massachusetts.

Amanda burst out laughing. "Yes, yes, yes," she chanted, steadying her ample midsection.

Artemas nodded his head excitedly and began a round of applause that showed his wholehearted support. George joined in. And Ebenezer sat back smiling the widest, most relieved smile Hattie had ever seen on his face. She was so ecstatic she moved around behind her chair and began to jump up and down. It was a form of complete delirium that she had never before experienced. For a long moment, absolute joy took over the room.

"All right. Quiet please," Ebenezer was saying now, just as the mayhem was feeling good and loud. "One more thing. Just one more thing, if I may."

Hattie, on her way to hug her mother, managed to gather herself, wondering what could possibly be added to such a grand moment.

"I have an announcement of my own to make," he began, still smiling sheepishly. "Just as your mother said, our renewal after much heartache is coming about. This blind spot about giving Hattie her freedom was only temporarily, I always knew. Grief and bereavement require much patience and time. But, for Hattie, there is not the benefit of time. We must act, not wait. Once we received such an enthusiastic reception by the headmistress of Amherst Academy, I realized that Helen would do the right thing by Hattie. But I needed to do my part, as well.

"Given that we were already into the summer months, I hastened to make application for Hattie to Amherst Academy. In God's good plan, she was a most desirable candidate. It is not a coincidence that my dear Helen reached her own conclusion in the exact, same period of time. So, Hattie, Amherst Academy has formally accepted you. Congratulations. You are going to school in Massachusetts this fall."

The moment he finished speaking, the room exploded with laughter and applause. Squeals and stomps followed as wonderful feelings of happy disbelief filled the Sheldon family.

"You'll give those professors a taste of their own medicine," Albert joked, clanging his spoon against his water glass.

"We can come and visit you AND Aunt Mary," Amanda squealed, her voice full of joy over her sister's good fortune.

"Massachusetts, here you come," Artemas shouted as he took Hattie's hands and whirled her in a circle.

Hattie wanted to dance on the table! She wanted to shout in ways that weren't acceptable indoors. But since she had accepted herself as a young lady, the noises didn't feel as satisfying as they should.

Suddenly, she had a new idea. Without giving notice to her family, she turned and sprinted through the front door. She knew they didn't follow her plan and would trail after her onto the front porch. She was going to do something outrageous and it felt so good.

After they had time to file out, Hattie suddenly rushed back toward the street from around the corner of the house. But she was not on foot. Rather, she was higher than normal and moving swiftly, her dress blowing in the breeze. There, in the fading light of evening, Hattie wheeled up and down the street on her brother Artemas' bicycle.

"Tonight is heaven-sent," she called, waving to them with the wind in her hair. Part of her joy was their absolutely surprised expression. Nobody knew how or when she had learned to ride the bicycle. But Hattie showed them she was good at maneuvering it back and forth.

At any other time in any other place, Hattie would likely have been disciplined and scolded. But this time, the absolute rapture of excitement erased any ideas that girls must be proper and could never ride a bicycle. Hattie ended those ideas as she rode back and forth, in the middle of a public street, on her brother's bicycle.

Before long, several neighbors, including Mrs. Chambers, emerged from their homes after being alerted by the Sheldon's excited voices. Polite inquiries were made, but the Sheldons did not apologize for Hattie. Instead, Hattie heard her mother tell Mrs. Chambers, "That's our Hattie. Wild horses can't hold her back. She's going to Massachusetts to attend Amherst Academy in the fall."

After her mother retired, Hattie's father and LeGrand Moore sat up talking business while Hattie and Amanda rocked contentedly on the porch. It was the most beautiful of summer nights, the aroma of grass and blooming flowers wafting through the fresh air from Mrs. Chambers' garden.

"In God's perfect way," Amanda whispered, "the climate provided a flawless setting for the resolution of your worries."

"I couldn't have dreamed for anything better," Hattie breathed, still half-stunned over what had happened.

"It didn't show, but Mother had your best interest in mind all along," Amanda replied.

"Yes, but she also had the advice of Reverend Fowler," Hattie added, and then inhaled in haste. "Oh! I almost forgot to tell you! The letter she got was from Aunt Mary. It went on and on with lovely compliments about me, urging mother to relent from her control. Please don't tell, but I read part of it."

"I know about that letter," Amanda whispered. "Mother showed it me. In fact, she gave it to me."

"You're kidding! What did Aunt Mary say on the second page? The first page left off when she was about to make a request!"

"I'm swearing you to secrecy, promise?" Amanda begged. "Mother felt terrible that she hadn't recognized the depth of her reaction to losing the girls. She told me to take the letter for safekeeping. On the one hand, the letter was so complimentary about you. On the other, it brought mother's character into question, which made her miserable. She gave me the letter and her permission to bring it around if she ever needed reminding."

❁ ❁ ❁

(page 2)

. . . you entrust Hattie and her schooling at Amherst Academy to us? You saw how Miss White practically begged to have her attend this fall. Jason and I will watch over her like our own. As we both know, Hattie will never be satisfied with the ordinary and cannot abide small thinkers. Remaining in Utica involuntarily, she would pursue learning at the expense of convention, rejecting suitor after boring suitor, only to suffer as a spinster and never realize her potential.

Many new paths open daily to women in today's changing social climate. Hattie desires to be one of those women, which prompts my final concern. Held back, Hattie's resentment toward you will grow, Helen. Given freedom, I am confident she will always be loyal and loving. Please accept my words in the spirit I intended—a future for Hattie and a deep desire for the most harmonious outcomes a family could desire.

Lovingly, Mary

8

A Chance Meeting

As the train rounded a curve, its engine slowing, Hattie could barely make out the station's stately façade against the clear, night sky. The last time she arrived at the Springfield, Massachusetts, station, it was with absolutely no thought of returning. Now, everything had changed. After a long day of travel, she was here to start the pursuit of her most coveted life opportunity. As much as her longing to attend Amherst Academy had grown in a short time, she nevertheless admitted that only a miracle had brought it to fruition.

Aunt Mary and Uncle Jason came into focus, waving excitedly from the platform as the train puffed the last few yards to a stop. Soon, Hattie and Aunt Mary would be in each other's arms. Hattie had frequently pondered how they were kindred spirits. She said a little prayer of gratitude that such giving relatives had come the long distance to collect her, to envelop her in love and support. They had much to talk about on the way to Amherst from Springfield.

"Welcome, dearest girl," Aunt Mary called as Hattie opened her window and stuck her head out. "You must be tired from the long ride!"

"Oh, Aunt Mary, I'm too excited to be tired," Hattie gushed.

"Your life has been filled with new things," Aunt Mary agreed. "We can't wait to hear everything, including all the details of Amanda's baby."

"Come along, girls," Uncle Jason urged. "Jump in. We need to get started."

That night, they stayed in Springfield with an old friend of Aunt Mary's. The quarters were tiny and cramped, but Hattie didn't care. She wasn't bothered about sleeping on the floor in a makeshift bed, either. It reminded her that there were many people with no bed whatsoever.

Finally resting her head on the pillow, her thoughts turned to tomorrow and the coming day when she would enter her new classroom. Precious few words passed between her and Aunt Mary after they settled for the night. In a matter of seconds, Hattie was fast asleep.

❖ ❖ ❖

Bright and early the next morning, Aunt Mary smoothed Hattie's hair away from her face and patted her hand to awaken her.

"We've got nearly twenty-five miles to cover today. As soon as you're dressed, come downstairs and have a quick breakfast before we leave," Aunt Mary directed softly.

Energized with excitement, Hattie was ready in no time. She hoped the day would pass quickly. Driving north past lovely meadows and groves of trees, Aunt Mary and Uncle Jason's wagon made good progress. The team of horses didn't flinch at the extra weight of

Hattie's clothes, books, and sturdy old trunk. Occasionally, they took a shortcut around a small mountain or large hill. A cooling breeze to her back, Hattie had the feeling of climbing steadily. She wasn't sure if the elevation was increasing or if perhaps the feeling was simply her hopes.

Just before dusk, the leafy familiarity of Amherst came into view. It was hilly in places, which created elegant shadows across the grass. Despite the waning light, Hattie got her bearings immediately, remembering the streets she had crossed when she was last here. Candles burned in windows, and the scent of cooked onions wafted by. Somehow, Amherst already felt like home.

She and Aunt Mary exchanged a knowing look. How exciting for someone close to share her intense anticipation. Should she laugh or cry? Hattie clasped her hands together and then nervously covered her nose and mouth out of sheer excitement—or it might have been disbelief.

"If it wouldn't look foolish, I could sing for joy and dance down the street," Hattie mused, shaking her head at the reality of being there. Just then, she spotted the white, three-story school building she remembered so vividly. It faced the fertile valley dotted with farms. She couldn't wait to walk up the steps and go inside. Every day.

The amazing privilege and newness of educational continuation for girls was the subject of much discussion at Amherst Academy. In addition to Hattie, all of the thirty-three girls who were boarding there knew how lucky they were. Most were enrolled in the English Department. They were fully cognizant that they were privy to opportunities previously reserved for young men only.

Gladly accepting their separate classrooms from males, the girls' conversations continued well into the wee hours on many nights. They talked about women's opportunities, westward expansion, women's conferences, and whether women would ever get the right to vote. This mattered, as many within society and government continued to insist that education for women was unnecessary in the absence of voting rights. It was joined in the debate by another topic that Hattie and many of the other Amherst Academy women both accepted and rejected at times.This idea held that the energies of a young woman should be devoted to, and were certainly better suited for, family life.

Hattie was of two minds on this topic. Listening to the conversations that swirled around her brought clarification, although slowly. The serious issues were interspersed with lighter topics, however. Just as intellectual issues dominated during the day, fashion and the potential of having male suitors ruled at night.

"Have you met anyone from the Classics Department yet?" Hattie's friendly blonde roommate, Priscilla, asked as the young women of the English department gathered for dinner in Valentine Hall. "I heard we might be allowed to hear men's lectures at Amherst College on occasion."

"My aunt said that, too," Hattie replied. "Amherst College came into existence because of the academy. While trying to raise academy funds, it became clear that a larger vision was needed to convince contributors. The community is invited at least once each year. Sometimes they debate, although debate societies no longer exist."

"Evidently, this is a well-read community that keeps track of Academy and College issues," another classmate inserted. "I was told that people here subscribe to many more newspapers and periodicals than the *Missionary Herald* or *Sabbath School Visitor*."

"I'm definitely attending the first public lecture," Priscilla returned. "I wonder how many men from the College will be there? My mother says I need to concentrate on finding a husband."

"My mother wants me to realize I should go back to Utica and marry a nice ordinary boy there," Hattie laughed in an unexpected moment of candor, surprising even herself.

❦ ❦ ❦

Without question, Hattie's favorite textbook at Amherst Academy was *Elements of Intellectual Philosophy, First Edition, 1827.* In addition to the book's rich content, she marveled at how much her professor knew about the book's author, Thomas Cogswell Upham. After just a few weeks of class, she already felt a distinct kinship to Upham. His insight was rich on what he termed the "interior life" of an individual. She felt Upham most deserved respect for his ideas about combining moral philosophy with social activism.

How mature she felt for her seventeen years to be encountering such heady topics. Social activism seemed the correct term for her family's commitment to freedom for all, most particularly for those Negroes shamelessly abused by slavery in many parts of the United States. Slavery was so divisive that many at Amherst Academy talked about it in battle terms.

"Mr. Upham is a recognized leader in the abolition movement in New England," she excitedly wrote her father. "Have you heard of him?

Upham's conclusion that war was fundamentally incompatible

with Christianity piqued Hattie's interest the most. She expressed this further in the letter, quoting Upham, who had written:

> *Christ's work on earth is not accomplished, and of course the work of his followers is not accomplished, so long as wars exist. Let it, therefore, be the language of every Christian heart—language which shall find its issues in appropriate action—that wars shall exist no longer.*

Hattie wrote home often, usually to share news about school. Writing out the gist of her lessons helped fix the information in her mind. She also remained mindful that keeping her parents apprised of her progress was a way to show her profound appreciation for this educational experience of a lifetime. Or really, she allowed, it was the chance of several lifetimes. After all, she was getting the schooling that her two dear sisters, bless them in heaven, never had the chance to enjoy. Even Amanda chose to marry and begin a family rather than continue with schooling. Of the four girls, how had she, Hattie, become the only one to gain the quality and amount of education that, heretofore, only young men had been afforded? And what did it mean, what did it suggest about her future that she was in such a position? To these questions, she had no firm answers. But she did have commitment to the idea of finding out soon.

Braving homesickness, Hattie knew it was something she must endure toward a higher goal. She thought about her family and the friends she missed, especially Margaret. As coincidences went, she found a delightful, although meager, connection between the revered textbook author Mr. Upham and Margaret.

Mr. and Mrs. Upham, according to Hattie's professor, were known to have befriended an author who was gaining in popularity, Mrs. Harriet Beecher Stowe. Mrs. Stowe's name had become familiar to Hattie as the sister of Catherine Beecher, the groundbreaker who had started Margaret's school in Hartford, Connecticut. Hattie delighted in the link, small as it was, because it made her feel akin to accomplished people making a place in the wide, wonderful world. And, of course, there was the coincidence of sharing Mrs. Stowe's name, Harriet. The nickname "Hattie" better suited her, she decided.

Returning to her letter writing, Hattie related how Thomas Cogswell Upham's leadership in American academic psychology and its melding with practical spirituality fascinated her. The very term "practical spirituality" seemed to best express her religious faith. By definition, Hattie sought to be known as a Christian person, as having straightforward, firmly held moral principles. Displays of emotion in religion were not appealing or even respectable, she believed, but sharing the faith through example was. A person's faith needed to be deeply grounded, as the professor said Upham's was after he graduated from Andover Theological Seminary, just outside Boston. Now that she lived in Massachusetts, Boston seemed less like a city from an American history story, and more like a real place—one she hoped to visit.

Weeks passed, then months. Burnished leaves that had fallen in October turned to crackly nuisances under foot. Hattie's studies were anything but a nuisance. She was thrilled at how her knowledge of the world grew. The coursework deepened her understanding from earlier study of the Greeks and civilizations from Egypt to Greece to Babylon. With visions of Babylon's hanging gardens, she read on about the ancient world and fed her growing relationship with history. Soon, the Reformation took shape in a deeply meaningful way, as did the Renaissance. Each new text and well-prepared professor opened the world to her through a sophisticated set of ideas and a prodigious vocabulary. Generations of intrepid explorers inspired new concepts in Hattie's heart about what lay within the possible.

Venturing to the library on a damp, windy Saturday, Hattie thought again about the defunct men's debate societies previously active at Amherst College. Curious as always, she wondered if the library held any information about them. Taking a break from her studies, she decided to do a little search.

After leaving the main reading room, she walked down a long, dimly lit hallway lined with shelves. When she located the one she sought, her lamp shed enough light for her fingers to travel through a stack of paper inside a large cloth box. Halfway down, tucked under other loose pages, a large file just waited to be examined. This was the kind of search she dearly loved, partly for the mystery of what she might find and partly for the fact that none of her friends cared about such things in the least.

Contained in the file's records were meeting minutes, agendas, membership rosters, and whole compendiums of debates, containing word-for-word accounts. Surprised to find such detailed information, Hattie began to peruse the topics, seeing how intricate the debates had been. She found everything from the rhetoric of social reform to children working in textile factories.

Before long, she came upon the minutes of a particular debate. Attached was a loose page noting that the debate occurred when

Indian policy had occupied the nation's attention. The date helped Hattie place both the debate and her whereabouts in time when it had occurred. Calculating back, she realized she had only been a child when the issue was debated at Amherst College.

She recalled vividly her first discovery of information on Indian policy. It was in a Presbyterian newsletter among a stack of unread materials near her father's favorite chair. The headline "Indian removals" had stopped her in her tracks.

Hattie had lost track of time because the astonishing story practically bled with sadness. Her heart had broken for the Indians and their desperate sufferings when the government moved them from their ancestral homes to a remote unsettled territory many hundreds of miles to the West.

She had been devouring the article's contents when an image captured her attention. It pictured a grand brick building with multiple impressive columns along the front and chimneys rising from the third-story roof. Many young people in rows had posed out front. A caption briefly described it as a Cherokee school in Park Hill, Indian Territory. That building was unforgettable in its size and modern elegance. It even put Amherst Academy and Amherst College to shame. It meant the Cherokees were recovering.

Refocusing on the present, Hattie questioned whether this debate document could answer how the intersecting lives of Indians and whites had led to removal. Certainly, her awareness of history had grown last summer upon learning her own ancestors had battled with the Indians in nearby Deerfield. But she still didn't fully understand the particulars that led to the deadly confrontation.

If asked, she could only respond that, on the one hand, the Indians deserved nothing less than the same equal treatment she believed Negroes were owed in a freedom-loving nation like America. On the other hand, momentarily confused, she was forced to acknowledge the prevailing position in all recent Christian literature, that explorers and pilgrims who came to America had discovered heathen beliefs and practices among the bloodthirsty, uncivilized Indians. Everything she had read concluded that the Indians were in desperate need of Christianization and education to enlighten their lives with knowledge and better practices. Hattie paused, pondering what to make of the validity of both sides.

Starting to read, she noted that the minutes commenced with a lengthy background statement. President Andrew Jackson had signed the Indian Removal Act on May 28, 1830. Hattie nodded, as this was in keeping with her understanding. The explanation spilled onto the next page, where she came upon a curious sentence that read,

> *Our debate society's policy is not to pursue any direct, critical examination of a sitting or recently retired president's actions. Rather, the more appropriate treatment of the topic should be a thorough investigation of former presidential administrations' policies with regard to similar actions.*

She couldn't wait to relate this point to her father, as he, unlike the debaters, had no trouble whatsoever making his strongly held opinions and critiques of presidents known.

Finally, Hattie came to the question that had been posed to each side in the debate: "Can the actions of generations previous to ours be rationalized with regard to how Indians were handled?" But nothing followed this central question. Only blank white pages filled the rest of the file. Hattie dug deeper and deeper looking for the rest of the account. It seemed quite strange for only the opening portion of the document to be present. She had so looked forward to poring over each side's comments. It was not to be, she realized, reaching the last sheet of paper at the bottom.

Turning it over, Hattie was surprised to find a handwritten note: "Any gentleman who wishes to examine the contentious issue contained in the missing documents will please report to Professor Alexander Colquhoun."

How curious, she thought, drawing back in surprise. Was she to believe that a professor had actually removed documents from student examination at the library? Why did the note address itself to "gentlemen only?" She was a legitimately enrolled student at Amherst Academy, which shared the library with the male students at Amherst College. Hattie's curiosity, tinged with more than a little frustration, immediately began to fuel a desire to pursue this matter. First, however, she had to find out where to locate this Professor Colquhoun.

"Hattie, the Deerfield cousins responded. They're coming to Thanksgiving supper. I hope they'll stay a few days," Aunt Mary related the next time she and Hattie were together. "If you're free and can help, I'll share some of the old family recipes you've wanted to try."

"That's perfect," Hattie exclaimed, thrilled at the chance to finally meet the cousins she had missed on the last trip. "I can ask lots of questions while we cook."

Before she could blink, the days passed. Soon, a chattering group of extended Sheldon relatives took their places at Aunt Mary's table, a veritable feast before them. The pumpkin soup's spicy, aromatic scent made Hattie's mouth water. Uncle Jason lifted the carving set and aimed for the goose before being reminded to offer thanks first. Shortly, the lid came off the steaming potatoes and everyone reached to fill their plates.

Aunt Mary broached a topic of conversation a little later, explaining that it was based on a brief comment Hattie had made in passing.

"From your knowledge of family history, how do you think our relatives and countrymen regarded the Indians, at least before the Deerfield Raid of 1704?" Aunt Mary began after the meal was well underway. "Hattie only recently become aware of her link to it. She's doing independent research alongside her fall classes. Maybe we can help her."

"I've read some earlier letters from the late seventeenth century about the Indians. That was before the famous raid," cousin Sybil responded. "You do know it was called a massacre back then, Hattie? The settlers had taught the Indians new skills with more modern tools. They helped lead the Indians out of their primitive, ignorant ways."

"An old uncle once told me that, without bringing Christianity to the Indians, there was no possibility of whites and Indians living side by side in peace," cousin Huldah noted. "Not only did the Indians love war, but they had no concept of the way settlers viewed land. Ownership of land by individuals was utterly foreign and repugnant to them. They also did not have knowledge of history or mankind's progress at bettering civilization in England and Europe through trial, tribulation, and triumph."

"The brave souls who wagered their very lives to seek freedom in America met with much less than they deserved," Sybil added. "America was a vast land, far greater than what most realized. Millions of pristine, open, unpopulated acres were just waiting.

Settling required people brave enough to risk everything for a new life free from government control and religious restriction. Some Indians were peaceful, while others just held our forefathers at bay, fought against all settlers, and unfairly blamed us with aggression."

"My father always says that all men desire freedom," Hattie inserted, thinking carefully about her words. "The Indians lived a free existence in America before it became a nation. That's what the settlers and other religious and political pilgrims sought, as well. Wasn't there enough land for everyone?"

"Yes, but the issue was control. Look at how many countries were vying for the land. Each one felt it deserved to control large tracts," Aunt Mary added. "The French, the Spaniards, and many others came to these shores. From all accounts, it was clear that the Indians who only populated part of the land nevertheless wanted to own and keep control over all of the land."

"Before long, the settlers lived fearfully most of the time," Cousin Sybil added. "The threat of Indian attack affected all their actions. All sides were fighting for the land itself, as well as a chance to profit from the resources."

That night, Hattie pondered all she had heard. She clearly understood the aims of the settlers and the settlers' version of the Indians' aims. Where was she going to learn the Indian's version of their own aims?

After making subtle inquiries among her professors at Amherst Academy, all Hattie had learned was that Professor Colquhoun had taught at the young Amherst College in the 1830s. That was nearly twenty years ago. But he was no longer a professor there. Where had he gone, she wondered. Was he still alive? If not, what had become of the debate record he had removed from the library? She wondered if he had taken other records. His actions were inexplicable.

If she were to learn any more information about him, it must now come from Amherst College, to which she had no formal connection, especially as a female. All the more, she was a new student and wasn't yet seasoned enough to figure her way around the divide between the college and the academy. There was only a remote chance of simply encountering a member of the Amherst College teaching faculty to make a subtle inquiry. So, Hattie waited.

The next week, although she meant to take a walk and breathe some crisp November air, she became engrossed in writing a short research paper. Before long, books and notes were strewn across her bed. But her mind was on Professor Colquhoun. Interrupting her seriousness, Priscilla rushed in late one afternoon from the library.

"Did you hear?" she gushed. "Amherst Academy students are invited to attend a lecture next week at the college."

"Really? How exciting," Hattie returned, flushing with anticipation. "Do you know the speaker or the topic?"

"He's from New York. I don't know his name, but someone said he will address the Compromise of 1850 that Congress just passed in September."

"That was a huge bill," Hattie remarked. "My father was terribly upset because the president avoided Congress during the debate. It went on for months. I'm sure the newspapers will cover this talk."

"I suppose. But that's not my focus," Priscilla commented, busying herself in her wardrobe. "I've got to mend my wool dress before then. It's supposed to turn cold and I want to look my best. We have to go early and stay late. All sorts of young men will be there. It's our first unsupervised chance to make their acquaintance!"

❀ ❀ ❀

The day before the lecture, the local newspaper in Amherst advertised the upcoming event. Its headline for Friday, November 29, 1850, read:

OPEN LECTURE TO EXAMINE SLAVERY:
Visiting Lecturer Lewis Tappan to Speak on Great Controversy

All week long, every setting in which Hattie had found herself buzzed with excitement about it. Some even speculated that fights could break out, so contentious was the subject. She vowed to go early, no matter how long the queue. She just had to be admitted to hear the whole thing.

On the afternoon of the debate, she and Priscilla made their way toward the auditorium. The sun's rays could offer little warmth as they stood in line. Cold had set in, and December was just two days away. Joining many students and townspeople who were waiting, Hattie felt their timing was good. They would get seats.

Chatting with a few others, she realized this was an opportunity to take the pulse of the community, as well as Amherst College. One man said he never missed a lecture and sent newspaper coverage of the lectures to relatives. Hattie decided to do the same. Surely her father would read every word. He loved lectures, but seldom attended due to the press of business.

After shifting from one foot to the other and feeling chilled, Hattie was glad the doors were finally thrown open. The excited crowd surged forward into the Amherst College auditorium. Conversation filled the air as she and Priscilla surveyed the crowd, the stage, and the seats. Hattie couldn't help but note the large majority of men, some of whom looked askance at her. Maybe they thought she was intruding into their world of issues. But the world was opening up for women, so she decided to not feel strange or offended. Her father never treated her like an interloper in a man's world.

The auditorium was an expansive space filled with hundreds of polished seats under the gaze of large windows high on the walls. These were already opened to release the crowd's heat. The stage contained an impressive dark wood podium centered and surrounded by bouquets of dried flowers. Hattie and Priscilla, with their widely different agendas, had to decide quickly where they wanted to sit. There wasn't much time, as the hall was filling rapidly with excited people.

"Oh, look," Priscilla exclaimed. "There's an empty row with some seats right on the aisle. Let's take those, Hattie. Any young man who wants to sit further down in the row will have to pass us. That creates a chance to introduce ourselves."

Hattie agreed reluctantly, feeling rather uneasy about Priscilla's scheme for meeting men in such a formal setting. But she immediately forgot this concern, becoming immersed in watching the crowd. Unaware of time, she eventually noticed that the largely empty row on which they sat was filling up from the other direction. Priscilla was crestfallen, but Hattie thought it humorous, continuing her observations of the activity swirling in her midst.

Finally, the row had filled from the other end so that only one seat remained. It was next to Hattie.

"I hope a handsome student comes soon," Priscilla groaned. "I wish I had planned better for our seats. My idea didn't exactly result in any introductions."

Just then, a stately, elderly gentleman with a shock of coarse white hair came to the end of the row, next to Priscilla. He bent forward ever so slightly and began to speak softly.

"If you would be so kind, young lady," the gentleman began, "I wonder if I might occupy that seat next to your companion."

Priscilla looked up in surprise, raising her eyebrows at Hattie. They both noted the great dignity and interesting presence of the man. Turning to Hattie, she whispered, "This one is handsome, but he's fifty years too old for us."

Hattie suppressed a laugh at the silly comment. How different their motives were. Then, taking the lead, Hattie stood and elbowed Priscilla to do the same. They took leave of the row and made way. The elderly man offered a polite little bow and a word of thanks as he slowly slid into the seat and settled himself.

Within a few seconds, the evening's host took the podium. In a booming voice, he instantly commanded the attention of all the audience members present.

"Gentlemen, let us come to order, please. Oh, and a few ladies, I see. Welcome to you all. I am Edward Hitchcock, president of Amherst College. It is a pleasure to host our honored speaker for this special occasion. I join our distinguished faculty in anticipation of this evening's lecture."

"By way of introduction, our speaker, Mr. Lewis Tappan, is a leader in the cause of abolition. He has long been active in church-oriented abolitionism and formed the American and Foreign Anti-Slavery Societies. He is recognized for his gripping daily accounts in *The Emancipator* during the Amistad case in 1841. Never idle, after that groundbreaking decision, he helped found the American Missionary Association in 1846 and hopes one day to Christianize Africa. Without further ado, I give you the distinguished Mr. Lewis Tappan."

Thunderous applause rose from the crowd, along with a few whistles. As she applauded politely, Hattie noticed that the elderly gentleman next to her remained quiet in his seat, one hand folded neatly as his elbow remained still on the armrest. His other hand clutched a distinguished cane with a brass ornament shaped like an eagle's head. He made no effort whatsoever to applaud.

Enthusiastically, Mr. Tappan launched into his topic. With much verbal energy, he addressed the question of liberating Negro slaves. How best might it be accomplished, he inquired. The Compromise of 1850 had greatly threatened those who had escaped to freedom in the North. Now, the portion of the package called the Fugitive Slave Law was playing havoc even with those who had gained legitimate freedom.

For a while, Hattie sat on the edge of her seat expecting more as he put forward his case. She felt slightly disappointed after the first ten minutes because he was not bringing forth many enlightening interpretations. She and her father had already examined rationale like his year after year in Utica. It came as a surprise that she knew the subject of slavery far better than she ever realized, at least if this speaker served as an example.

Not bored, but still inattentive after the first half hour, Hattie gradually became more aware of the elderly man beside her. His reactions to the speaker's points were subtle but detectable. Often, his head was down as he listened. To convey agreement, he either nodded slightly, tapped the eagle head atop his cane with his index finger, or actually raised the cane slightly and stamped it down. There was a certain poetic character to his subtlety, if not to his striking head of white hair and tall, thin frame. If she were a betting woman, Hattie would have wagered that perhaps he had Italian blood, so rich was his skin tone. Somewhat olive and swarthy, he looked more distinguished than the speaker.

Mr. Tappan droned on with an account of lessons learned working in his father's dry good store and in his own Mercantile Agency in New York City. For some reason, Hattie's attention was drawn more and more to the elderly man. When she registered interest at the best points made by the long-winded speaker, they were the same points to which the elderly man reacted positively. That one so much her senior would react to the points she appreciated bolstered her confidence.

Who was he, she wondered? The possibilities were many. From his tailored appearance, he could be anything from a diplomat to a reverend. Rarely did he look up, but when he did, Hattie noted no recognition in his eyes. He did not seem to focus on the speaker or much of anything else. The old man was a mystery and soon, he became far more intriguing than the speaker at the podium.

The minutes passed slowly when the lecture became drawn out. It was merely a retrospective, not an analytical approach. Maybe Mr. Tappan didn't understand about student audiences. A sharp delivery couldn't make up for dull points. As the talk approached one-and-a-half hours, Hattie had trouble maintaining her composure and grew weary. Mr. Tappan fell far short of her expectations. She wondered how many others, including the old man, shared her feelings.

Because of her boredom, she began to feel restless. Try as she might, she heard herself sigh on more than one occasion and hoped she wouldn't actually nod off during the presentation. Growing weary, she shifted uncomfortably in her seat.

Then, finally, blessedly, Tappan made a brief, charging summary of his main points and concluded his remarks. The applause that met his departure was only polite. Quickly, the crowd began to thin and people as restless as Hattie pushed their way to the exits.

Awaking from her reverie, Hattie turned to comment to Priscilla, only to see that she was already standing in the aisle talking to a tall, handsome student. It was possible, Hattie noted with a chagrined attitude, that Priscilla had actually accosted the fellow first. But she was good looking, so he seemed quite pleased to have a polite chat with her amid the pushing and surging crowd.

"Excuse me, miss," the elderly man tapped upon her forearm. "Has the crowd thinned perceptively yet?"

"Oh, yes sir," she returned warmly, noting the exquisite quality of his tailored suit. "As many as a quarter of the attendees have already left."

"I thank you for the helpful statistic," he replied, smiling to himself. "You must be a student of mathematics. If I don't miss my guess, you are attending Amherst Academy?"

"Why, yes, that's correct," Hattie replied, pleased to be positively noticed. "I do like mathematics very much, but it is not my primary concentration."

"Then perhaps you're a philosopher or maybe an observer of politics," the elderly man continued politely. "Please don't be offended, but I noted that you speak like a New Yorker. Am I correct that you are a supporter of abolition?"

The comment amazed Hattie. She had never detected that the man even looked in her direction, much less took notice of her responses and characteristics. But he must possess great powers of perception. Turning to address him face to face, she noted his perfect grooming before seeing that, behind his dignified pince-nez, his dark but murky eyes made little contact. Peering closer, she realized that the man must be all but blind. How curious. He was observant though blind. How did he manage to read her subtle reactions? And why?

"I presume that, by now, you've realized I'm virtually blind," the man said to a wholly shocked Hattie. "Sooner or later, people recognize that I haven't made eye contact with them."

"To be honest, I just reached that conclusion," she responded sheepishly to this man she liked more by the second. "Did you enjoy the lecture?"

"It was respectable enough. And you?"

"Among his many points, your reactions showed that you and I agreed on the few that were significant."

The old man reacted with a little polite grin, which soon escaped into a wide, open smile. He then leaned his head back to release a knowing laugh.

"I always enjoy the wry comments of a rare, witty pupil," he quipped. "Only a mere handful of his points were fresh and insightful. The fact that we agreed helped pass time. This speaker missed the mark with a lot of pointless mush."

This time, it was Hattie who laughed. To meet a man so possessed of candid observations was a great joy.

"Hattie, we must be going," Priscilla urged from the aisle, tapping Hattie and interrupting her enjoyable conversation. "Hurry. There's a group up ahead that we don't want to miss."

"Oh, all right," Hattie returned dejectedly, not really wanting to go. Turning to the old man again, she took a last look at his interesting face. What an unexpected turn her evening had taken.

"Sir, I'm afraid my roommate wants to leave now," she said softly. "But it has been a privilege to agree with you all evening. And it was a pleasure to meet you. My name is Hattie Sheldon."

Even as he thanked her in return, the old man came to his feet quickly, continuing with polite generalities. As Hattie exited the row, he followed closely behind her. She wondered if he needed a guide and then comprehended that he must have some level of sight.

Making her way through the noisy crowd, Hattie occasionally spoke to an acquaintance or waved to another in the distance. Soon, they emerged into the frosty evening, puffs of vapor rising from various conversation circles.

"I know my way home from here. Thank you again for your delightful company, Miss Sheldon," the old man uttered, extending a hand. "What a pleasure to make your acquaintance. It does me good to be with students again. Once a professor, always a professor, I fear. My name is Alexander Colquhoun. Goodbye now."

Hattie would rather have talked more with the old gentleman. But Priscilla waved toward a group of young men in conversation. It happened so fast, Hattie was temporarily dislodged from her thoughts. As they approached, she struggled to look polite, because her thoughts were elsewhere.

Try as she might, the identity of the old man would not leave her mind. *What was his name*, she demanded of herself, turning back to see if he was still present. Did he say Alexander Colquhoun? Wasn't he the debate leader who had removed the minutes from the library? Why, it just had to be the same man! But he was gone, the crowd having swallowed him whole.

Hattie struggled to hide her disappointment. If only she could find him. But someone next to her seemed to have said hello. She had no choice but to turn and be polite. There, a short, ruddy-faced boy smiled and looked straight at her. Smiling back, she sought to pry her thoughts away from the professor and appear to be interested. Priscilla would be unhappy if Hattie didn't give her full attention to meeting eligible men.

"Wasn't the lecture fascinating?" the eager young man said brightly, his tie slightly askew. "I'm Wilfred Pence. What's your name?"

"Hello Wilfred. I'm Hattie Sheldon."

"Pleased to meet you, Miss Sheldon. I'm a new student at Amherst College."

She gave Wilfred an encompassing glance. He looked intelligent, but was unappealing in a toothy kind of way, or maybe it was just boyish immaturity. But he seemed genuine and might turn out to be fun. "I'm at Amherst Academy, as you've probably guessed," she returned with a friendly grin.

"I'd love to get acquainted, but it's getting late. I'd be honored to see you safely home," he offered politely.

"Do you have a bicycle?" she responded, much to his surprise. She could tell the question threw him.

"Well, not here tonight," he chuckled. "But, yes, I have one here at school. Why?"

"Just curious," she answered coyly. "Since you said yes, I'd be grateful for you to see me home. Several of us can go together. I'd also like to know about your bicycle."

❀ ❀ ❀

Hattie felt proud of herself for actually flirting with a young man. Perhaps she would get to ride his bicycle. But something else much more important was on her mind.

She had inexplicably ended up seated beside the very man she sought to find! Fate was strange sometimes, she mused in the dark. Not long ago, she had encountered a family story that had been a secret all her life. Now, in this encounter with Professor Colquhoun, a mystery was solved and the solution brought to her in a few short days, as if by design.

The most amazing part of making Professor Colquhoun's acquaintance was his perception of her unspoken opinions. A respected professor had actually commented that Hattie, a female student no less, was strong and bright. He was an intellectual, so she prized his acknowledgement. Her father would love knowing this. She wasn't so sure about her mother.

But, now, she had to find a way to speak with the professor about the missing debate account. Assessing her position and itemizing her options, Hattie knew she must not seek to reach the Professor through any connections relating to Amherst Academy. Doing so would raise too many questions, the answers to which would likely be misconstrued. After all, one look at Priscilla proved that Amherst Academy coped with young women who would manipulate any connection under the sun to gain access to Amherst College's young men. Hattie, on the other hand, cared about ideas, which was becoming more evident all the time. The last thing she wanted was to bring herself into question as the kind of person who pursued men.

Having reached that conclusion, however, Hattie paused before moving on. An idea had popped into her head that might prove interesting. There just might be a chance to find the Professor without involving Amherst Academy. It involved Priscilla's fascination with the opposite sex.

❂ ❂ ❂

Hattie had begun to hear a new term. It was used by professors in lectures and, soon, by her peers at Amherst Academy. When one of them spoke of "civic virtue," all understood such a concept to be a combination of religious values and patriotism. From before the revolution, it was said, there existed a growing tenet of freedom that the values of the citizenry were the foundation of a republic. Hattie knew who had taught the citizenry, traditionally, but she now began to wonder aloud who *should* teach them.

Women were not schooled well, if at all, by any formal entity outside the home at the time of the revolution. But times had changed, and Hattie was living proof. Seminaries and academies for women were cropping up all over New England, united in their quest to build a new path for women where none existed before. Further afield in the young nation however, education was an uphill battle, especially for women identified as indispensable "elsewhere." That meant the home.

Hattie felt like she was solving an arithmetic problem regarding the relationship of A to B and, therefore, to C. Why were the new institutions of learning united in their belief that women should be limited to teacher preparation courses? Somewhere in all the rationale, a missing link became obvious. Sooner or later, as scores of women graduated and became teachers, an admission had to be forthcoming that they could build children's character for leadership in the nation. But the category of children happened to include boys.

"There is agreement that families and churches are primarily responsible for building children's moral character," Hattie reasoned in a letter to Amanda. "There is also an understanding that teachers, heretofore all male, were to prepare the citizenry. So, now that women are graduating from schools that insist they become teachers, where are we to work? The roles teaching children and forming citizens are already filled. But there appears to be an opening, a need, if you will. Someone new could fill the gap that turns children into citizens. That's what I'm aiming for."

Her conclusion was just one of many reached during that first year at Amherst Academy. It was true that teaching had become the newly accepted profession into which most educated women found their way. Hattie tried the idea on for size, trying to envision herself having all the answers, keeping discipline, challenging even the most lethargic pupil to greater learning achievements. To her great surprise, she rather liked the idea. At one earlier stage of her development, becoming an author or even an anonymous journalist held her fancy. But, now, she delved into the heart of what teaching might mean to her if it became her profession.

9

Regio Et Religio

Hattie's thinking was maturing by leaps and bounds. Some days after class, she marveled at how knowledge gave her a fresh perspective on life and its challenges. *Think deeply*, she implored herself. *Be consistent and stay with the task at hand.*

"I'm trying hard not to be hot one day and cold the next," she wrote Amanda. "But things change so rapidly with each new level of understanding."

Yet, she could count on one thing never changing. That was Priscilla's endless quest for a suitable young man to marry. Her roommate's latest suitor was a charming fellow named Quill Hamilton.

"Hattie, Quill wants to take a stroll together. But we will violate the academy's chaperone requirement unless you and Wilfred come, too. Won't you please go with us?"

Hattie knew this day would come, and she was ready for it. Having given much thought to her priorities—study, teaching, enriching the world, and righting wrongs—versus those of her marriage-desiring roommate, she had happened upon a completely brilliant point of intersection between their interests This was a delightful turn of events.

Except for having her name linked romantically with the very eager Wilfred Pence. He was a polite boy and bright, but not exactly a looker like Quill. She was flattered that he showed so much interest, but there was not going to be any kind of romantic future for them as a couple. Soon, she would have to tell him they would never be more than friends.

Hattie had contemplated this point at length in a letter to Margaret. "I neither desire nor reject the prospect of keeping company with young men. Courtship just isn't among my priorities. Wilfred pursues me and I keep my distance. Yet, I realized that if a really handsome boy like Quill sought me out, I might feel differently."

But she had not shared this with Priscilla. In fact, once she realized that Priscilla's romantic goals could help her solve the library mystery, Hattie played along as best she could.

"All right, Priscilla," she replied seriously. "Since the rest of your life's happiness hinges on this walk with Quill, I will go, but only if the weather holds. And don't give Wilfred false hope. We can have fun together, but he's not my beau. Also, I have another important condition you must agree to. In fact, I need you to do me a favor."

"You mean you'll go?" Priscilla responded breathlessly. "Of course! Anything you want. Your wish is my command!"

Once Hattie had verbal agreement, she jumped into the heart of her request, detailing what she needed in exchange for making the stroll a possibility.

"Your end of the bargain involves Quill's cooperation. Recently,

I happened on something unexpected at the library. The details would bore you. The only person who can help is that old professor we met at the slavery lecture! It's against the rules for an academy woman to contact faculty of the college. But Quill can contact him. All I need is the chance to talk with the professor for an hour or so."

"That's it?" Priscilla queried, looking puzzled. "It can't be that difficult, Hattie. For goodness sake, this sounds easy. I will make sure he helps you."

And that's exactly what happened. Hattie marveled at how easily her plan fell together and was implemented. Quill agreed readily. The next day, he made inquiries at Amherst College, which was pleased that he sought out a revered former professor forced to the sidelines by blindness. Professor Colquhoun's address was supplied, so Quill wrote him asking for an appointment for himself and three friends. He received a favorable reply immediately, along with an invitation.

On the appointed day, Hattie and Priscilla bundled up in warm coats to join Quill and Wilfred for that leisurely stroll. A stern December wind pushed them through the chilled streets toward the professor's charming cottage. Just a few blocks from the college, it was framed by tall, stately trees. The frost had withered a few vines coming through cracks in the fence. If she could catch a glimpse behind the house, Hattie felt sure a lovely, but dormant garden rested there.

Approaching the door, Quill knocked heartily. A sweet-faced, gracious woman who introduced herself as Mrs. Colquhoun opened the door.

"We have so looked forward to your visit," Mrs. Colquhoun offered graciously. "My husband and I don't entertain many students these days."

She showed the foursome inside the fascinating dwelling that must reflect its occupants' wide-ranging interests. On one table sat an elegant old globe, while in the corner, a marble bust reminiscent of ancient Rome rested on a pedestal. Hattie detected an interesting scent of spices and crushed roses.

In a matter of seconds, the party of students stood in the center of the professor's shadowy, book-lined library, replete with a leather-topped desk and comfortable chairs. Handsomely framed certificates and renderings on the wall must tell stories about his earlier life, Hattie surmised. It would take a long professorial career to amass such a collection. On the desk rested a diverse collection of objects including an old wooden gavel, a porous rock marked by sprinkles and chunks of gold, and multiple tools from an Indian tribe. How sad, Hattie thought, that this grand, learned man could only sit with his books and memories now that blindness had robbed him of the capacity to read.

"Welcome, my young friends," the professor called to his visitors, rising and facing the direction of their footsteps. "It was quite a surprise to receive your letter. I don't hear from many students," he trailed off, a hint of sadness in his voice.

Quill approached first and took his hand, shaking it vigorously before offering introductions of the others. The professor greeted each person individually. That was when Hattie nodded to the others as she stepped forward.

"Professor, do you recall the night of the Tappan lecture? You and I met because we were seated side by side."

"Why, yes, what a marvelous evening. I most certainly

remember," he returned brightly, lighting up all over. "You are Miss Hattie Sheldon. Is that correct?"

"Yes, sir. Thank you for remembering," she responded warmly. "I must confess that I'm the one who wanted an audience with you today. It was awkward to arrange in light of the restrictions. But, thanks to my friend, Quill, I'm grateful to be here. You already know I'm a serious student. May I beg your indulgence for a few minutes about my discovery at the library?"

"Your interest flatters me," the professor revealed, offering the smile of a person who had almost been forgotten.

"Where can we talk?" Hattie inquired.

"You young people make yourselves comfortable here in the library while I talk with Miss Sheldon in my study," he answered. "When we finish, I'd like you to join Mrs. Colquhoun and me for tea."

"Oh, thank you. That's kind," Hattie responded, not believing her good fortune.

The professor looked pleased and ready to delve into her subject. She followed him to a smaller room, where he seated himself behind an antique French desk and offered her the seat opposite.

"Very well. Let's begin. Oh, by the way, did you attend yesterday's lecture by the transcendentalist?" he inquired, looking toward her in anticipation of a report.

"No, I'm afraid not," Hattie returned, surprised. "Did I miss something valuable?"

"Honestly, no. It was an update on the movement, but a little outside the faith, in my estimation."

Hattie began by summarizing her research question. Next, she broached the library mystery politely but directly by mentioning the removal of the minutes. The professor seemed to take the inquiry in stride, which showed that he stood with his decision.

As they talked about it, she relaxed, finding his presence comforting. The patterned rug beneath her feet looked like the one in the dining room at home in Utica. Even more familiar, his chair looked quite similar to her father's cushioned reading chair.

The professor responded by offering some background information by way of explanation, and then responded with a question.

"What do you know—or think you know—about Indian relationships in the new American republic? I seek what you understood as a child, what was taught at home, in school, and at church, and what you believe is the truth."

Hattie responded slowly and thoughtfully, adding as much detail as she could recall. Something about the professor engendered her complete trust. From his comments, it seemed clear that they thought alike and shared the same religious tradition.

"Very well," he returned, standing by a window that cast a shadow on his desk. "Now that I understand your interest and where you stand, let me address several points. Be warned that I may forget you are a female student. I can't quite help teaching in my old way, you see. If I challenge you too deeply, please don't be offended."

"Nothing would flatter me more, Professor," Hattie returned, shivering with excitement. "I think my learning capacity is equal to any young man, if you'll forgive me being brash."

"Brash! I think not. On the day I was married, I learned an unforgettable lesson about the intelligence of females. Never underestimate a woman. But because I've always taught boys, perhaps I appear uninformed like the rest of our society. Please know that I think women have equal intelligence to men."

"What about the Indians' intelligence, sir? Do you believe them to be of equal intelligence to whites?"

The professor squinted and shook his head. Hattie liked the way he referred to the Indians using old, romantic terminology.

"The children of the forest," he explained respectfully, "were advanced, despite their seemingly simple interests. God imbued all humankind with equal intelligence. They were simply behind in the progress of mankind because of their geographic location."

Any argument, he posited, that insisted upon one race possessing inferior intelligence to another was flawed. Indians were simply misunderstood by Euro-Americans. The real issue, he insisted, was the heart. And somehow, this pivotal point had been missed in the debate at Amherst College those many years ago. Because such a glaring omission could mislead students, he had prevented that from happening.

"Just before my retirement, I went to the library quietly and removed the debate minutes. It was never my intent to destroy the record, but rather to send a worthy student—one who persevered to the bottom of the collection—a message. You were the first student in ten years who dug that far, caring enough to pursue the truth about the flawed debate."

Pleased, Hattie struggled to accommodate her own accomplishment and find an adequate response.

"I don't know what to say, sir," she returned slowly, blushing.

He smiled a knowing, professorial grin, and they sat quietly for a moment.

"For years," Hattie began again, slowly at first, "I have listened to my family and many others speak about the egregious crimes Indians committed against settlers. War was the Indian way of life, I heard. Because of the violence, settlers were forced to drive the Indians off their land. It was viewed as their only choice, I guess. Therefore, it seems the settlers began to see it as a right. They had to preserve their own lives. But something about it troubles me," she concluded, her head leaning to one side as she toiled internally.

"I can well understand," the professor continued, shaking his head. "You've touched upon the very point I abhor. It overlooks an exceedingly important aspect of the larger story: the truth."

"Help me understand, please," Hattie urged, growing anxious. "What am I sensing but not piecing together?"

"Nothing but the other side of the story," the professor returned, his words blunt but his tone equal. "Do you not have information about what we did to the Indians first? Only by learning about that crucial missing link can you be in possession of the full story. So, start again with your initial recital to me, and let's analyze your points one at a time."

Hattie began again, listening to herself repeat the lore and history that previously had constituted what she believed to be the full story. She believed that the Indians in North America, many of them nomadic, were savages, as she had heard at church her entire life. Territorial, they could behave kindly, but never was there a firm security against their sudden attack. The whites saw that Indians were in desperate need of Christianity to stem heathen ways. For instance, Indians lacked the understanding of forgiveness, a necessary component when two different groups sought to live side by side peacefully. They resorted to blood revenge and war to solve problems.

"My father often spoke about the unbroken expanse. He talked of millions of picturesque acres, the lands of Jefferson's vision, teeming with every kind of mineral and animal," she added. "He was enamored with the concept of Manifest Destiny, believing that adventurous and enterprising whites were validated in their conquests. Once they overthrew a given people who stood in their way, the land became theirs. His generation spoke in terms of how white explorers were thwarted by Indians who were poor land stewards, having never brought the vast, rich resources to bear. So they concluded that the Indians failed to turn America into the world leader she should have been all along."

"Very well stated. That is a comprehensive synopsis in the view of many. But it is short sighted. Now I have a few questions for you. Who was here first? Do economic and political goals trump all others? What gave the settlers any right to believe they must transform all aspects of the Indians' lives, especially since the Indians were happy with themselves?"

"You mean the settlers did not have a right to inhabit the land?" she questioned slowly, trying to put aside everything she had known from the white viewpoint.

"Who was here first?" the professor repeated.

"The Indians had been here for hundreds and perhaps thousands of years before explorers came," Hattie replied with a frown, although certain of her answer.

"Correct. What authority gave the settlers and explorers the idea that, because they had undertaken overwhelming odds to leave their old, problem-ridden countries, they were destined to greatness? How were they emboldened to succeed or die trying, even if it meant ruining the entire way of life in a land belonging to others?"

"I ... suppose they felt that since their pursuit of religious freedom was a primary goal, that surely God would ... oblige their aims, honor their faith, and bless them?" Hattie reasoned with great concentration. "They were on the same side as God, in other words. Heathens inhabited the land they wanted, and there was so much land that was sorely needed by their oppressed countrymen. And so their mission gained validity? They couldn't return to their old lands or lives, so they *must* succeed. God had brought them the distance, so they must fight to spread his word. Developing the land seemed to be their duty, or they would let God down. Is that right?"

"There! You're on the right track in tracing their misguided rationale," the professor encouraged, an animated expression on his face. "Let's continue. What was the result of a superior attitude on the part of the whites?"

"Well, they viewed the Indians as ignorant and themselves as educated and enlightened. They believed it was their charge to teach the Indians modern ways, and viewed them as backward if they resisted."

"When two sides are equal in the sight of God," the professor reasoned, picking up where she left off, "what gives one side the idea that they are wiser, better, more advanced, more religious?" He trailed off, looking at her with an expectant expression.

"I suppose it must come from within the one side that judges the other as inferior," Hattie replied, her eyes widening as she began to perceive more than she could have imagined. "And that, I guess, is sin."

"Exactly," the professor congratulated, leaning forward in his chair. "It was the settlers' flaw to assume they were better and more advanced in every possible way. They had developed a standard for comparison, living there on the other side of the world among many races, beliefs, and languages. But the Indians had no standard for comparison. They had never known another race, another place, another way of life. Why, they wondered, would these strange white people who believed themselves to be in authority come to their land and tell them they were wrong?"

Feeling the weight of heavy new ideas, Hattie slid down in her chair because she had no answer. She was deep in thought, her heart full of new misgivings. The feelings had something in common with grief, an emotion she knew well. Here, after this brief encounter, she found herself questioning all she had known before.

"Have you studied Latin yet?" the professor inquired softly.

"I tried to educate myself, but wasn't very successful," she replied truthfully.

"That's admirable. Make no excuses," Professor Colquhoun soothed. "You will receive a worthy course of study at Amherst Academy. My question relates to a certain Latin phrase that I believe sheds considerable light on our conversation."

"From the Holy Roman Empire," Hattie guessed.

"Precisely. Roman law was quite advanced, growing in scope during the early years following the crucifixion of Christ," the professor explained, as if to a class. "There is a lofty phrase applicable to our examination here. It is *regio et religio*, which roughly stands for "whose realm, his religion." This is meaningful to me because Roman Catholicism existed among my ancestors at one time, and its teachings reached my ears. But it has application with our issue today, as well. The phrase represents an agreement between warring factions from two different belief systems after a long history of destruction of one another and of their property."

"You mean one region's religion against another region's religion?" Hattie asked, trying to make sense of the phrase.

"Yes. Peace was achieved when they stopped trying to change or eradicate one another because they were different," he explained. "They took their culture and its religion, then went to the agreed boundary and minded their own business. Peace came when they left one another alone. Neither sought to dominate the other. Their common interest was survival."

"So the white settlers must not have heard of *regio et religio*," Hattie summarized, readily grasping the direction of his point.

"Or they overlooked it," the Professor returned, looking over his pince-nez, which no longer could correct his vision, but which he habitually wore anyway. "Sadly, we are able to say with conviction that they did not practice religious toleration toward the Indians, even as they desperately wanted it for themselves." He looked sad as he summarized this.

"I see. So the quest for religious toleration led the settlers to America," Hattie restated, finding a growing fault line along history's path. "But once here, they insisted that the Indians must become Christian."

"It is true, I fear," Professor Colquhoun returned quietly. "For centuries, in the interest of peace, peoples on other continents had well un derstood that certain magnanimous indulgences were required toward others who were different from their own tradition. As a matter of morality, they put aside their personal opinions to pursue a larger aim. They decided to live peacefully alongside those different others without words or actions that molested them personally, publicly, or privately."

"That practice was never brought to American shores, was it?" Hattie questioned quietly.

"I'm afraid not," the professor clarified. "Rather, we battled, stole, and killed the Indians over land, resources, control, and misunderstood behavior. It became clear that whites were killing every beaver, deer, and otter. When the white man's bullets attacked the sacred state of nature, as well as the people, they retaliated through attacks, murders, kidnappings, and the destruction of many explorers and their settlements in return."

"I just learned recently that my ancestors were among the dead at the infamous Deerfield Raid of 1704," Hattie shared, making the connection that members of her own family had likely not practiced tolerance.

"That's as poignant an example as any in existence," Professor Colquhoun replied. "Our nation's history is rife with other tragic but illuminating stories. Among the more recent, we saw the President of the United States refuse to acknowledge or enforce a Supreme Court decision in favor of one southeastern Cherokees. Blatant disregard of carefully negotiated treaties occurred, as well. The tribe had adjusted well to white encroachment for decades, yet their land was what President Andrew Jackson wanted, casting their sovereignty and very lives to the winds. He ordered federal troops to forcibly remove them from their ancestral homes. They were marched across 800 miles of rugged terrain during the most unendurable cold, with no shelter from the harsh elements, rotted provisions or no food whatsoever, and unfathomable misery. Believe it or not, many of them had no shoes, and some had virtually no clothing to cover their bodies. Yet, when I risked much to tell this sad truth, charges of disloyalty to my country were hurled at me. Some even suggested I was guilty of treason for speaking against the president."

"The President was dead wrong, wasn't he?" she questioned.

He nodded in the affirmative.

❖ ❖ ❖

For the next several days, Hattie thought of little but the astonishing, transformative information learned from Professor Colquhoun. Often, when she was awake in the night, her thoughts focused upon the unknowing children caught up in the Deerfield Raid. Some were murdered, while others were kidnapped and taken to Canada. All were innocents victimized by a battle they could never understand.

Now, she, Hattie, a descendant of the survivors, was faced with the reality of injustice. Even more concerning, the injustice had cut both ways. In addition to the plight of white settlers, over the years many thousands of Indian people were also killed, maimed, and left without a place to call home.

The emotion of Hattie's new awareness began to dawn. Unsettled, she felt the very ground of previous misunderstanding break beneath her feet. Within her body, ripples of nausea formed in response to her naiveté. Then, pulling herself up, she digested the reminder of the facts: it wasn't her fault that history only remembered one side of the story.

All of her life, only the white side had been passed along. Likening her internal upheaval to that of an earthquake, Hattie felt the force of great change pushing upward, pressing great boulders of truth forcefully to the surface, to the light. This vision came to define her feelings, which alternately flared, pushing out old ideas and perceptions.

Often during class Hattie challenged herself in the midst of a lecture with her new motto for life: there are always two sides to a story. This new foundation provided security and grounding to her emerging maturity. The profound life lesson from Professor Colquhoun was leading her to examine all evidence in every situation. Contemplation filled her free hours, as she envisioned her future role in correcting historical misunderstandings, righting wrongs, and teaching what had really taken place. Perhaps she could help, in some small way, to keep historical misunderstandings from ever happening again.

After a period of reasoning through the issues, an idea sprang up. She believed nothing was beyond the transformative power of God. Given opportunity, reasons for optimism still existed for Indian peoples in America, no matter what they and their ancestors had suffered and endured. Could she perhaps bring opportunity to them? As she asked herself question after question, she also had to allow that not all whites were guilty of being intolerant or criminally negligent. How the practice of warring with Indians became so ingrained, she didn't know. But she felt compelled to do her part, and that meant ...

Why, it meant facing—and teaching—the truth. It meant doing right by the truth and making the real story well known. Where had she learned only one side of the story? In Utica. What city was full of limits and needed to welcome new opportunities for women? Utica. Where could she begin to make a difference by telling the real story, the whole story? Utica.

Gradually, Hattie developed a new attitude about her hometown. If she became a teacher, she could return but break free of Utica's narrowness. She didn't have to dread the social clamoring and shallowness. Her life would have meaning. She would be too busy meeting children's needs to bother about Utica's shortcomings. Maybe she didn't have to follow convention like those who focused on marrying instead of education and who accepted boring domestic lives instead of dynamic working lives. Those were serious reasons for not liking Utica, after all.

But, as a teacher, she could create a new kind of life, a life outside expectations. Maybe the children of well-traveled people needed education. Maybe she could become a new kind of teacher. If that were the case, maybe she could be happy there. The students, as well, could benefit from a more realistic version of the old settlement story.

Invigorated, she began to see that her next step was no longer a cloudy, unformed idea. She would focus her future studies at Utica Female Academy toward teaching. Her discoveries formed a vision leading her back to Utica to share the truth. How fitting that she would return to the city, perhaps even the school where her historical understanding had gone astray. After all, how many others had also learned just one side of history?

"This must be it," she wrote her parents not long after talking with Professor Colquhoun. "This must be the missing element. Maybe I don't have to look so far beyond Utica for my life's devotion. Since I learned the truth, my thoughts and interests are oriented toward the idea of teaching. The professor has motivated me to approach the subject matter altogether differently. Whites need to be taught the role their forefathers played in disintegrated relations with Indians. I can do just that. The Indians deserve compassion, which I certainly now feel toward them. I can live consistent with what you taught, with the great truth that all men are created equal. I can heal the wrongs of history by reiterating that message through teaching."

When Hattie first glimpsed the envelope of her parents' response letter, it came as a great surprise to see her mother's handwriting. Her mother was definitely not the family correspondent and never had been. Something must be quite weighty for her mother to have written. In addition, the letter was plump.

The first page began with an explanation that both her parents had written separate letters contained in the one envelope. Hattie decided to read the pages in the order her mother had chosen. After just a few sentences, it was obvious that her mother found few words expressive enough to convey that she was far better than fine. In fact, evidenced by the angle of her handwriting and the words themselves, her mother was ecstatic. She was overjoyed. She was as elated as a person could become, especially one who had previously lived through the lowest of the lows. That which Hattie's mother had long dreamed about had come to pass because of Hattie's newly announced plans.

"Dearest, my fervent prayers have been answered by a benevolent God," her mother wrote. "I have wept many tears of joy upon hearing you will come back to Utica."

It was understood that Hattie intended to follow through with her lifelong goal of attending Utica Female Academy, the equivalent of college for men, after completing her schooling at Amherst Academy. Now that the teaching decision and conclusion to return to Utica were made, her mother wrote, the time would fairly fly for her until Hattie completed her schooling at Amherst. A great burden had been lifted.

"Praise God," her mother concluded in the letter. "Once again, I will have my Hattie right here in Utica, near home, close to family, and blessedly returned to me. With much love, Mother."

When Hattie brought the next page forward, it was a newspaper article instead of a sheet of paper. The headline screamed:

BULWARKS OF LIBERTY THREATENED
BY FUGITIVE SLAVE LAW.

A feeling of concern suddenly gripped her stomach. Her father usually turned to her first when he was concerned about a political development of import.

Based on the scratchy quality of his penmanship on the next

page, he must be quite upset. Reading rapidly, she confirmed that he was distressed. He raged against the Fugitive Slave Law that had passed Congress on September 18, 1850. Any day, he warned, the entire Underground Railroad might be compromised.

"This has turned us into bloodhounds," he wrote, his penmanship obviously suffering under the emotion. "We citizens are now *required* to actively assist with the return of escaped slaves. But too many people are spontaneously and mindlessly obeying the absurd law. Are they without conscience? Do that many in the North *agree* with slavery?"

After some contemplation, he related to Hattie, he had polled his friends and others. When their answers came, he shuddered and could scarcely contain himself. They didn't question the overreach of the law enough. They didn't believe in slavery, but they also didn't fight against it! They merely looked the other way.

"I think thousands of our countrymen are on the fence," Ebenezer griped. "There is no question but that the law is patently immoral. I believe all citizens of conscience and faith must disobey it."

This was a new level of disdain even for him, Hattie noted. Never before had he been this distraught over a political development.

"You need to be aware," he urged, "that this flawed law demands the action of all white people against all black people. That means you, me, and our entire family. How, in heaven's name, are we to accommodate the outrage? It strips Negroes of any right to ask for a jury trial or to testify in their own behalf!"

Continuing, Ebenezer's view of the law's failings was bolstered by a recent speech that the noteworthy orator, Ralph Waldo Emerson, had delivered in Concord, Massachusetts. The newspapers had covered it, he related to Hattie. Had she read the stories?

Emerson had posed a question: "How can a law be enforced that fines pity and imprisons charity?" This point consolidated what was most upsetting to her father. From the day the law was passed, no matter what, there could be no lawful assistance lent by any church, any charitable individual, or any organization to aid escaping slaves.

But how ridiculous, Hattie deduced. In reality, what with slave hunters running loose, this meant that all Negroes were now endangered, whether free or escaped or enslaved. It was obviously about skin color. That's what slave hunters looked for, caring nothing about whether a given Negro man had papers proving his freedom. By criminalizing moral actions she or others might take to help an escapee, the law essentially stripped them of religious freedom. It didn't sound legal, but it was now the law of the land.

As she neared the bottom of the last page, Ebenezer's scribbles were so bad that Hattie realized her father was exhausted.

"Our work in the Underground Railroad has placed us in line with the Negro man who has risked everything to escape maltreatment. I cannot help but shed a tear, Hattie, over Emerson's impassioned words:"

> *This is befriending in our own state on our own farms, a man who has taken the risk of being shot, or burned alive, or cast into the sea, or starved to death, or suffocated in a wooden box, to get away from his driver; and this man who has run the gauntlet of a thousand miles for his freedom, the statute says, you men of Massachusetts shall hunt, and catch, and send back again to the dog-hutch he fled from.*
>
> —*Ralph Waldo Emerson*

"We all must pray for our nation and for the Negroes this law will destroy. Love, Father"

❧❧❧

Hattie dropped the letter, grabbed her coat, and virtually ran to the library. The overcast grey sky promised to deliver snow, so she was glad to have on her most sturdy boots. How could she have gotten so addled by the missing debate notes that she forgot to read about this law? Her concentration caused her to overlook the world around her. She hadn't even taken time to sit with other students and banter about current events.

Quickly locating the resources she knew would inform her, she settled in a quiet corner. As she flipped through old and new newspapers, she read headlines about the Fugitive Slave Law screaming that something terrible had taken place on September 18, 1850. In such a short time, she had fallen seriously out of touch with political news.

Hattie hastily read one story to find out the latest developments. Within a few minutes, it seemed obvious that every state from Massachusetts north had taken a dim view of the limiting legislation Congress had passed as part of the Compromise of 1850. The hallmark of concern was that no room for dissention existed. Supporters of abolition had simply been overruled and their viewpoints silenced. Somehow, the representatives in Washington, D.C., had found a way to force any American citizen who encountered a runaway slave to participate in his capture and return. Worse, if a free Negro were somehow wrongly taken into custody, he could not request a trial and was denied the right to testify in his own behalf.

Oh my goodness, Hattie exclaimed to herself. Looking around, she sought to process so many repercussions. *Father was right, I need to do something. But what? I can only imagine the frenzy of action and reaction that must be encompassing him right now.*

❧ ❧ ❧

Archibald Alexander's widely acclaimed book *Evidences of Christianity* was the main text for Hattie's theology class. A Presbyterian, Alexander's name had long been known within the Sheldon household. He was a pillar of the denomination for his steadfast maintenance of its doctrines. Hattie was thrilled by the choice of text and inspired by her Professor, Cornelius Thorne. Her already deep interest in matters of religion, theology, and faith was increasing steadily.

Arriving early to her class, Hattie chose a seat in the front corner, warmed by the south sun. Opening her textbook, she reviewed the assigned reading again. Various classmates filtered in, immersed in conversation and full of liveliness. The professor came through the doorway followed by Priscilla, who rushed toward a back seat awkwardly. To her surprise, Hattie saw that Priscilla had been crying. Her tear-stained face looked frightful, as did her red and swollen nose.

The professor brought the class to order and began to call the roll. Since Hattie was seated on the front row directly in front of him, she couldn't interrupt by going to comfort Priscilla. What could have caused such an upset? Priscilla was an outgoing, enthusiastic person. Hattie had never seen her unhappy, much less in tears. Hattie struggled to keep her mind on the lecture.

When class finally ended, Hattie grabbed her books and rose to go comfort Priscilla. But just as she turned, Professor Thorne called her name.

"Miss Sheldon, this is for you," he said in a serious tone, unsmiling.

Hattie turned back and approached his desk. The professor extended an envelope in her direction.

"Oh, for me? How kind. Thank you," she replied, smiling widely as she took it. Momentarily, her spirits lifted. Was it an invitation? She glanced back up, wondering if an explanation might follow. But Professor Thorne avoided her eyes and busied himself at the desk.

So Hattie walked toward Priscilla, who had not moved from her seat. She held her head in her hands. Behind Hattie, the door opened and shut, which offered a degree of privacy now that the professor had departed.

Drawing up a chair, Hattie began quietly. "What's the matter? Why are you crying?"

"Oh, Hattie, I'm so sorry," the tearful girl replied.

"What do you mean? Did something happen?" Hattie soothed, rubbing her roommate's shoulder.

"It wasn't intentional. I promise. I still don't understand why it is such a crime," Priscilla sobbed.

"Did something illegal happen?" Hattie questioned, growing more concerned. "I don't understand."

"He told me he was the professor's neighbor. His questions didn't appear suspicious at first," Priscilla explained, her voice shaking. "But after I answered and told him about our visit, he suddenly became hostile and accusatory. You should have seen the dark contortions of his face."

"Wait. Start over please," Hattie urged. "I'm confused. Who was whose neighbor? And who is angry?"

"Our theology professor, Mr. Thorne, is very, very angry, and says disciplinary action will be taken."

"Why is he angry with you?" Hattie queried, still not understanding.

"He's not angry at me. It turns out that Professor Thorne is Professor Colquhoun's neighbor."

Suddenly Hattie felt worried. "But why would Professor Thorne take action against Professor Colquhoun?"

"No, that's not it either," Priscilla wailed, waving a helpless hand in the air. "Thorne knows we went to Professor Colquhoun's house and that you met with him. Thorne says it crossed the line. He intends to take action against YOU, Hattie!"

❊ ❊ ❊

When the whole story emerged, Hattie felt so deflated and stunned that words escaped her. The details had unfolded quite rapidly once she learned that Thorne was Colquhoun's neighbor. He had seen the girls go with the boys from Amherst College into the professor's house. To Thorne's mind, it looked "irregular." Since Priscilla was the first one he encountered after the visit, he asked her to step into his office.

"Professor Thorne began with a polite spirit. There was no disdain in his initial inquiry. I didn't realize his questions were leading me into a trap," Priscilla moaned. "The more he learned, the more he changed into a different person, I tell you. Soon, he was accusing us. His voice became guttural, and he scowled at me. It wasn't fair or in keeping with the way a theology teacher should treat a Christian student. I was scared. It felt more like a legal interrogation."

Hattie was stunned that Professor Thorne had been threatening and employed anger. According to Priscilla's account, after she answered his initial, innocent questions, he demanded a full explanation of why the girls were that far from campus with the boys, why they went to the home of a controversial ex-professor, and what their motive had been. It was no wonder that, out of sheer terror, Priscilla coughed up the entire story of the library discovery and Hattie's plan to discuss it with Professor Colquhoun. After that, Thorne acted like he had just won a guilty verdict against an adversary.

Following Priscilla's points, a nauseating feeling began to grow in Hattie's stomach. Her mouth went dry, and little tingles of nervousness ran up the back of her neck. Her heart skipped a few beats. Beads of perspiration joined along her forehead as she connected the confrontation and the envelope from Thorne that was still in her hand. Looking down, she lifted it and tore open the flap to read what it said.

Friday, December 20, 1850

Miss Sheldon,

It has come to my attention that you have abrogated the terms of your student agreement at Amherst Academy. I will bring your violations before the Faculty Disciplinary Committee after the Christmas recess. Once the matter is considered and appropriate punishment options for your wrongdoing determined, you will be notified. At a future date of unknown origin, you may be asked to appear before the Committee for questioning. Before that time, your parents will be notified and you will be placed on academic probation.

Signed,
Cornelius Thorne, Professor

❁ ❁ ❁

Feelings of outrage and fury choked Hattie the moment she finished the note. These charges were an altogether new experience for her. Prior to this unthinkable episode, she had only read about such injustices.

Professor Thorne had blown things totally out of proportion. He had terrified Priscilla, which was unnecessary and inappropriate. If the matter were really important enough to investigate, why didn't he also question Hattie, Quill, and Wilfred? Thorne was jumping to conclusions without gathering much evidence, without giving the accused a chance to be heard.

Hattie spent the rest of the afternoon calming Priscilla. That night, when she could ponder everything in the privacy of darkness, she contemplated the subject of injustice. Lately, a significant number of unfair situations had crossed her path. The slaves had no recourse against prejudice and bounty hunters. The Indians had been discriminated out of their homeland and then marched forcibly in winter to foreign territory. And, now, although it seemed minor in comparison, Hattie relived feelings of being wronged by her mother's limitations.

During the difficult days that followed, Hattie struggled to hold her head high. She didn't feel like a criminal, but she almost looked like one. Getting too little rest left her exhausted and bleary-eyed. Her emotions became evident as she suffered.

This new, astonishingly unfair situation put her previous idea of restrictions into perspective. Thorne's charges could damage her entire future. Why did the two schools limit students with such stringent divides between their respective faculties? If she were found guilty of breaching boundaries, Amherst Academy could dismiss her, ruin her reputation, and stop her admission to the Utica Female

Academy. Without any certificate or teaching credentials, she would likely be unable to find employment. The looming threat of returning to Utica, shamed and rejected, was too painful to accommodate. Hattie felt hemmed in. She began to avoid people and the library a little too much.

Soon, however, she began to comprehend that crying in isolation offered little comfort. It was simply a waste of time, emotion and energy. *STOP*, she told herself. *I need to change my thinking. It has to happen immediately or I'm sunk.*

It was time to get back to normal. It was time to fight back. Mulling the accusation over and over wouldn't solve anything. Fingers on her temples, she must focus elsewhere and come up with something wonderful enough to replace the fear. What had always been heartwarming, unforgettable, and full of love?

Nothing came to mind initially. She searched for a memory that was pretty and loving and innocent, but one did not come. However, a good justification popped into her mind and planted a small seed of hope.

It was not her fault that the debate files from the men's college were available to female students. She had no control over the fact that, previous to her discovery, no other student, male or female, had pursued the missing minutes. These facts were reasonable and, as she pondered the details further, offered significant comfort.

"I think you're onto something," Priscilla replied enthusiastically after Hattie shared her conclusion.

"I'm going to keep thinking, but at least this has potential," Hattie sighed. "Hopefully, I can get some sleep and not worry about it all the time."

"Don't let Thorne win," Priscilla urged. "Force your thoughts onto something wonderful, like Christmas."

Hattie extinguished her lamp, pulled the covers up, and took a deep breath. In her lifetime, nothing felt quite as comforting as sitting around the fire on Christmas Day. Her family always read the Bible's Christmas story together before exchanging gifts. Everybody was happy and full of chatter as they enjoyed the best meal of the year. In her memory, the parlor at home on Christmas felt warmer when the window frost was the thickest. After supper, she and her siblings played games that became more fun because their parents joined and were not in a hurry. Before bed, they gathered together and sang favorite hymns.

Christmas would be different this year, of course, because she wouldn't be in Utica. But she and Aunt Mary intended to make it special. Those particulars needed to be planned now. She could get busy with festive ideas instead of fretting over this unfair charge. The more detailed she could make her vision for Christmas in Amherst, the freer her mind would be, hopefully. Hattie finally slept.

Sadly, the respite from worry didn't last long. Well before sunrise, she awoke with a start. The threatening situation was still there, a harbinger of ruin. How could this have happened? It was absolutely unfair, shameful, and even odd. What would her family think?

The longer she pondered it, the madder she got. Trying to harness her anger and look carefully at her options, however, was much harder than she imagined. The only light at the end of the tunnel involved defending herself. To date, her performance at the academy had been satisfactory. She was not at the top of her class, in her estimation, but neither was she the poorest performer. Prior to this incident, she had never been subject to any corrective discipline or even questioning. Her "misdemeanor" was not immoral or felonious or scandalous. Rather, in her thinking, she had just pursued learning that extended beyond her assigned course work. And, by way of justification, the library box into which she dug contained a challenge for a serious student to discover. Professor Colquhoun hadn't wagered that that student would be female, however.

Thinking of him led her to reflect on his good character. Why had Thorne disparaged the professor to Priscilla by calling him an old, rejected ex-professor? The extreme wording felt suspicious. If a reason existed for Amherst College to hold Professor Colquhoun in poor standing, surely Quill would have learned about it when he was given the professor's home address. Quill was told the professor was a revered but retired faculty member who suffered from blindness. These were two very different versions of the professor's standing.

Rising from her bed, Hattie pulled on warm clothes. Thank goodness Priscilla was asleep and didn't witness her angst. She exited quietly into the hallway and, with folded arms, began to pace up and down. If only there were some solution or encouragement inspiring enough to blow away the ominous clouds of the threat. She paused, gazing out the window at the end of the corridor. The wintry scene before her, swirling with snow, looked as cold as her heart felt.

A wall plaque beside the window caught her attention. The indirect light of dawn was just enough for Hattie to make out its words. The plaque honored a former student of Amherst Academy for valor. The young woman had risked everything to save several family members from a burning building.

Hattie became very still, her memory racing. The woman's bravery reminded her of the night around Aunt Mary's table when her father revealed the tragic details of 1704. Riveted from shock after the raid on Deerfield, their ancestor, John Sheldon, had made a profound choice after the worst moment of his life. He had to overcome the horrid sight of his murdered wife and child in order to rush out and help others. Surely that situation could inspire Hattie to put this one in its place. This was no time to shrink in the face of mere controversy, she realized. Unlike the Deerfield Raid, nobody in her crisis was dead or missing.

John Sheldon had braved blizzards and frostbite to rescue his terrified children. Such desperate circumstances as that required fortitude. Surely Hattie could follow suit. She vowed to muster new strength. It was a time for faith and humility.

Returning to her bedside, she kneeled, took a deep breath, and asked for God's help. Without His strength, wisdom, and power, she could not withstand this onslaught. Then, she climbed back in her bed and tried to be still. She didn't fall asleep, but the pulsating worry lessened. Soon, she became aware that a lovely calm had come over her spirit. She blinked in amazement, feeling renewed.

That very day, strength began to return to her threatened state of mind. Perhaps God had brought her the story of her ancestors only recently for a reason. It had certainly given her courage and the will to persevere. Compared to murder and kidnapping, her quandary paled. Nothing was yet lost, so why think along the lines of defeat? Instead, she knew she had to tackle her moment of injustice without hesitation. It was time to show strength of character. *I will not allow one drop of fear to poison the well of my resolve*, she told herself. There would be no acceptance of accusations until she had had her say.

On that point, Hattie paused. Having her say must begin with a long letter of explanation to her parents. That would be among the most daunting obligations she had ever completed. Compared to their feelings, her own could be put aside temporarily. She must assure them that she would fight tooth and nail. For as long as it took to restore the Sheldon name to its place among respectable people, she would contest the terrible charge.

To bolster her resolve, she wrote a long letter to Margaret, as well. It helped to get her feelings on paper. She also considered sharing the situation with Aunt Mary, but talked herself out of it. Why associate Aunt Mary with something like this when she had only recently overcome the grief of her daughter's death? No, it was selfish to burden Aunt Mary. Surely this situation would be resolved soon.

10

Justice Delayed

After Christmas, Hattie noticed that Professor Thorne, previously bright and cheerful, seemed much more troubled. He was overly serious and could be critical beyond measure. Class lectures sometimes got off the subject as he raved about one oddity or another.

The winter cold bore down with fury. Weeks passed and brought heavy snow, but little sunshine. No resolution presented itself. The circumstances felt frozen in mid-air like icicles. Unpleasantness was so hard to bear when Hattie couldn't take walks or smell the grass or sit in the sun. Even worse, Professor Thorne sneered at her in the hallway and wrote unnecessarily nasty comments on her papers.

Determined not to succumb to his tactics, Hattie poured every waking moment into her studies, working terribly hard to learn her class material. It seemed the only way to salvage her character in his eyes. What had happened did not make sense, but the fact remained that it wasn't yet resolved. If she could perform error-free on the theology material, as she vowed to do in all her classes, surely Thorne would reconsider.

The fact that the charges against her were confidential remained one of the few bright spots. Only Hattie, Priscilla, and the Amherst Academy faculty were informed. Then, one afternoon, a new idea came to mind. Why hadn't she informed Professor Colquhoun about the sad turn of events? There was nothing to lose by doing so. He might have suggestions or recommendations for her.

With this in mind, Hattie sat thoughtfully at a corner table in the library. Resting her feet against the bulky table legs, she dipped her pen in the ink and drafted a polite letter to the professor. Concisely, she detailed the events that had occurred following her enlightening meeting with him. Careful to cast no blame, she also accepted none. Since he had been so good to tell her the other side of the story, the letter ended with appreciation. Immediately, she posted it and was hopeful for a speedy reply.

When the Professor's response arrived, Hattie rushed to her room to read it. The letter was gracious, but not at all satisfying. She read it again and again, but could not find comfort in his words. He seemed to care, she allowed. But, on the other hand, he sounded distant.

Dear Miss Sheldon,

I am saddened by the accusation that has befallen you. Thank you for writing and entrusting me with your confidence. I promise to consider the situation from all sides. If I may offer a suggestion, it would be wise to leave it in God's hands. My prayers for a resolution go with you during the interim.

Sincerely and fraternally,
Alexander Colquhoun

A period of waiting ensued. Although it was only 1851, Hattie felt like years had passed. Some days she wondered if she had grown old, as if it were 1891. A loving letter of encouragement from her father inspired her to persevere. He agreed with her approach to the problem. Her mother wrote a sweet note at the bottom, as well. Finally, Margaret expressed great concern and support in a thoughtful reply.

Hattie kept with her original decision and took no other person into her confidence about the plight. Priscilla seemed to mature under the circumstances and remained a faithful companion and secret keeper. They examined every side of the issue on many occasions, but still no progress presented itself.

Worst of all, the invitation to a questioning session that Hattie had been promised was not forthcoming. This caused considerable confusion, as justice demanded that the accused, as well as the accuser, be heard. Surely her day would come. In preparation, she constructed detailed explanations to anticipated questions. But the delay wore on, as did her nervousness.

She began to count the number of days until the end of the spring term. Was it possible there might not be a resolution to the problem? How could they possibly leave this matter hanging?

During the week of final examinations, Hattie managed her rising and falling emotions enough to perform satisfactorily. Her mind remained sharp, even though the strain left her frame weary and her energy sapped. Emerging from class after each test, she tallied the questions, one by one, to be certain her answers were correct. It was no small satisfaction to reach the end of the classwork. But that victory felt tainted by the charges still impacting her status.

Following the very last examination, Hattie was desperate to put her feet up for a few minutes. A little catnap was what she needed. Instead, an envelope was waiting under her door. She tore into it hopefully. Maybe this was the long-awaited notice. Would she finally get to answer questions and offer a defense of her actions?

The note said she must appear before the committee tomorrow for their final decision! Final? Horrified, Hattie let out a grunt and stomped her foot. Final decision? She wanted to SCREAM. This was so unfair! It felt like the faculty committee agreed with Thorne's grudge. What if this impacted the way they scored her examinations? But then, she stopped short. The Fugitive Slave Law denied Negroes the right to defend themselves. Suddenly, she felt their injustice in a shockingly graphic way.

As she suffered the awful helplessness, Hattie turned on her heel and went outside in search of a distraction. A hint of spring was in the air, but it remained quite chilly. Standing in the cold, she shivered until her teeth chattered. But it was better than losing her temper, crying, or screaming out loud.

An exceedingly agitated Hattie made her way to the faculty office the next day. She arrived with resolve, but her bloodshot eyes and shaky hands didn't show it. The walls, lined with framed certificates and scholarly recognitions, brought home how deeply she desired to become a teacher.

To her surprise, Miss White, ever calm and gracious, came

out and greeted her. Miss White seemed fair, although she did not allude to the matter at hand and simply walked Hattie down the hall toward the bland conference room. They did not talk, which made the hall seem a mile long.

Miss White ushered Hattie inside, then closed the door and left. Alone there for reasons she didn't appreciate, Hattie walked a few steps and wondered why the conference room's starchy white walls were completely bare, as were the windows. The starkness agitated her. She also contemplated the imposingly long conference table surrounded by large, dark chairs with arms. They had leather seats. There wasn't a stitch of fabric or tapestry anywhere, so her footsteps echoed hollowly. The seriousness of the atmosphere was anything but comforting. Her mouth went dry.

This was obviously the place where matters of school policy and student conduct were resolved. Perspiring nervously, Hattie wondered where to sit. She decided to stand until someone else arrived. It would show the kind of person she was, as if to say that she made no assumptions about her place on foreign soil. She certainly didn't want to offer the faculty any new or additional reasons to disparage her.

Shortly, Miss White returned, still smiling. This time, she made general, congenial conversation. Hattie dared not take encouragement from her constructive attitude, but she did appreciate the cordiality. Miss White showed her to a chair at one end of the intimidating table.

Moments later, the door opened again, and all of Hattie's teachers filed into the room. Wearing scholarly robes, they came to stand behind a line of chairs while Miss White seated herself opposite Hattie. Gulping, she wondered if her version of the Spanish Inquisition were about to commence.

Just as she wondered why Professor Thorne was not present,

the door swung open again. To her absolute surprise, Professor Colquhoun entered, following behind Professor Thorne. Upon seeing the older gentleman, Hattie's sweaty palms went cold. She felt her face turn white. This felt like a bad omen. Was Professor Colquhoun against her, too? *No*, she scolded herself. *You are a person of faith. Stop second-guessing! Maybe they're going to question him as well.*

But she couldn't stop. Were they going to give her the third degree? What if dear Professor Colquhoun was forced to answer entrapping questions like Thorne had hurled at Priscilla? Shifting in her seat nervously, Hattie fought to maintain her composure. She also struggled mightily to suppress a churning stomach and keep her face from giving away any fear.

"Thank you for coming to today's meeting," Miss White opened, nodding to all around the table. "I would like to begin with a review of what has brought us together. It is my intention to resolve this matter today."

The account presented by Miss White was fair, in Hattie's estimation. She had all the facts and was given to no exaggerations or embellishments. As she spoke, some teachers nodded. One glanced nervously at Hattie, then darted his eyes back to Miss White. Hattie couldn't tell what this might suggest. Out of respect for the individuals and the process, she tried not to make eye contact with any of the teachers from then on. *Can I count on justice*? she asked herself. The only thing that seemed certain was that the matter would finally end today.

"My original order of business was to undertake a question and answer period," Miss White continued. "But Professor Thorne has asked to make a statement, so I invite him to stand and offer that."

Mr. Thorne stood slowly. His squinty eyes remained downcast as he removed a wrinkly piece of paper from his pocket. With a wobbly hand, he unfolded it and seemed to read its contents silently. Hattie watched how his nervously blinking eyes appeared glued to the words. She had never seen him in this kind of state. Not only was his expression that of a terribly troubled individual, but his clothes seemed to have wilted, as well. He opened his mouth to speak, but his dry lips stuck to his teeth, and nothing came out. Coughing, he pursed his lips together tightly, perhaps to cover the action of running his tongue over his teeth so that he could speak. Why was he so nervous? After so confidently accusing Hattie and letting the matter languish for these many months, what in the world would make him so jittery? Hattie was the one who had the right to be frazzled, not Thorne.

"Many years ago, when I had the great privilege of entering Amherst College as a student," he began in a weak voice, "I quickly became involved with the Platonic Society, a popular debate organization that no longer exists. That activity was as important to me as my coursework. Before long, I was honored to become a debate team leader. Those of you with whom I currently serve on the faculty may not know that Professor Colquhoun, to my right here today, was the professor in charge of debate oversight."

Hattie all but gaped at this admission. There was a link between Thorne and the professor that went back nearly twenty years? What an unexpected statement. But what did it have to do with Hattie's situation?

"During that formative time, one particular topic held my focus more than any other. A significant debate was on the calendar, which led me to do much preparation. The topic question was "Can the actions of generations previous to ours be rationalized with regard to how Indians were handled?" In that day, I believed the many violent and discriminatory actions toward Indians were merely unfortunate.

At that point of my immaturity, I insisted that winning our freedom from the British was achieved because the new Americans were not intimidated by Indians. I was quite radical and nationalistic in my thinking about the revolutionary period."

Hattie no longer cared whom she made eye contact with. This statement by Mr. Thorne seemed to be some sort of odd summary of his history. She could not read why he was offering so much information, but she began to have a little glimmer of connection when he spoke about the Indians.

"I asked to make a statement today because several things need correcting," Thorne stuttered, taking a deep breath. "I need to offer an explanation, make an admission, correct more than one wrong, and seek forgiveness publicly. I am ashamed to admit that I led my debate team in the same vein as my personal opinions, telling the others that we must support Indian-hating President Andrew Jackson no matter what. But such a stance tainted the very idea of an honest debate. To his credit, Professor Colquhoun was not a man easily fooled. He saw through my flaws, and my team received a reprimand and a poor grade."

Such a confession shocked Hattie, who happened to glance at the faculty. Miss White's eyes registered doubt, and her face revealed something akin to disgust. Several others around the table shifted uncomfortably. Professor Colquhoun held his head erect and blinked rather respectfully. Hattie was immobilized with anticipation.

"After that outcome, I was angry and unable to see around my own idealism, as I have come to know it. Regretfully, I blew the significance of the situation out of proportion. Before long, I let it fester in my heart. It is with much apology that I admit to holding it against the professor for many, long years. He deserved better.

"More recently, when I learned that Miss Sheldon had delved

into the old debate team records and had gone to the professor for clarification, I exploded. To learn that the professor had removed the minutes from the library left me just as furious. It was a deeply flawed response, especially for one who professes to be a specialist in theology. The idea that anyone, much less a woman, would dig back into the past and possibly uncover my flaws brought me to the end of myself. Miss Sheldon is so bright that I feared for my job if she made her findings public. My attitude and actions were unjustified and wrong, as I have come to see. So, with all of you present, I offer an apology and ask for your forgiveness, just as I have asked God for his."

Hattie found herself unable to move. Just when she had begun to follow Thorne's line of reasoning, he had made a swift turn in her direction and then, it was over. Did his apology mean he did not really think she had done wrong? Was he taking her "wrong" upon himself in a strange way? Would there be a vote? Would she not be questioned after all?

Miss White opened her mouth to speak, but Mr. Thorne did not notice. Taking a deep breath, he obviously had more to say and remained standing. Miss White closed her mouth and leaned back, seemingly in awe over this unexpected presentation.

"Since I brought the charges against Miss Sheldon, the professor contacted me and requested a meeting," Thorne continued. "Very reluctantly, I agreed to sit down with him. Since then, we have been discussing things regularly. His mentoring about my reaction has been more than beneficial. As for the debate topic, we have examined it, point by point, and discussed what he calls "the other side of the story." This has been more than a period of growth and healing for me. A friend like the professor is something I have never known. He has changed my life for the better through his patience and influence."

"Thank you, Mr. Thorne," Miss White interjected as she rose

to resume the conduct of the meeting. "We must move on. Your unanticipated confession leads me to dispense with my agenda. The appropriate action is to bring this matter to a swift and affirmative conclusion. Hattie Sheldon, this committee will not need to ask you any questions. Rather, it is my prerogative as chairperson to apologize to you on our behalf. All charges against you are hereby dropped. It was wrong to hold you hostage for such a long period of time, during which Professor Thorne did not come forward about this matter. I am not ashamed to say in your presence that I will recommend probation for him. No student should endure such a situation ever again."

"May I offer a comment, Madam Chairman?" Professor Colquhoun inquired politely, raising his hand.

"Certainly. I yield to Professor Colquhoun," Miss White continued, sounding like someone in government.

"Madam Chairman and members of the faculty," the professor began, clearing his throat. "This young woman, Miss Hattie Sheldon, impressed me from the moment we first met. Her astute personality and bright mind led her to research what no student, male or female, had pursued in the ten years since my retirement. She dug to the bottom of the box. I commend her for being a serious student and offer my friendship as a mentor. In your hearing, she is welcome always in my home on any occasion when she wants to debate a topic of her choice."

"Why, thank you, professor," Miss White returned, smiling widely. "I would like to add to your accolades about her. Miss Sheldon, I am honored to reveal today before this body that, against difficult odds, you scored perfect marks on all your examinations. That has earned you the coveted number one position in your class. Congratulations."

The faculty broke into applause and rose from their seats. Even Mr. Thorne looked respectful but wistful as he stood. Hattie found herself paralyzed and nearly stupefied. Had a reversal of everything just taken place or had she merely dreamed it? She sought to force the edges of her lips to turn up, even as her brain seemed to scatter in many directions.

The afternoon had taken a most unexpected turn. In her wildest anticipations, she had never considered this. A standing ovation from her teachers? Who would have guessed it? She felt a little bit embarrassed, if the truth were told. But her manners came first. Standing, she expressed genuine words of appreciation to all in the room before Miss White came to her side.

"You may go now. I'm so sorry this happened. Let's sit down and talk through it tomorrow," Miss White whispered as she escorted Hattie to the door.

Having departed graciously, Hattie's emotions felt as erratic as spring weather. She did not know if she was going to rain, thunder or lightning. She needed to do something to release all the pent-up emotion she had harbored. Her outlook had been grey for so long that she scarcely envisioned brighter days. All she wanted now was to break free and get out in the open.

Then, just as she approached the stairs, a voice called her name. It was Professor Colquhoun. He must not care what anyone thought, because he had simply called out into the hallway. Of course, he could not see her. Hattie didn't want to turn back, but she forced herself to forego her escape and approach him.

"Yes, sir. You called my name," she began pensively.

"Are you all right?" he inquired sensitively. "I've been so concerned."

"Thank you," she replied, searching his face for clues. Why had he not sought to meet with her until now? Months had passed with no contact. "I'm confused, I guess."

"This problematic situation required intense patience and attention," he continued.

"It certainly did. I almost threw my hands up many times," she agreed, feeling more understood.

"Actually, I wasn't referring to you. I was explaining myself," he revealed.

"I don't understand," she replied with some hesitation.

"I wrote you that my prayers for a resolution were with you. I meant every word, for the best thing I could do was pray for you. Meanwhile, on your behalf, I slowly and methodically worked to gain the trust of Mr. Thorne again."

Hattie gasped and then restrained herself. The professor went on to address his silence and distance. He wanted her to know that he hadn't ignored her after all! He had just taken an approach he couldn't explain at the time. For a reason she still didn't understand, he had been mentoring Thorne. It must have taken place during the time she so needed to hear something, anything. Now, she understood why Professor Colquhoun offered no words of support.

"That's the opposite of what I expected," she confessed. "You knew that didn't you?"

"Young people need mentors and advocates in many unanticipated settings," he returned philosophically. "I could best help you in absentia while I helped Mr. Thorne in person. Please know that I did not forsake you."

Both of them were quiet for a moment. As much as Hattie wanted to delve further into the unclear elements, she reserved herself. The professor's countenance suggested that he might be keeping a confidence. He might be holding a private sentiment within himself. Whatever it was, she needed to respect it. So she simply thanked him, shook his hand warmly, and promised to be in touch. Then she departed.

Covering a city block quickly, the moment she turned the corner and was no longer visible to anyone at Amherst Academy, Hattie broke out into a dead run. The last time she recalled running this fast was during the awful slave roundup in Utica. That day she had to deliver bad news. But today, given this blessed reprieve, she could share wonderful news. And the person she wanted to tell, the loving arms into which she wanted to collapse, were those of Aunt Mary.

"Why didn't you tell me, dear?" Aunt Mary begged, wringing her hands over Hattie's extended period of suffering. "That situation was a tremendous burden to bear alone."

Aunt Mary almost whimpered as she hugged Hattie close. Together, they shed more than a few tears. She was very patient.

"Why did you keep it secret?" she asked later. "What good did that serve?"

"It was shame and pride. I know that now," Hattie allowed, wiping her tears as she pulled up to the kitchen table and took a sip of cool water. The feeling of being safe and protected in Aunt Mary's home was calming. Just looking around the pretty, homey kitchen helped erase the trauma of the lifeless conference room.

"After the charge came, I just kept thinking that it would be over soon. But that didn't happen."

"Promise me you'll never suffer alone again," Aunt Mary instructed, taking Hattie's hand. "Let others share your burden, dear. You never know how they might help. In this case, I knew things that would have made a big difference to you."

"What do you mean?" Hattie pursued, unable to grasp any connection. Beginning to relax, she reached down and loosened the laces of her shoes.

"Well, we have lived in this community for many years. That familiarity includes some eye-opening lessons and unpleasant findings. It is known around town that the Thorne family suffers from, shall we say, outbursts. They have a long, ugly history of holding grudges. Some call it uneven emotions. Mr. Thorne is just the latest member of his family to experience a similar episode that becomes excruciating for others. Many in his father's line have caused terrible problems like this one with you. Some have become incapacitated. See how you could have been encouraged had you told me?"

"That's shocking," Hattie responded, her eyes wide. At the same time, her mind raced back to Professor Colquhoun's careful wording. He must know this secret about the Thorne family! That had to be the answer to his reticence and careful wording. His integrity demanded the confidentiality that even protected an adversary. That was why he wouldn't reveal it even to Hattie.

The professor must have endured much discomfort as he drew Thorne back to reason inch by inch. It was probably the only way to convince Thorne to drop the charges! What an amazing sacrifice! Professor Colquhoun had saved her future!

Hattie fell back in her chair as the realization struck her. It took several minutes, but hearing herself explain it aloud to Aunt Mary confirmed everything. Professor Colquhoun really was a diplomat as well as a teacher. He had secured her exoneration.

Aunt Mary shook her head in wonder. Hattie all but cried, except that her heart was free from burdens for a change. Soon, however, she returned to the unanswered concerns about Thorne's problem.

"You mean he was hired despite his problem? And it was just kept quiet?" she questioned.

"No. There's nothing to keep quiet if nobody knows," Aunt Mary countered.

"Oh! I see. The other faculty members are not from Amherst. So no one knew to question him or delve into his background, did they?"

"It looks like that's what happened," Aunt Mary agreed, now standing at the basin peeling vegetables for supper. "Just promise me that, if something happens in the future, you will never hesitate to trust a friend. Two heads—or three—are always better than one."

"All that misery was unnecessary ... those awful months of waiting and worrying ..." Hattie lamented. "On the other hand, the threat motivated my best academic performance ever."

"Yes, but that's another thing altogether. Some people compensate better than others," Aunt Mary confirmed. "I'll give you credit for endurance—unsupported and alone. But it only works for a short time. It's much harder in the long run all by yourself."

"You can say that again," Hattie returned seriously. "I felt isolated and utterly overwhelmed. Sometimes, finding anything encouraging was a real struggle."

"Here's something to remember always. It takes many good things to cancel just one of life's ugly trials. That's why we need others," Aunt Mary testified, handing Hattie a carrot to assuage her hunger.

Hattie nodded philosophically. "I needed to hear that. Things are getting more complicated the older I get and the farther I go from home."

"Life is usually like that, dear," Aunt Mary soothed. "We suffer, but learn the great value of finding balance. In the years ahead, heaven knows where life will take you. But this episode will remain a powerful lesson about its complexities and how to handle them."

❋ ❋ ❋

June 15, 1851

Dear Margaret,

It seems ages since we've corresponded. I can't believe I've finished a whole year at Amherst Academy. It has been full of lessons too numerous to explain. You were pivotal in the chain of events that led me to this wonderful school. Isn't life amazing sometimes? I thought I couldn't endure it when you moved away from Utica. But hearing about your wonderful school helped lead me to my school. Thank you from the bottom of my heart!

Amherst Academy has been both maddening and magical. I say that after overcoming significant hurdles. Hardships here taught me to stay focused upon the positives and my goals. Now, my focus for the future is teaching. I encountered a treasure trove of historical information here in Massachusetts that has set me on a new path. In addition to the high quality instruction in many intriguing subjects, a wonderful retired professor has mentored me about America's founding and the real story of Indian relations. (It's no wonder I'm passionate about this, given my fervor over slavery's injustice and the miracle of Underground Railroad escapes. In many ways, the Indians were treated as badly as the Negroes.) Of course, women here are not allowed to debate. But the professor and I discuss much hidden history and spar over it. I find the exercise completely energizing and envision bringing the content to the classroom. Once I discovered this subject matter, I settled on teaching it. Doing so frees me from Utica society's entrapping expectations. Employment as a teacher can occupy my time and attention, offering the perfect excuse for avoiding the people and activities that are so confining. I have a growing comfort about going home and settling there now. With any luck, I will also achieve my lifelong dream of attending Utica Female Academy. But I must close for now, as it is quite late. Do write me of your progress and plans, dear friend. Love, Hattie

Some weeks later, Hattie caught sight of Professor Thorne at a distance. She didn't feel dread or disgust, but she did feel hostility. He had a problem, which was what prompted his unfair charges. Nevertheless, she held significant bad sentiments against him in her heart. Until she actually saw him, she hadn't realized the power those feelings had over her.

Her only standard for comparison was how she had once felt when her mother controlled her so tightly. That situation had threatened to steal her good attitude and hopeful spirit in the past. It had occurred before she understood her mother's suffering.

She couldn't let her attitude slip again. The pull of it was too strong in a bad direction and too hard to correct. So Hattie decided to forgive Professor Thorne as she had forgiven her mother. It was something she would have to work toward, perhaps daily. Old feelings were persistent, but releasing him would free her. She might even get up the nerve to tell him one day.

11

Rodrique Hortalez et Companie

During her final year at Amherst Academy, Hattie intended to take advantage of every opportunity for tutoring from Professor Colquhoun. His insights were invaluable, especially on subjects she studied methodically on her own time. These included Indian relations, teaching, and the Christianization of America.

"Professor, in my Indian readings, I found precious little about the early colonists' efforts to share Christianity," Hattie shared one summer afternoon, sitting opposite him and looking out at his vine-laden garden.

"You should be satisfied with that result," he returned soberly, "because, in truth, those early colonists, unlike others who followed, were much less focused on religious differences. The French were even less aggressive about it than the English."

"Were they mainly oriented to survival, to meeting their own needs?" she pursued, trying to envision the colonists.

"Most definitely," he confirmed, "and their actions invited disdain. Soon, they were coping with the onslaught of warfare. Remember, the Indians coped aggressively with many unintended consequences of the foreigners' presence. Previously unknown diseases brought by whites began to strike down the Indians, killing many. They knew the whites were to blame. But the whites were helpless to stop it, as they, too, succumbed to the diseases. The issue, along with many others, could not be resolved."

Continuing, he clarified that it took a period of living side by side for the deepest differences between the two civilizations to become apparent. Even in a spirit of cooperation, vast misunderstandings occurred. The Indians lived corporately and couldn't grasp the individualism of whites. Indian religion was communal and oriented to the divine in nature, which whites couldn't accommodate in their quest to subdue the environment and make use of nature's resources for their profit. Like great wars from past epochs, the divide between their customs sometimes victimized both sides.

"How have you become such an expert, Professor?" Hattie queried, honestly dazed by the professor's wisdom about Indians.

"Ah, a fair question and not an unexpected one," he responded slowly, frowning to himself. "That question once brought fear to me because I could not answer it safely. I had to remain discreet. In the glare of retrospect, I recall how the truth might have brought disregard upon me."

Hattie looked sideways slowly, watching the professor in a new light. Whatever did he mean, she wondered. When and why had he feared for his safety? He must have something unexpected in his past. What would warrant silence for so many decades, she puzzled?

Yet she felt that questions would be inappropriate, so she remained silent.

"You are not my formal student," he continued after a moment, his voice full of contemplation. "You are not linked with any authorities. Your interest is greater than ninety-nine percent of my former students. Perhaps it is time to break my silence. I no longer have much to lose. Your response to my story might prove useful. Would you honor me with your honest reaction if I relate the details?"

"I would be delighted," she responded with wonder, "and truly honored. My Presbyterian upbringing held that confidences were part of one's sacred trust with another."

Sighing, the professor stood and walked to the window. For a long moment, he stood there soaking in the sunlight, turning his head this way and that, as if keeping time to his reasoning. Then he strode across the room and stood in front of the fireplace, obviously considering risks and repercussions. Whatever he had to say, it was the source of life-changing importance to him.

"Warmth comes from the sun and from fire," he ventured after a time, looking philosophical. "Man needs warmth. But one source, the sun, cannot be touched, while the other, fire, destroys upon contact. Perhaps I have viewed my own history from the same position of quandary. But my future is short, while yours is long. I am ready to share what happened in my younger years."

"I appreciate that, sir," Hattie responded sensitively. "Perhaps the story has become a burden?"

Regretting the comment, Hattie grew silent. Again, she waited. Shortly, Professor Colquhoun began to speak.

❖ ❖ ❖

"Just as America had won her freedom from the British, I was born. A few short years before that, my father had been on the cusp of leaving France unexpectedly, with no inkling of the adventure in store for him.

"Let me go back. You see, at the beginning of America's war of independence, the Continental Congress sent commissioners to Europe in search of support for their great cause. They were desperate because King George III of England undertook vicious maneuvers against American coastal waters, ports, and cities. Without a new, significant supply of war material and weaponry, the Americans could not win their freedom.

"The French eventually agreed to help. After much maneuvering under cover, the Bourbon King of Spain joined the effort, as well. Together, they led the way for others who provided funds for the American war effort through a false trading company, Rodrigue Hortalez et Companie."

Hattie began to grip the arm of her chair. This was much better than anything she had read at the library. Could she actually be hearing, firsthand, a true story of international intrigue involving the high seas? She waited for the next sentence, gaping at the professor, unblinking. For once, she was glad he was blind. It left her free to stare in amazement and not be detected.

"Beyond the focus on supplies," the professor began again, "the issue of expertise brings me back to my relationship to all of this. America needed to fight European expertise with European expertise. The Continental Army lacked seasoned officers, artillerymen, artificers, and engineers. Soon, experienced individuals in France heard rumors about the tremendous need. Rodrigue Hortalez et Companie was deluged with volunteers.

"It so happened that my father, a French military officer, was among those hired to accompany the trading company's first shipment aboard a French frigate, *L'Amphitrite.* She left port on 24 January, 1777, loaded with cargo. The shipment was to aid Washington's army which was grappling unsuccessfully with wretched conditions, lack of armaments, and near starvation.

"For weeks, the ship fought angry, threatening seas. But, in April of 1777, against all odds, it docked unharmed at Portsmouth, New Hampshire. Shortly thereafter, the Continental Army won its campaign in Saratoga, the turning point in the war.

"That end is where my personal story has more of a firm beginning, for my father was injured early on. Because of language and translation problems, he struggled to communicate with the Americans. As a result, he was discharged. But, luckily for me, he made a swift recovery with a new plan.

"He had no desire to return to France on the foreboding and dangerous seas during war. Rather, he availed himself as a man with leadership skills to a previously unknown French fur trading company. That company assured him of a bright future and took him into the western wilderness. He made good money immediately. Unbeknownst to him, however, it was not a legitimate company, and the man with whom he traveled was an escaped French convict. One day when my father believed the man was checking traps, the man shot him in the back as he watered his horse at riverside. Barely conscious, he recalled the man searching his person to steal his money and identification papers. Then he was left for dead.

"My father regained consciousness and realized he was not mortally wounded. Nevertheless, he could not mobilize himself well. By God's grace, the wilderness climate was temperate. At length, he dragged himself to a place where he crafted a crude shelter. While sleeping shortly thereafter, he was awakened by noises and found himself nose-to-nose with a baby black bear. Not far behind was his massive mother. Amid his weakness, my father was no match for her giant, powerful paws. He was mauled and wondered why the bear didn't finish the job. Awaking afterwards, he alternately sipped rain-water and ate roots before lapsing back to sleep from the pain and loss of blood. His memory was quite cloudy about everything but one fact.

"A woman began to nurse him back to health. He could not see her because of bandages she used on his eyelids. Bit by bit, she gently coaxed life back into his weakened body. Her healing skills were a marvel, he told me. She used herbs, poultices, and roots to treat his wounds, stemming the pain and redness while offering him nourishment.

"He feared he had spoken like a deranged person when he was so injured. Perhaps it frightened her. She spoke little, and her language was not French. He believed she was just shy because she spoke so very little. All he knew was that she was gentle, continued to treat him, and saved his life.

"When he regained some sight, he learned a little more. They came to understand each other and fell in love. He would never forget that he would have died alone in the wilderness without her. Another blessing was that her family liked him and treated him well. They knew a few words in French.

"But there are many other details he didn't ever tell me," the professor related wistfully. "I lived many years wondering about her, finally coming to the satisfaction that my answers would only be found in heaven. I will meet her there, for the first time."

"Oh, no. You mean she died?" Hattie cried breathlessly, on the verge of tears. "Professor, I'm so sorry. What happened?"

Taking his handkerchief, the professor dabbed at his own tears.

Hattie's empathy rose. What a life-changing experience. He had endured much to tell his secret life story. She felt great compassion for him. How had she become the trusted one for this revelation?

"You see," he continued, "they were married and happy together but for a short time. While she was expecting me, she began to suffer from a fatal illness. She wondered if I would ever be born, but due to my father's vigilance at her side, I came into this world untouched. Tragically, my mother's health was broken, and she perished shortly thereafter. He only had me as a reminder of her. As the years passed, he remained a man of few words, and his broken heart did not heal. Because he said so little about my mother, I pictured her neither a traveler, nor a British or French citizen. In my childhood dreams, she was the product of explorers from another land, like my father.

"He eventually decided we would return to France when I was quite a young child. That is another miracle. I know next to nothing about it. It has plagued my imagination over the years to picture him traveling with a child on a long, dangerous voyage. There were always hostilities on the seas. But God was merciful.

"In France, an order of kind, loving nuns cared for me during my father's absences for work. They taught me English, which is still inexplicable and always will be. When he secured more gainful employment in England, we moved again. I received my early education there. But, quickly, I learned that the British looked down on the French. It would have been all the more damaging had my schoolmaster or mates known that my father aided the Americans in their war for freedom from the British. The British were most wounded to lose that war. It was not spoken about, so I learned to keep that part of my history hidden.

"Then, just as I had begun to see myself as British, we came back to America. I was almost grown and could have stayed behind, but would never have endured a separation from my father. Our bond was very strong. Once back in America, I was admitted to prestigious institutions because of my distinctive schooling and strong performance on examinations. I spoke English, Spanish, French, and Portuguese by then.

"By the time I began my teaching career, that long story seemed superfluous. There were many aspects of my origin that remained unspoken as my father grew older. I worried about repercussions should I be asked questions for which no answers existed. My father remained quiet. He was sustained by a deep Catholic faith. It pained me that he remained silently brokenhearted after losing my mother. He couldn't speak about her and never remarried. So, I determined to keep quiet about my background.

"In his last years, I cared for my father when his health failed. He knew many things that I could not have understood, that no one could have accommodated. Upon his deathbed, I asked once again if he could try to share more about my mother. With a burning gaze, he mustered the strength to tell me a few cherished facts. That is when he gave me some of the artifacts I keep on my desk. Those ancient tools belonged to my mother. He had hidden them away for many years. To my astonishment, just before he breathed his last, he whispered that my mother was an Indian."

Hattie gasped out loud before realizing she had leaned forward, her neck craned out of astonishment at his story. Embarrassed, she clamped her hand against her mouth. She looked at the ceiling for want of a better reaction, knowing he couldn't see her anyway.

Professor Colquhoun paced the floor as he spoke, then took a seat behind his stately desk. When Hattie glanced in his direction, his right hand cradled his forehead, while in his left hand he turned one of the old, well-crafted Indian tools over and over. Suddenly, the meaning of his artifacts took on great significance. Why, everything he had taught her gained significance in the light of his amazing revelation. No wonder he knew so much about the Indians. He was half Indian himself! And he had not known it for a great portion of his life!

"Forgive me," Hattie pursued respectfully. "But your name doesn't sound French. It sounds Irish."

To her relief, the professor laughed light heartedly for a moment.

"You're a clever young woman," he returned, smiling. "You notice all the details. I respect that."

"Am I wrong?" she pursued, questioning.

"You're right," he apologized gently. "When we moved to England and I was put in school there, my father enrolled me under the maiden name of his mother, who was Irish. It helped hide the fact that I was essentially a native of France, their hated neighbor across the English Channel."

The room was quiet for a moment. The professor appeared lost in his memories. Hattie, on the other hand, was wide-eyed over his story. It had literally fallen into her lap. He had shared it without reservation and in complete trust. Another aspect of her reaction was that she knew what it felt like to pursue something important, to feel that it was all she had. The professor had dug and toiled and scraped for information once he learned the true identity of his late mother. Hattie had pushed and prodded to gain her freedom and win the chance for more education. She could relate to his experience. It warmed her that they had so much in common. There was also a certain bolstering because he respected her for pursuing information about the Indians, for needing to know the whole story.

"Miss Sheldon," he eventually called in her direction, having roused himself from the desk. "Please forgive me for being distracted.

I recall saying it would be good to know your thoughts. But, now, with all respect, I only need a cup of tea. Having recalled every detail I ever knew, I freed the secret. My heart is at peace, even joyful. I can scarcely express it in words. Come, let's go into the parlor and have tea with Mrs. Colquhoun now."

September 20, 1851

Dear Hattie, How we miss you! I just sat down to send you news from home and mail an enclosure. We are all well, although Father has had quite a period of alarm, as I'm sure you have already gathered. His agitation over this slave law has cost him many a night's sleep. I promised to write you in his stead because he is so caught up with the anti-slavery society's response. He swears he will run for a ward seat on the Abolition Party ticket to fight the measure. Mother remains bound to the orphanage, her talents put to good use. Business is good at the shop for LeGrand and father. Artemas displays thoroughly delightful talents with leather craft and saddle construction. Albert has met a lovely young woman called Ann Porter. He raves of her beauty and also talks alternately of farming and his deep interest in the militia. You may have read everything in creation about Indians, but he has read everything in creation about military matters. Little Mary is one and has two fine teeth in front. She is adorable and looks a lot like you, Hattie. Finally, George sends his love.

When the June 5, 1851, edition of National Era magazine arrived, everyone in the family began to read a particular installment with great interest. It turned out to be a stunning serialization of a new novel about slavery. Each week, we compete for who will read the latest chapter. I am enclosing several at father's request. The authoress is Reverend Lyman Beecher's other daughter, Harriet—remembering of course his daughter, Catherine, who heads your friend Margaret's school in Connecticut. This slavery story, called Uncle Tom's Cabin, details graphically the day-to-day perils of slave life. It is the talk of the antislavery society, the town, and the papers. Our like-minded friends cannot stop raving about its realistic portrayal of slavery's ravages. I hope you find it as captivating as we did, Hattie. It goes a long ways toward explaining why abolition is our stance and why every Christian should fight slavery. Last, but not least, I have wonderful news. Father and Mother received your acceptance to Utica Female Academy day before yesterday! I had to laugh upon over-hearing them wonder aloud about who you must take after, because it doesn't seem to be either one of them. The school shared that you were the first applicant and the first student admitted for the 1852–1853 term. We are all so very proud of your academic accomplishments.

With love, your sister, Amanda

Hattie hugged the letter close and shed a little tear of excitement before reading it again. After all these years, she was actually accepted to Utica Female Academy. How many times she had read stories about it in the newspaper. She must have walked past it a hundred times, stopping to imagine what it felt like inside. Margaret would be proud—or maybe a little jealous.

After the second reading, her gratification faded a little. Should she worry about her father? Although she couldn't tell anyone, a slight disappointment rose up because he hadn't broken the news to her. It felt like he had passed the responsibility down the chain of command. Was he really too busy or too upset to write her about the achievement of her lifelong dream?

But perhaps she was overreacting or being too sensitive. There was no denying that she had been away from home for a long time. Homesickness could take different forms. A while back, her mother had praised heaven that Hattie had agreed to return. She hoped nothing had changed her parents' minds about wanting her. Truth be told, she was growing tired of school. But it was no time to think like that. She had this whole school year to complete at Amherst Academy.

Hattie read the first installment of *Uncle Tom's Cabin* in one sitting. It so captivated her attention that she scarcely moved, her eyes devouring the words, page after page. In her heart of hearts, she believed that slavery was evil beyond comprehension. But, having never come face to face with it, she could not envision its many complications.

The story line in *Uncle Tom's Cabin* gave her sudden access to the heartbreaking hazards endured by slaves and their families, as well as insights into the lives of their masters and the masters' families. It was staggering confirmation of the unthinkable. She digested searing details of slavery's sinister practices and attitudes.

That night, she couldn't go to sleep for the bad omen plaguing her thoughts and raising questions she could not answer. What drove such vicious treatment of other human beings? Was slavery really rationalized just because the southern plantation economy needed it to survive? The author of *Uncle Tom's Cabin*, Harriet Beecher Stowe, believed so. She must have actually witnessed the horrendous things in her story, Hattie concluded. Maybe she lived near slaveholders or knew some of the slaves personally.

Hattie suffered the novel's heart-rending account of loyal Uncle Tom, a kindly Christian slave sold away from his family because of his master's debt. The malevolent slave hunter who pursued him was barely human, in her estimation. She couldn't calm down for reliving the vivid, harrowing escape of Tom's acquaintance, a young slave woman intent on keeping her precious little son from being sold.

From that time forward, Hattie waited for the next chapters of *Uncle Tom's Cabin* with bated breath. It wounded her to the core when Uncle Tom was sold again and again. But her spirit buoyed because his Christian faith sustained him. Cruelly abused, he not only persevered, but helped other slaves. By contrast, the slave owners in the story believed themselves to be moral and Christian, while separating themselves from responsibility for slavery as an institution. In so doing, they revealed unacknowledged prejudices and bigotry against Negroes.

Well beyond feeling shocked, Hattie puzzled over the depiction of seemingly decent Christian people who nevertheless practiced slavery. They told themselves it was too ingrained to ever be stopped. *Uncle Tom's Cabin* revealed the astonishing level of rationalization and self-delusion of these slave owners. The duplicity of it stunned her. As for those non-Christians in the story, including a particularly wicked slave owner who vowed to break Uncle Tom's faith, their pride in cruelly manipulating and controlling other humans nauseated her.

Each time the plot involved a slave hunter, it took Hattie back to the unforgettable slave roundup in Utica. All over again, she could hear the curses, smell the dung-covered street, and feel herself rolling to safety. Seared in her memory was the vision of several helpless kidnapped Negroes held in the filthy cart without food or water.

According to this new law that her father hated, if a roundup happened today and Hattie tried to help him and Silas, they would be arrested. Any official could drag Silas away, lying about him, imprisoning him even though he had earned his freedom. Having papers to prove one's freedom would not stop bloodthirsty slave hunters. They simply wanted to grab as many Negroes as possible and sell them down South for profit.

The day finally arrived: April 1, 1852, when Hattie read the last installment of *Uncle Tom's Cabin*. By then, the story had turned her stomach into a knot as hard as a tree stump. She couldn't shake its impact on her spirit. Day after day, the story stayed fresh in her thoughts. It was so disturbing that, during supper with friends one night, she kept interrupting the conversation about Uncle Tom's Cabin with troubling observations and points for discussion.

"The Christians were as bad as the non-Christians," she told friends. "Their so-called Christian way of handling slaves wasn't that different from wicked people's maltreatment of slaves. Both abused them physically and emotionally."

"You know, Hattie," Quill finally retorted. "The story was stimulating, and I don't deny its popularity. But, I've never seen you this mesmerized. Why has it captivated you so and dominated your thinking?"

Captivated? Was she? It gave Hattie pause. After supper, she tried to focus her thoughts off the story, but to no avail. There was no escaping its effect.

Quill was right. Her thinking was dominated. She just hadn't viewed it from that perspective before. When she examined her concern further, she understood that *Uncle Tom's Cabin* took her further back than the slave roundup in Utica. It recreated the myriad feelings she experienced as a little girl on the one and only Underground Railroad rescue in which she participated. *Uncle Tom's Cabin* was so real it had become personal.

At length, she delved into why the story impacted her so deeply. For starters, her primary source of aggravation was the injustice. She could not bear stories of people denied their own humanity. Deep in her spirit, she really did believe that all men were created equal. Someone had to help people caught up in violence they couldn't fight against. But even if Hattie wanted to do something today, she asked herself, what would it be?

The school year had flown. Weeks later, on a warm afternoon, Hattie made her way to Professor Colquhoun's home. On a whim, she took a slight detour through an area of Amherst she hadn't explored before. She had grown to love the town, just as Aunt Mary did. People were friendly. Neighbors and others looked out for one another and offered little kindnesses. This grounded their common loyalty in the community. These kinds of sentiments filled Hattie's thoughts as she ambled along, smiling.

Rounding a corner, she noticed a Negro man standing by his horse. Calmly submitting to the halter, his horse flicked its tail to switch flies away. A small boy, probably his son, reached to pet the horse's velvety nose as the man supervised. The boy squealed with delight.

A few steps away, his mother watched with a gentle smile, the baby on her hip bouncing excitedly. Hattie and the woman exchanged smiles and nods. But after the man saw her, he led the horse behind the house, turning back twice to keep an eye on her. Did she look suspicious?

As questions formed in her mind, Hattie reoriented herself. The people were obviously free Negroes. Once again, her deep feelings about the impact of the fugitive slave law rose up. *Every* Negro had to be watchful at all times and in the presence of all white people. This was the epitome of her father's concern. A schism of deep and divisive import had formed the day legislators passed the fateful law. It put all Negroes on guard every second of every day.

As far as these innocent Negroes in Amherst knew, Hattie was a suspicious stranger walking past their house. They were obligated to question the motive of strangers in order to protect themselves, their children, and their very lives. She could barely put herself in their place. It gave her pause.

From her earlier reading of today's newspaper, Hattie recalled a prominent, foreboding ad. In large, urgent type, it warned colored people to avoid previously trusted public officials like police officers and watchmen. The law had empowered such officials to act in the capacity of slave catchers. Hattie didn't look like an official, but she was a stranger in the neighborhood. It was fair to assume she might be a slave catcher's informant. No wonder the Negro man had fear in his eyes.

She decided the best characterization of a slave catcher involved the word "rabid." She had only encountered one rabid animal in her lifetime. It had bloodshot eyes, a dripping, curled lip, and made guttural sounds. The memory alone brought her disgust. How much more gripping was the fear of these Negroes that some slave catcher would come like a possessed demon to drag them away.

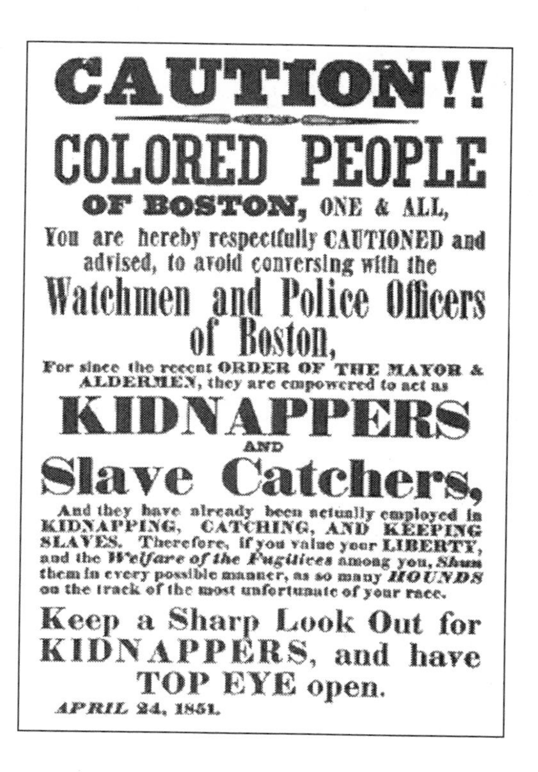

❖ ❖ ❖

Spring sunshine encouraged new, moist leaves on the tree outside Hattie's window. The closer she got to finishing school, the faster time flew. Soon, her course of study was completed, and she found herself packing for the train back to Utica.

As her departure grew imminent, so did her awareness of all the changes and improvements Amherst had brought into her life. If she tried to write a list of blessings, it would be very long. She had treasured Amherst Academy and the degree to which rigorous study had opened her mind. Of the many benefits she had accrued, she was grateful for learning to write well, for becoming a better thinker, and for experiencing what academics really involved.

But, oh, how she would miss the people, as well. Each one had a special place in her heart and had affected her in a unique way. She was a better person for having known them. Her heart was full of love for her newfound relatives in Massachusetts and the family history they shared. Aunt Mary, almost a second mother, had showed her how painful experiences could influence her for long-term good. She had drawn Hattie close, close enough to reveal the many ways her daughter's death brought heartache. The intimate hurt made Hattie appreciate her own mother from a new, more understanding perspective.

There were other memorable relationships and moments Hattie recorded in her diary. Priscilla and her other roommates deserved credit for shaping her into a well-rounded person who took time out for fun. They had laughed themselves silly on occasion, and cried together, as well. Something about the experience of living together without their parents brought them particularly close.

Finally, there was Professor Colquhoun. To say he had changed her thinking and her life was an understatement. Before she first arrived, her most compelling life experiences involved escaping slaves and the Underground Railroad. Now, thanks to him, she was leaving with a wealth of new information about a completely different race. The Indians' suffering compelled her compassion. She pondered the life-changing understanding the professor had given her about them.

Thankfully, the world did not stand still for God's creation and peoples. The world stayed in motion, and civilization with it. She had her eye on helping the Indians make progress. Certainly, she intended to set the record straight about the true historical relationship in America between Indians and settlers and explorers.

Hattie never dreamed that so many would gather to say goodbye at the station. It truly warmed her heart. Looking from one kind face to the next, she grew wistful about leaving. One last time, she took each one's hand and thanked them.

Without Aunt Mary's influence, she would likely never have found herself in an Amherst classroom.

"Write me often, dearest girl," Aunt Mary whispered in Hattie's ear, giving her one final hug. "I don't know where life will take you, but you will make a success of it. That's a certainty."

Turning to dab at her eyes, Hattie collided with Wilfred, the eager suitor she had spurned. He stood there looking a little stiff and uncomfortable, a sheepish look on his face. Then he extended a hand to shake hers.

"Good luck, Hattie," he wished with a genuine smile. "I'll always remember meeting you at the lecture and going to Professor Colquhoun's home together."

"Wilfred, you've been a sweet, patient friend," she reminded the young man who had accepted her disinterest gracefully. From him, she had come to understand the value of friendship and how it could endure even after disappointments occurred.

"Keep studying," he sighed. "You've got too much determination and too little time for an admirer."

Before she turned from Wilfred, Hattie heard footsteps. Priscilla was calling her name as she ran to the platform.

"Thank goodness I'm not too late. Oh, Hattie, I'm going to miss you," she cried. "Promise you'll stay in touch after Quill and I are married?"

Just then, the conductor announced that all passengers must climb aboard. The train would leave the station in two minutes, his booming voice warned. Hattie felt pressed for time, but knew that the clock waited for no one.

She cast a long glance at Professor Colquhoun. Without his mentoring, she would never have known the story that now motivated her future. Finding herself unable to speak, she shook his hand before giving him a little hug. He seemed to understand and patted her shoulder in return.

"I've got one last thought for you," he offered didactically. "President George Washington believed that the Indians could make up for lost time. He said it was possible to progress as a people and catch up with the new Americans within fifty years."

The professor was always an optimist, she thought. His encouragements were little treasures she now cherished through the tears he could not see. She would remember them—and him—all her life. But the time had come for a new chapter, and that meant closing this one. As she climbed onto the train, she was struck by her good fortune.

"I know you'll excel at Utica Female Academy, just as you did as Amherst," Aunt Mary called as the train pulled away.

Hattie let her tears fall while blowing kisses to everyone. They would write each other. But she feared the professor wouldn't be able to correspond. Perhaps it was better that he couldn't see her tears. She wished only happiness for him. He deserved much love in his last chapters of life. Certainly, his early life had held enough loss and change for more than one lifetime.

❧ ❧ ❧

As the distance between the train and the well-wishers grew, Hattie felt pangs of loss. The best way to put her goodbyes in perspective was to be thankful, she realized, as she settled into her seat. It really was true that Amherst had brought a type of miracle into her life. Many hours lay ahead on her journey, and the trip offered plenty of time to ponder the ups and downs of going back home. Her lifelong goal of attending Utica Female Academy would finally reach fruition. *This is the best of all worlds*, she mused to herself. *I'll be back with the family, my teaching goal is set, and this is my dream school. Surely there won't be rough spots like the accusation at Amherst Academy.*

But something about that didn't ring true. It wasn't realistic. *What am I thinking,* she asked herself. *Anybody who expects smooth sailing in life is naïve.* Of course there would be challenges and problems! That's what life was about. Difficult situations were supposed to produce maturity, to remind people how to respond the next time a trial came along. It was time to contemplate her difficulties from a new perspective, Hattie decided.

Had she taken lessons from the troubling experiences in her life? Yes, especially when it came to the family. And she understood that trouble came from bending the rules at school. Connecting with Professor Colquhoun through a back channel had gotten her into trouble. By contacting him through Quill, she had played with fire. The emotional burns she suffered were a powerful reminder to use better judgment and be vigilant.

Looking absentmindedly at trees and rocks as the train lumbered along, she felt the gnawing reminder of her hurt over Professor Thorne's accusation. It had been so personal. And so false. All that waiting and suffering without any sign of progress took an ugly toll.

Memories sprang up of wounding helplessness and unpredictability about the timing and outcome. She, Hattie Sheldon, the young woman who thought she was prepared for the world, had been at the mercy of everyone and everything. Even now, recollections about her lack of control over the situation depressed her.

When it came to control, she turned the events over and over. Before long, a revelation of sorts struck her. The Indians had no control, either! At the mercy of authority and power beyond their experience, their lack of control had lasted much longer than hers. As one who intended to teach about the Indians, she should have grasped that earlier.

The oversight frustrated her as she gazed out the window, hardly noting the wild geese flying overhead. It would behoove her to pay better attention. Now was the time to stop thinking of things solely from her own perspective.

After more careful consideration, Hattie was able to view Thorne's accusation in a different way. To her surprise, despite all the hurt, it actually had a redeeming aspect: she had been forced into a position she had never experienced before, the victim role. All sorts of things had plummeted when she became the victim, including her confidence, optimism, and even hope. The Indians might have plenty to say about that. Their losses were far more pervasive than hers, even to the point of degradation.

Hindsight was turning out to be instructive. Maybe her painful vulnerability had more lessons to offer. What about the way other people had reacted? When the circumstances couldn't be changed, they had shown her compassion and forbearance. She needed to keep that in mind. A day might be coming when she would need to respond like they had, and doing so would be quite a change, she admitted.

Priscilla had kept Hattie's confidence and supported her

each step of the way. Miss White had maintained an open mind and treated Hattie respectfully throughout the ordeal. Professor Colquhoun exhibited loyalty by the way he coped with her, as well as Mr. Thorne.

But Hattie herself had been impatient, overly emotional, and too guarded. She could still hear Aunt Mary saying she made a bad choice by keeping the episode secret. Aunt Mary was right. Hattie had added insult to injury. By prioritizing her own perseverance and walking the difficult road alone, she looked like a martyr.

If that didn't prompt a new level of maturity, what would? She must prioritize sounder and well-balanced responses in her quest for growth. Even so, she was already a different person than when she had left Utica two years ago. She felt more mature and even looked older and wiser. Another inch taller, she had slimmed down and begun to dress like a mature woman.

For the most part, Hattie liked her adult self better than her younger self. The transformation was easy to detect in her attitude, choices, and opinions. It was possible, however, that people in Utica would need time to get adjusted to the adult she had become. Her mother would probably push back the most against her newfound independence.

This was not a newly minted conclusion. It had come to mind several times in recent months. Just a few days ago, a sudden recollection had stirred her worries again. That day was firmly set in her mind, as were her actions afterwards.

❖ ❖ ❖

After she arose that day, her mind was filled with packing. Quite by chance, she had found her mother's gushing letter about returning to Utica to teach. It had drifted her back to forgotten feelings about living at home, cooking meals, missing her father's shop, and enduring many limitations. The emotions weren't necessarily good ones. A few were somewhat haunting.

That same day, while reading an article about a woman actually attending medical school, Hattie had inserted herself into the story. The woman was a groundbreaker who simply wouldn't take no for an answer. Hattie had pictured times her mother had told her no and held her back. The recollection gave her something of a chill. There and then, she had realized it was time for action.

"I've made so much progress," she had concluded aloud, surprising even herself. "I can't let myself fall back into that old, juvenile crisis. Now, I have leverage with mother. Since she dreams of my return, I need to use that to my advantage."

Without hesitating, Hattie had brandished her pen and drafted a clever letter of intent to work at her father's shop. It was a condition of her return, she specified. The facts spoke for themselves: she had lived in another state, moved freely about the town of Amherst and beyond, and learned significant life lessons. She had traveled, become a good cook, learned how suitors approached young ladies, and endured a near-scandal. She was a full-fledged graduate of Amherst Academy, with honors no less. Those credentials qualified her in new ways to work at the shop and to watch out for herself. If her parents didn't agree with her new independence, she added, she had alternatives.

There. She had said it! Declaring herself brought a freeing release. It also removed the idea of compromise from the negotiating table. It was time for her to live her life on her own terms. Taking pride in her decision, Hattie quickly posted the letter and gave it no further thought.

After the excitement of arriving back in Utica, nothing was mentioned about the letter. To her delight, she received the warmest of welcomes. She expected the subject to be raised the next morning, but accidentally overslept.

Hattie found herself alone in the empty house. Perhaps they had forgotten about her letter and the way she stood her ground. Or maybe they were just too busy, her father with the shop and her mother with the orphanage. Perhaps they just hadn't realized the depth on her intentions. But that too, must work in Hattie's favor, she schemed. So, without further hesitation, she dressed and left for work at her father's shop.

As Hattie made her way downtown, she took stock of Utica's hustle and bustle. The familiar flow of commerce up and down Genesee Street had not changed. It was teeming with elegant carriages and well-worn wagons, bedraggled horses and shiny bicycles, barking dogs and hurrying pedestrians. Nothing looked different.

Even though Utica felt secure and familiar, would she like it better this time? What actually lay beneath the surface? She asked this question frequently over the next weeks. By the time school started, she still had not made up her mind.

Luckily, she liked Utica Female Academy very much. The course of study promised to be rigorous and thought provoking. Beyond the excellent academics, an unexpected level of prestige was attached to being a student there. Perhaps it was because the parents of UFA students paid tuition instead of the school receiving support from taxes. With more than 170 students enrolled, the school was doing so well that it had a faculty of ten teachers. Hattie knew she was more than privileged to attend a higher school. Maybe young men could attend universities, but the young women at UFA believed they were almost equal in every way.

On her first visit to the library after the fall semester started, Hattie scanned the local newspapers at the reading room's big public table. Bad news screamed from the headlines. Feeling agitated, she seated herself in her old spot. The familiarity was unexpectedly comforting. How nice to return to the same chair with the big arms. Utica was changing, but her familiar reading place was still there.

Picking up the papers, she began to read a series of troubling stories. "City Debt Crisis Deepens," one paper beheld. "Street Condition Complaints Double," a second echoed. "Tax Protests Grow Vocal," a third warned. Finally, and perhaps the most threatening, the newest edition of a fourth paper led with "Arsonist Strikes Again."

Hattie leaned back, her mind reeling. It was 1852. Why, at this late date, had the city gone into debt? When she left for Amherst Academy, it was still prospering. What was the reason for the street deterioration? Citizens were angered over taxes and an arsonist was on the loose. What had become of Utica?

Certain she must be missing something, she began to work her way through older editions of the papers. They, too, were full of dismal stories. Seemingly, Utica appeared far from any kind of upswing. Hattie began to second-guess her decision to remain there after graduation.

For some time, she had built up lofty images of entering a proud, respected school. Her teaching days were within reach. Before she went to sleep at night, she imagined eager children who came running excitedly, each one ready to follow instructions and excel. Hattie's lectures about America's founding and fight for independence would be sprinkled with real stories and attention-grabbing details. Now that she had personal experience with abolitionism and knew how to portray the Indians, her students would be more realistically prepared for life.

But how could any of that happen if Utica was falling apart? Under the circumstances, she couldn't feel very secure. Any future teacher needed to be certain that the education system was sound. What about the city's economic future?

Suddenly, the familiar chair no longer felt comforting. What measures was the city employing to address these wider, deeper problems? Why hadn't her father mentioned any of this in his letters? Hattie felt justifiably nervous.

The city's disintegration was the opposite of what she needed right now. Even if Utica could change for the better, how long would it take? Should she associate herself and her ambitions with a city plagued by such big problems? What if the city's troubles imposed themselves on her?

Momentarily, she stood and collected her things. Remaining in the quiet of the library felt oppressive. She needed fresh air and exercise to process the unexpected. Her restlessness was linked to decisions about her future. Could she—or should she—make Utica her permanent home?

12

Setting the Record Straight

The best part of being home was spending time with her niece, Mary. Hattie had waited patiently in Amherst while the little baby grew into a young child, all the while imagining them together when she returned to Utica. Now she could see Mary nearly every day.

They read books, went out to the swing, walked through the neighborhood, and made big messes together in the kitchen. Hattie never tired of new things to teach Mary. A few minutes together each day let her picture herself instructing other children.

❀ ❀ ❀

During Utica Female Academy's Christmas holiday, Hattie's classmates had gone every which way to spend time with their families. Most were from the state, but some traveled long distances to be home for the holidays. Meanwhile, the Sheldons were invited to attend several parties and a large assembly.

Inside the civic reception hall decorated with greenery and pinecones, music set a festive atmosphere. As her family greeted friends, Hattie looked around for familiar faces. She caught the eye of a neighbor girl in a deep green gown and waved. The girl looked so happy as she danced with the young man she always intended to marry.

Hattie surveyed the other side of the room. Several boring fellows with slouching posture shifted from one foot to another as they lingered by the etched punch bowl. Even after several years away, she observed the same old maids lining the dance floor expectantly like wallflowers. Shivering, she couldn't help but wonder what it felt like to be in their places. She didn't want to end up like them, but she also didn't want to take her eye off education.

After making light conversation with several people, Hattie wandered into a side hall to think. Looking out a large, draped window at the falling snow, she took stock. So many more considerations seemed to bombard her: the condition of Utica, her future as a teacher, the expectation that she should have a beau. Sighing, she felt pressured in this traditional place.

"Well, hello Miss Sheldon," a lilting voice called from across the hall.

Hattie turned to see Mrs. Cornelia Cooper Graham approaching her with a welcoming smile.

"Mrs. Graham, how nice to see you," she replied, taking the esteemed woman's hand. "It's been a long while. Is everything going well at the orphanage?"

"When I saw you across the room, that's the very thing I wanted to mention," Mrs. Graham replied. "You've always been good with children and concerned for their welfare."

"Did you know I've decided to become a teacher?" Hattie returned.

Mrs. Graham clasped her hands excitedly. "All the better! That's wonderful news, and perfect for what I wanted to ask. I need a young person to lead some little activities and read stories to the children."

Hattie beamed with excitement. "I would love to do that. It sounds like perfect teacher training."

"Oh, good," Mrs. Graham replied. "We have needed someone like you for a long while. How about twice each week?"

"That will work nicely," Hattie agreed. "I'll ask Miss Kelly if she might give me credit."

"Oh, let me ask her. It will add emphasis, like a recommendation," Mrs. Graham strategized.

"Why, thank you. I can't tell you what this means to me," Hattie cooed.

"How about Tuesday and Thursday afternoons?" Mrs. Graham proposed. "Come to my office around three o'clock and we'll go from there."

❖ ❖ ❖

"Hattie, may I have this dance?" her father invited from the doorway.

Glancing back lovingly, she approached and took his hand. He was so thoughtful in social settings to detect even her minor discomfort. Her father understood her even when she hadn't said a word.

As he led her around the dance floor, the smell of cinnamon

caught her attention. She didn't feel so ill at ease, especially after the conversation with Mrs. Graham. As she was on the verge of telling her father about it, Artemas cut in and took Hattie's hand. Laughing, they danced off as her father went to her mother's side.

Hattie enjoyed seeing all the pretty dresses as they swished past. They made her miss her classmates, all of whom were lovely girls from widely varying backgrounds. Hattie loved hearing story after story as they shared details of their lives. When they had spoken of their upbringing and travels, it felt so good to share her experiences in Amherst. She drew confidence from her accomplishments and felt capable of more.

"Hattie, where did you get that satchel?" one friend had inquired, eyeing the new book bag Ebenezer had made for her. "It's the most luscious leather I've ever touched."

"My father crafts these at his shop," Hattie returned brightly. "Come with me sometime. He also makes and repairs leather trunks."

"Mother says I can visit New York City sometime this year if a friend goes, too," the girl expounded excitedly. "I would love to carry a satchel like yours."

Nearly all of Hattie's classmates spoke of themselves as future teachers. She didn't take them seriously, however. They entertained big dreams, but she believed their most fervent hope was to become wives and mothers. In all likelihood, they would never teach. Admirable aspirations didn't always pan out when romance came into the picture.

At least Priscilla had been honest that education wasn't her priority. Hattie remained firm, however, about her decision to teach. But she knew it was only a matter of time before people would start urging her more openly to find a husband.

Strange, but her mother had not mentioned young men lately. This was a change, as she had frequently urged Hattie to be more focused on marriage. In fact, her mother seemed to have new respect for Hattie's plans.

Suddenly, Hattie stopped dancing and came to a dead halt.

"What's the matter?" Artemas asked, leading her off the dance floor.

She searched the crowed for their parents. "It just occurred to me that I'm in big trouble."

"With who? Do you have to fix it right now?"

"I don't think I can fix it," she whispered. "Mrs. Graham asked me to help at the orphanage. It never occurred to me until now that she might not have asked mother first."

"That's a problem," he agreed. "But if mother thinks you're old enough to get married, why aren't you old enough to help at the orphanage?"

The apple tree and lilac blooms came late during the spring of 1853. Intemperate weather had persisted as winter waned and the streets refused to thaw. Business at Ebenezer Sheldon's shop picked up in late April. Ships docked, trainloads of travelers arrived, and school would soon adjourn. Hattie got excited as new characters came to town. This was on her mind as she walked to the shop one afternoon.

Across the street from the shop, she noticed a well-dressed bearded man in a wagon. He drove past slowly while straining to look inside. Why didn't he just stop and go in, she wondered. The man slowed down even more, so she stopped, too. An old sense of protectiveness rose up toward her father and his business.

But then the man sat upright again and moved on. Hattie continued to watch him, even though he wasn't particularly suspicious. In fact, he looked much like Ebenezer's average customer. He drove to the end of the street.

Laughter rose from a familiar gathering spot next door, catching her attention. Leaning against the street lamp, she paused to enjoy the people and think again about life in Utica. It was pretty ordinary, truth be told. If she were asked how she felt about the city, the best word she could offer was "accustomed." Her hometown was not exciting or even very interesting. How deflating to approach her twentieth birthday in this state of mind.

Unexpectedly, the man she had just been observing returned. But this time, he directed his wagon into the alley that led behind her father's shop. Now Hattie's interest was piqued. What was the nature of his business? Why had he avoided the front entrance? Scampering across the street, she followed him down the alley, creeping alongside the building's outer wall quietly. Just short of the back, she peered around the corner of the building. The man was gone, but his wagon was at rest, its horse tied to the post. He had gone in the back door of her father's shop. Why?

Hattie rushed back to the main entrance and entered breezily. To her surprise, the front of the shop was empty. Nobody was present to greet customers. The elegant aroma of leather and its nostalgia stopped her, prompting childhood memories of times spent there. But this was no time for emotionalism. Something was amiss.

Gathering her wits, Hattie headed for the back workroom. A conversation in low whispers stopped her. Concealing herself, she strained to listen.

"The parcels arrive tomorrow," the bearded man was saying. "We need to outfit the horses."

"I have two harnesses ready," her father replied. "Which stations will you be forwarding from?"

"Number two to number three," the man returned, his voice even lower. "Our baggage consists of four. Joseph is the conductor this time."

"Are you the shepherd?"

"Yes. My wagon is out back. Can we load now?"

Hattie heard their footsteps and took a peek. Their backs to her, each man carried a brand new harness in one hand and a bridle in the other. Then they disappeared out the back door.

Her father had not mentioned payment. This fact confirmed Hattie's theory. She knew exactly what was going on.

❁ ❁ ❁

One evening the next week as Ebenezer read his newspaper, Hattie sat down at his feet on a little stool.

"Father, tell me about that man from the Underground Railroad," she said in a quiet voice, looking directly at him. "How long have you been involved in abolition work with him?"

Ebenezer's pipe fell from his mouth, dropping hot tobacco ashes on his trousers. The newspaper crumpled as he jumped to his feet and brushed the tobacco remnants onto the floor.

"Dash it all, Hattie," he cried, clearly undone. "What are you talking about?"

"I saw that bearded man tie his horse and wagon around back," she explained, clearly energized. "I wondered why he didn't use the front door, and hoped nothing was wrong. Before you knew it, I had slipped inside the shop. I listened to your conversation and heard all the code words."

"Now, Hattie," Ebenezer interrupted. "This is no time for you to lose focus. You need to concentrate on your studies and your studies alone."

"My schoolwork is coming along fine. It's just one part of my interests, though. Abolition is the other. I'm appalled by the Fugitive Slave Law and what it means for everyone in the North. You're so courageous in spite of it, Father! After overhearing you and that man, I see how brave you are to soldier on helping escaped slaves. It's dangerous and illegal, yet you keep doing the right thing. You donated the harnesses and bridles to support them, didn't you?" she asked, her eyes sparkling.

Ebenezer was now looking out the window to avoid her. He jammed his hands into his pockets and began to jingle coins. She was troubled that he did not look at her. Silently, she watched him clench his muscular jaw muscle.

"Don't take umbrage, Father," she whispered, her hand on her heart. "I just want to say that it's admirable. I'm so proud that you're doing it."

Ebenezer flushed bright red while relighting his pipe. She knew he was trying to downplay the situation. But the tremor in his hands was an added sign he was nervous.

"There's something I've wanted to ask you for a long time," she went on, slowly. "Sometimes I think about it late at night, especially on really cold nights. Please don't think me impertinent, Father. I just can't help but recall when we helped the slave family escape. The memory of that little girl, Sena, is seared in my memory. Why didn't we ever do it again?"

Ebenezer sat back down in his chair, leveling his gaze directly on Hattie with the most severe and serious expression he had ever pointed in her direction. Then his head dropped and he shook it, obviously searching for words.

"I feel almighty compromised … by the city," he began, his speech halting. "We were … in a different situation then … living in the country."

"You mean we stopped because we moved to Utica?" she questioned, a little disbelieving.

"Well, uh, in part. There was certainly … more to lose in the city … than in the country," Ebenezer returned, trailing off.

"But you still support the cause," Hattie objected, feeling herself deflate slightly. "I saw you give him supplies from the shop. I want to be a part of that."

"No! No, you cannot be part of it! The Underground Railroad is no place for you," he ordered.

"But I feel so strongly about it," she begged. "I'm old enough to act on my convictions, Father. How can you deny me that?"

"I can stop you from making a mistake because I'm your father. My number one job is the protection of my family. That includes your reputation."

"But you taught me that equality is the principle of patriots. I took it to heart. Equality for all is my life's goal now," she persisted.

"Well, it can get a person arrested, fined and maybe hung nowadays," he practically yelled, getting right up in her face. "It is no place for an educated young woman."

"I still intend to stand up for my principles," she retorted defiantly. "Ignoring the wrongs and remaining silent is sinful. I've already decided to teach about the Indians. You've just helped me clarify where I'm going to fight."

Ebenezer left the room. Reeling, Hattie became a little

lightheaded and nauseated at the same time. She understood everything her father had said, but he had acted like she was a child. In addition, she felt hollow knowing what had really happened. Of all things, it sounded like economics had ruled out her family's activity with the Underground Railroad! Back then, were they poorer, but more selfless? Her father had made comparisons between the country and the city, as if that changed their beliefs. After all his teaching about values, equality, and doing the right thing, had success in the city trumped engagement in favor of reputation? It was hard for Hattie to understand that that's what put a stop to future rescues.

All evening, she turned their conversation over, finding it deeply troubling. Her father's stated belief had never wavered, she allowed. He always said his entire family was one hundred percent in favor of the abolition of slavery. But they had stopped acting like it! Even worse, her parents hadn't explained their lack of involvement to the children. All those years had gone by and during each one, Hattie expected to go on another rescue mission. She still did, which was the root of considerable restlessness.

The week before school adjourned, Hattie sat with classmates one afternoon enjoying the sunshine and chatting about the future. At the suggestion of UFA preceptress, Miss Kelly, weeks earlier, several had begun to assist with the children at various churches in the city. It was an excellent chance, she insisted, to practice their new teaching skills.

Hattie had jumped in with both feet and loved every minute of it. The opportunity not only confirmed her decision to teach, but acquainted her in a new way with Reverend Fowler. They shared a love of research, study, and writing. Hattie's help freed more of his time.

Other girls had their own stories, both funny and trying, about children's antics. They laughed at their own exhaustion after church on Sunday, but were glad the experiences created study breaks. It had been a rigorous academic year.

As the conversation wove its way from topic to topic, Hattie tried to assess her classmates' political leanings. To her knowledge, few were informed about the Indians. She shared her intent to teach beyond generalities and outside the usual subject matter.

"I want to be a teacher who sets the record straight about the Indians," she asserted.

"You want to teach Indians," a shocked classmate questioned. "Full or mixed bloods? I hope it's not the really violent ones. Lots of tribes hate each other, you know."

Taken aback, Hattie found herself silent. She had no idea how to respond. What kind of comment was that? This girl was informed, but did not agree with her. Someone coughed nervously and another laughed. Soon, the conversation went on.

But the girl's attitude quickened her resolve. That girl was exactly the kind of confused person who needed enlightenment. But, on second thought, her question had not related to Hattie's vision of teaching *about* Indians. She had asked about teaching the Indians themselves. Such an idea had never crossed Hattie's mind. Until now. The profound possibility sent her to the library where, in a quiet corner, she examined the possibility with vigorous interest.

Later in the afternoon, Hattie grew unusually tired. Had this new idea exhausted her? Whatever the cause, her energy flagged as if she might be getting sick. A dull ache throbbed behind her eye sockets. Nothing was worth risking illness.

Giving up at the library, she walked home, despite having told her parents she would study until late. Artemas was down in Burlington fishing, so the house was silent and peaceful. She went straight to bed and fell asleep immediately.

Awakened by faint, raised voices, Hattie knew she wasn't just dreaming. The sky had grown dark outside. Sitting up, she took a deep breath as her parent's conversation rose from downstairs. They were having an unedited discussion, probably because they had no idea she was in the house. Silently, she hid behind her door and listened.

"You can't be serious, dear," her mother was saying. "I've never known our Hattie to be confrontational."

"I didn't say that. She was more curious than strident," her father returned. "But there was almost an edge to her inquisitiveness. It stunned me for her to recall the events of that rescue years ago. She wasn't even in school then, was she? How did she recall so much?"

"Well, I certainly have never broached the subject with her again."

"Then, on top of that, she figured out who Mr. Dandridge was and why he took the harnesses. Maybe I've grown careless and become cavalier out of blind certitude. Or am I jaded like the South, believing God is on my side? If Hattie can figure out my activities, so could others," he concluded, troubled.

"You must be more vigilant. They'll throw you in jail if they catch you! Oh, how I hate this! We have come too far for our lives to fall apart now," her mother moaned.

"But that's not the end of it. She's interested in the cause now."

"In abolitionism? Well, what did you tell her?" her mother burst out frantically. "You mean she might get involved? We can't allow that! It's too dangerous."

"All right, all right," Ebenezer crooned to soothe her. "Don't get so upset."

"I can't help it," her mother raged. "After all these years, this is no time to let her turn back the clock and risk her life."

"She doesn't understand what happened back then," he returned. "I intimated that our business success and community standing guided the decision. It's just as well that way. She could never have been admitted to these schools if we had a questionable reputation or legal trouble."

"Oh Lord forgive," her mother whispered. "You have covered for me so many times since the girls died. I can never make it up to you. None of the children must ever learn that I almost lost my mind. All Hattie knows is that I was terribly controlling. She'll probably resent me forever, but I'd do it again rather than lose her."

"Let me handle it," he urged. "You just stick with being protective. Now let's calm down."

"Calm? How can I possibly be calm?" her mother fretted, pacing back and forth from the living to the dining room. "You just said Hattie wants to help escaping slaves! She hasn't a clue how much more charged and dangerous it has grown!"

"I told her no," Ebenezer clarified. "It was a hard conversation for me. As abolitionists, we have set extremely poor examples."

"But we still help the cause," her mother rationalized. "It's just from afar, that's all."

"I only hope I can hold her back."

"You must," she begged. "She cannot be allowed to do it. I won't give up another daughter—or the success we've fought for."

Then silence fell between them.

Stunned by her mother's words, Hattie groped for the edge of her bed. There in the dark, the wounding admission she had just overheard was almost more than she could accommodate. Her mother's statement about losing her mind crashed forward like a tidal wave. Had grief almost driven her mother insane?

All these years, Hattie had watched in puzzlement as her mother transformed into someone different at unexpected times. First, she was a loving mother, then a hovering caregiver when the girls became ill. After they died, she was devoid of emotion until the orphanage seemed to prompt fresh enthusiasm. Her presence remained remote and mechanical, however.

In the glare of reflection, everything fell into place now for Hattie. Her mother had emotional problems. The only thing that had soothed all those moody flare-ups and tempered the heavy control was helping orphans. What Hattie previously assumed about her mother must be forgotten and forgiven. Hugging her pillow close, she began to sort out the pieces of her shattered understanding.

At intervals, Hattie whispered the truth aloud to believe it. Her mother had almost lost her mind. That's why they had stopped doing Underground Railroad rescues. The decision obviously had little to do with moving to the city, becoming successful in business, or protecting their reputation. She almost resented her father for clouding the facts, but he obviously had no other choice.

Hattie sorted through memories of things that had never before made sense. Her heart felt crushed by every sort of emotion. Worst of all, she recognized that no questions could be asked. No details were forthcoming. This matter was just too sensitive and, besides, she had learned about it by eavesdropping. At first light, she decided to rush to Amanda's. Tomorrow couldn't come fast enough.

❖ ❖ ❖

Arriving during Amanda's breakfast, Hattie burst into the kitchen right after LeGrand had left for work. She barely got her breath before unleashing the torrent of her astonishing story. Quoting their mother word for word, she covered every detail. Amanda gaped and stopped chewing her bacon. Questions flew as they shed a few tears and puzzled over their mother's condition.

"We're stuck. We can't do or say anything to anyone," Amanda ventured. "There's no other way to look at it. We don't want to compromise her or bring disdain on ourselves."

"I guess you're right," Hattie agreed.

"She would be crushed to learn that we know," Amanda theorized. "She would be even more crushed if father told her that we know."

"I've never felt so helpless. Or confused," Hattie related. "All this time, I've been caught in my own interpretation of what was happening. I was rebellious because there wasn't an ample reason for her opposition. Suddenly, I've got to reverse course and feel compassion."

"That makes two of us. We must forgive her in our hearts," Amanda added. "And that's all there is to it."

❖ ❖ ❖

Moses Bagg, MD, commonly just called "Doctor" around Utica, was as clean-shaven a man as Ebenezer was whiskered. The cheerful doctor had cared for all members of Hattie's family at one time or another. Dr. Bagg was a Geneva Medical College graduate, and his sharp diagnostic eye and watchful care had brought many coughs to an end before lung trouble could set in. The Sheldons and many others literally trusted the doctor with their lives.

He had opened his medical practice in 1845, the same year Hattie's father established Ebenezer Sheldon and Son: Harness, Trunks & Bags. Both men had been born in Massachusetts, and their common heritage created an added kinship in Ebenezer's mind. Even though they didn't see eye to eye politically, Hattie's father regarded Dr. Bagg as a true friend and Christian of the first order.

Ebenezer sought out the doctor's advice from time to time on matters that had a civic component. The extended Bagg family had been in the Utica area a long time, having established Bagg's Hotel, a noted Utica crossroads stopover. Dr. Bagg enjoyed respect because of the hotel, but he never took advantage of the notables who stayed there. If character were his middle name, then compassion was a close second. Hattie thought of him like an uncle, so kind was his manner.

By the time her second sister had died, Dr. Bagg came and went from the Sheldon family home as if he, too, lived there. If anyone could have saved the girls, it would have been him. He had done everything possible to relieve their suffering. He said losing the girls broke his heart as if he were one of the family.

Hattie's mother appreciated Dr. Bagg's skills at the orphanage, too. She said it warmed her heart to observe his bedside attentiveness. He poured himself, heart and soul, into healing and had a soft spot for children.

Hattie thought back on times during her childhood when Dr. Bagg had looked in her throat and ears, examined the glands behind her ears for swelling, and reminded her to drink all her milk. At the time, she didn't grasp that he recognized her good mind and intellectual potential. Shortly before she left for Amherst, she had seen him and enjoyed a brief visit.

"When you complete your studies there, promise you'll return and attend Utica Female Seminary," he had urged, bushy eyebrows raised. "You're geared toward study, you know."

"You have always encouraged me," Hattie replied reflectively. "You really mean it, don't you?"

"Of course I do. From the time you were little, I knew you were cut out for scholarship. After teaching rhetoric and composition for a few terms, I know how to spot students of high caliber. You need that higher level of instruction."

When they had a recent conversation after her first year at UFA, she pointed out that his predictions had come true. She was gratified to have excelled academically. But, taking him into her confidence, she bewailed the city's shortcomings. Too many problems were plaguing Utica. More and more often, she was faced with its inadequate potential for meeting her long-term goals.

"I'm always available to explore options with you," he offered through a squinting smile. "And on another note, Mrs. Bagg and I will host a little supper next Friday. I vowed to see friends more in 1853. Please tell your parents. Come at seven o'clock sharp. We'll look forward to it."

Hattie could smell something fishy shortly after she stepped into the Bagg's home—and it wasn't the food. Mrs. Bagg must have an ulterior motive given that Hattie and one other young man were the only singles in the room. Hattie had never seen this pale, squinty person before. With any luck, he was just an out-of-towner and she would easily be off the hook.

Hiding her annoyance, she took notice of the beautiful table set for dinner. How could she handle this without offending Mrs. Bagg? On the other hand, discomfort was no cause for an impolite attitude, so she vowed to use good manners yet show no interest in the bookish young man. Shortly, Mrs. Bagg introduced them.

"Mr. Finis Cumbers, I'd like to present Miss Hattie Sheldon," she said expectantly. "Mr. Cumbers is our guest for a few days."

"How do you do, Mr. Cumbers?" Hattie greeted.

"I'm happy to make your acquaintance, Miss Sheldon."

Then Mrs. Bagg rushed to her supper preparations and they were left alone.

"It's so nice that you could visit Utica," she stammered. "What brought you here?"

"My father was at school with Dr. Bagg," he replied, blinking nervously. "I'm trying to narrow down my professional intentions, so Dr. Bagg invited me to shadow him for a few days in his medical practice."

"He's generous like that, our Dr. Bagg," Hattie responded. "What professions are you considering besides medicine?"

"An uncle of mine completed a horticultural course of study in England, and then remained there," he explained. "His profession is fascinating. But going to England to study would be a large undertaking. So, I'm giving the decision time."

"Are you interested in herbs or the medicinal use of plants?" Hattie asked, putting two and two together.

"Well, yes, but I'm inclined to focus more narrowly. My growing passion is the study of mosses and liverwort."

Hattie just nodded, unable to reply politely.

❧ ❧ ❧

Having broken free from dull Finis, Hattie hoped to speak with several other guests. Her gaze came to rest on Mr. Charles Mann, a gentleman revered personally and professionally as a founder of Utica Female Academy. She had known him for years. If she got stuck in another boring conversation with Finis, she knew she could direct a comment his direction and he would rescue her. But then Mrs. Bagg called everyone to the table.

"After church last Sunday," her father shared between bites of green beans, "George Wood and Robert Williams were transfixed by news of Admiral Perry's mission to Japan. Have you read any recent reports?"

"I'm struggling to find time for the headlines," Dr. Bagg replied, a little embarrassed. "It is spellbinding, though. The language differences alone are daunting, all the more the cultural chasm."

"I have a little news to relate," Hattie's mother chimed in. "I had forgotten to mention this until now. After church, while Ebenezer talked to George and Robert, I approached Abigail Whittlesey who was back for a visit."

"You don't say," Mrs. Bagg interjected excitedly. "I haven't seen her in years. It's good to hear she maintains Utica ties. How is *The Mother's Magazine* faring? With her success in journalism and printing, I figured she had disappeared into New York City society and forgotten us."

"Not at all. She knew everyone's name and her affection was genuine," Hattie's mother related. "While I waited to speak with her, Abigail told a compelling story about Samuel Wells Williams of the Williams printing family. I didn't realize he was born in Utica.

He's the one accompanying Admiral Perry on this mission to Japan as his official interpreter."

"Great Scott," Ebenezer snorted. "That's impressive. I wonder how he came to speak Japanese?"

"I know a little background on that," Charles Mann reported brightly. "Several years back, Williams visited this area. I attended a series of lectures he gave on his life and work. He's that kind of intellect who masters languages easily. He related how, in the early 1830s, he entered the employment of the American Board of Commissioners for Foreign Missions. They sent him to China to oversee their operation at the Canton Mission Press."

Hattie grew more interested by the minute about this adventurer. Translating between the Japanese and British on critical trade agreements must be a riveting profession. She envisioned Williams and the delicate thread of trust he was weaving between the two cultures.

"In China, he was editor of a leading periodical, *The Chinese Repository,*" Mann continued. "He mastered the Chinese language first, which helped get that journal into print."

"How old is Mr. Williams?" Hattie finally managed to ask.

"Abigail said he left for China in 1833, shortly after finishing his education. That was the same year you were born, dear," her mother winked.

"The printing business must be fascinating, especially abroad," Hattie mused out loud. "But printing in another language boggles my mind."

"I agree. Imagine gaining the necessary expertise," Dr. Bagg replied. "Bravo for him! Williams has brought us up in the world. Maybe you'll get involved with printing, Hattie."

Hattie smiled, already lost in thought. Gazing just past Dr.

Bagg's head, she stared at a large picture of a ship braving the high seas. Without doubt, Williams' pathway to the wider world had opened because of scholarship. He had parlayed a good education into printing expertise, only to have that catapult him to matters of state.

Printing had also led Mrs. Abigail Whittlesey to great acclaim and success with her magazine in New York City. This was exactly the kind of accomplishment Hattie aspired to. Perhaps, as Dr. Bagg suggested, she might inquire with organizations that employed people interested in printing. If anything kept her from teaching, she might just become a printer.

"That young man seemed interested in you," Hattie's mother commented lightly the next morning.

Hattie rolled her eyes. "He wants to study horticulture, mother. He was as dull as a plant."

"You say that now, but just wait," her mother warned. "If you keep that attitude, you may regret it. The privilege of having choices isn't lasting or universal. You won't be young forever. Only the young can remain picky about suitors."

"What does pickiness or youth have to do with it?" Hattie questioned. "I simply haven't met young men with whom I have much in common."

"That's because of your extreme positions," her mother retorted. "I don't know where on earth you will meet a man who understands this Indian obsession of yours."

Hattie balked. "It's not an obsession! I want to teach a truth that hasn't been well understood before."

"I'm sorry, dear, but that doesn't seem like a wise choice," her mother responded. "Before long, you're going to regret it and see that I'm right."

Hattie avoided as many boring young men as she could during her next three years at Utica Female Academy. She knew she would never regret it. Her devotion to study was unbending in comparison to many classmates. As predicted, many left school to marry and start families.

UFA's preceptress, Miss Kelly, maintained a long tradition of calling upon students in their homes. Hattie looked forward to the visit during her final year. Because she had signed up for more than five subjects in one term, Miss Kelly urged her to reconsider. At first, Hattie was confused, but found herself grateful later, as Kames' *Elements of Criticism* and Abercrombie's *Intellectual Philosophy* required much more study than she had anticipated.

Miss Kelly had one primary mission, and that was to make her students into the best female teachers in America. She practically preached that young women at UFA should go across the land to train other female teachers. Throughout their lifetimes, they must encourage a yearning for more education, she urged.

The idea of going anywhere in the United States of America took Hattie by storm. It gave birth to possibilities she had never before considered. The nation was immense and full of needs. Maybe Hattie could do something never before attempted by any woman in Utica, or even in the state. After all, she had earned academic honors that proved her capable even though she was a little embarrassed by the recognition. To her father, awards were no cause for becoming over-confident. However, she had to chuckle when he reminded Artemas of her accomplishments to prod better school work from him.

❊ ❊ ❊

One day in February 1856, after she submitted a paper at the faculty office, Miss Kelly asked Hattie to sit down.

"I understand you've been talking about the Indians, Hattie. What exactly is behind your plan to teach the real story?" Miss Kelly questioned.

"At Amherst, I learned of flaws in the accepted history of white/Indian relationships during America's founding," Hattie explained confidently. "It is incomplete, according to several sources. There's another side to the story that I want to bring forward."

"What are those sources?"

"A former professor at Amherst College has spent decades compiling facts that set the record straight. The Indians weren't always bad, and whites weren't always good, as we've been led to believe. The whites stole Indian land and reneged on agreements and treaties. They viewed themselves as having some kind of divine right to the Indians' land. The Indians response came in the form of reprisals, but often turned to murderous rampages. Both sides are to blame for the poor state of their relationship."

"This professor is your only source?" Miss Kelly questioned.

"Oh, no. Excuse me," Hattie apologized. "Another source is my actual family history. In Massachusetts, I learned about the infamous Deerfield Raid of 1704. The French and a large number of Indians came down from Canada to attack the English settlement. There's more to the story than is usually told. Too often, the Indians' side is discounted. I'm not saying their actions were totally justifiable, just that there are two legitimate sides to the story. Even members of my family blame the Indians solely."

"You do recognize that is controversial, don't you?" Miss Kelly asked, nursing a deep frown.

"But we must counteract that idea," Hattie countered, gaining fervency. "There is ample evidence if only people can be taught."

"Hattie, every person we know is descended from settlers and patriots. Because of their perseverance, we are free today. America is a republic, and we have democratic processes, not a king who rules as his fancy dictates. If your teaching favors the attackers and casts blame upon the brave souls who won our religious and political freedom, you will meet with stiff resistance. I, for one, don't want my forefathers to be the subject of disdain, and I know many more who feel the same way. Your point of view may have validity, but I don't have the stomach to take on the established history of our country. And I doubt the directors of Utica Female Academy or any other school will, either."

Crestfallen, Hattie shared the details of Miss Kelly's scolding with her mother. She hesitated beforehand, but felt she might explode if she didn't get it off her chest. Even though her mother had ruined her Underground Railroad dreams and balked when Hattie wanted more education, Hattie had forgiven her nonetheless. Her forgiveness was based on compassion. Hattie still craved her mother's support.

But her mother just threw her hands up and shook her head.

"What did you expect?" her mother queried. "Your position is overzealous!"

At that, Hattie removed herself from the room. The more obstacles she encountered, the more her mother failed to take her side. It was foolish to confide in her, because the outcome was predictable.

Exasperated, she turned to Amanda once again.

"Hattie, this is your blind spot," Amanda scolded, rolling her eyes. "You're missing the obvious."

"I have no idea what 'the obvious' is," Hattie replied argumentatively. "I would be relieved to grasp why mother is so unconcerned about my misery."

"You're interpreting it the wrong way," Amanda chided. "She's grateful that you're home. But she has little patience for your ups and downs. The same with teaching. She views these things as temporary."

"Temporary? What does that mean?" Hattie puzzled. "Does she think this frustration will suddenly disappear? Does she think an appropriate teacher position will just ... float into my hands tomorrow? And since my worries will go away soon, they don't matter right now?"

"No, silly," Amanda returned patiently. "It is clear to everyone *but you* that Mother wants you to give up on teaching! She wants you to marry and start a family here in Utica like me. That's her dream. Once you've settled down, she's sure you'll get over the hurt feelings and forget all this about the Indians."

Groaning, Hattie's fell backwards into the waiting arms of a soft chair. How could she and her mother so misunderstand each other? It never ceased to amaze her how different they were. She was hoping against hope to teach about the Indians, and her mother was hoping against hope that she wouldn't.

Hattie dreaded telling him, but decided her father would offer much needed perspective. He was always good at refining arguments and sorting out conflicts.

"I feel like nobody understands or respects my goal," she complained, her shoulders slumping.

"Don't let one skirmish determine the outcome of the bigger battle. That's where perseverance counts," Ebenezer boomed, raising a hand like a mounted soldier in battle.

"How do people keep pushing ahead when things look bleak?" she questioned. "I wish I had a role model."

"You do," he confirmed. "There's perseverance in your blood all the way back to our first role model in this country. Isaac Sheldon risked his life leaving England for America before 1650. Imagine the hardship of that?"

"You're right. But I'm still worried. Miss Kelly threw cold water on my plan. Like mother, she doesn't buy the other side of the story. I don't think she'll recommend me for a teaching job."

"It's way too early to give up. Remember that fellow Williams? He didn't learn Japanese and Chinese in a day, my dear. Sometimes, our plans don't unfold quickly. If you believe in your path, persevere against all odds."

Mustering her resolve, Hattie sat down on a chilly night in early March and began to draft letters to all area schools. She must not let Miss Kelly or her mother discourage her. She also couldn't afford to wait until graduation to look for a teaching job. Testing the market now made good sense. She had plenty of time to wait for replies. Using her time wisely also meant thinking hard about other options.

One of them was printing. Soon, she reflected on the dinner at Dr. Bagg's home. Perhaps it wasn't a total loss after all. The conversation offered leads she hadn't followed. She had let the boring encounter with Finis Cumbers cloud her thinking. Maybe some opportunities might come from that evening after all.

Could she really write for publications? Why not send a letter to Mrs. Abigail Whittlesey asking about positions at *The Mother's Magazine* and seeking advice on the printing profession? Perhaps she could even talk with someone in town from the Williams family about the printing business. Maybe it wasn't too far-fetched to attend a women's conference for ideas.

Meanwhile, her spring class assignments didn't appear as grueling as she had anticipated. With extra time on her hands, Hattie mustered fresh conviction and threw herself into work at the shop. She examined the place top to bottom. There were tasks left undone, housekeeping that had been ignored, and customer service that could be improved. She also intended to increase sales. All the place needed was a greater degree of sensitivity and more interest toward customers.

"They'll respond because I'm a good listener," she explained to her father. "I'll make them feel valued to win their repeat business. I can even improve the bookkeeping."

"Well, that remains to be seen. I realize you have more education than anybody else. But don't take over my whole operation," Ebenezer scolded lightheartedly. "You can help out in most areas. Leave the money side of things to me."

❖ ❖ ❖

Hattie kept her head down and worked harder than ever. She made a point of starting conversations with customers, often beginning with a practical compliment. If they could be drawn into some kind of exchange, perhaps she could better respond to their needs. To her delight, over the next couple of weeks, more and more customers began to respond to her efforts. Hopefully, her father would notice. She wasn't going to brag on herself, however, by pointing out her victories.

Then, much to her chagrin, other customers did not respond well. Women seemed more interested in chatting than buying. Some men misinterpreted her interest. The first time it happened, she was barely able to salvage the situation.

A strapping young explorer, clean but unkempt, had come into the shop. He had an appealing, crooked smile. Hattie waited on him and soon found his personality charming. The man seemed to linger, which made her wonder why he had so much leisure time. But to her disappointment, he left without making a purchase.

The next day however, he returned. This time, he was the one making conversation. Politely, he asked quite a few questions about her, Utica, and her father's business. As he purchased a new harness, Hattie was sure he was flirting with her and felt flattered. Before long, she was headlong in a discussion about his upcoming plans.

"Oh! So you're going out West!" she had responded innocently. "How exciting. I want some adventures like that, too."

"My fortune's in California," he shared.

"I've read about the gold rush," she commented. "You're brave to travel so far. I've dreamed of chasing a dream like that."

"With this new harness, my team of horses can make the trip in record time. All I need now is a good wife to support my efforts."

"I was thinking about you last night," he continued, getting down on one knee.

"Oh, uh, that's wonderful,'" Hattie interrupted nervously, stunned by what looked like the beginning of a proposal. She turned and pretended to arrange merchandise while talking as fast as she could. "I'm sure you'll succeed. Someday, after I graduate, I'll teach school and maybe go on adventures of my own."

"Oh, too good, are ya?" the man responded to her chagrin. He stood and threw his head back defensively. "I'm not schooled like you. But I'll be back with pockets full of gold. Then you'll be interested."

"I didn't mean any offense," she stammered. "There's no doubt you'll be a success."

"I'll be rich," he retorted stridently. "But I'll take my business to another harness shop where the young ladies are friendlier."

Hattie rolled her eyes as he left, hoping her father had not overheard the conversation. But when she turned, his brow was furled in a heavy grimace. To make matters worse, a second encounter with an interested man occurred. It totally unnerved her. She didn't want to go on adventures as someone's wife. They thought she was interested in *them*, but all she cared about was where they were going.

❖ ❖ ❖

"While you were at the library, one of father's customers asked about you at the shop today," Artemas announced gleefully to a surprised Hattie at supper. "He said you were as good-looking a sturdy woman as he'd met, and a risk taker. He wondered if I'd talk you into going out West with him."

"Sturdy? Of all the nerve," Hattie retorted icily. "Well, I hope you told him no."

"I told him you were a teacher," Artemas returned nonchalantly. "He said you might be a teacher, but because you were working in the shop, you were obviously looking for a husband."

"I AM NOT!" Hattie thundered, her eyes blazing. "The last thing in the world I want right now is a husband. And you can tell any customer who asks."

"Why, Hattie," her mother replied, looking hurt. "Don't say such a thing. God created families, and he blesses marriage. This independent streak of yours is going too far."

"Independent streak," Hattie mocked. "That's what you call all the effort and sweat and time of getting an education that cost Father good money? I believe in principal, and I intend to teach about equality for every soul. There's far more than mere independence on my mind."

"Now, ladies," Ebenezer interrupted seriously. "We won't have any more talk like this. We all have different opinions and varying motives. Hattie and I will discuss matters relating to the shop later. Let's keep our home a place of civil and loving discourse, if you please."

13

The Cherokees

"I have a special announcement to make before we begin this morning's offering," Reverend Philemon Fowler stated in a particularly excited tone the next Sunday at First Presbyterian Church.

"A few weeks back, a particularly prominent missionary friend wrote that he was planning a stop here later this month. It is his first visit back to our environs in over thirty years. That's how long his service and his loyalty to the Cherokee Indians have kept him from his family in Vermont."

The word "Indians" caught Hattie's attention.

"Reverend Samuel Austin Worcester serves the Park Hill Mission in the heart of the Cherokee Nation way out in Indian Territory," Reverend Fowler continued. "You may have read of him, as he is revered far and wide. I responded immediately, inviting him to speak to this congregation. I am delighted to report that he has agreed."

Hattie perched excitedly on the edge of the pew.

"This servant of God will preach here on Sunday, April 30. He is the first trained linguist ever to attempt a Bible translation into the Cherokee language. He also runs a printing press. I am sure his materials will touch many thousands in that far territory on the rugged frontier."

Hattie felt riveted by Reverend Fowler's words. She scarcely breathed while taking in every syllable about Indian Territory. If ever there was someone with whom she wanted to have a long conversation, it was this Reverend Worcester. For more than thirty years, he had devoted himself and his endeavors solely to the Cherokees? That was impressive. Without question, he would know their perspective in a most intimate way.

He also ran a printing press, which aligned with one of her new interests. What must Indian Territory look like, feel like? How advanced—or how backward—was the tribe, she wondered?

As her imagination looped around her thoughts, more questions began to pile up. She longed to meet someone inspiring who had lived a meaningful and directed life, like Reverend Worcester had. If she could talk to him, what should she expect? Her mind began to fill with ideas, hopes, interests, inquiries, and emotions.

After the benediction, during which she had prayed to God for guidance, Hattie sprang from her pew. Without explaining anything to her parents, she headed toward the narthex where Reverend Fowler always shook hands as congregants left the church.

"Oh, Reverend. Your announcement is too good to be true," she gushed. "My family will help organize meals for the Worcester family. Or we can entertain them. Anything. Please?"

"Why, Hattie," Reverend Fowler smiled, "you are first in line, aren't you? Yes, of course, I would be happy for you to help. In fact, I believe Reverend and Mrs. Worcester are bringing one of his daughters on the trip. She might need a friend. "

"That's perfect," Hattie replied excitedly. "Shall I call at the church this week for my assignment? I just have a strong sensation that something good will happen because of Reverend Worcester's visit."

"Thank you. That's wonderful," he returned appreciatively. "I will watch for you later this week."

❖ ❖ ❖

"I volunteered our family to help host the Worcesters from Indian Territory," Hattie announced after church.

"You did what?" her mother questioned, confused.

"Didn't you hear Reverend Fowler's announcement in church?" Hattie queried, certain they must have hung on every word as she did.

"To be honest, I just heard bits and pieces," her mother returned, looking disinterested. "He said someone will be speaking. Isn't that right?"

"No, Reverend Worcester is more than just an ordinary speaker," Hattie replied impatiently. "He works with the Cherokees in Indian Territory and hasn't been home to Vermont in more than thirty years. Reverend Fowler invited him to stop in Utica and teach us about the Cherokees. It's an astonishing and rare opportunity. That's why I volunteered our family to help host them."

"What did you say? Slow down," Ebenezer interrupted. "You volunteered us for what?"

"This incredible missionary and his family will be guests of our church," Hattie replied impatiently. "Church members are needed to help feed, entertain, and organize all kinds of things for them."

"What's the big hurry?" her mother replied impatiently. "Why did you do that without even talking to us about it?"

"Because I want to host him! I want to talk with him," Hattie replied in rapid fire. "I want as much time as possible to find out about his work and Indian Territory and the Cherokees and his translation work and the printing press."

"All right, all right," her father counseled as he patted her arm. "I'm sure we can reach an agreement for a reasonable amount of service. What's so urgent, Hattie?"

"I can't explain it. You wouldn't understand anyway. Just please help if we are given the chance. Promise me," she returned, growing weary of their reticence.

But she knew her father was right about her. She was overly excited and knew it. Her feelings related to teaching the whole story about the Indians. If Miss Kelly was to be believed, her plan would fall flat on its face. What might Hattie learn from Reverend Worcester to counter Miss Kelly and other detractors? For a long time, considerations went round and round in her mind and heart.

Now that Reverend Worcester was coming to Utica, she could test her theory against a true expert. Thinking back, her first feeling of destiny had come from Professor Colquhoun. What an inspiration to learn he had Indian blood. He had studied for more than half his life to unearth historical failings. Now, a second towering figure was coming to Hattie's town, Hattie's church, perhaps even Hattie's home to share more than thirty years' experience in Indian Territory!

"Tell me more about Reverend Worcester and his work with

the Cherokees," Hattie begged the next week in Reverend Fowler's study. "As missionaries go, why is he so unusual?"

"Oh my, Worcester's accomplishments could fill many books," he marveled. "His reputation precedes him in an awe-inspiring way. Not only is he the seventh pastor in his family, but he created a class all his own with the American Board, as well as with the Cherokees themselves."

"What's the American Board?" Hattie quizzed.

"His employer is the American Board of Commissioners for Foreign Missions, a large missionary organization—largely Congregationalist—that is based in Boston," he shared. "It has sent missionaries around the globe. Lots of them."

"Isn't that the same group that hired Samuel Wells Williams? He went to China and worked on the printing press there," Hattie recollected.

"Why, yes. How in the world did you know that?"

"One night at Dr. Bagg's we were talking about Admiral Perry's expedition to Japan," Hattie explained. "Mr. Williams is the Admiral's translator. He was born here in Utica. Before Japan, he was sent to China by the American Board."

"You have a good memory."

"How can I help with the Worcester's visit?" she persisted.

"I will ask him to preach twice on Sunday. I'd like to have a supper gathering on Monday, so perhaps you might coordinate with Mrs. Fowler on that. His daughter, Mary Eleanor, will likely need a young companion like you. And maybe your mother can help host her stepmother, Mrs. Erminia Worcester. As the time draws nearer, our plans will become more detailed."

"That's wonderful," Hattie accepted. "I will follow up right away. But tell me some more stories."

"If I start, we might be here until next week," he laughed. "I'd love to share more, Hattie, but have to go to a meeting. Here's an idea though. For years, I've clipped newspaper articles about Reverend Worcester. Why don't you take them and acquaint yourself with how he made history."

"I can't wait to get started," she beamed.

"All right. Let me share one final tidbit that will surprise you," he added. "I have never met Worcester face to face. After he went to prison for his loyalty to the Cherokees, I began to write to him. He thanked me, and it began a fascinating and edifying correspondence that has lasted many years. Does that surprise you?"

Hattie couldn't believe her ears. "I'm not surprised, I'm speechless."

❁ ❁ ❁

Hattie digested the articles as if she were a starving animal at a five-course meal. She read most of the night, only stopping when twilight approached and the birds chirped outside her window. The information was satisfying, heartwarming, and motivating. Sleep came easily.

When she woke up, it was nearly nine a.m. She knew her father would frown when she arrived late at the shop. But, as fate would have it, he had left early to make a delivery some miles away. He wouldn't return until afternoon, so Hattie breathed a sigh of relief.

Immediately, her thoughts returned to the incredible life of Reverend Worcester. His story was positively riveting. Born in Vermont, he was a descendant of the late, esteemed Governor John Winthrop's sister, Lucy, as well as Reverend John Edwards' sister,

Esther. Desiring higher education, he had left Vermont and moved to Massachusetts, just like Hattie.

Reverend Worcester's alma mater was Andover Theological Seminary. It was a half day's journey from Boston, the headquarters of The American Board of Commissioners for Foreign Missions. Although Hattie had never gotten around to visiting Boston, she could almost picture its wide streets and famous ocean pier, the site of the Boston Tea Party. That was one of her father's favorite stories from the colonial period.

Within two years of graduation in 1823, Worcester had married, gained ordination, and left New England to serve the Cherokee Indians first in Tennessee, then in Georgia. Earlier, as the population of the United States continued to expand, competition for land grew. This created tension for the Cherokees, who owned massive numbers of acres across several southeastern states. Ancestral tribal lands had become part of those states. Soon, the Indians found themselves at cross-purposes with state governments because they intended to remain on their own lands and govern their own nation. The states were opposed to the tribes' independence and their claims on land within state borders.

Cherokee land in Georgia was of particular concern. The township of New Echota, Georgia, had been selected as the Cherokee's independent capital in 1825. They would not compromise their sovereign status, as evidenced by the well-publicized written constitution they adopted in 1827. That was the same year Reverend Worcester took up his missionary work with them.

The idea of Indians having a constitution and a capital was looked upon with disdain by opponents. After all, these were signs of increasing tribal sovereignty and permanent status. The State of

Georgia did not approve and turned to the national government for help as land values increased. Georgia wanted to remove the Indians.

Meanwhile, Worcester established the first Indian printing press. He toiled using Sequoyah's new alphabet to translate the Bible into Cherokee and get it into print. Soon, participation in tribal matters led him to correspond with officials on behalf of the tribe. He grew more and more loyal as their challenges mounted.

In 1828, gold was discovered not far from New Echota. Swarms of white squatters began to plot ways to take Cherokee land. Georgia sought authority over the Cherokee Nation and led the way for several other states, including Tennessee, North Carolina, and Alabama, to also decide to remove the tribe.

Hattie already knew that the controversial Andrew Jackson, who was elected to the Presidency in 1828, harbored antipathy toward Indians. In 1829, he revealed his Indian removal policy, which passed Congress the next year. Emboldened, Georgia demanded that residents swear allegiance to the state. Worcester challenged the law because it forbade whites to set foot on Cherokee land without a state license. His loyalty to the tribe was more than confronted when a lawsuit was filed in retaliation. Asked to leave the state, he refused and was arrested along with several other missionaries.

They were convicted and sentenced to four years in prison at hard labor. Declining a pardon, Worcester appealed in 1832 so the case could be heard by the U.S. Supreme Court. The Cherokees had hoped for a legal remedy defining their sovereignty by clarifying the nature of the state and federal relationship.

In its final ruling, the Supreme Court ruled that the Georgia law was unconstitutional since states could not pass laws disrespecting the sovereignty of Indian tribes. This meant that the Cherokee Nation was independent. Only the national government, not states, had authority in matters relating to Indians. Thus, the sovereignty of the Cherokees made Georgia laws void in Cherokee Territory.

But the state of Georgia ignored the decision, and the governor kept Worcester imprisoned. Even worse, President Andrew Jackson refused to enforce the ruling of the Supreme Court. In 1833, a new Georgia governor finally offered to pardon Worcester if he would refuse to work among the Cherokees. He declined, but was freed eventually and left Georgia, realizing the Cherokees could not win.

Worcester believed his future efforts would be best spent in the place where the Cherokees would likely end up, the new Indian Territory. This fertile region, west of the 95th Meridian and other white settlements, was not part of any other organized territory. The government made it available in exchange for Cherokee lands ceded in the Southeast. Worcester moved there in 1836 to prepare for the Cherokees' arrival on the unbroken frontier.

Meanwhile, a highly educated minority faction of the Cherokees continued its work behind the scenes. This group believed survival trumped loyalty to the land. Its members favored voluntary removal to Indian Territory. On December 30, 1835, they voted unanimously in favor of a secret instrument called the Treaty of New Echota. The secret treaty agreed that the Cherokees would willingly depart all Cherokee ancestral lands located east of the Mississippi River. In exchange, the tribe would receive remuneration in the amount of five million dollars, title to the new frontier lands in Indian Territory, educational funds, and payment for lands the tribe would vacate east of the Mississippi.

The Congress of the United States not only entertained the fraudulent treaty but voted to ratify it on May 23, 1836. The fate of the Cherokees was sealed. But when the majority of the tribe found out, cries and protests made headlines. The principal chief, angered by the dissident minority, declared the treaty a fraud and lobbied angrily in Washington, D.C. But there was no reversing it.

What followed was a deadly break in the tribe, marked by vows of revenge. Many also began to mourn because, soon, they must remove to Indian Territory. The only life they had ever known was ending and, with it, separation from the sacred ground containing the graves of their forefathers.

❖ ❖ ❖

For days, Hattie read nothing else but the newspaper clippings. She absorbed all the details of the Cherokees, their ancestral land, Reverend Worcester, the legal wrangling, and the new Indian Territory. The story had to be pictured to absorb its details and complications, so she drew a map and a timeline. The minority faction sounded very sophisticated in the particulars of legislation, while the majority seemed loyal to an agrarian life. The Cherokees and their history were complicated. Perhaps that answered why a man of Worcester's caliber had devoted his life to them. Hattie realized there was much more to learn.

❖ ❖ ❖

At her next opportunity to speak to Reverend Fowler, she was ready with a page of questions.

"When did you first write to him?" she inquired.

Reverend Fowler responded seriously. "His imprisonment was the subject of great scorn in religious circles. How terrible for such a good man to be swept up by unsavory political maneuverings. I was just finishing at university then, and he was a role model. I wanted to encourage him."

"He kept writing back to you?" Hattie commented. "That's so interesting."

"Yes, and his spirit was astonishing. I could tell that he was an extraordinary individual," Reverend Fowler explained. "He was so appreciative of my prayers. It mattered not to him that there was a difference in our ages. And so we simply continued to communicate, share information, and encourage one another."

"Tell me more about the American Board of Commissioners for Foreign Missions," Hattie asked.

"When we speak of foreign mission agencies," he detailed, "the American Board ranks as the first, having received a charter fairly early in this century, I believe. Unlike many other organizations that represent only one denomination, the American Board is Congregationalist and Presbyterian. But it is also supported by Dutch-Reformed and Associated Reformed denominations, among others."

"Do they have missionaries all over the world?" Hattie asked.

"To my knowledge, it is quite comprehensive, yes," Reverend Fowler replied. "East Asia is heavily involved, as is Africa. And even here on the North American continent, there is a significant presence among non-Christian peoples who remain uneducated."

Then Reverend Fowler paused, turning sideways slightly. "Why do you ask so many questions? What is behind your interest?"

"Honestly, I should have a better answer than I do," Hattie answered, slightly apologetic. "For some time, I have nursed a growing interest in other cultures. I'm drawn by the needs of people beyond the realm of expectation for young women. You already know that I want to teach. I'm riveted by people who have suffered great injustice, such as slaves and Indians."

Tipping back in his chair, Reverend Fowler questioned, "Do you have firm plans for your future yet?"

"Besides teaching, I am interested in printing," Hattie replied slowly. "Teaching about the Indian seems beyond my grasp, for some reason. I can't figure it out. I'm treading water, looking for the right fit, but no schools seem interested. From all indications, my future is not here in Utica."

"I have questioned that for some time," he returned. "I'm glad to hear you're open to something else. You never know what awaits you. In my line of work, one becomes practiced at recognizing the God-given gifts of others. Your gifts are a sharp intellect and a strong constitution. You were wiser than your peers at a young age. Maybe that came from the devastation over losing your sisters. Now, it appears you are focusing upon a still foggy, distant goal that you know, in your heart of hearts, is beckoning you."

"That's exactly it," Hattie whispered.

"I believe our great teacher and protector of the Trinity, the Holy Spirit, has his hand on you," Reverend Fowler smiled. "You don't know what you're looking for, but you have an unexplainable certainty that it's out there and it's meant for you. Commit your future to God. Things will come clear in his time."

When she should have been sleeping, Hattie was kept awake by the Cherokees' sad story and their unthinkable miseries. Some of them had departed willingly for Indian Territory. But many more refused to leave for the new homeland the government had selected for them. Soon, the military began an operation to forcibly remove the remaining majority. White squatters wanted their fully furnished homes, complete with clothing and keepsakes. Even worse, women and children were rounded up at gunpoint.

Hattie related her easy, secure circumstances to the Cherokees' tenuous and disrupted lives. Without doubt, they would consider Hattie's comfortable home and room and bed to be unattainable luxuries. It hurt her to imagine them herded into temporary camps. What followed was a forced, wintry march across hundreds of miles. She could not fathom how many Cherokees died.

Meanwhile, preparations for the Worcester family visit began immediately. At church the next Sunday, Reverend Fowler offered more details.

"Our congregation's long support for missions will be rewarded. And our younger members will come face to face with a man whose entire life has been in service to God's work in extremely difficult places."

After the service, Hattie's family lingered to talk with friends. On their way out, Reverend Fowler stopped Hattie.

"Since you have such an interest in organizing, I'd like your help with another important project."

"Of course," Hattie nodded. "For the Worcester's visit?"

"Actually no. It's something else. Did you hear that my assistant is moving away? Our annual baptism down at the river is coming up," Reverend Fowler explained. "Would you consider helping me with the arrangements?"

"Have you set a date yet?" Hattie inquired. "It seems like some church is down there most days during warm weather. Do all denominations baptize the same way?"

"I've narrowed it down to two days," Reverend Fowler returned.

"As to your second question, baptism styles vary. The immersion versus aspersion versus affusion debate continues. Baptists only immerse. Presbyterians generally practice aspersion or affusion. "

"That's interesting. And yes, I would be happy to help you," Hattie replied. "I love organizing things."

"Oh, bless you. That's a weight off my shoulders," he returned. "Pray that the weather cooperates. We will walk in our usual chain, hands clasped, across the footbridge. I chose an area for the congregation just a few yards from last year's location. It's a nice little sandbar. The river isn't deep there."

When she wasn't studying or working at the shop, Hattie's mind settled on the Indians. She recalled the newsletter article that had caught her attention years before. There had been violent fights between Indians and whites over land. The idea of forced removals still made her shudder. A library article she discovered called the Indians' grueling journey a heartless death march.

Finally, finally, she was going to have the chance, firsthand, to find out more about native Indians, their ties to the land, and the aftermath of Indian removals. She could hardly contain her excitement. Try as she might to remain calm, she was formulating all kinds of questions in her mind as she waited for Reverend Worcester's arrival, and some of those questions had been bubbling around for years.

Refocusing on her school obligations and future, Hattie followed up on her applications for teaching positions. Two schools had no jobs available. A few only hired male teachers. Others said they wanted only the traditional version of Indian history to be taught.

Hattie didn't want to give in to doubts, but soon, she had heard back from all her applications. There were no available teaching positions in the local Utica schools. Even her inquiry about teaching after graduation at Utica Female Academy had met with skepticism. She wasn't sure where to turn next.

"There is always the possibility of serving as a governess," Ebenezer reminded to ease her frustration. "I'm sure we could identify families with means who would love someone like you."

"That's so sweet, Father," Hattie replied, trying to be sensitive. "But frankly, I'd much rather work in the shop."

14

Reverend Samuel Austin Worcester

Reverend Worcester's coming was an event in itself. It was almost a spectacle. When he first stepped off the train, his conservatively cut but tattered black topcoat only emphasized his unusual height and thin frame. Several young girls surged forward to present him with flowers. Applause broke out. As polite introductions were made, Hattie sought to hide her surprise at how angular this man's frame was. Nobody missed Reverend Worcester's presence.

Hattie smiled at the humble joy on his boyish face upon meeting his longtime correspondent, Reverend Fowler. They embraced, Worcester thanking Fowler for his friendship. As they talked, Worcester's deep-set eyes sparkled. Gesturing expressively with his worn hands, he seemed both a man from the wilderness and one who possessed city graces. He also looked faded enough to suggest a rather hard life.

Standing close beside him on the platform was his wife, Erminia. She looked current but conservative in a green day dress with a wide collar of crochet extending across the plaid dress's shoulders. Next to her stood Worcester's daughter, Mary Eleanor, in a dark skirt, white batiste blouse and waist-belt with buckle. Noting how little the brunette women resembled each other, Hattie remembered that Erminia Worcester had married into the Worcester family recently. Reverend Worcester's first wife, Ann, died shortly after giving birth to Mary Eleanor. The two women standing before Hattie functioned as mother and daughter, but actually were not blood relatives.

Mrs. Worcester was tall and, as Hattie's mother would word it, substantial. Her dark, coarse hair lay in barely managed curly waves beneath a well-worn hat. Compared to her husband's fine features, she had a strong, broad nose, forehead, and jaw. By contrast, Mary Eleanor was slender, pale, and almost delicate, her face reflecting many aspects of her father's features. When Mrs. Fowler welcomed them, both said they were pleased by the clamor but shocked by the applause.

Mary Eleanor accepted a bouquet of flowers from a little girl and then looked as if she didn't know what to do. Her mother took the flowers and offered something of a bow, which Hattie found slightly funny. Maybe it was for want of rest. Undoubtedly, their journey had been long, so they must be terribly tired. Perhaps they were also a little out of sorts, she concluded.

As helpers gathered their severely worn bags, some difficulty arose about handling. Mary Eleanor inched back behind her step-mother, as if the activity threw her off guard. Erminia Worcester frowned. Someone pointed the way to the waiting carriage, but she seemed fixated on the bags.

"Please be careful," Mrs. Worcester scolded the man with the bags. Her tone was sharp but then she seemed to catch herself. "I mean to say, thank you, but my bag is about to break."

Unlike Reverend Worcester's narrow bag, Mrs. Worcester's looked like it might burst at the seams. Perhaps she wanted to be prepared for any eventuality, or maybe she brought everything she owned. After all, she had never met her husband's family in Vermont.

Once the crowd thinned somewhat, Hattie stepped up to introduce herself according to Reverend Fowler's instructions. As she approached, there was no mistaking that Mrs. Worcester suddenly disciplined Mary Eleanor with a snarling, exasperated sound. Hattie almost jumped back. But when Mrs. Worcester saw her, an instantaneous transformation took place and her expression turned charming, while her tone became melodic. Nevertheless, Hattie knew what she had heard and realized that Mrs. Worcester was forcing the gentility.

Mary Eleanor Worcester responded to the snarl with panic and nervousness. She became silent upon Hattie's approach, her eyes apologetic. Hattie hid her discomfort while exchanging a minimal version of her planned conversation. Then she took her leave. There was no denying that Mrs. Worcester was annoyed and anxious. Likewise, Mary Eleanor's hands were as cold as ice and trembling.

"The progress of mankind through time must be mirrored by the advancement of Christianity," Reverend Worcester asserted. He stood much taller in the pulpit than the diminutive Reverend Fowler ever had. "The lack of education among the Cherokees perpetuates time-worn practices that are decidedly non-Christian. My charge, supported by generous donations from churches like yours all over New England, is to share and reiterate, through endless acts of benevolence, the worth of the Cherokees. By reaffirming my acceptance of their unique humanity, it opens the door to the only real path of faith for them."

Continuing, he added more to the congregation's understanding. "This effort requires great endurance, as the Cherokees, from their origins, never contemplated any kind of life that was superior to the one they lived. But whites insisted that it was so. Sadly, as they responded to change, Cherokee exposure to white Christians only brought them into contact with aggression, covetousness, and lack of trustworthiness. In turn, whites found the Cherokees imperceptibly different because of their total lack of individualism. Cherokee culture is communal, as is their view of the spiritual. To bring salvation, we can only succeed if we love them deeply."

In the sanctuary, not one sound interrupted his words, so captivating was his presence. Hattie nodded in agreement at his main points. When he gestured heavenward reverentially, his long arms, adorned in black, resembled the outstretched wings of a magnificent bird. He was regal to Hattie, even in his humbleness.

Worcester's points aligned with stories and lessons shared by Professor Colquhoun. The only difference between the two men, as she distilled the many issues, was that Worcester lived among Indians. Therefore, his knowledge had a more gripping edge to it. Until today, Hattie had never envisioned that another highly educated man could assume a more compelling place in her thoughts than Professor Colquhoun. But Worcester had unusual, motivational power. He used words like tools, crafting them into perfect products, just like her father did with leather.

From the moment he climbed to the pulpit, Hattie had watched his placid demeanor transform into a convincing expression. There was fire behind his galvanizing words, but it was the kind that changed a person's heart. He had convicted her right then and there with the absolute rightness of his point.

"Indians are our fellow man," he was saying. "There is no truer evidence of God's love than how we treat our fellow man."

❖ ❖ ❖

Hattie prepared some of the food herself for Monday evening's supper, the highly anticipated time when she might talk with Reverend Worcester about the Indians. The gathering was small in the comfortable atmosphere of the Pastor's parlor. Several people sat quietly and listened attentively to the interesting things Reverend Worcester had to say. He was calm and fatherly, Hattie thought.

"Tell us about the rest of your family, Reverend," someone asked.

On this point, Hattie was most curious. If she could picture his family, she would be able to form a complete vision of his life and understand better how he lived.

"God has blessed me with six wonderful children," Reverend Worcester replied, smiling. "I have four daughters and two sons."

Two of his daughters, Ann Eliza and Sarah, were teachers in Indian Territory. The majority of missionary teachers there had eastern educations. His eldest, Ann Eliza, was schooled in Vermont and, like her father, enjoyed languages and translation work. Now married, she and her husband were working in the Creek Nation, about a day's journey from Reverend Worcester. Sarah, his second daughter, had graduated from Mt. Holyoke in Massachusetts and then taught Cherokee girls until she married a local physician.

As fate would have it, the third daughter, Hannah, was just one year younger than Hattie. She was dear to him because, even as a little girl, she shared his love of the printing press. At this mention, Hattie took special note because of her growing interest in printing.

Hannah had become an essential helper to Reverend Worcester, he related, and played a key role in his ability to complete the many printing jobs, both sacred and secular, with which he was tasked. Hattie knew the press was a pivotal part of his ministry in Indian Territory.

Continuing with his response, Reverend Worcester beamed when speaking about his sons.

"Leonard, my eldest son, will graduate this spring from St. Johnsbury Academy in Vermont. My youngest son, John Orr, will begin his education at that same institution soon."

❀ ❀ ❀

As a teaching pastor, Ebenezer had pointed out, talking to people in all settings was Reverend Worcester's forte. They seemed to be drawn to him. Patiently, he had fielded question upon question after his second sermon on Sunday afternoon. Of interest to Hattie was the fact that the questions came mainly from young men. She didn't mind being the unusual curious female in the fray, though. Whenever she got the chance, she was ready with a new question and couldn't wait for his always compelling response.

"How do the Cherokees characterize their own situation?" she asked seriously. "Reports claim the government paid them handsomely to relocate to Indian Territory. What do they say?"

"Most of the Cherokee people had no choice about coming to live in the new place. That's why you hear the word 'removal.' They were literally removed, forced to leave. But, thankfully, they are gifted with great patience," Reverend Worcester returned thoughtfully. "They also have tremendous endurance. Compensation was promised, but it is not their way to publicly disparage the government, even though many take issue with reports in newspapers."

He did not confirm any payment, Hattie realized. Instead, he praised the character of the Cherokees. She felt deep compassion between the lines of his response. She also sensed a stirring in her own spirit. It was more than a feeling and, with each new piece of information about life in Indian Territory, it grew in strength. She felt she understood the Cherokees, even though she had never met even one member of the tribe. Reverend Worcester's story was more than compelling—it drew her.

If asked, she would describe it symbolically as though looking up when sunbeams broke through the clouds. A streaming effect, a glittering flash of light, a resonating illumination—all were akin to her growing realization. She felt like dawn was breaking in her soul. Perhaps this related to what Reverend Fowler meant when he said that her future would soon become clear.

❖ ❖ ❖

The next day, having rested from the trip, the Sunday services, and Monday's dinner, the Worcester family was given a tour of Utica. Local merchants had added festive touches to their displays in preparation for May Day on May 1st. The very idea of May arriving meant summer warmth was close behind. The prospect of warm weather improved everybody's mood in a cold climate like Utica.

After class, Hattie hurried to the church. As luck would have it, she was present when something unexpected occurred. The supper planned at the Fowler parsonage that evening had to be cancelled.

Reverend Fowler had just received word about the sudden, serious illness of a close relative. Folding the message he had just read, he sagged into his chair, a worried hand on his forehead.

"I have to leave immediately. We won't be able to host the Worcesters tonight," he sighed in frustration.

Without hesitation, Hattie stepped forward. "I can help if you'll let me. My family can easily host the meal."

Although distracted, Reverend Fowler agreed. They reviewed the details and what was already prepared. He seemed relieved that the evening could be redeemed for the Worcesters.

Hattie knew exactly what steps she would take. First, she headed for the Fowler home, grabbing Artemas from the shop on her way. Together, they packed and moved a rich soup and two joints of meat that Mrs. Fowler had already prepared.

Rushing the cooked food into their home, Hattie explained the situation to her mother.

"Can we please serve your mince pies?" she begged, looking at the freshly baked desserts cooling on the stove.

"You are stretching the limits of my patience," her mother moaned. "We have less than two hours."

Artemas made another trip at Hattie's instruction to see Amanda, who was asked to bring bread, homemade jam, and fresh butter. Before the Worcesters arrived, the meal and table looked almost perfect.

Ebenezer couldn't hide his pride over the change of events. He was honored, and it showed, Hattie thought. In fact, he looked so pleased that he must have something up his sleeve.

"I'm most curious about your modes of transportation in Indian Territory," he questioned gingerly during the meal.

Of course, Hattie laughed to herself, this question would come first. Her father's leather and harness business equipped every manner of transport. Politely, Reverend Worcester described the various wagons common in Indian Territory, making allowances for the endurance of many people who only owned oxen or perhaps just a horse. Ebenezer congratulated him for helping close such an unhappy chapter for the Cherokees while opening the frontier.

This recent journey that brought the Worcester family to Utica was compelling in itself. They had come by stage, boat, rail, and wagon. The last leg of their travels, which wasn't yet in sight, would reunite Reverend Worcester with his family of origin for the first visit since he had left over thirty years before. At this, Hattie marveled; she was already missing Aunt Mary in Massachusetts so much. How he must have missed his loved ones. But Reverend Worcester, a godly man, had placed his mission first for thirty years!

"Reverend, I have pondered how we might show appreciation for your willingness to spend a few days in Utica," Ebenezer offered later. "Hearing of your arduous journey, I think I made the right gift choice for your family."

"Oh, that isn't at all necessary, Mr. Sheldon," Reverend Worcester replied, concern crossing his face.

"I insist. Consider it a mission contribution, if you must," Ebenezer argued. "Artemas, please bring the items in from the other room, won't you?"

Hattie had been straining to hear two sets of conversation. Ebenezer's unexpected announcement took her off guard, coming at the moment Erminia Worcester inquired of her mother about Utica's lunatic asylum. That was where Hattie's oldest brother, George, worked. Of all the topics in the world, Hattie wondered why this one would interest Erminia.

"There is no institution, no provision whatsoever for people who suffer nervous system terrors or are emotionally incapacitated in Indian Territory," Erminia Worcester offered as Artemas left the room. Hattie couldn't miss the fact that Mary Eleanor flushed a bright red after the remark. It seemed that Erminia showed great curiosity about anything related to health.

Curious about what Artemas was bringing, Hattie continued to watch the nervous Mary Eleanor. Had she ever traveled before, Hattie wondered? From her brief observation of Mary Eleanor, she had yet to form a complete opinion about what kind of temperament the young woman had.

"Ah, here he comes," Ebenezer trumpeted as Artemas entered with three trunk-like carrying cases.

Erminia Worcester's head swiveled, her attention riveted upon the carrying cases. To Hattie's surprise, she let out a sudden hoot of joy. The shock of it so surprised Ebenezer that he flinched involuntarily.

"Ohhh, how absolutely tremendous of you, Mr. Sheldon," Erminia gushed, jumping from her chair to examine the carrying cases. "When I asked about your merchandise, I didn't expect, uh, I didn't think of goods like these. Just saddles and harnesses and the usual."

"Don't mention it," Ebenezer responded lightly. "I couldn't miss an opportunity. You folks can do a little free advertising for my products on your travels!"

"Mother, may I have the grey one please?" Mary Eleanor asked tentatively, looking sideways for approval. She stroked the buttery leather that Ebenezer had crafted so beautifully.

"Oh, I rather wanted that one. But, all right," Mrs. Worcester sighed, taking a bit too long to choose between the remaining two cases. The way she said it sounded like her concession was a great one. Finally, she picked the brown one and handed the black one to her patiently waiting husband.

"This is a most generous gift," Reverend Worcester offered, his eyes moist in wonder. "You have no idea how much we will treasure these. Our own bags and hampers are in bad shape, but I couldn't justify the expense to the American Board for new ones."

Hattie watched the glint of excitement in Reverend Worcester's eyes, as if he were a lucky child at Christmas. She was glad to see the human side of this intensely dedicated man who had sacrificed many comforts.

As the evening progressed, the two families seemed to learn from one another on topic after topic. The Sheldons knew little of the frontier, and the Worcesters had long been away from life in any city. Hattie couldn't get enough of what she was hearing.

When Reverend Worcester turned to talk with Artemas, she felt it only right to concentrate on Mary Eleanor.

"Are there efforts toward statehood for Indian Territory?" she inquired. "I know that neighboring Arkansas and Texas are states. What about pro- and anti-slavery debates?"

Mary Eleanor gave Hattie an utterly blank look followed by a long, searching stare toward her father for help. But he had not heard. The silence was uncomfortable, so Hattie pushed forward, hoping to have better luck on other subjects. After asking a few more polite questions, she learned that Mary Eleanor had a limited interest in things she found fascinating.

For instance, she was dying to discuss the Cherokees, their education, and the improvement in their way of life after their forced removal. Her curiosities about the needs of the Cherokees, after all, were deep. She wanted to understand their situation in detail, as well as how the missionaries met their needs. It also seemed obvious that northern-educated missionaries must share the Sheldon's abolition stance. Hattie envisioned a place where slavery did not cause political maneuvering. This must be the case with the Cherokee Nation.

But Mary Eleanor brushed aside anything about statehood, abolition, or the Cherokees. Whatever she was asked, she avoided, demurred, or laughed at it nervously. Hattie had never interacted with someone like this before and wasn't sure what to do. Mary Eleanor didn't make eye contact and seemed to have no other curiosity than getting a new dress and meeting her cousins in Vermont for the first time.

"All my life, I've dreamed of beautiful dresses, romantic parties, and the thrill of city life," Mary Eleanor whispered. "One of the boys at church yesterday asked if he could write to me!"

This struck Hattie as the absolute antithesis of Reverend Worcester. How could such an outstanding, wise man have a daughter who seemed to have no depth whatsoever? She was old enough to be past this stage. But Hattie felt obligated to pursue light conversation with her anyway. Little more was needed than an occasional nod during Mary Eleanor's jumpy, excitable chatter.

Soon, supper ended and brought a welcome break from Mary Eleanor. While clearing dishes, Hattie shook off the girl's silliness and then realized she was missing an opportunity. Since her mother had ample help from Amanda, Erminia, and Mary Eleanor, Hattie could make better use of the time. Who cared about the dishes? This might be her one chance to talk with Reverend Worcester one on one!

So, Hattie returned to the table to engage Reverend Worcester in conversation. Upon seeing her intent, her father sat back, looking curious. Hattie made initial inquiries about Indian Territory. Unexpectedly, instead of offering facts and stories, Reverend Worcester proceeded to show great respect for her observations, educational accomplishments, and interests. To her surprise, he began to ask her questions instead of the reverse.

"Oh, you're a graduate of Amherst Academy," he nodded. "It's just down the road from Mt. Holyoke, where my daughter Sarah was educated. Many Amherst graduates went on to attend Mt. Holyoke."

"I hear it's a wonderful school. Some of my friends are there now. But I'm happy at Utica Female Academy," Hattie returned. "Our preceptress promises she'll make us into the best teachers in America."

"Traditionally, the Cherokees have preferred eastern-educated teachers for their schools," Reverend Worcester explained to a wide-eyed Hattie. "Candidates need unique spiritual, social, and educational capabilities, as well as a strong constitution. The unexpected is standard fare in Indian Territory."

"Maybe demand for women teachers there is greater than it is here," Hattie commented, then decided not to pursue that topic. "May I ask a few other questions about the Cherokees?"

"Why, certainly," Reverend Worcester responded, taking a sip of coffee. "They are my favorite topic of conversation."

Just then, Hattie's mother brought fresh mince pie to the table. Once she was seated again, she resumed a conversation with Erminia Worcester. Meanwhile, Hattie did her best to focus on Reverend Worcester so she would not be drawn away by the women.

"I've read some about Indian removals. America's leaders didn't pursue much continuity with regard to Indian policy, did they?" she inquired.

"That is a sad fact that contributed to their loss of sovereignty," Worcester related. "Jefferson respected the native inhabitants of this land. Madison, unfortunately, was focused on the War of 1812 and neglected the Indians. Monroe's attention was riveted by foreign policy and trade, which contributed to the damage Andrew Jackson inflicted through his personal vendetta."

"What about the Indians' impression of whites? Have there been repercussions?"

"The Cherokees are wonderful people whose trust has been broken repeatedly," Worcester replied haltingly. "Whites assuming authority over them was something new and foreign in their experience. Many lifetimes of service to them by scores of missionaries have still not healed their legitimate wounds."

"How do they feel today about whites' characterization of the history taught about them?"

"The majority of whites and Christians believe the Indians are heathenish," Worcester returned. "In truth, they had significant spiritual practices which we have tried to mature and direct toward Christianity. They were more advanced than many tribes, for instance, in respecting life and death. The story of their pain over removal and leaving behind the graves of their families speaks for itself."

While listening to Reverend Worcester's fascinating reply, Hattie happened to glance at her parents. Both wore unusual expressions. She was pleased as she read their faces, hoping that the back and forth with Reverend Worcester showed she could hold her own.

"Do you speak the Cherokee language? How were you able to do the Bible translations?" Hattie pursued.

"I communicate with my Cherokee brothers in everyday dialogue," Worcester explained. "But I don't preach in their language. It would be presumptuous to do so. For translations, I have had the help of Cherokee translators. I trust their ability to appropriately characterize the intent of my words. We also receive guidance from other professionals with the American Board in Boston."

The most challenging part of his work, he went on to relate, was learning to read the Cherokee language. It sounded impossibly complicated to Hattie. He told the remarkable tale about the alphabet originator, Sequoyah. A silversmith and the grandson of a Cherokee Chief, he was crippled from birth and illiterate in Cherokee, as well as English. But he believed the Cherokees needed a written language, like he had seen among the whites.

Once he began work in earnest, he encountered many doubters, even his wife, who burned his initial work thinking it was bewitched. When he finally finished, he taught the new syllabary to his little daughter. Soon she was able to translate words using the new alphabet; its validity was proven. Later, tribal leaders agreed it was legitimate, so he was allowed to teach others. No longer would Cherokee ways be passed down to later generations by word of mouth only.

Using the syllabary, Reverend Worcester began to translate the hymnal, as well as the Bible itself. After that, he printed them on his printing press. He had lost count of the number of pages. Hattie tried to picture his press.

As the evening lengthened, Reverend Worcester told more heart-rending stories about the Cherokees. Since the late 1830s, the vast majority had settled in new homes and become farmers. Some had other professions. All remained suspicious of the promises of whites that led to the loss of their homeland. They needed teachers who understood that.

Despite rumors, the Cherokees were quite civilized, he added. Many lived at a high degree of enlightened culture. Worcester described daily life and detailed how he guided the education of the Cherokees. Hattie hung on his every word.

❖ ❖ ❖

After the Worcester family's activities in Utica came to a close, Hattie attended a send-off in recognition of their great contribution. Reverend Fowler was just back from visiting his sick relative.

"I was deeply touched that you thanked the congregation for supporting foreign missions," he offered, taking Reverend Worcester's hand during the reception.

Hattie wasn't sure why, but the event drew a sparse crowd. She and Mary Eleanor were the only young people present. Good manners required that she continue to engage the troubled young woman. In just a few minutes, however, she began to struggle for conversation topics again. Mary Eleanor offered nothing and barely responded. How uncomfortable to just stand there. So, Hattie decided to swallow her pride and offer a compliment.

"Mary Eleanor, your family has made a deep impression on Utica. I'm so glad to have had the privilege of meeting and knowing you."

To her surprise, tears suddenly sprang from Mary Eleanor's eyes. She turned her back to everyone else, which left her facing Hattie squarely. When she raised a hand to wipe away the tears, it shook nervously.

"It's always this way with Father," Mary Eleanor sighed. "People think he's a prophet. It's really true, I guess. But to me, he's just my father. He's always so encouraging and I adore him, even though we have so little time together."

"So, he must be terribly busy? But I can see he takes it in stride," Hattie surmised. "He's an optimist, isn't he? That must have helped through his imprisonment. He made it sound like a passing discomfort."

"He only focuses on the positives, unlike Mother," Mary Eleanor replied, suddenly candid and engaged as she wiped her eyes. "In prison, he slept for sixteen brutal months on a rough puncheon floor. He was chained and led on long marches behind the horses of officers. It makes me ill to think of it."

"How awful," Hattie sympathized. "I had no idea. But those sufferings didn't deter him."

"My father never gives up. He honors all commitments and is so sensitive to others. I never have to worry that he will be critical of me. But the prospect of being away from him makes me sad."

Hattie had no idea what Mary Eleanor meant or how to respond, so she just smiled warmly.

"You remind me of my sister, Hannah. I miss her so much," Mary Eleanor offered, changing the subject. "She's patient, especially with Mother."

Again, Hattie could think of nothing to say.

Reverend Worcester turned to say goodbye. He waved briefly and nodded appreciatively as he headed for the door. Hattie smiled at the warmth in his eyes, for it reflected kindness, patience, and compassion—all the good things that she valued. What an odd juxtaposition that his wife looked annoyed, uncomfortable, and more than anxious to leave. She was actually scowling.

Hattie watched as Mrs. Worcester's eyes came to rest upon Mary Eleanor. An undeniable frown came across her broad brow. It was an odd, poorly timed display of irritation. Was it related to Mary Eleanor's tears, or something else?

Hattie dug deep for a final, kind reply to Mary Eleanor.

"Your family has certainly touched the church and made us happy during this visit. I hope the rest of your trip is all that you are hoping for. Have a lovely time and a safe journey."

Then she followed the family out, hoping for a final chance to shake Reverend Worcester's hand. She wished she could talk to him at length. This one man, given the chance, could have helped her find the right use for her education. Moments later, the Worcester family departed for Vermont.

❖ ❖ ❖

For days afterward, Hattie thought about Reverend Worcester and the meaning of his life. He was the most selfless person she had ever met, utterly secure in his life's mission and meaning. She wanted to live a life like that, a life filled with commitment to a worthy cause.

She still wondered about the various needs of the Cherokees. It was inexplicable why Mary Eleanor had not been more help. She seemed incapable of focusing. Why did she look so anxiously at her stepmother all the time? If Hattie had tried to contemplate the ideal family for someone like Reverend Worcester, she would never have chosen Mary Eleanor or Erminia. But that was not realistic or kind. He was.

As she worked late into the night on assignments, Hattie

pondered how well educated Reverend Worcester was. His chosen field had justified every minute of study, every hour spent in contemplation of a mission larger than himself. He had gone far from Vermont because of his commitment and loyalty to his chosen cause. She couldn't picture how far away Indian Territory must be. Maybe like her, day-to-day cares in his Vermont hometown had brought disappointment. Was he driven away by that?

Hattie could not hide her discontent about Utica. Her attitude toward it was not from a lack of gratitude. Utica had nurtured her in childhood. Now, she didn't feel the same way and couldn't explain it. But her certainty about it grew each day. In fact, after recent conversations with Reverend Fowler, she no longer felt guilty for wondering about leaving. Did she need to do more soul-searching?

When she tried, all she pictured was Reverend Worcester's extended family and other missionaries in Indian Territory. What was life like in that faraway place? She tried to imagine their faces. Soon, the Cherokee Nation they called home became a fully formed vision. She knew they lived side by side with Indian people there. They worshipped together in Reverend Worcester's church. They swam in the same river and gardened in the same soil. The mission itself was a place to walk together into the future.

Then, without really intending it, Hattie began to see herself there. She pictured a doorstep as she approached a sturdy, weathered door and knocked. The door opened and she went inside.

Emerging later, she found herself walking across a field of wildflowers, and then approaching a quaint, old schoolhouse. Reverend Worcester's daughters invited her inside. How lovely it felt. She wanted to be their friend. Hopefully, they weren't as troubled as Mary Eleanor.

15

Disappointment and Dreams

After neglecting her studies to focus on the Worcesters' visit, the orphanage, children on Sunday, and the baptism event, Hattie was behind. Deadlines piled up, requiring her to skip work at the shop to catch up before graduation. She felt bad about abandoning the responsibilities she had created for herself at the shop. Hopefully, things could wait until the baptism and school were over.

Then a thought struck her that was wholly uninvited. Nobody had said they missed her at the shop. She stood still for a long minute mulling this over. What did it say about her?

For that matter, what did all the other recent, unexpected developments mean? Life had been busy enough with school and the shop. She had applied for teaching jobs and received no favorable replies. Thank goodness for her other new tasks. Yet Utica still felt stale.

Then, suddenly, Reverend Worcester had come to Utica and transformed her whole orientation. Hattie realized she had stopped seeing herself as trudging the path of disappointment and climbing the hill of unrealized dreams. Change had come unexpectedly. Was it redirecting her path or offering a new route altogether?

Finally, blessedly, the day was coming when her schooling would end. Her parents had committed so much energy, sweat, and support to her education. But she was tired of it. It was time to let life, rather than books, become her teacher. She was ready for the next phase, but still unable to define it.

Although Utica Female Academy had promoted itself as having links to potential employers, that had not helped Hattie. On the contrary, she had encountered a dearth of opportunities. Given this puzzle, she was surprised when Miss Kelly called her in right before graduation.

"Hattie, I have been contacted by a well-placed English family with three small children," Miss Kelly shared excitedly. "They are seeking a governess. It is a good opportunity, and they live within walking distance of your home. "

Try as she might, Hattie's expression could not rise to the level of optimism she knew Miss Kelly expected. A governess job was something others wanted for her in the absence of a regular teaching job. It sounded isolating, but she couldn't say that.

"Oh, how kind of you to consider me," she replied warmly. "I would be honored to meet them and discuss their requirements."

At their home later that week, she found them to be delightful, friendly souls. Maybe she hadn't taken the governess job seriously, but they had. They had already sought character references on her. Dr. Bagg was their doctor, so Hattie knew he would vouch for her.

There was no denying that the job would be a good fit. The children, twin girls of twelve and a boy younger than ten, were well-mannered and precocious in an endearing way. She could almost picture herself creating juvenile versions of ancient classics and Greek myths for them. They might like American versions of the old rhymes she was taught as a child. She knew she could meet their requirements, but they could never meet hers.

All this she kept to herself, however, while thanking the gracious couple and expressing interest in talking again. They were not yet ready to hire, which was a relief. As she departed, one main thought was on her mind. Ordinariness. This situation was much too sedate. Everything about it pointed to a lack of keeping true to her dreams.

Before Hattie knew it, May was halfway gone and graduation was at hand. Given her rigorous studies, Hattie felt she had earned the right to be twenty two years of age. Good news arrived that she was among the top graduates in her class. The best news, however, was that Aunt Mary had decided to come from Massachusetts. This was a cause for real celebration, especially since Hattie's lack of a job had taken some luster away. After all, she had linked graduation to the beginning of a grand adventure. That had not materialized.

Following the Sunday afternoon ceremony, her parents hosted a grand supper in Hattie's honor. Freshly cut branches from flowering trees formed a soaring arrangement on the sideboard across from the carefully set table. The dining room had never been so beautiful.

Hattie laughed to herself that it looked rather like a wedding reception, which her mother would have preferred.

Alongside Reverend and Mrs. Fowler, Aunt Mary, and her parents, Hattie was thrilled that all her siblings were present. Albert came down from Lysander with his wife, Ann, who sat next to Hattie. George's wife, Lydia, was beside Artemas. Across the table, George conversed with Amanda and LeGrand. Hattie kidded little Mary and George's two sons.

"Hattie has been a great help," she heard Reverend Fowler tell her father. "I don't know how I could have organized the baptism on my own. She's excellent at logistics."

Hattie's favorite baked chicken was the hallmark of the meal, which also featured some of Aunt Mary's pickled beets, her mother's divine bread, Amanda's potatoes, and much more. Each person had his fill while catching up with the others.

After the dishes were cleared, Amanda surprised Hattie with an enormous layer cake. As she began to cut generous slices, Ebenezer called for everyone's attention.

"Hattie, your mother and I talked endlessly over what to get you for graduation," he began excitedly. "You are now the most highly educated person in either of our family lines. But it was Amanda who came up with the perfect gift idea. In fact, she undertook quite a project to attain this special remembrance. So, without further ado, please accept our gift, sweetheart."

Hattie reached for the embossed box tied with a pretty white ribbon. It was an elegant presentation. Feeling through the paper, the gift felt squared off and rectangular shaped. It had to be a book, but which one?

"You know how much I love books," she breathed expectantly,

smiling from ear to ear. "I can't imagine how you decided on this particular one."

"Oh, we're certain about the choice. You have definitely already read this one," Amanda returned mischievously.

Hattie looked puzzled, as she untied the ribbon. "Hmm. That's intriguing. Why would you choose a book I've already read? It's like a riddle, then? Mary, why don't you help me open this," Hattie asked her precious niece.

Mary rushed to her side and began to help lift the wrapping paper from the book. When Hattie spied its front cover, she gasped. The swirling, gold letters announcing the title and author were ornate and familiar. A beautiful, dark volume, it felt marvelous to hold in her hand. The significance of the book also made sense to all at the table. It was the best-selling novel, *Uncle Tom's Cabin.*

"This is so beautiful I could weep," Hattie whispered, turning the book over in her hands.

"Open it, dear," her father instructed.

Hattie gently lifted the edge of the book's handsome leather cover. There, in friendly, looping letters was an inscription that read:

> *May 1, 1856*
>
> *To Miss Hattie Sheldon—May you forever honor the dignity of all human beings and become a person of influence in the pursuit of your choice. Please accept my best wishes on the occasion of your graduation from Utica Female Academy,*
>
> *Sincerely yours,*
> *Harriet Beecher Stowe*

"Oh my goodness," Hattie cried, clutching the book to her

heart. "She's so famous now! How in the world did you manage to get her signature?"

"Amanda wrote Margaret, who arranged it in Hartford through Catherine Beecher," her father explained. "I'm so glad it pleases you."

"Oh, it's the most prized thing I've ever owned," Hattie replied, clearly touched. "Yes, it most definitely pleases me. Thank you from the bottom of my heart."

"On that note, a bit of news reached us. It's extremely pleasing, dear," her mother inserted expectantly. "I have barely contained myself since Miss Kelly told me about the people needing a governess. Won't you share it in your own words?"

Hattie suddenly felt frozen to her chair. An instantaneous rush of emotion bombarded her with a sense of betrayal. It had not occurred to her that the governess job about which she held no interest would be made known to anyone else. Miss Kelly must have assumed that Hattie would pursue the job, so she shared the news.

Now, with all eyes upon her at this happy occasion, Hattie realized that a crucial moment was suddenly upon her. Should she pretend to be interested, but demure about the details? Should she deflate the family by announcing her rejection of the job? Or should she act flattered that her loved ones were interested, yet not reveal anything more?

Hattie chose the gracious response. It seemed appropriate, given the celebratory meal in her honor.

"What a surprise that you already know," she smiled, hiding her real feelings. "I had a nice conversation with an English family seeking a governess. They were delightful people with darling children. It's not yet time for them to hire, so we agreed to discuss it again later."

"How encouraging, dear," her mother replied, beaming. "It was such a relief to hear about it."

Hattie wanted to retort with a saucy comeback, but realized it would be utterly tactless. She had no desire to disrespect the guests or the occasion. Sighing to herself, she mentally threw cold water on her wounded feelings and vowed to take up the matter with Miss Kelly tomorrow. If there was anything she could not abide, it was broken confidences. The last person she wanted involved in her future plans was her mother. She cast a quick glance at her, almost trying to read her mind. There must be a bright imaginary vision there of Hattie's prospects. Quite probably, her mother already pictured Hattie working during the mornings as a governess while spending afternoons planning a wedding, even though there was no groom.

Each day thereafter, Hattie decided to be thankful for everything she could dream up. Her work with children at the orphanage and the church had ended. But it had been great. School was finished. But it had been wonderful. She still had the baptism project and, thankfully, the shop.

Always her haven, the shop felt familiar and satisfying. Lately, however, she noted that her father stayed close by when she was helping male customers. Did he worry over past misunderstandings about her availability? What if he thought she was hurting business? Maybe he just intended to interrupt an inappropriate overture or even a proposal.

Contemplating this, the fact dawned on her that even the shop had grown confining. Her father was watchful and a little worried. That had never happened before. She couldn't be sure, but something told her there were concerns he would never voice. It had been wonderful for the two of them to be together as father and daughter, but she wanted an adult role now. He probably wanted his shop back.

A frown on her brow, Hattie wondered what she would do in the long term. Without school and other projects, she would only have the baptism. When that ended, she would be bored to tears. A much more serious solution was needed to her growing problem. How would she spend her time?

❖ ❖ ❖

The details for the baptism were completed. Each name was spelled correctly on the certification cards. All the candidates had been given instructions to follow. She had even posted invitations to their families. Finally, her only remaining task was selecting appropriate hymns they would sing during the procession.

The mighty Mohawk River, a time-honored location of baptisms for the First Presbyterian Church, was low this year. Birds lingered at the water's edge, pecking at the old, dry water line. The river still ran, but it was not a rushing river and it was not deep. This made it perfect for the baptism.

"As long as the weather is decent, things should play out like clockwork," she consoled Reverend Fowler.

Luckily, it had been a warm spring and promised to be temperate for the baptism. Rains had brought life back to the region. Each day, the landscape grew more lush and green. Full of anticipation, Hattie envisioned the crowd gathering on the grassy bank in one week. When all were accounted for, they would form a long line. Hand in hand, she would lead them across the old, quaint footbridge to the sandbar.

Reverend Fowler would position himself in a secure spot there where the water was just waist deep. Hattie's responsibility was to send him the candidates, one by one, adorned all in white clothing. He would ask each person a final question of faith, get their full name, place his arm around their shoulders protectively, and then baptize them quickly while saying a prayer.

That same week after graduation, Hattie thought about writing Margaret. But then her mother stopped into the shop, saying she needed help with supper. She also wanted Hattie to accompany her to a recital the next day. Amanda needed her to mark a hem on a new dress. There seemed to be a thousand other trifling things to be done, and none of them related to her dreams or the future. They were ordinary tasks that went along with family life.

Arriving home, Hattie rushed to comb through the day's mail. One envelope in the stack was addressed to her, so she plopped down in her father's chair. The return address was Vermont, which was momentarily confusing. Wondering who she knew in Vermont, she suddenly recalled that the Worcesters were there visiting. A rush of warmth and excitement filled her heart. How wonderful of them to write her!

Dashing up to her room, sometimes two steps at a time, she tore through the envelope and grabbed the letter. Flipping to the back page, she blinked in disbelief that the signature was that of Reverend Samuel Austin Worcester.

It must be a thank you letter, she thought. Only a truly thoughtful man would notice the effort she expended to organize, improve, and even salvage different aspects of his visit to Utica. With a grateful but pounding heart, Hattie began to read the letter as fast as she could.

All the customary greetings and kind words were there. On the lower part of the first page, however, the letter took a different direction than she expected. Reverend Worcester was offering details about the American Board of Commissioners for Foreign Missions. Then she read a sentence that made her knees go wobbly.

"Therefore, I am pleased to offer you a position as missionary teacher at the Park Hill Mission."

Hattie went completely limp and had to sit down. As she grew short of breath, tears sprang to her eyes and a chill went from the top of her head to the bottom of her feet. After she read a few more sentences, her whole body tingled with nervous anticipation. Absentmindedly, she used her forearm to brush aside a tickling strand of hair and wipe away beads of perspiration.

This letter is unbelievable! It has come straight from heaven, she whispered to herself. Her strength returning, she grew so twitchy it was impossible to stay seated. She began to pace the floor.

The idea that Reverend Worcester might return her interest was the farthest possibility she had ever considered. But it was clear from the letter that he really did regard her favorably. Tapping into her most fervent hopes, he had asked her to join forces with the American Board of Commissioners for Foreign Missions. The organization was offering her a job teaching the Cherokees in Indian Territory! Hattie reread it several times to be sure she wasn't dreaming.

Her mind raced with ideas as her heart nearly burst with thanks. She tried to envision the place itself, the seriousness of the work, and the depth of commitment she would need. There was so much to learn, and she had so many questions. One thing, however, was certain. The decision to accept was hers and hers alone. She would determine her own course and choose her future path before anyone else could talk her out of it.

Taking out pen and paper, Hattie committed her every thought and idea to a page for deeper examination. It was a scrupulously thorough review, unlike any she had undertaken before, even on a thesis paper. In fact, her initial effort lasted the rest of the day and into the evening. When called down to supper, she begged off with a headache so nobody would see her state of excitement or question what she was doing.

There had been many pivotal moments in her life. But none of them held a candle to this one. That fact informed how she intended to deal with this momentous development. As a teacher in her own right, she was a full-fledged adult and capable of making decisions independently.

But independence did not mean making the decision alone. For, now that this offer had come, Hattie knew that God had plans for her life. Just as Reverend Fowler had said, the Holy Spirit had kept his hand on her and was honoring her dreams. She fell to her knees, thanking God for answering her prayer and bringing this answer to her troubles. She felt so blessed. This job wasn't just down the road or across town. It was truly an adventure on the frontier, just as she had imagined all those years ago in her father's shop.

For the next few days, Hattie pondered her response. All of her life, there had been a place in her soul that cared for good people who lacked advantage. As she matured, however, she found herself wanting to do more than just care about them. She wanted to help them, to bring prospects where none had existed. The world had enough dreamers. Her desire was to act and work in every way possible. Her response would begin with that commitment.

At the library, she began to search in old newspapers for information about the American Board. To her chagrin, she learned the Board had actually met in Utica recently. Just down the street, no less! Leaning back, she pinched herself over the missed opportunity. Why hadn't she read about it? Maybe she was so focused elsewhere that she simply overlooked it. If only she could have attended and learned more. But this was no time for regret. She moved on to more articles.

The Daily Press contained an interesting piece about significant monies going to missionary work worldwide. Churches, in particular, sent money to hundreds of denominational and nondenominational organizations at the farthest reaches of the earth. Her confidence in the American Board grew just knowing that so many people supported its work. Thanks to this article, she needn't question how well-funded its missionary efforts were, which offered a commentary on the strength of the body. After all, she needed to be certain that her trust of her new employer was warranted. If the American Board received consistent, sizable donations, it must be strong.

On the other hand, Reverend Worcester hadn't looked like a man who was well paid. In fact, he had looked almost threadbare, especially in comparison with her father. His family had not been able to afford new traveling bags. But perhaps this was just an indication of personal conservatism, further evidenced by Erminia Worcester's rather worn hat.

Hattie contemplated her church's impressive offering for the Worcester's personal use. Would they spend it or save it? Maybe they were waiting until they reached Vermont to replace needed items. It felt good to know that her father's gifts would save them having to invest in new luggage.

Suddenly, she felt guilty for analyzing the Worcester family's finances so closely. Money was obviously the last of Reverend Worcester's priorities. His mind was on higher things. Furthermore, she told herself, money must not play a deciding role in her choice, either.

Fascinated, Hattie read more and more to satisfy her hunger for information about the Cherokees. Many forces imposed themselves on the Cherokee Nation. Several accounts described the place as a vast prairie crossed by rough and rutted roads. It was traversed by a gamut of travelers from soldiers to pioneers, fur traders to gold miners, missionaries to desperados. Maybe words like these made for good newspaper copy. But how true were they?

Reverend Worcester had said the Cherokees preferred teachers from the East. His daughter, Sarah, had graduated from Mt. Holyoke. Perhaps Hattie's capabilities would be similar to hers. How many times, she wondered, had Sarah Worcester made the trip between Indian Territory and Mt. Holyoke? Whatever the number, just knowing about Sarah was a source of encouragement to Hattie. If Sarah could make the long, arduous journey regularly, so could she.

The last two nights before the baptism, Hattie fell into bed completely exhausted from the exercise of making her decision. She implored God to inform her choice and strengthen her for the time when she would break the news. Her family had no inkling about what she intended to do. She had already concluded there must be no opportunity for wavering on the decision. By the time she revealed the job offer, she must already have accepted it.

On Thursday before Saturday's baptism, Hattie wrote Reverend Worcester a gracious letter of thanks for his offer. She stated her acceptance of the job and asked for more details. A brief letter was best, she concluded. So, she kept it simple and posted it late that afternoon.

Keeping the secret was harder than Hattie imagined. She couldn't even tell Amanda. Her heart had been racing most of the time since she received the offer. Scores of disparate ideas, reminders, and concerns crossed her mind every hour. She was even too agitated to read.

Preparations should begin right away, she told herself, but not until she had done the hardest thing of her life: tell her parents. That might best play out in a traditional setting. The most comfortable place at home had always been the supper table. So, on Friday, Hattie offered to cook a nice dinner for them. She would tell them that night. As she cooked, she could refine her words.

Most Friday nights, Ebenezer came home from the shop a little early. Her mother returned from the orphanage late in the afternoon, too. Artemas would be playing ball with friends that evening. Perhaps she could encourage them to tell some stories from the shop or the orphanage. Her father also liked to read aloud from the newspaper, which would distract everyone.

Finally, Hattie served the dinner. Neither of her parents appeared to suspect anything. They ate together in peace, making small talk. Among the topics of conversation were the Worcesters in Vermont, Hattie's graduation, and hoping Aunt Mary got home to Massachusetts all right. Her father asked a few questions about the upcoming baptism the next day, as well as Hattie's opportunity to be a governess for the English family. Finally, she took a deep breath and began the speech she had rehearsed.

"I want to talk with the two of you about my future," Hattie began, using her fork as a distraction to push potatoes around her plate.

"Well, Miss Kelly gave you a good launch with that governess job," Ebenezer replied, sipping his tea.

"Yes, that was generous," Hattie agreed, gulping. "But I have decided not to pursue it. Another much more appropriate job is waiting."

"What other job?" her mother queried, looking up in confusion.

"Earlier this week, a letter arrived for me in the post," Hattie continued, digging her fingernails into the palm of her hand to relieve pressure. "It was from Reverend Worcester in Vermont. He offered me a teaching position among the Cherokees in Indian Territory. I have accepted."

"Now just one minute!" Ebenezer challenged, throwing down his napkin.

Her mother lost her grip on a water glass, spilling it all over the table. She made no effort to retrieve the glass or mop up the water. Instead, she began to make a moaning sound and pounded her fist against the edge of the table, as if beating a drum.

"No. I don't believe it," she cried. "Nothing happens that fast."

"It did happen and it is done," Hattie replied solemnly, her stomach tightening. "I cannot live an ordinary life here in Utica and fulfill my goals. You both know that. This unexpected job offer seemed like an answer to prayer. I believe God just showed me the direction for the life he has given me."

With both parents' heads buried in their hands, Hattie leaned back and tried to endure their strong disappointment. Even Ebenezer was crying, which broke her heart.

"Reverend Worcester's letter said he had consulted Reverend Fowler before offering me the position," Hattie continued, licking her lips nervously. "Because he had met the two of you, he believed my character was of the highest quality. He told me that he felt sure my emotional strength could sustain me, that I showed a ready ability to make good decisions and had a comfortable security over carrying them out. He complimented me on my visible drive and the palpable certainty of my goals."

"God help us, Hattie," Ebenezer whispered, his face pale. "Aside from being the death of me, do you have any concept of the danger into which you have just delivered yourself?"

"I view myself no differently than Reverend Worcester views himself," Hattie replied sternly. "He puts his beliefs first and commits the rest of it to God. All of my life, I have been drawn to helping people who are oppressed. I know I can make a considerable difference among the children I will teach in the Cherokee Nation."

"Why couldn't you just teach some nice children in Utica?" her mother sobbed. "I can barely contain my misery. All these years of worrying for your health and safety, only for you to choose—willingly choose—to leave us. You actually favor an utterly uncivilized, vast frontier setting where violence is an everyday occurrence. How could you, Hattie? How could you do this?"

❖ ❖ ❖

The next morning, Hattie was up early. She felt the strain at home so acutely that she left for the church, even though hours remained before the baptism. There were simply no answers to her parents' anguished questions.

Her first stop was Reverend Fowler's office. He was expecting her anyway, but not for the reason she now expressed.

"I received a job offer from Reverend Worcester," she blurted out.

"Oh my. That was fast," he replied, surprised. "Did he tell you he contacted me?"

"Yes," she returned somewhat curtly. "I have already accepted the job."

"You what? I can't believe it," Reverend Fowler replied slowly. "Are you sure about that? I had hoped to talk it over with you and your parents first."

"I understand," she returned, looking down. "But my desire to make my own decision took precedence."

"I can see that," Reverend Fowler replied quietly.

Hattie smiled proudly, but he did not respond in kind. She waited for a word of congratulations.

"Since there is nothing further needed on that issue, I guess we'd best get planning for the baptism," he said, straightening papers on his desk.

She noted his lack of comment, but her excitement filled the gap where questions might have been raised. Surely he would remain supportive. Who wouldn't back someone who wanted to be a missionary? She was counting on his help, but decided not to question his reply to Reverend Worcester's inquiry. Hopefully, he had recommended her. If not, and in the event her parents approached him about it, what might happen?

Truth be told, she almost expected them to confront him. Was it possible they might try to reverse her decision or put roadblocks in her way? Would they go that far?

But her mind was made up. She was going to Indian Territory to start a completely new life. Her intent would be fulfilled by the need there. Nothing about Utica could satisfy her. Apart from her family and church, she felt she was leaving little behind.

❧ ❧ ❧

There was no better time for baptisms than a bright, sunny day in late May. Some years, it felt almost hot when the sun created a glare off the water. Today, however, it was temperate and perfect outdoors. The sand would be nice and dry, which made for warmer walking than on wet sand.

At one-thirty in the afternoon, people from the church began to gather near the river at the appointed place. Some came on foot, a few by buggy, a handful by bicycle, and the rest by wagon. The sound of voices and occasional laughter rose up as the fluffy clouds floated by. Hattie could tell they had prepared in advance because of what they brought. There were games and umbrellas, picnic baskets and blankets, jump ropes and harmonicas. It was definitely a time for families to celebrate together. They would picnic under the big trees after the baptism.

Referring often to her list, Hattie kept watch for new arrivals. Shortly before two, she had made a check mark beside the name of every baptismal candidate.

"All are present! I'll wait for your signal," she told Reverend Fowler.

The ceremony would begin shortly.

"My friends, may I have your attention?" he called to the crowd a few minutes later. "Will everyone please take hands and bow for a word of prayer?"

Reverend Fowler thanked God for the people, the weather, and the setting. He asked for a blessing on their gathering and ended the prayer with a strong "amen."

"We will now proceed to the other side," he instructed. "I view of it as a sacred passage across the footbridge. Think about our linkage and common bond in the family of God. We are going together to the other side, which is reminiscent of many Biblical themes."

The footbridge was a favorite landmark and meeting place in Utica. Constructed of local stones from an ancient quarry, it had a rustic essence of solidness, like the foundation of the city. No denomination could claim exclusive use of it or the sandbar below. It had been the sight of so many baptisms over so many years that many claimed the river flowed with holy water.

Reverend Fowler led the procession. The low hum of conversation signaled a feeling of controlled excitement. Some of the younger children giggled as they approached the mid-point. Hattie walked close to the woman who would lead the singing. Often, during her childhood and since, she had made this trip. A question came to mind as she wondered where the Cherokee baptisms took place. Did Reverend Worcester baptize members of his church in the river? What was the name of the river?

About two dozen people had reached the sandbar behind Reverend Fowler. He turned, motioned supportively and nodded encouragingly. People graciously stayed in line as others continued to file off the footbridge.

Suddenly, an urgent noise broke everyone's concentration. Something solid was fracturing, and it signaled danger. Hattie knew the sound of rocks cracking, but had no time to think further. A shifting movement suddenly destabilized her feet. She yelped, intending to turn and investigate. Just as she did, Reverend Fowler cried, "Stop. Go back!"

But it was too late. The center of the footbridge had suffered a crack that split one side apart from the other. Whole sections came apart and began to fall, along with the people who had stood on them. Like Lot's wife in the old Bible story, just as Hattie looked back, her heart gripped with fear and turned hard as a pillar of salt. The foundation beneath her feet had disappeared.

There was nothing below her but air. She screamed as she fell, the sensation taking her breath away and replacing it with terror. Before she could even pray, she landed and everything went dark.

16

Mind Over Matter

"Hattie, can you hear me?" came a distant voice from a foggy, ethereal place. "Please wake up, honey."

The voice seemed miles away, as if someone were calling to her, almost echoing, around the curves of a deep canyon from a distance. Hattie was asleep on the top of a mountain below a perfect blue sky punctuated with thin, ethereal clouds. The place's peacefulness lulled her away from the voice until a sharp pain in her left leg demanded notice. Were it not for that pain, she would be happy dozing on her mountaintop forever. But the pain's sharp, pulsing edge continued to intrude on her reverie. It throbbed and gnawed at her, insisting that she not sleep. She became angry at the pain.

"Open your eyes, Hattie," the voice insisted.

"It hurts," Hattie whispered, reaching into the air. "My leg . . ."

"It's Father, honey. Open your eyes."

"Wake up, Hattie," Amanda added, stroking Hattie's hair.

"Something has happened to my leg," Hattie moaned, blinking.

Then, without fanfare, she simply opened her eyes and woke up again into her real life. Instantly, the mountaintop and the canyon were gone, as were the voices calling from afar. Looking around weakly, she did not recognize her surroundings and frowned with confusion. Blurred figures stood around her. Then, she recognized her father's voice and felt his hand on hers.

"There you are. Look, it's Father and Amanda," he comforted.

"Everything's going to be all right," Amanda reassured.

But Hattie didn't make eye contact. Instead, she looked at her outstretched arms, now covered in red scratches and purplish bruises. More than the voices, these injuries caught her attention.

"What's wrong with me?" she queried, finally looking up at her father groggily.

"You had a terrible accident, sweetheart."

"An accident,' Hattie echoed, puzzling over her location. Then, growing alarmed, she cried in a raspy voice, "Where am I?"

"You're still in Utica," Ebenezer confirmed, patting her hand.

"You fell a long ways into the river. Do you remember that?" Amanda inquired softly.

"When did I fall?" Hattie replied, looking at their faces for the first time.

"You went to the river with Reverend Fowler for the baptism," Ebenezer clarified softly.

"Yes, we were there," Hattie replied. "We were singing."

"That's right. But the footbridge over the river gave way, I'm sad to say," Ebenezer added.

"Oh! I do remember," Hattie sobbed, lost in grief. "All the screaming scared me. People were thrashing in the water. Someone grabbed me and I was pulled under."

"Don't think about that anymore," Ebenezer instructed softly. "It's over now."

"You're safe and sound at my house in the big feather bed," Amanda explained. "You have a broken leg, but it will heal."

Suddenly, Hattie's full capacity for awareness returned to her. She began to shake her head in denial, not wanting to believe what he had told her.

"What? Is that why it hurts so much? I want to see it, show me," she demanded, reaching for her leg and tugging at the bed linens.

"All right, slow down," Ebenezer responded, pulling back the sheet.

Hattie gaped in amazement at the bandages and splint on her left leg. Covering her eyes she began to chant, "No, no, no!"

❖ ❖ ❖

When Hattie awakened later, Ebenezer hugged her close. She had gained ground emotionally and felt lucid despite her pain. Together, they talked about the accident, going methodically through the turn of events before the horrific moment when the footbridge gave way.

Hattie and the others had been twenty feet above the water. The sudden break sent them hurling through the air. Some, like Hattie, fell into the shallow water. A few unlucky ones fell hard on the sandbar. Many had broken bones.

"Reverend Fowler came through in the worst of circumstances," her father detailed. "So many injured people needed immediate attention. He chose the quickest and closest option, organizing another parishioner's wagon to get you here to Amanda's house because it's so much closer than home."

"How many were hurt?" Hattie breathed, still incredulous.

"Forty. Sadly, one man had broken his neck and was pronounced dead at the scene."

Hattie looked at her father in horror.

"He was the grandfather of one of the girls," he related respectfully. "Did you meet him?"

"No, but I saw him. I'm so sad for his family," she lamented. "It's tragic."

"Yes, it certainly is. But you are alive, thank the good Lord."

"How bad is my leg, Father?" she implored. "I don't have time for a broken leg. I should be packing. There's so much to do before I leave for Indian Territory."

"You sustained a serious break," Ebenezer confirmed. "Luckily, it is not a compound fracture. Dr. Bagg will explain it. "

"I could be dead, couldn't I?" Hattie whispered, recognizing the full import of the accident.

"I'm afraid that's true," her father agreed soberly. "Now take a nap. I'll be back later."

When she wasn't asleep, Hattie told herself this was just a temporary setback. Shortly, however, Amanda broke the news that her injury was significant. Dr. Bagg had stopped by, but didn't want to wake Hattie. He gave strict instructions that she must remain in bed and could not be moved home yet. Her healing depended on early immobilization of the broken bone. She would have to stay at Amanda's house for an undetermined period of time.

Hattie wept, devastated by the turn of events. She had never experienced so many conflicting emotions at once. Her future felt threatened. Her health was in question. Suddenly, the power of unforeseen circumstances impressed itself on her like nothing ever before. She buried her face in her hands and sobbed.

Eventually, she drifted off to sleep. Once when she awakened, whispers outside her door wafted in.

"I'm so glad I'm the one to take care of her," Amanda murmured.

"You'll never know how grateful I am. This is tedious," Ebenezer replied in a low voice.

"How's mother taking it?" Amanda returned.

There was no reply.

❧ ❧ ❧

Another time when Hattie woke up, her little niece Mary was holding her hand. Amanda waited on her hand and foot. Dr. Bagg stopped by regularly and urged her to rest. When her eyes were closed, she felt motion, almost like drifting in a boat. Her leg throbbed with sharp pains, but her heart ached with disappointment.

On the third day, Hattie announced she was hungry, which pleased everyone. After downing two fried eggs for a late breakfast, she napped again. Later she discovered Artemas by her side. He had been drawing with her pen while she slept.

During their conversation, Hattie adjusted the bed sheet, exposing her left foot. To her amazement, she spied dots of ink in a funny design all over her toes and the top of her foot. Casting a sharp, confused look in her brother's direction, he confessed sheepishly. The poor fellow had done it out of sheer boredom, so she sent him home. Hattie was beginning to become too familiar with boredom herself.

What would Dr. Bagg say? The silly prank might raise eyebrows. It also raised serious questions. How long before she could wash her foot? Or wear a shoe? Most importantly, when could she walk again?

But each time a touch of panic rose into her throat, Hattie's sweet little niece, Mary, seemed to appear. A calm and loving child, she offered to scratch Hattie's back or adjust her pillow. It warmed Hattie's heart and made her put aside her worries for a few minutes.

Mary began to ask Hattie to read to her. The warmth of a child snuggled close to her did Hattie's heart much good. With Mary hanging on every word of a story, Hattie saw herself as a teacher in her own schoolroom. If this child responded to her, surely the children in the Cherokee Nation would, too.

After a few days, an ugly reality reared its head. The broken leg was bad enough. But there was something worse that hurt in a more profound way. Hattie's mother had not come to her bedside. She had sent several loving notes and a little bouquet of flowers, but Hattie needed her mother to be there. The longer she stayed away, the more Hattie worried about her state of mind.

The next time her father visited, she put hard questions to him. He grew a little pale.

"I don't know what to tell you," Ebenezer faltered, whispering. "Your mother took the news badly. She thought she had lost another daughter."

"Is she reasonable?" Hattie pressed.

"Of course. What do you mean?" her father resisted.

"Does she have her wits about her?" Hattie clarified.

Ebenezer did not budge. He insisted her mother was terribly upset but fine.

Too many things had hit her all at once, he explained. The announcement that Hattie was leaving for the Cherokee Nation had been followed by the accident. Her mother's adjustment to anything traumatic was slow and painful. In the last few years, she had been hit by an avalanche of change, which she defined as loss. Hattie understood her choice well. Somewhere within it, there was a lesson to learn.

Her father tried to hide his anguish, but it showed and cut at her heart. She ached with compassion because he was caught in the middle. After he left, she felt certain that, at home, her mother had taken to her bed.

Oh, dear, she thought to herself. *This situation with Mother will not go well.*

❖ ❖ ❖

During a visit from Reverend Fowler, Hattie shared some of her worries. He listened intently, which helped her express the many confusing things on her mind. It occurred to her that he was the only one who knew all the key people in her current situation. He was her parent's pastor and friend. He had been there when the bridge gave way. He had corresponded with Reverend Worcester for years. Most importantly, he understood why she wanted to work in the Cherokee Nation.

How should she interpret her surprising circumstances, she asked. Did the injury mean God didn't want her to leave Utica? Should she show deference and give in to her mother's wishes?

"Faith and feelings often work at cross purposes," he replied with measured emphasis. "You must do what you believe is right. How you feel—and how others seek to change your feelings—is another matter."

"Then let's talk about teaching the Cherokees, because I know that is right," she replied. "I'm tired of talking about sad and hurtful things."

"Very well. I can try to help with that."

"As I've contemplated leaving here and starting to teach, what questions have I failed to ask?" she queried. "To be truly ready for what's ahead, I want to examine my responsibilities from every angle. I'm going to be completely separated from everything and everyone familiar in Utica. Your articles said the Cherokee people also feel far, far from home."

"Can you help alleviate those feelings?" Reverend Fowler questioned.

"Well, once I've finished the long journey, I will understand their plight better."

"That's good. And it raises another point of Worcester's that I meant to share earlier. He never places himself in a position to look suspect in the eyes of the Cherokees. You need to prioritize the fact that they need a trustworthy teacher. If they don't trust you, they might not let you teach their children. "

"I never thought of that. I guess I have to help them respect me."

"How would you do that?"

Hattie sat silently and searched her life for things applicable, for an observation or experience that would lend her credibility or proficiency. How could she show understanding of them as a people who had been manipulated? Had she ever encountered needs as great as theirs before? Her list of answers was so short she wanted to cry.

To her great annoyance, she felt tired and found concentration hard. This injury had taxed her energy.

"I'm struggling for an answer. I'm sorry. This pain wears me out. I get too emotional. But it's made me realize something. I've lived a protected and privileged life."

"I would call it a blessed life. And perhaps this hardship is preparing you for your future. Think on that."

"Maybe you're right," she pondered. "One day, I wonder if I'll look back on this and feel differently about it."

"Possibly. But for now, you need rest," he added. "When you feel stronger, it will help to itemize what's motivated you and what makes you so certain you'll succeed."

Hattie knew she had to come up with sound answers. Articulating them was pivotal to her future and essential for her parents' peace of mind. They would feel all the worse about her going if she wasn't prepared philosophically. That very idea might also have prompted Reverend Fowler's questions. Her parents and Reverend Fowler needed to know enough—and hear enough from her—to support her decision.

She needed to ask herself many more questions. For a start, what inner resources qualified her—in her heart, conscience, and soul—for this work in Indian Territory? It was a perplexing question because, previously, she had relied solely on her intellect and education.

"I guess I do need rest. I have more questions than answers," she confided emotionally. "A good night's sleep will help me."

"Several weeks of rest is more like it," he reminded. "I'm concerned about your stamina for the trip ahead. As for your intellectual and spiritual capabilities, they are above reproach. It's your rationale that needs work."

❀ ❀ ❀

Visitors came and went from Hattie's room. Most talked about her injury. Nothing much was said about the Cherokees. Soon, the whole situation began to feel so drawn out, even though her injury became less acute. She had not yet found answers to Reverend Fowler's questions, which was concerning.

Her whole life had grown completely stale and boring. She was still not allowed to stand on her leg. This fed doubts about being strong enough to leave for the Cherokee Nation. All these factors forced her toward deeper contemplation. She must concentrate. Nothing should be off limits in the physical, emotional, spiritual, or professional realms of her search for answers.

Way too much time and attention had been spent on her feelings. Following the lead of other people's kindness, she had accepted sympathy and reacted to their apprehension. Doing so cost her a discernible part of her fighting spirit. Letting go any further would be a bad choice.

Choice. The use of the word *choice* caught her attention. For a long moment, she thought about ways to see things differently. Then, quite suddenly, she realized she hadn't looked at the whole gamut of outcomes after the injury. Pain and pity had ruled the day. She had given in without even realizing it!

The truth prompted her to new levels of understanding. Why choose to feel despair when she could choose hope? She must elect to abandon her dream of teaching in the Cherokee Nation or form a new commitment to it!

Sitting up straighter, Hattie sipped water absentmindedly. She must make a decision. If she let herself dive further into this deep pool of barriers, she might never come up for air. But if she stayed above the fray and kept her focus off her accident, she might realize her dream.

This situation might be bad, but it was only temporary. There would be an end to the debilitation. Nobody had said her injury was permanent. She would walk again! There was every reason to push ahead as if her leg was healed.

The discomfort of the break and the threat of immobility had robbed her. She must fight back. Nothing must stop her from going to the Cherokee Nation. Nothing. God had shown her clearly that she was meant to teach there, so she would do just that.

Hattie grabbed her pen and paper. From now on, she vowed, each waking moment must be devoted to anything but her broken leg. She might be a convalescent, but she didn't have to think or act like one. From her bed, she could accomplish many of the tasks she needed to finish. The time would go faster while waiting for more information from Reverend Worcester.

First, she penned a cordial note to the English family, explaining that she could not be considered for their governess position. She said she had taken a job with the American Board and would be moving to Indian Territory. She wrote a similar note to Miss Kelly at Utica Female Academy.

Each time a family member or friend came to visit, she decided to engage them in a conversation about the Cherokee Nation. That would be her sole focus. She must turn every doubt into a hope, every detractor into a supporter. Nothing would jeopardize her future in the Cherokee Nation.

❖ ❖ ❖

While visiting with her father the next day, several pieces of her unfinished puzzle suddenly fell into place. There was an answer to Reverend Fowler's question. In fact, it had been there all the time.

As they talked, her father mentioned the shop and his free Negro employee, Silas. Instantly, Hattie pictured that frightening night when she had helped with the Underground Railroad rescue. Had not that slave family been forced out of every kind of home or homeland? They were the epitome of disenfranchisement! If ever there were people who couldn't bear to put their trust in white people, it was slaves.

Hattie had come in close contact with escaping slaves. They had chosen to trust her father's plan. It was trust or die, essentially. And given that graphic memory, she realized she really did have an experience that mattered and the understanding to go with it.

Like slaves, what if the Cherokees had no other option than the mission where she was going to work? She understood, had experience, and was trustworthy to stand by their side. Fulfilling that very role was what fueled her fervor for their plight. When she saw them in the light of having few options, she would—she must—go to all ends to win their trust!

"Hattie, after three weeks in bed, it's time for you to go home," Dr. Bagg announced unexpectedly while taking her temperature soon afterwards. "I know your leg still aches and is weak. But after you disobeyed me and stood on it, I realized you had healed more than I knew."

"That's a relief," Hattie replied excitedly. "I can't wait to walk."

"Take it slow. You don't want to risk re-injury. And don't go headlong with your plans for a few weeks," he instructed.

"My future isn't as pressing as facing my mother," she confided. "I dread sorting things out with her."

"Will you allow me to comment?" Dr. Bagg returned. "You may think I want your mother to take care of you now. But that is not the case. Rather, it's time you went home and began to minister to her. This impasse must be resolved. We both know she lacks the resources to do that."

Hattie wondered how much Dr. Bagg knew. "She has such a blind spot when it comes to my dreams and plans. She balks and is stubborn as a mule."

"Don't disparage her until you've walked in her shoes. Go home and face the problem, even though it's hurtful," Dr. Bagg reiterated. "Later in your life, it will inform your decisions on things that are much more trying."

Hattie knew he was right. She had to repair the present before she pursued the future. Keeping things in order was wise. Plenty of time existed for unforeseen circumstances ahead. The Bible didn't promise anyone an easy life. She must accommodate that.

"I always tell my patients that the head, heart, and stomach all need to align on weighty decisions."

Hattie remained silent, but smiled as he left. Dr. Bagg's final sentence put everything in perspective. All three elements were working together for her. It was right for the heart to lead because courage must be her guide. She had only erred during the threat to her health by giving too much attention to her head. Thinking too much was dangerous. Now, she had aligned all three and could see the future. Taking a deep breath, she bowed her head and asked for God's guidance.

As soon as George and Albert carried Hattie from the wagon into the familiarity of her own house, she spied a letter waiting on the sideboard. Next to it was a dried-up bouquet of flowers. Her mother didn't appear to be present, or at least didn't rush to the door at the sound of scuffling feet.

Hattie's father gave her a concerned look and then turned toward the kitchen. She knew he was going in search of her mother. Without hesitating, she grabbed the letter, tore into it, and began to read. It was Reverend Worcester's reply! It had arrived so much sooner than she expected. But, of course, he was in Vermont where mail service was quite reliable. She wondered how long it would take for her letters to reach Utica from the Cherokee Nation.

His letter was long and full of information. He was obviously in the habit of writing lengthy letters. Possibly they were the only contact he had with family and the American Board. She wondered if the organization's officers ever visited the Cherokee Nation. Thirty years was a long time to carry on via letter.

Thirty years of letters, she repeated. No wonder he seemed so patient. Her experiences at the shop paled in comparison. There, she counted on a quick answer from her father as she went about her duties. What if she posed a question but had to wait weeks for an answer? Shaking her head, she returned to Reverend Worcester's letter and read on.

Regarding his adopted home on the frontier, Reverend Worcester explained that Park Hill was only four miles—a short wagon ride—from a fairly new town in Indian Territory called Tahlequah. It was more commercial than little Park Hill, which just had general stores. The area was close to the border with Arkansas, which had attained statehood in 1836. The actual boundaries of Indian Territory were unmarked.

Worcester assured Hattie that Park Hill and Tahlequah were highly civilized cultures. In recent years, tribal leaders from Park Hill had hired teachers from the East so the students could learn every manner and custom of eastern society. Toward that end, they had traveled the great distance to Mount Holyoke on more than one fact-finding mission. This occurred as they built new male and female seminaries fashioned on eastern models to insure that high standards of education existed in the West, as in the East. He had been asked to supervise.

Hattie wished she could find that old article from her childhood about the Cherokee removals. It was her first introduction to the town of Park Hill. She recalled the photograph of an impressive three-story brick school building with columns out front. If Park Hill had buildings this modern, it must be a very developed place.

In closing, Reverend Worcester included a list of supplies, belongings, and garments that Hattie should bring. The items were in keeping with the windy, dry climate in Indian Territory. Her travel route would be arranged later, probably by the American Board, which would notify her of details. Finally, Reverend Worcester's last item, to her surprise, indicated that her traveling companion would be his wife, Erminia.

"She has agreed to accompany you in my stead," he wrote. "Unexpectedly, I must remain in Vermont to conduct overdue business and tend to family matters here."

At first glance, this seemed fairly reasonable, although unusual. Hattie had assumed that the Worcester family would travel back to Park Hill together after their stay in Vermont. But Reverend

Worcester was staying in Vermont, his wife was going back to Park Hill with Hattie, and nothing whatsoever was mentioned about his daughter, Mary Eleanor.

Hattie reached deep into her core to understand her mother, prompted in part by uneasiness about Erminia Worcester and Mary Eleanor's relationship. How had they weathered difficulties? She decided there was much to contemplate.

Meanwhile, the accident that led to her broken leg, at least from her mother's perspective, had taken on an identity of its own. Her mother spoke of nothing else. The unwelcome circumstances dredged up her past suffering, bringing harsh and punishing emotion. Hattie respected her mother's agony, but struggled for patience. She knew she couldn't give in, however, or let her mother's feelings control her future.

The most difficult thing to accommodate was her mother's choice not to see her at Amanda's. It had left a gaping hole in her heart during the hardest part of her recuperation.

"I know it's hard to understand, but it had very little to do with you," Amanda reminded.

Yet Hattie felt rejected. Was there another word for avoiding your daughter's worst crisis? But she vowed to keep quiet until her mother was ready to talk.

Several days passed uneventfully. Much to her surprise, her

mother appeared sweet and calm most of the time. But she was also distant.

"She's using her hurt to manipulate me," Hattie confided in Amanda.

Amanda wasn't so sure. "She doesn't do anything with her hurt but give into it."

"I'm not going to succumb to her pressure and give up my dream, even if she acts the martyr," Hattie asserted.

"Do what you must," Amanda advised. "It's your life. Try to honor her, though, like the Bible says. She deserves that."

❖ ❖ ❖

To stay busy while she hobbled around, Hattie focused on the list Reverend Worcester had provided. It included three pairs of hard-wearing shoes, wool and cotton stockings, a cloak of waterproof material over wool, three sets of undergarments, two sets of warm underwear, a durable walking dress, a dark dress of flannel or comparable fabric, two dresses of calico or gingham, and a sturdy underskirt. Other necessary items would be provided upon her arrival, she was told.

Hard-wearing shoes. That term was a far cry from the shoes her friends fussed over for parties and balls. Hattie pictured a utilitarian life that did not feature parties. Warm underwear. How could winter there possibly be as cold as Utica's winters? On the other hand, Hattie allowed that heat might be harder to come by in the Cherokee Nation. It wasn't an appealing idea.

She could only guess about her living quarters. Beyond the fireplace, would she have a stove? Of course, she would have appropriate furniture. What about suitable linens? Those weren't on the list.

Maybe more information would be forthcoming about things like linens.

It was too early to start second-guessing each little thing. Reverend Worcester had offered assurances, so she must accept them and be patient. If she got to the Cherokee Nation and discovered a need, surely it could be met in the town of Tahlequah.

For now, why not start packing? Once she could lay eyes on everything, she would feel many steps closer to departing. Given the situation with her leg, however, she needed help. Her mother still couldn't talk about her upcoming departure, so she tasked Amanda with gathering or purchasing items from the list.

The two of them had always made a good team. They were seasoned at anticipating each other's needs. Now, they had to figure out how to be supportive while living hundreds of miles apart. Getting specific about the packing brought them face to face with their upcoming separation. What would life feel like without a sister nearby, Hattie wondered? How would Amanda handle her role as the Sheldon's only daughter in Utica? Hattie didn't envy her sister that role or responsibility.

"Will you go downtown and see what's available?" Hattie requested. "Then let's talk before anything is purchased."

"I'll comb through White and Mortley, as well as J.B. Wells & Son. I think Wells will have the superior selection," Amanda predicted.

J.B. Wells & Son Co.

77-79-81-83 Genesee Street

Oldest and Most Reliable Dry Goods House in Central New York

— ESTABLISHED 1843 —

Silks, Dress Goods, Cloaks, Carpets, Lace Curtains, Hosiery, Underwear, Men's Furnishings, Gloves, Laces, Cottons, Blankets, Bedding, Stationery, Toilet Articles, etc.

❀ ❀ ❀

"Now that I've gotten over your big announcement and the shock of your broken leg, I need some more information," Ebenezer inquired one evening.

"Of course," Hattie assured him. "I'll answer the best I can."

"Don't accuse me of prying, dear. But have you thought deeply enough about all this? There are many dangers in the region where you're going. It's keeping me awake at night."

His words made Hattie realize for the first time that she might have appeared secretive.

"I'm sorry, Father," she responded openly, propping up her leg to relieve the swelling. "What I know so far is that I will be employed by the Park Hill Mission. It's near the Arkansas border and not far from Kansas Territory. The mission needs a new teacher."

"I shudder for you to go anywhere near Kansas Territory! Did Reverend Worcester happen to mention the killings there? Vicious battles are raging between pro-slavery and Free State men. It's dangerously close to where you'll live."

"From the newspapers, I know about the sacking of Lawrence," Hattie replied soberly. "But there's danger at every turn, Father, even in Utica. I don't intend to go near Kansas Territory, if that makes you feel better."

"It doesn't. There's a level of hazard out there well beyond anything here. Have you asked enough questions about the Cherokees?" he continued, showing great restraint.

"Well, I hope so. I've tried to examine every fact I can find. That includes what Reverend Fowler taught me, as well as what I learned from Professor Colquhoun. Father, it's like a sense of destiny. God prepared me to do the job, made schools available, and equipped me to thrive in educational settings. God let me meet Reverend Worcester and led him to hire me."

"I wonder what God had to do with your broken leg," her mother called from the kitchen.

Hattie did not reply. She simply let the comment echo and sat silently until her father continued.

"You've gained from your innate need to learn," he summarized. "The library has been your friend. Books have been your constant companions. You are utterly qualified in every way to teach. I just worry about you teaching way out there on the frontier. That worry is doubled because of your leg."

"I understand," she hesitated, vowing never to reveal the day and night ache in her leg. "My leg's healing just fine. Let's get back to the wider issue. First, look at my position in this family. After the girls died, I had to figure out why I had lived. Why was I the one who ended up getting the remarkable education? I was absolutely driven to go beyond the ordinary. Second, Margaret shared how Reverend Lyman Beecher raised his children. His words have echoed in my head ever since: "Do something to change the world." I decided that my life was not meant to be spent here while people elsewhere needed what I could teach them. Then, Reverend Worcester expressed confidence that I had much to contribute to the Cherokees. A new door opened widely, so I went through it. Please trust me."

"But we know so little about where you're going."

"Actually, I know more since Reverend Worcester's letter arrived. I'll tell you everything he shared."

So, she began to describe Park Hill and Tahlequah. Along with Reverend Worcester's descriptions of the two towns, he depicted a big, white, two-story house, Hunter's Home, which was one of Park Hill's crowning jewels. The owner, George Murrell, was supportive of the mission. He had married into the well-to-do family of the future Cherokee Chief, John Ross, before the majority of the Cherokees were removed to Indian Territory. Murrell started over, establishing a large operation in Park Hill. Hunter's Home was built in the mid-1840s. Reverend Worcester said Hattie would become well-acquainted with the family.

Another magnificent home, Rose Cottage, belonged to the chief. Just down the road from Murrell's, it had an impressive orchard containing nearly 1,000 apple trees. Hattie felt she understood the emphasis on these grand homes. Reverend Worcester must not want her to become frightened that Park Hill was outside of civilization.

As soon as she got there, she determined to scout the place for herself and find out the whole story. It was going to be exciting to walk the place top to bottom. She intended to know Park Hill like the back of her hand, just like she did Utica. It was such a state of security to get that feeling of familiarity. Why, she knew the colors of their neighbors' draperies in Utica. She knew the names of their dogs. It would make her feel stable to know these things in the Cherokee Nation, as well.

Ebenezer seemed calmer after Hattie shared information from the letter. He yawned and said he would retire. Hattie relaxed at his reaction, and then let her thoughts drift back to the letter.

Was she as strong as Worcester to endure a long separation from her family? She'd better be, because only after three years' service in Park Hill would she qualify for a visit back to Utica. What would it be like to leave the family behind and make a 1,300 mile trip? Soon enough, she was going to find out.

❖ ❖ ❖

After a delay that lasted a little too long, Hattie determined it was time to have the difficult, inevitable conversation with her mother. She did so when her mother brought the mail to her room one afternoon.

"Mother, as painful as this is, we must talk it out," she coaxed in a soft, but serious voice. "We can't keep avoiding the obvious."

"Oh, Hattie. Let me be," her mother begged.

"Your feelings about my future and my feelings about my future have no intersection. We've got to break the impasse."

"Why do you torture me?" her mother fretted, acting uncomfortable. "You are bound and determined to throw yourself headlong into a foreign culture. Sometimes, I am certain it's just to spite me."

"You know in your heart of hearts that isn't so," Hattie replied evenly. "I have no spite in my temperament. You've misread me. I react negatively when you prioritize only your perspective and your hopes for my future."

"It is not respectful for you to disregard my feelings and dreams for your future. You don't know anything about motherhood, either. Sometimes, you have no compassion for the losses I have suffered."

Before she could blink, Hattie knew she had come to a totally new juncture in her relationship with her mother. Before her, the quandary posed by her mother could not have been more obvious. Hattie was clear about what was happening and what it meant. Having reached this moment, she told herself that the many, many difficult experiences leading here had taught her well. She had learned her lessons, every one of them.

All of her energy now focused on the fact that her path was crystal clear. The search had ended, as had all its machinations and confusions. Hattie knew exactly where she intended to go. Fully aware of the words she was about to speak, she recognized that childhood was behind her forever. She wasn't a little girl any longer. Rather, she was an adult daughter who made a daring choice in keeping with her convictions. It was time to have her say and end the misunderstanding with her mother. She felt confident, while filled with love and compassion.

"Mother, I have the utmost respect for you," she began softly. "But your own wording is the telltale issue here. You are not the only one who suffered. Our entire family grieved painfully and deeply. Because of that, I decided to make something unique out of my life. I am going *because* the girls had such short lives. What if my life ends up being short, too? I am going *because* I want to use my years uniquely. Why can't you understand that?"

Despite her certainty, Hattie sat back after she finished, a bit shocked by her own fortitude.

Her mother stared at the floor looking conquered, which signaled to Hattie that perhaps she had gotten through. Her mother sighed, pressing fingertips into her temples.

"No mother gives up her child easily, Hattie," she finally whispered. "I cannot just let you disappear from our lives without trying to dissuade you. I also cannot suddenly change my protective nature. Until my dying day, I will do everything in my power to protect my children."

This time, Hattie grew silent and stared out the window. Not a whisper of air stirred the trees. It was as if nature held its breath while she and her mother talked.

Hattie had to allow that her mother had put forward a strong position. It pulled at her heartstrings. But something about it didn't feel quite right. So, she silently walked back through her mother's arguments, one by one. It took several minutes. Then, she realized what was bothering her. She also recognized that fate had given her the best possible example to use against her mother's reservations.

"On any ordinary day when I've worked at the shop, if a horse went wild, crashed through the window and landed on me, I would die," Hattie explained patiently. "Even if you were sitting right here, you couldn't do anything about it. Do you see that?"

"I don't agree at all," her mother replied, thrusting her chin forward defensively. "There is always something that can be done."

"Not always. Here's an even more graphic example," Hattie continued. "When the footbridge gave way, right here in Utica, I could easily have died. You weren't there. You can't be wherever I go for the rest of my life. Even if you had been there, like the woman right next to me, you couldn't have stopped it. You know I'm right. I could have died right under your nose. No one but God can protect me, and you refuse to admit that!"

Weeping quietly, her mother stood and shook her head as if unable to accept Hattie's words. If ever Hattie had seen a picture of suffering, this was it. And even though frustration flooded her mind, she still felt compassion. Her mother's stubbornness was an outgrowth of great loss. Having been wounded in the past, her mother insisted on trying to control the future. It didn't look like she would give up. Hattie could see it on her face.

"I am going to cook dinner now," her mother responded quietly. "It is too difficult for me to hear you invoke the name of God against me when I am just seeking to keep you near."

During the night, Hattie was awakened by a sharp, throbbing

ache in her leg. Perhaps shifting her position might break the cycle of discomfort. After several minutes had gone by, however, it hadn't helped. Reaching onto the bedside table, she lit her lamp and wiped sleep from her eyes. Any bad thing always felt worse in the middle of the night.

Sitting up, she reached for her crutches and used them to pull herself up. Her nightgown became slightly twisted in the bed sheets. Untangling the mess only brought more pain. Finally getting to her feet and gaining balance, she moved herself around the room, shaking her leg slightly to increase the circulation. The pain improved a little.

But her armpits ached from the hard pressure of the crutches. How long would she have to use them, she wondered? They had grown cumbersome, heavy, and annoying as she made her way through the house each day. Going up and down stairs was the hardest challenge of all. Sometimes, she felt she might topple over. What if the day of her departure came and she still needed these crutches?

After a few minutes, her leg didn't feel as bad, but her arms were sorer than ever. This situation was wearing thin, its aggravation trying in the extreme. She felt cross and impatient. The next time Dr. Bagg came, she would question him extensively about the healing process. When could she expect to have full use of her leg back? How long would her leg hurt this badly?

On second thought, maybe she would talk mostly about the crutches. If he knew the extent of her pain, he might keep her down longer. She could not let anything like that happen. It would more than suggest that she was worse. It might be far wiser to withhold any information about how much her leg hurt. Surely it would subside soon.

But Hattie continued to struggle. Healing must have caused her body to work harder, because her clothes felt loose. She realized she had lost a few pounds. That was the good news. But her pain, which was bad news, continued to be a plague.

At night, she felt she barely slept. The throbbing made her cry into her pillow. Luckily, Amanda stopped by to see her.

"You look drained," Amanda whispered in a startled voice. "What's wrong?"

"You've got to talk to Dr. Bagg for me," Hattie begged. "My pain should be better by now, but it's getting worse."

"You're afraid mother will find out, aren't you?"

"Yes! That would put another layer of questions and concerns into the mix!"

"I'll go right now. Keep a stiff upper lip. And avoid those stairs."

July 1, 1856

Dear Margaret,

You're expecting this letter to be full of enthusiastic details about my graduation, I know. That did happen and it was truly wonderful. But everything else that's taken place is what's occupying and dominating my life right now. I've just got to tell you. It's almost too unbelievable to be true. Some of it is really good and some is really bad. You recall my glowing letter right after Reverend Worcester's visit? That was such an uplifting time. Then I was caught up in examinations, graduation and making application for teaching jobs. Just when I was exasperated by the lack of opportunities, a governess job came along. Everyone thought it was perfect, but I held tight to my dream of much more. The pressure to take it began to gather. I didn't know what I was going to do. But then, as if from Heaven, a letter came from Reverend Worcester. I couldn't believe my eyes. Margaret, he actually offered me a teaching job in the Cherokee Nation! It was the highest, most fulfilling moment of my entire life! Of course, I accepted immediately. Breaking the news to my parents, however, nearly broke my resolve. It certainly brought me down to earth. They absolutely went to pieces. The next day, while the strain was still quite unbearable, I went to help Reverend Fowler with baptisms. Never again will I underestimate the power of the unexpected. It makes my chin quiver to think about what happened at the river. As the baptismal procession crossed the old footbridge where you and I used to pretend we were getting married, the footbridge broke in two! The stones and mortar split apart, maybe from the weight of so many people on it at once. Suddenly, a number of us were plunged twenty feet to the water and sandbar below. I can't find words to describe my fear, to relate how people screamed, to feel the cold water and wonder if I might drown. There were many injuries, some quite serious. One man died! It made all the papers. So, here I sit with a broken leg! I hobble about on crutches. And the pain—I can't tell you how badly it hurts. Dr. Bagg says I've had a setback, that the muscles or tissue around the bone seem to be inflamed. I'm beside myself, just when I need to be packing to leave for the Cherokee Nation. That will take place in a matter of days, I just learned. Reverend Worcester's wife, Erminia, will be my chaperone. The itinerary I received begins with rail travel. Then, we transfer to riverboats and maybe even wagons. It's really going to happen! I'm trying my best to appear as strong as ever for the rigors of the trip. I'll write you the first chance I get.

Love, Hattie

❀ ❀ ❀

"Hairbrush," Hattie called from her new checklist of needed items.

"Check," Amanda replied.

"Pen and ink?"

"Check."

"Bible?"

"Check.

"That's it. We have everything," Hattie sighed contentedly.

"What about the crutches?" Amanda whispered warily.

"I've tried to go without them more. Surely I can wean myself off them."

"But you heard Dr. Bagg's warning! I wish you could see the pain on your face when you put weight on your leg."

"It's been better since he gave me that White Willow Bark. After I drink the tea, my pain is so much better."

But Dr. Bagg had warned her not to drink the bark tea more than three or four times a day. By evening, she had usually used up her daily allowance. The pain returned and she had a hard time hiding it.

So, Hattie found reasons to remain upstairs in the evenings. No wonder she had lost weight. One too many times she had begged out of supper saying she was just tired. Those stairs were too great an obstacle and caused more pain. She didn't want anybody to witness her struggling.

With her departure eminent, she told herself she needed to preserve as much energy as possible. The truth, however, was anything but the smiling veneer she projected outwardly. Still, she was determined to mask the situation long enough to get on the road. There was ample time to heal while she traveled, she told herself.

After all her things were packed, Hattie spied one final item she had intended to include. It was perhaps the most important thing of all. Partially hidden by a handkerchief on her dresser was the little, handmade cross from those many years ago on the Underground Railroad rescue. The woman who wrapped tiny scraps of leather around two little sticks was like a missionary. She had fashioned that cross in a threatening situation to leave a message of hope. Her point was that faith must come first. She would always remain in Hattie's memory, especially when it came to keeping a sense of perspective.

In one of the most harrowing situations of her life, that woman had risked much to say thank you. She could have been apprehended during the time it took to give Hattie's mother the cross. But her message had been just as important as her personal safety. She wanted to attach a memory to the gift, and she had succeeded.

The message was about remembering how God was the only one to count upon when everything seemed impossible. She made her gift and her life an example. Likewise, Hattie had been warned that she would face difficult challenges before, during, and after her work with the Cherokees. It would behoove her to take the message of this little cross to heart.

For relief from the hurt and boredom, Hattie found it helpful to exercise her leg by bending and then extending it. Staring at her suitcases, she was encouraged that the pain had leveled off. But weakness had taken its place. Nevertheless, her level of excitement rose as her departure neared.

Ebenezer checked on her each morning, looking at her askance when she spoke of leaving. Even her mother came upstairs more often and seemed concerned. Hattie just smiled and raised her eyebrows as a show of high spirits. Sometimes, when others were downstairs, she made noises with one of her crutches so her parents would think she was busy and moving about.

When afternoons came and a nap was acceptable, she dozed. A light breeze from her window cooled the humid upstairs air. She was awakened on occasion by a buzzing cicada or barking dog.

One afternoon she heard a carriage draw up out front. A horse snorted and pawed the gravel. Then, footsteps proceeded up the walk to the front door. Someone knocked, and then the door creaked slightly and her mother's voice greeted Reverend Fowler.

Fully awake now, Hattie reacted with a start when she heard him say, "Shhhh!" As quickly as she could, Hattie grabbed her crutch and moved from her bed to the door to listen. Her mother's voice had lowered to a whisper as she spoke with Reverend Fowler in the foyer.

"Let's sit down in the parlor," she suggested.

Since the parlor was directly beneath Hattie's room, she couldn't hear much of the conversation. But she understood enough to realize that Reverend Fowler had not come to see her. It was concerning. What was he discussing with her mother? Why were their voices muted? Obviously, they were talking about her.

Hattie felt threatened and vulnerable. This was no time to be unaware of what was going on. The suspense alone was maddening. Quickly, she discarded her crutch and lowered herself to the floor, wincing silently as she stretched muscles that were not used to new positions. With some effort, she used her good leg to inch her body into the hallway and across to the stair rails. There, she was concealed to listen as their whispers drifted up.

"Erminia Worcester's train leaves Vermont for Utica day after tomorrow," Reverend Fowler explained. "I just heard."

"Oh, dear. This is happening so fast," Hattie's mother returned.

"Yes. She wants to depart with Hattie early the next morning. That is, if Hattie is able."

"You know my feelings on that," her mother fretted. "I seriously doubt she can go."

"I'm worried, too. Dr. Bagg was tight lipped when I approached him about it, but his raised eyebrows confirmed my suspicions," Reverend Fowler continued.

"She still has noticeable pain and weakness," her mother explained. "It's no time to begin an arduous journey."

Hattie bit her lip. How did her mother know she felt weak? Had she given herself away somehow? What if she had talked in her sleep and the family heard? Her mind raced with worries.

"We all want the best for her," Reverend Fowler offered.

"All she wants is to go to Indian Territory. No matter what," her mother replied. "Honestly, this situation is beyond all reason. It's my job to protect her, but that casts me as the one causing problems. If Hattie learns I notified Reverend Worcester of the accident, she may never forgive me."

Hattie gasped silently, her mouth falling open. Oh no! Her own mother had written Reverend Worcester about her broken leg? This was the worst of all possibilities. She could scarcely believe it. The situation had gone way, way beyond her wildest fears.

Something had to be done. But what?

"You acted out of concern and courtesy," Reverend Fowler comforted. "None of us knew the extent of her injury then. There was so much confusion. You mustn't chide yourself."

"You're right. She was unconscious," her mother agreed. "I

grew more and more distraught because that poor man died and the newspapers picked it up. Reverend Worcester could easily have read about it. He deserved the truth."

"Does Hattie know he's remaining in Vermont and won't be making the trip?" Reverend Fowler inquired.

"Yes, he had written her right before the accident," her mother confirmed. "She's been packing ever since."

"From what I gather, everyone knows her healing is delayed. Does she realize that?" he queried.

"She has not acknowledged any delay, to say the least," her mother muttered. "She is bound and determined to go."

Reverend Fowler sighed. "Erminia Worcester wants confirmation before she will leave Vermont for Utica."

"But the answer is obvious," her mother argued. "Hattie can't possibly make the trip."

"It looks questionable," he acknowledged. "Whatever your decision, I still must get word to Vermont right away that the plans are altered."

Hattie's heart raced. Feelings of betrayal began to spread, sickening her stomach and making her mouth go dry. Even though she knew nobody wished ill for her, she suddenly felt alone in the world. Without even seeing her again, Reverend Fowler was poised to call off her trip, and her mother was all too happy to comply. Hattie had to stick up for herself.

Mustering every ounce of energy she had, Hattie grasped the top stair rail and began to pull herself up. She struggled against weakness and a sharp ache in her leg. She had to get downstairs one way or another.

Over the last few days, her efforts to move had been aided by picturing a train engine. As she had observed many times, a train engine would start out slowly and then gather momentum. Soon, it became a powerful force that couldn't easily be stopped. She had to emulate that engine now. With all her might, she had to gain strength and somehow make her way down those stairs to stop the people who were going to cancel her future.

Taking deep breaths, Hattie drew herself up internally now that she had come to stand at the top of the stairs. She smoothed her dress and hair, and then pinched her cheeks to bring color into her face. With her good leg, she took the first step. Her weak leg followed. She was careful not to let her broken leg lead or to stand alone too long on any given stair. Her hands gripped the rail so tightly that her knuckles turned white.

To her surprise, she felt unexpectedly strengthened. With each step, her resolve grew and her leg seemed to be taking orders. Maybe good intentions really could make pain disappear. She continued methodically, her mind formulating the persuasive words she must speak.

"I hear the two of you down there," she called in a strong but kind voice. "And I'm here to tell you that I'm just fine. There's no cause to change the plans."

By now, she had reached the bottom step, where she turned to see them in the parlor. Both her mother and Reverend Fowler were standing now. They looked completely amazed and a little uncertain of what to do. Hattie pasted the widest, healthiest smile she could muster on her face. It took an exaggerated effort to cover the pain.

"Don't underestimate me when I'm down," she chided, walking toward them with no crutches, her determination bidding the pain to remain at bay. With all her might, she resisted the need to limp.

"I ... er ... we are just concerned," Reverend Fowler stuttered, rushing forward to take her arm.

"Everyone has been so supportive, which has given me the strength I needed," Hattie gushed, minimizing the problem. "See for yourselves. I'm strong and I'm going. Tell Mrs. Worcester to head for Utica."

❂ ❂ ❂

As the train gathered momentum, smoke billowed upward in the same way Hattie pictured her prayers rising. Leaning against her trunk, she balanced her weight cautiously while waving from the train's last car. Finally, finally, her journey was beginning. It was taking her toward a long anticipated but barely formed picture of her future. Simultaneously, her loved ones were receding, their figures and influence growing smaller and smaller in the hazy distance. Soon, they would be completely out of view.

What a grand event the send-off had been! Ever so many wonderful friends had come to say goodbye and wish her well, some with tears but most with smiles. If only she could sit down now and talk over every detail with her family at home. But that would not be possible.

Along with the excitement of what was coming, she felt an emptiness about what she was leaving behind. All adventurers had to cope with such emotions, she imagined. Stepping out of tradition and comfort into a new life was not for the fainthearted. She must think ahead rather than look back. Most of all, an abiding sense of gratitude must bolster her as she blazed a new trail.

The fact that she had been able to follow through with her plans was something of a miracle. Determined, Hattie had somehow kept the accident and her broken leg from determining her future. It had to be reinforced strenuously at times. On many occasions, she insisted she was completely well, strong, and capable of travel. It shocked her now to realize she had even fooled Dr. Bagg.

Looking down, she stared at her handkerchief, now damp from the many tears she had shed. Those tears were shed for more than goodbyes. Her leg throbbed so painfully this morning that she had fought tears while boarding the train. It still hurt, and she still needed to keep that fact under wraps. She must continue to present a strong front to Mrs. Erminia Worcester, just as she had to folks at home.

Savoring this private moment before finding her seat, Hattie closed her eyes. She had departed on the most important undertaking of her life. The packing had ended, the vision was taking shape, and it was time to get better acquainted with her boss's wife. They would be traveling companions for the long, long journey to the Cherokee Nation. It was time to think of that new place as home.

Acknowledgements

Visiting quiet, rural Park Hill, Oklahoma as a child, I never dreamed that its grassy meadows and quiet streams once were enjoyed by a woman I could never meet. But her character made an impression when she taught Cherokee children there before the Civil War. And her influence became a permanent memory my grandmother talked about so lovingly.

Harriet Ann "Hattie" Sheldon's life led me many thousands of miles on a drive from Virginia to her hometown of Utica, New York, then to Park Hill, Oklahoma. I'm grateful to Brian Howard and the Oneida County Historical Society in Utica for opening its library to me on a day it should be closed; to Mary Ann Buteux for helping me discover proof of Hattie's family and their business in Utica; to Gerald Waterman, who produced documentation and drove me to the graves of Hattie's family at Forest Hill Cemetery; to Building Administrator Steve Best at First Presbyterian Church of Utica for opening the vault and sharing traces of Sheldon's past; to the Oneida County Record Center; and to the Utica Public Library's microfilm collection. My thanks also go to Bill Shores, who confirmed the Revolutionary War service of several Sheldons and led me to their deserted resting places near Bernardston, Massachusetts; to Rose Newton and the Sheldon Family Association; to the Memorial Hall Museum and Library in Deerfield, Massachusetts; to the docents at the 1699 John Sheldon House in Deerfield, Massachusetts, for their patient sharing of details and realistic portrayal of Hattie's forefathers; to the McFarlin Library at the University of Tulsa for its marvelously catalogued Alice M. Robertson Collection of correspondence and papers from Oklahoma's first woman in Congress, who was a granddaughter of the revered missionary, Rev. Samuel A. Worcester; to my friend, Gloria McQuade, for helping me research the collection; to the Oklahoma Historical Society's George M. Murrell Home; to Oklahoma anthropologist Shirley Pettengill for sharing mountains of information and giving patient historical guidance about the Cherokee Nation and Worcester family from the era they were based in Park Hill, Oklahoma; to the archivists of Houghton Library at Harvard University; to the Library of Congress for maintaining magnificent sources found nowhere else in the world; and to the Indian Records Unit of the National Archives in Washington, DC. I am indebted to Ancestry.com, FamilySearch.org, GenealogyBank.com and Fold3 for the documentation required to bring the characters in this book alive. Finally, for their patience, ideas, editorial guidance, and encouragement, I thank Steve Funk, Lea Helmerich, Dale Duvall, Barbara Nelson, Rebecca Schenk, Mickey Miller, Regina Jahr, Lucile Higgins, and David Miller.

Many, many thanks to Gary Bowers, for gracious permission to use his original painting, "New Growth," for the cover art. For more works by this award-winning artist, visit: www.garybowers.net

ABOUT THE AUTHOR

A descendant of Oklahoma homesteaders on both sides, Lane Dolly grew up hearing stories of perseverance from her accomplished physician father and revered preacher grandmother. Dolly worked in the Reagan White House then earned a Masters in Public Policy. A voracious researcher, she followed all-but-forgotten leads to fill a mysterious gap in her family tree. Hundreds of hours of research, in The Library of Congress, Harvard's Houghton Library, The George M. Murrell Historic Home, and the University of Tulsa's McFarlan Library helped Lane to discover the "mother lode" of historic connections from which this account grew. Through her efforts, Dolly's great, great grandmother emerges as the heroine in *A Distant Call: The Fateful Choices of Hattie Sheldon.* This debut novel takes us from the abolitionist movement in the Empire State to Hattie's decision to teach the Cherokees in pre-Civil War Indian Territory.

31165306R00246

Made in the USA
Middletown, DE
20 April 2016